BETWEEN THE TREES

KATHY MOCZERNIAK

Lavish Publishing LLC

Contents

For Mike, my reward

Acknowledgments

It's hard to know where to start acknowledging the people who have had a role in a book that, in many ways, I've been writing my entire life. First, I have to thank my husband, Mike, and our beautiful children, Jonathan, Maddy, Amy, and Matthew—my inspirations, my greatest loves, my rewards. You are simply my everything. We sacrificed our own time together for everything involved in me writing this book, but you supported me endlessly, and I love you all with everything I am. Always.

Of course, I must thank my mom, Mary, who has been there for me and loved me through every day, every success, and, perhaps most importantly, every failure. I would not be the woman, mother, wife, friend, and writer I am today without her, and I am so thankful to have such a loving, strong, compassionate, and supportive woman by my side no matter what. I love you, Mom. I'm grateful for our journey.

To my Aunt Karen, Uncle Bill, and my cousins Tim and John, you've always been my safe place to fall. So much more than extended family, you are great gifts blessed upon me, and I love you dearly.

To my dad, Bob, the man who taught me baseball, how to swing a hammer, to appreciate the oldies, and that love is a powerful motivator for growth, I love you for who you are and who you have worked hard to become, and I will always be your baby girl.

Friends are family that you choose, and I've been blessed with the most amazing friends. Lauren, we found each other as children and grew side by side. You were there for me in the darkest time of my life, and your light played a vital part in me finding my way through. That creates a bond that will never be broken by time or space. I am eternally thankful for you. To my girls, Megan, Jacki, and Kelly, our friendship that began so long ago continues to bring me endless joy, and I am so grateful we have each other as we continue this life together. I know we'll remain there for each other forever...and always. Beyond unwavering friendship, Kelly also followed me through my journey as a writer, reading my work while offering honesty and encouragement, believing in me from my early drafts to the novel it has become. Thank you, you four wonderful women, for your friendship and for your roles in the story of my life.

To my other family members and friends who have always been by my side, I am forever grateful. A special shout-out to my December Sisters, who have been with me since this book first began. You read my earliest drafts and gave me encouragement and confidence, and I'm so grateful. You ladies are the best.

To my friends, my beta readers and proofreaders, Samantha, Kelcee, Sarah, Rachel, Robin, and Marty, my stepdad, thank you for your time, your advice, your intellect, and your support.

I want to offer my sincerest gratitude to those who helped my book look its best. Thank you to the talented CK Green of KP Designs for designing my beautiful cover and to Desiree Scott for the superb formatting. I truly appreciate the time and effort you both put into my book.

To Lavish Publishing, not only did you take a chance on me when you hired me as your editor, you then let me into your family as an author. For the knowledge, experience, and friendships I've gained with you, I am forever grateful. Thank you for making my dreams come true.

My dear readers, I cannot thank you enough for honoring me with the gift of reading my words. Know that truth and fiction grace these pages, but in the end, it doesn't matter what is real and what was crafted. What is important and what I truly hope you take away from Kathryn's story is a peace in knowing every branch, every veined leaf, whether bringing light or darkness, has led us here to this moment and made us who we are today. If you're not where you want to be, it only means your story isn't complete yet. Fight for your happiness and don't let your past define your future.

I truly hope you enjoy *Between the Trees.*

Prologue

She stood frozen at the end of the driveway, struggling for breath, her eyes unblinking.

He was there. He was waiting for her, his image blurred slightly by the window glare.

Without further thought, she bolted. Pebbles and dust kicked up behind her as she dug her blue sneakers into the shoulder of the road, her backpack slamming against her. She didn't dare look back. She simply ran—ran for her life, ran for her safety, ran for her freedom.

The long, blue ranch-style house came into view, and the purple door drew closer as she fought through the burning in her legs and lungs, only pushing harder. She leapt up the stairs two at a time, landing on the porch, and frantically banged on the front door. Peeking around into the window, she saw her aunt walking to the door, and she whipped her head back toward her house.

No one.

She looked back into her aunt's eyes.

"Kathryn? Honey, what's wrong?"

"I...I can't go home. I can't." Her shaking hand found her midsection, and she bent forward, bracing her other hand on the doorframe as she fought for her words through gasps. "Please. I can't go back there."

"Come in. Come in." Aunt Hannah stepped aside and put her arm around Kathryn, gripping her bicep and assisting her over to the flowered living room couch. She sat next to her niece and took her hand. "My dear, what happened? Why can't you go home?"

Years of holding it all in…years of secrets kept…years of lies… No more. It all burst forth, pouring out of her like a river that broke through a dam that centered its existence around suppressing the flow of something meant to be beautiful.

Aunt Hannah's eyes grew larger and larger until they fell closed and overflowed with anguish.

With one last sharp intake of air and one final word, Kathryn sobbed uncontrollably, giving in to too much. It was all just too much.

Aunt Hannah slid closer to Kathryn and pulled her into her shoulder, holding her as she wept, rubbing her back. "Oh, my dear. I'm so sorry. I'm so glad you came to us. You're safe now."

Up and Over

She walked in sunlight. Straight, lemony brown hair hung down her back, moving lightly in the soft breeze. The hem of her yellow dress swished down to her ankles not yet scarred with life's betrayals. Her little hand fit perfectly inside his. Innocent crystal eyes shimmered in the sun's brilliance as she looked up at him, blinking bangs off her eyelashes.

"Let's go this way, Daddy! I want to lift our hands over the tree again," she said, tugging on his hand.

He gazed down upon her delicate porcelain face. "Of course, Kathryn. Anything you want, baby girl."

They continued hand in hand, walking at a gentle pace. Her little three-year-old legs could only carry her so quickly across the lush grass. The sound of their strides was accompanied only by rustling leaves and falsetto melodies cascading from surrounding treetops. All else was quiet.

When they reached the young elm standing in the back corner of his lot, their hands lifted in unison as their voices blended harmoniously singing, "Up and over!"

Her sweet giggles pulled at his lips and mended his broken spirit even if only until she must leave again.

She squeezed his hand and laid her cheek upon it. "I miss you, Daddy."

"I miss you too, baby girl," he said, threading his overworked fingers through her hair.

They carried on, leaving a light path behind them with every step.

3

Slivers of early morning cut through the plastic blinds and scattered across the oak hardwood as she observed the floating dust particles softly twirling in the streams of light. She blinked hard, returning from her reverie. Engrossed in the vision behind her blue eyes now absent of their past innocence, it took her a moment to remember where she was. Kathryn lay awake in a foreign bed in an unfamiliar room and rolled over, staring at the ceiling, thinking about the scene that was playing through her mind—as accurately as she could recall a three-year-old's memory—aching for those simple moments. The past twelve years may have played with the memory, blurring it, altering it, dressing it up with glitter and lace, but still she smiled.

Her eyelids fell, and she held on to his hazel gaze and the joy in his voice when his rough hand guided hers over the tree barely taller than she at the time.

Kathryn pulled herself up and swept long, thin strands off her face, tucking them behind her ears. Sliding on oval, wire-rimmed glasses, the blurred shapes came into sharp focus. She thought of getting up out of bed and having to function like a normal girl and was overtaken by that familiar ache in her stomach. Her heart rate increased, and her body flushed despite the cool air wafting from the vents. The role she had been playing the past week and a half was wearing on her, slowly corroding what she desperately fought to keep in her grasp.

A tender knock came to the door, sending her recoiling against the wall with a ragged gasp.

The doorknob shook rapidly.

Kathryn's feet slid on the plush carpet as the door began opening in sharp jabs. "Stop!"

Kathryn's lashes fluttered, refocusing her vision, and she inhaled deeply, trying to calm her breathing at the haunting memory triggered far too often.

"Kathryn, dear? It's time to get up. Breakfast will be ready soon. Everyone is already out in the kitchen."

"Okay, Aunt Hannah. I'll be out soon."

The floor was cool against her bare feet as she walked over to the closet and sifted through the few clothes she brought with her, pushing the teenage-boy shirts aside. She pulled on her favorite jeans and a pink, short-sleeved V-neck top before going across the hall to the bathroom to splash some water on her face, brush her teeth, and put in her contacts.

Back in the bedroom, Kathryn stood in front of the mirror atop the oak dresser and feebly attempted to conceal the aftermath of another night of tears. Alabaster powder only slightly softened the redness, and she flinched as the tip of the eyeliner scratched against her worn eyes, but she pressed on, determined to complete her mask. Gliding on strawberry lip balm, she breathed in deeply, let the air escape through glossed lips, and forced a lifeless smile.

That's not going to fool anyone. Try harder.

She ran a brush through her hair and pulled a small section back with the black hair tie that rarely left her wrist. Behind her reflection, she spotted Mittens curled up at the foot of the bed. She turned and knelt, reaching out to pet Mittens' belly. The cat startled awake and released a soft moan before pushing her face into her best friend's hand. Kathryn leaned closer, and Mittens delicately pressed her nose to her forehead. Her hand passed over the black, shiny coat that was broken in a few places with snow-white fur on her tummy and paws and painted her forehead with an upside down "V." With six toes on each of her front paws, combined with the placement of the white against the black, she looked as though she were wearing mittens.

Mittens hopped down from the bed as Kathryn poured food into the bowl next to the door, and she sat on the floor with her while her cat ate, spinning her gold Claddagh ring on her right hand. "We don't have to be afraid here, baby girl." She ran her fingers over Mittens' back as it arched against her touch. "Maybe you could start exploring outside the room today." Mittens looked up at her with wide, jade eyes, crunching on her food. Kathryn smiled and scratched the white fur under her lifted chin. "Well, when you're ready." She gave her a quick kiss and a rub on her nose. "See you after school, Mitter Bitters."

Closing the door behind her, Kathryn started down the long hallway toward the kitchen, stopping to behold the framed pictures draping the walls. Her aunt and uncle and their two boys grinned back at her as she reached out and touched the clean glass. Sliding her finger over, it swept across a picture of the young girl holding a baby doll, hair hanging down her back, bangs thick across her forehead. Kathryn's petite arms were clutching Benji, his bald little head marked with four years of love. The fair, little girl stared at her, the warmth in her eyes belying the disturbing truth of her reality.

The smell of cooking eggs and sausage pulled her away from the pictures and into the kitchen. Sunlight flooded through the window, bouncing off the amber honeycomb tiles that wrapped the walls, contrasting with dark cabinets and linoleum flooring. Aunt Hannah stood over the stove in her pale yellow pajamas and white apron, fussing around making breakfast. Her short, dark blond hair was held off her face by a pink headband, her glasses fogged from the ribbons of steam rising from the frying pan.

"Good morning, Kathryn," Aunt Hannah said, looking up from the stove.

"Morning, Aunt Hannah."

Jake and Sam, already dressed for school, sat at the kitchen table, chomping away on some toast with raspberry jam, and Uncle Alex looked over his glasses, reading the newspaper. Kathryn joined them at the round, wooden table scarred with years of crayon markings and spilled apple juice.

"Hey, good morning there," Uncle Alex said with a familiar chuckle in his voice. He shook out his newspaper, folding it in half, and placed it on the table. "Would you like some OJ?"

"Sure."

"Kathryn, is it okay if I grab something out of the room?" asked Sam.

"Of course. It's your room."

"Well, it's yours while you're staying here. I don't want to intrude."

Kathryn stared at Sam, wondering when her chubby little cousin grew up to be the young man before her. "Just be careful of Mittens. She's still really scared. She'll probably just run under the bed when she hears the door open though."

Sam nodded.

Kathryn took a sip of orange juice and placed a piece of buttered toast on her plate.

"We were talking earlier about your concerts that are coming up," Uncle Alex said. "How are you feeling about your orchestra concert? Do you feel comfortable with your part?"

"Yeah, I think so. I still have to nail down the Brandenburg, but I'll work on it some more before next week. I'm excited though."

"Aw, that's great. I know my students always get excited about their choral concerts. And Bach's Brandenburg Concertos are some of my favorites. Absolutely beautiful pieces." He swept an extra layer of butter onto a piece of toast. "So, does being second chair cellist as a freshman have anything to do with your excitement?"

She grinned. "Maybe."

"Well, you should be excited, Kathryn, and you should be proud of yourself, too. Second chair is a wonderful accomplishment, and you've earned it."

She had earned it. She earned it with countless hours of practicing until her callused fingers were sore and her strong bowing arm felt as though it couldn't possibly pull one more stroke. The cello was Kathryn's great love, her passion, her escape.

"And, Jake, your band concert is the week after, right?" asked Uncle Alex.

"Sure is, Papa."

Sam returned, book in hand, and sat down just as Aunt Hannah placed breakfast on the table. "I'm pretty sure I heard Mittens hiss at me from under the bed. I thought about peeking under to see if she'd let me pet her, but I like my fingers, so…"

Kathryn snickered. "Probably a smart decision." She scooped a spoonful of scrambled eggs onto her plate and nabbed a couple of sausages before it was too late. "This looks great, Aunt Hannah. I'm still not used to these fancy breakfasts on school mornings." Kathryn looked down sharply and shook the thought from her mind, crushing it with guilt as an image of her mom's face flashed behind her eyelids.

"Just one of the perks of being able to be a stay-at-home mom. I don't have anywhere else I need to be, so I can cook for my family. I'm very blessed." She offered an empathetic smile as she turned to the stove.

"Well, we will certainly be at both of your concerts, won't we, Sam?" said Uncle Alex, looking across the table at his youngest son.

With a full mouth, Sam's attempt at answering resulted in specks of egg flying onto the table. Jake started coughing after nearly choking on his sausage as Uncle Alex observed his boys.

Sam swallowed while just barely accomplishing an even expression. "Sorry, Papa. Yes, we will be there."

There was little talking when the boys went at their food. The sounds of chewing and forks striking the porcelain plates were all that could be heard until Aunt Hannah announced it was time to get out to the bus. The three teenagers dashed into the living room. After slipping on her blue sneakers, Kathryn grabbed her bag, said goodbye, and headed out the purple front door. Jake and Sam followed—after running back to the kitchen to grab some more toast, of course.

The morning sun was already strong, but the dancing breeze cooled the air and tousled Kathryn's hair as she stepped off the porch. She breathed in deeply as her vision traced the front yard littered with birch trees stretching their white limbs toward the clear sky. Spring in the small Western New York town of Edgebrook, a suburb outside of Buffalo, brought trees speckled with leaves, and the grass had finally warmed to a healthy shade of green after the harsh winter. A thick bumblebee buzzed past her ear, its fuzzy, contrasting stripes bold and defined. Birds nattered in the distance as sweet scents of new life enveloped them from every angle. Aunt Hannah's flourishing daffodils next to the praying angel statue in the front garden confirmed that it would be summer in just a few weeks.

As the boys waited for their bus to the middle school, they kicked a rock back and forth in the driveway, sending it in all directions except toward each other.

"Whoa! Where'd it go?" shouted Jake.

"In the grass somewhere, I think." Sam shrugged. "Here's another one." He attempted to kick the rock, and the toe of his sneaker smashed into the concrete.

They all burst out laughing.

"I'd stick with music and academics, Spahn boys."

"Good call," Jake said. "Oh, there's the bus. Do you think you can walk, Sam?"

Sam reached down and grabbed under his thigh near the knee and dramatically lifted his leg as if his foot were on strike, clearly upset by its unintended collision with the driveway. "I think I can make it!"

Kathryn wiped tears from her eyes as she gained control of her laughter. "Bye, guys. See you after school." She waved as the bus drove away and watched them disappear from view, leaving her alone. Happiness abandoned her as she gazed along the road; standing four houses down and across the street was her home with her mom...and him. She looked away as her eyes stung, threatening to tear.

Staring at the ground, rolling a stone under her shoe, she struggled to suppress the memory trying to fight its way to the surface. A sharp breeze rolled in, feeling cool on her damp cheek, and she leaned back against a birch lining their driveway, blinking hard, releasing a final tear and clearing her sight of the early June morning.

The bus's breaks screeched in front of the house, and she quickly blotted her face with her palms. With a deep breath, she climbed in and grabbed the high seatbacks for balance as the bus pulled forward. She made her way to her usual seat with Valerie. A thick sheet of dark brown hair covered the side of her face as she focused on the trashy magazine on her knees.

"Hey, Val."

"Oh, hey," she mumbled, her eyes still fixed on her lap.

Kathryn sighed and looked forward.

After a silent bus ride, they arrived at school, and Kathryn and Val parted ways at a split in the hallway with a weak nod. As Kathryn walked through the halls, weaving in and out of other students, she tried to keep her head and the façade up. She could not have been the only one. There must have been other kids faking smiles, faking laughter, faking personalities. There had to be.

She approached the top of the stairway, meeting the locker-lined hall. Red locker doors creaked open and closed as students hurried to pack their bags and get to first period. As she reached her locker, she saw Lexie gathering her books for her morning classes. Lexie smirked at a boy walking past her and flipped her golden hair off her slender shoulder. He looked back at her and smiled, knocking into another kid.

"Yum," she said, giggling.

Aubrey and Erica pranced up to Lexie and started talking in high-pitched squeals and flailing well-manicured hands.

"Hey, Lex," Kathryn said, forcing a smile.

"Hey, Kathryn." Her eyes narrowed slightly as she watched her friend through wisps of blond swept across her forehead.

"Hey," she said plainly, nodding toward Aubrey and Erica.

"Oh my God, Kathryn. We were just talking about Dylan. He totally looked at me the other day in math. He's so cute!"

"Oh, come on, Erica! He's got nothing on Tyler," Aubrey shrieked. "He's so fine!"

"No way!"

"Uh, yes way!"

Their incessant shrills were piercing, and Kathryn had the sudden urge to bang her head against the locker. As they bickered back and forth and went into annoyingly precise detail about Dylan and Tyler's hair, Kathryn spun her lock combination, opened the door, and buried her head inside. Closing her eyes, she took a deep breath. He was there. He was everywhere.

The doorknob shook rapidly.

Kathryn's feet slid on the plush carpet as the door began opening in sharp jabs. "Stop!" She pressed her shoulder against it, digging her bare feet into the floor, pushing her weight against the door. "What are you doing! Leave me alone!"

She felt a soft hand on her shoulder.

"Kathryn, are you okay?" Lexie asked, barely above a whisper.

"Oh, I'm fine." She peeked around from behind the locker door and saw Lexie looking at her with doubt yet care and concern in her emerald eyes. Kathryn surrendered, releasing a deep sigh. "No, I'm not. I can't stop thinking about it. And it doesn't help that I'm reminded of it every time I look down the street."

"You're not thinking about going back there, are you?"

"No. I know I can't. But I just miss my mom so much. I mean, I'm still mad at her after what happened the other night, but she's my mom." Her eyes dropped, and she stared at the glittering flecks embedded in the floor tile as she started to choke on the pain closing her throat.

9

"I know."

Lexie put her arm around her friend and leaned her head against Kathryn's as her strength crumbled. Kathryn tried to fight the tears, but it was pointless; she was broken.

The bell sounded, signaling five minutes until first period. They had to be downstairs and across the school for orchestra.

"You go on ahead and just take a moment to yourself. I'll catch up in a sec," Lexie said.

Kathryn smoothed the pain across her flushed cheek, attempting to steady her breathing. With a deep inhale, she slung her bag onto her shoulder and started off down the emptied hall.

Erica scoffed. "What's wrong with her this time?"

"Seriously. All she does lately is cry," said Aubrey.

Kathryn stumbled to a stop in the middle of the hallway, their words piercing her like knives to her side. She jumped at the bang of the locker door slamming and spun around.

Lexie took a quick step toward them, her stance tall and hard. "Just shut up! You have no idea what she's been through! You stand there with your perfect little lives and your perfect little families, and you have no idea! So just shut up about things you don't understand!"

Aubrey and Erica stood motionless, their eyes widened. As Lexie turned away, Erica's mouth opened as if to say something, but nothing came out.

Lexie put her hand on Kathryn's shoulder, turning her around, and they continued walking down the hall. Kathryn looked over at Lexie, who offered an assertive smile. They walked silently. Words were not necessary.

They entered the large orchestra room bright with heavy lighting and thick with the scent of polished wood. Instrument lockers lined a majority of the perimeter, and grayish-blue acoustic padding splashed the white brick walls with a bit of color. Kathryn weaved through the blue chairs strategically placed around the room, avoiding bowing arms and viola scrolls. Most of her fellow orchestra players were already in their assigned seats, tuning their open strings and chitchatting.

Kathryn opened the wire locker door that housed her cello and grabbed it by the neck. She took her seat in the second chair. There was barely time for a quick nod to Cari, her stand partner, before Mr. Darrow stepped up onto the riser in front of her. He raked a large hand through his short, orange hair and tapped his baton against the black steel music stand. The chatter ceased immediately, and the students looked to their teacher, instruments at the ready.

"Here's your A."

Mr. Darrow sang the pitch-perfect note, and the room reverberated with dissonance. Slowly, the strings slid into tune.

"Let's start at the top and try to get through the whole program without having to stop. I'm looking at you, second violins," he said, pointing his baton and furrowing his ginger eyebrows.

"Totally not my fault," Lexie said with a giggle.

"Never is." He rolled his eyes. "What are you doing to your hair?"

Lexie flicked her palm toward the tall ceiling with a shrug, a hot pink highlighter pinched between her fingers, absent of the bow present in those around her. "I'm coloring my hair."

"With a marker?"

"It's a highlighter. I'd never use marker," she said, shaking her head. "Too harsh."

"Of course. Silly me." His sarcastic smile fell into a scowl. "Alexandria, put the marker down and pick up your violin and bow."

Lexie released the strip of hair, capped the highlighter, and dropped it in her lap before grabbing her instrument and bow, offering a toothy smile.

The young musicians set their bows on the strings with the rise of Mr. Darrow's long arms high above them, the platform adding another seven inches to his already considerable height. With a strict downbeat of the baton, Kathryn drew her bow across the D string and leaned into her cello as they became one.

At the closing crescendo of the final piece, their bows lifted off the strings in unison, and Mr. Darrow's baton held steady.

"Eh. Hold your bows up until *after* I release my arms and they're at my sides. If I see an arm move a single inch, you'll be cleaning the file room for a month." His arms remained high. "Saw that," he snapped at a violist in the back row.

Kathryn's arm started to shake as she tightened her mouth to keep herself from smiling.

He continued to hold his arms up until his stern, freckled face began to crack. His arms fell, and the room burst with sighs of relief and laughter.

"That was actually pretty impressive, guys. Okay, I won't make any of you clean anything. For today, at least." His smile was wide, and his amber eyes shone their typical warmth. "Honestly, great job, everyone. Except you," he said, turning toward Lexie.

"Love ya, Mr. D!" Lexie winked.

Mr. Darrow chuckled. "Oh, lucky me."

Kathryn joined in with the unique energy that surrounded Mr. Darrow as he grinned back, laughing and beholding his students.

"Just a few things I noticed that probably no one else will, but I will, so you need to fix them. Violins, you need to really draw out the crescendo in the Vivaldi. You have time to build, so make it start even softer and then really push it forward. Violas, you need to come in a bit stronger on your solo in the Brahms. That's your moment. Seize it. Cellos, the Brandenburg... Yeah, you know what I'm talking about. It's not as together as I know it can be. Please work on it over the weekend. Staccato. Short, short, short. That's the only way the rhythm works and the only way your bows are going to keep up with your fingers. It's blending a tad too much. Other than that, excellent job, my little minions." He tapped the tips of his large fingers together and narrowed his eyes. "With only a few minutes left, I suppose you all can get packed up early. Just this once."

The students put away their instruments and stood by the door, waiting for first period to end.

"Well, that was a fun practice," Lexie said, snickering as the bell rang. "I'll see you in bio, Kathryn. I hope your day picks up a bit." She offered a gentle hand on Kathryn's shoulder.

"Thanks, Lex. I'm already feeling better."

They departed in opposite directions.

The day dragged on as class after class Kathryn fought to stay mentally present. It was a conscious and exhausting effort on her part to fight against the darkness creeping up on her, threatening to overtake her.

When Kathryn's lunch period began, she headed back to the orchestra room just as she had done every day this past week. She grabbed her lunch bag from her cello locker and opened the door to the file room.

"Back again?"

Mr. Darrow's voice startled her, and she turned to see him standing in his office doorway. "If that's okay."

"Hey, if you want to hide away in a tiny room and eat your lunch all by yourself, who am I to stop you?"

That was exactly what she wanted to do—hide.

"Thanks, Mr. D. I'll turn the light off when I leave."

Kathryn entered the cramped room packed with filing cabinets, leaving only a small space free for her to take refuge. She pulled the top chair off the stack in the corner and sat down. Closing her eyes, she listened to the silence and drew a deep breath as if emerging through water's glassy surface after a long dive. However, in the nothingness that surrounded her, she felt him starting to close in on her again. She scrambled for her book to distract her before he could come where he was not welcome. Opening the novel to page ninety-four, Kathryn leapt into the pages, escaping her own mind. She took out her lunch and started on the ham sandwich Aunt Hannah had packed for her. Reading had a way of accelerating time, and the end bell caught her off guard. She quickly gathered her things, placed the chair back on the pile, turned the light off, and raced to her next class across the school.

When the seventh-period end bell rang, Kathryn slipped her math book into her bag and started toward the science wing for biology. She spotted Lexie leaning against the doorframe, and calmness settled through her body.

"How's your day been?" Lexie asked.

"Okay, I guess."

They entered the classroom, where florescent lighting reflected off the black lab tables. The walls were adorned in posters with the headings "Parts of a Cell" and "Photosynthesis." A human skeleton replica rocked a fedora in the back corner, next to a wooden table equipped with petri dishes, microscopes, slides, and spare textbooks. The girls walked past Mr. Elliott's desk and down the narrow space between the rows of lab tables.

"Well, it looks like your day will be improving very shortly," Lexie said, nodding toward the back table.

Kathryn smirked and shook her head as she came to the lab table she shared with her lab partner, Liam.

"Hey, Kathryn." His chocolate eyes squinted as he flashed a sparkly white grin, stark against his olive skin.

"Hi," she said breathily, pulling her supplies from her backpack.

Mr. Elliott stood in the front of the room, his hands clasped behind his back, light reflecting off his glasses and balding head. "Good afternoon, class. Books and pencils out on the tables, please, and turn to page three hundred and ninety-four. We'll be continuing our lesson from yesterday on plant cells. Yes, I know. Exciting stuff."

Kathryn leaned against the table, rolling her pencil between her fingers, watching the embossed lettering on the shaft spin while Mr. Elliott droned on.

"Observe and examine the slides and note the characteristics available in your textbooks. Take detailed notes. Compare and discuss with your partners. Slides are on the back table. You have forty minutes. Let's get to it."

"I'll go get the slides," Liam said, nudging Kathryn's forearm with his pencil eraser.

Shuffling feet scraped against the bare tile while the whispers of discussion were peppered with the clinking of glass slides against metal microscopes. Kathryn rested her chin on her hand, mindlessly retracing her name

13

atop her lab report as a shadow crept across her paper, pulling her attention upward.

"Kathryn?"

"Oh, yes, Mr. Elliott?"

"How's it going over here?"

"We're fine. Liam just went to get the slides."

He took a few steps toward her desk and leaned in a bit closer, his voice soft. "You look sad today. Are you okay, Miss Lucas?" His words echoed in her fragile mind.

"Are you okay, Miss Lucas?"

She looked up from her math book and met Mrs. Donovan's glare. "Um...what?"

"I said you look sad today. Are you okay, Kathryn?"

"Oh, yeah, I'm okay."

"Well, then tell me the answer to the division question on the blackboard," she said sternly, peering at her through dark, thick-rimmed glasses.

She examined the problem. "Forty-nine divided by seven equals seven," she answered quietly.

"Very good."

Kathryn looked back down at her desk, but she could feel the attention upon her.

"What's got you so down?"

"Um...nothing. I'm fine." Glancing around the room, she met pairs of eyes everywhere she looked. She blushed and lowered her head again, raising her hand to her forehead to shield the onlookers.

"Well, you don't look fine. You look sad. We better do something about that." Mrs. Donovan sneered. "I think you should be smiling."

Kathryn watched her as she turned on her heel and grabbed a piece of chalk from the blackboard tray. She swiftly approached her and put her hand under Kathryn's chin, lifting it, her black fingernail polish gleaming under the harsh lighting. Pressing the chalk into her skin, she drew white lines on Kathryn's face from the corners of her mouth up her reddened cheeks.

"See, now you're smiling."

The room erupted with laughter as she looked away, tears in her eyes, desperately trying to wipe the chalk marks off her face with her long sleeves that concealed last night's secrets.

"Kathryn, are you all right?" Mr. Elliott asked.

"I'm fine." She offered a weak grin.

"Well, okay then." He returned a caring smile. "Mr. Pratton, find everything you need to begin?"

"Sure did, Mr. Elliott," Liam said, lifting the small box of slides.

"Excellent. Carry on."

Mr. Elliott eyed Kathryn once more before moving on to the next table.

"What was that about?" Liam asked.

"Oh, nothing. Let's just get started."

Liam shrugged and placed the first slide on the microscope. "Let's see. I think this looks like...my grandma's wallpaper."

"What?"

"It does! Look!" He slid her the microscope. "It's the same shade of putrid green and has a similarly hideous pattern."

Kathryn closed one eye and inspected the specimen, adjusting the fine focus knob. She consulted the images in her textbook. "I think it's an elodea leaf."

"Well, if you say so. I still think it looks like Grammy's wallpaper."

She giggled as she looked over at Liam, her mind free of anything outside of that moment and the way his deep voice hummed in her ears.

"There's that smile." He ran his hand through his thick, coal-black hair before jotting on his paper. "So, anything exciting happening this summer?"

"No. Not really," she said, her eye peering through the microscope at the next slide.

"Yeah, me neither. I'll probably just hang out with friends. And play baseball, of course, now that my wrist is healed. You know, just a normal summer. Pretty boring, I guess."

She pulled away from the eyepiece and turned to him. "Sounds nice, actually."

Their gaze held for a moment, and Kathryn could feel warmth crawling up her cheeks. "Look at this one." She turned the microscope toward him. "I think it's an onion."

He leaned in close to her to observe the slide. Kathryn inhaled his scent— clean and comforting. She was noticing his long eyelashes on his closed eye when movement to her right caught her attention. Lexie's eyes were wide, and a goofy grin was plastered on her face.

"What?" Kathryn mouthed.

Lexie smiled broadly while silently clapping.

Kathryn breathed a laugh, rolling her eyes.

"Yup," Liam said as he lifted his head. "Definitely an onion."

Kathryn could feel Lexie staring at them, but she kept her focus on finishing their lab assignment. They were writing down the last of their notes when the bell rang.

Mr. Elliot strode to the front of the room through the center aisle carved out by the lab tables. "Please leave your papers on my desk. Have a nice weekend, everyone."

"The period's over already? Geez, that went by quickly." Liam stood and arched his back, stretching his tall, lean form. "Well, I have to get to baseball practice."

"On a Friday?"

"Oh, yeah. Coach doesn't cut us any slack," he said, shoving his textbook into his backpack. "See you Monday, Kathryn."

"Bye," she said, returning his smile.

She was packing her bag when Lexie rammed into her side, almost knocking her off her feet.

"I saw all that, you know." She giggled.

"Saw what?"

"Liam flirting with you for like the whole period!"

"Oh, stop. He was not. He's just a nice guy."

"Look, I know flirting. I'm a flirting master."

"That's true."

"He totally likes you. Trust me."

Kathryn shook her head. "You're crazy."

Lexie and Kathryn returned to their lockers to gather up the books they needed for homework over the weekend. They pushed open the double doors leading outside and walked into the afternoon air warm and sweet with spring.

"I'm telling you, girl. He's so into you." She elbowed her arm and laughed. "Seriously though, it was nice to see you happy." She linked Kathryn's arm and leaned her head on her shoulder.

As they arrived at Lexie's bus, she unhooked from her friend. "I'll call you this weekend, okay?"

"Hey, Lex?"

Lexie stopped on the steps and turned to face her.

"Thanks."

Lexie smiled, mirroring Kathryn. "Always."

Kathryn found her bus and climbed into an empty seat toward the back. Knowing Val would be there soon, she held on to the quiet moment. Being alone once more with nothing to distract her, the weight of it all set in again, the thoughts of Liam vanquished. She leaned her head against the window and watched the kids walking past. There had to be others. She could not be the only one.

Val flopped down next to her and slammed her black backpack on her lap. "Ugh. Today sucked. I had two tests, and I know I didn't do good on them."

"Sorry."

"Whatever. School's stupid. I just want to go home so I can finally have a smoke."

"Any plans this weekend?"

"Partying at my house. Well, of course at my house. It obviously won't be at yours."

The disdain in her voice grated at Kathryn's already worn nerves. "It's not like I asked for this."

"Yeah, but you went to them and told."

"I was scared!"

"I know. It just sucks, okay?"

"Yeah, it does suck." Kathryn felt her nails digging into her palms as her fists tightened. She was in no mood to listen to Val go on again about how much of an inconvenience this was to her.

"So, what are you doing this weekend?" Val asked.

"Probably practicing for my concert next week."

"Sounds boring."

"Well, not to me."

"Whatever." Val slapped her magazine on her lap as her dark hair fell, shielding her face from view.

Kathryn snapped her head away from Val and toward the window. Determined not to break again, she closed her eyes and inhaled deeply as the bus began to pull away. *I can't be the only one.*

Changed

The sun had barely broken the horizon when Kathryn woke with a start the next morning, muted daylight creeping through the edges of the drawn blinds. She lay with her moistened eyes closed for a few minutes, red and orange embers dancing through the darkness behind her eyelids—remnants of her fiery nightmares that continued to seep into her reality.

In her typical escape attempt, she sat up and grabbed her book on the nightstand and slipped on her glasses. After reading the same sentence seven times, she snapped the book shut and groaned. Kathryn rested her diary on her folded knees and tapped the pink pen on the blank page. She encased the letters "LP" in a bubbly heart and traced it into a thick, sparkly line before resigning and getting out of bed. Mittens mewed at Kathryn as she passed. Sliding her fingers into the blinds, she parted the smooth plastic and peered out at the front yard. A faint mist imprisoned the white birches that scattered the lawn, and gray clouds refused to let the sun penetrate their stubborn gloom. The dull morning painted the still street in haze and blurred the outlines of the houses on the other side.

It called to her. It beckoned. It demanded she share in its despair.

She threw on some black stretchy pants and a gray T-shirt and tied her hair back in a ponytail. After putting her contacts in, she carefully peeked into Aunt Hannah and Uncle Alex's bedroom. Aunt Hannah was sitting up reading a book, with her left hand stroking Uncle Alex's brown hair while he slept.

"Aunt Hannah, I'm going to go for a walk," she whispered.

"This early?"

"Yeah. I just want to get out and clear my head a little."

"Okay, dear. Be safe."

"I will, and I'll be back in a little while for breakfast."

Stepping out onto the porch, she inhaled the thick, warm air stagnant and heavy with moisture. Kathryn walked to the edge of the driveway and looked to her right. The modest two-story home dressed in dark wood siding stood a quarter mile down and across the street. She turned to her left and started down the sidewalk, her blue sneakers disturbing the gathering of whirlybird seeds damp with the morning dew.

The sidewalks were empty, the street deserted save for a few random cars passing by, offering sharp blasts of cool air, a welcome relief against the unusual humidity. Kathryn closed her eyes while she walked and leaned her head back, taking in the comforting scents and sounds of her small corner of Edgebrook. Her sneaker hit against the well-manicured grass, and she broke back into the scene around her.

To her left, she observed the ivory brick Cape Cod two houses down from her current residence. Red shutters to match the door lined a large picture window, the inside hidden by drawn curtains. House after house, Kathryn met only tightly closed drapes blocking out the world and prying eyes.

She stopped in front of a traditional red brick ranch that, unlike the others, was open to the shafts of sunlight that were just beginning to peek through the conceding clouds. The TV flickered with Saturday morning cartoons and innocent happiness. The plump, orange cat sat with his usual grumpy puss as his human waited on him, and the dopey, floppy-eared dog remained oblivious.

Kathryn watched as a child stood up in front of the TV and rushed into another room. Within seconds, the child returned, pulling their mother by the hand, her long hair in a high ponytail. The child jumped up and down, presumably excited to show their mother something silly that chubby feline had just done.

Her smile didn't last long before it faded. She closed her eyes as the darkness tried to sweep her away once again. Shaking her head, she continued down the path.

As she fought away that look in his eyes, her left foot caught the unnoticed imperfection in the sidewalk. Pain stabbed her ankle as it gave way, and her hands and knees hit the concrete.

Kathryn screamed as he grabbed her hair and threw her into the wall, and her hands and knees hit the floor, pain radiating throughout her shoulder and scalp.

"Why did you do that?" Jane screamed.

"She's a pain in the ass little bitch."

Kathryn gasped through her wails as she cowered against the wall, familiar rage coating his voice.

"Leave me alone!"

Breathing heavily, Kathryn rolled herself off her knees and brought herself to sitting, surveying her surroundings. Her vision drifted to her side, tracking the immense height of a newly budding ash tree towering over her, sheathing her in its shadow. Its roots had infiltrated the concrete, causing it to rise into a menacing hurdle to someone lost in their own mind or a young child on their bike still stabilized by training wheels. Crushed stone, sand, cement, and water—lesser materials united to create one of strength and stability. Yet there it lay—broken, cracked, destroyed, ruined by the tree's determination to survive, spreading its roots outward regardless of the casualties.

Kathryn, its latest victim, lifted her pant leg to reveal a scraped knee and took off her shoe and sock to examine her ankle. She rubbed it in a meager attempt to ease the pain and passed her finger over the centimeter long, slightly raised scar on the inside of her ankle, the memory trying to overtake her.

No.

She slid her sock and shoe back on before crawling to the grass and using the tree's trunk to pull herself up, the pain pushing the memory aside. Her face pinched with the first few steps, but the stabbing began to lessen as she slowly made her way back to the house. She saw her own home in the distance as she neared her temporary residence, and she clenched her teeth. Even a simple walk led back to him; it happened far too often.

Kathryn gripped the wooden porch railing and limped up the stairs, fighting through the ache in her ankle. She pushed open the purple door to find Jake and Sam sitting on the couch in the living room, watching TV and snacking on dry cereal.

"Hey, Kathryn. You have to come see this. It's hilarious!" Sam said through an overflowing mouth.

"Nah. I think I'm going to take a shower."

Without looking at her cousins, she walked straight to the bathroom and shut the door, leaning her forehead against the beveled detailing. She disrobed and slid the band out of her hair, tossing it on the ivory vanity. Sitting on the tub floor, she hugged her knees to her chest as the water rained down upon her, pounding against her head, blocking out all sound. She cranked the steaming water as it stung her skin. Kathryn welcomed the pain, freeing her mind from the distressing memories haunting her lately. He had finally broken her, fragmented her protective barriers, allowing triggers to attack the fragility of her mind. Weak was never what she wanted to be, yet her tears bled in with the water pooling around her as she sank deeper and deeper into a chasm of despair from which she feared she could never escape.

The soft knock on the door drew Kathryn's pen across the pages of her diary as she flinched, shrinking back against the wall again. Her breath rushed through her lips, and she rolled her eyes, annoyed with her involuntary reaction.

"Come in."

"Hi, dear. Your friend Rachael is on the phone for you."

Kathryn reached for it. "Thanks, Aunt Hannah."

"Hey, Rachael. What's up?"

"Hey, girl! It's been like a week since I've talked to you. How's it going over there? Probably crazy boring, right?"

"It's…quiet, but that's kind of a nice change."

"So, you like it over there?"

"I miss my mom, but yeah, I do. Kinda nice not being scared all the time."

"But don't you miss our awesome Friday nights?"

"I miss *you*. But to be honest, I don't miss everything else."

"Hmm… I just got off the phone with Val, and I know she misses Fridays!" She laughed.

"I'm sure she does."

There was a break in the discussion, a thick cut in the lifelong friends' usual upbeat conversational dance—a separation of sorts, a disease spreading through their relationship, slowly eroding away at what Kathryn once held so dear.

"Anyway, I'm going to hang out at the mall with some of my friends today. Do you wanna come?"

"What friends?"

"Just some guys I met in my dad's new neighborhood. They're super cool. They're pretty hot too!"

Kathryn hesitated. "I guess so. I'll just have to check with Uncle Alex and Aunt Hannah, but I think it should be fine."

After Aunt Hannah gave the okay, Kathryn put herself together and waited outside on the porch steps for Rachael and these friends of hers. A chill spread through her, and a tightness pulled at her stomach. She twisted the hem of her purple shirt around her finger, watching the blood drain from the lower half and pool in her fingertip.

As the car rattled into the driveway, she uncoiled the shirt, smoothing it out over her jeans. Rachael jumped out of the car and ran over to meet Kathryn, stumbling on the uneven stone pathway. Her platinum hair fell into her face, and she reached up for Kathryn's shoulders to keep herself standing.

Rachael laughed hysterically. "Whoa, great entrance, huh? Oh my God. That was close." She leaned over and rested her hands on her knees, continuing to laugh. Gathering control of her breathing, she stood and held her side. "Damn. That hurts. Okay. I'm good." She exhaled deeply. "Okay. Yup. I'm done. Hey! How's it going? Let's go shopping! You ready to go?"

"You're completely crazy." Kathryn wiped the tears from her eyes and reined in her laughter.

Rachael bowed deeply with a flourishing gesture. "You know you missed me!" She leaned in for a hug.

"Of course I did," Kathryn said, pulling away. "I'm ready. Let's go."

The black sedan was more rust than paint, and it shook as it idled. Rachael jiggled the door handle while lifting up with an unsettling amount of effort. On the second try, it creaked open, and she stood aside for Kathryn to get in.

Kathryn hesitated a moment before slowly moving toward the black death on wheels and clambered into the back seat.

The boy behind the wheel turned to face her, sweeping his long, dark hair off his smooth face and flicking it behind his pierced ear. "Sup? I'm Steve."

"I'm Caleb," said the boy in the passenger seat.

"Hi. I'm Kathryn."

"Oh, we know. Rachael's told us all about you." Steve slid on his sunglasses and pulled out into the street.

"All good. I promise." Rachael nudged her arm and snickered.

"So, Kathryn, we need to know what Rach was like as a kid. Still a pain in the ass?"

"Very funny, jerk." Rachael forcefully shoved the back of Caleb's seat.

"Um…pretty much like she is now. Rach is Rach. Always has been and no apologies."

"Ha! Damn straight. And she oughta know. Been my girl since we were babies. And we stayed friends even when I moved to Florida." Her arm landed on Kathryn's shoulder, and she gave her a squeeze.

Kathryn gripped the torn seat the whole way to the mall while Steve,

Caleb, and Rachael jabbed back and forth at each other and recounted last night's shenanigans.

"No, dude, seriously. I was so drunk when I got home. Oh, and totally stoned. My mom caught me in the kitchen, looking for some munchies. I thought she'd figure it out for sure, man, but she didn't say anything," Steve said, laughing.

"Damn, man. You're lucky. I've been caught before. It wasn't a pretty sight. My mom was so pissed. Grounded forever, she told me. Yeah, right. I was drinking and getting high a few days later." Caleb looked back and winked at Kathryn.

Her eyes darted toward the window and stayed there.

Steve parked the car, and Kathryn followed behind the group as they entered the mall.

Rachael slowed and stayed back with Kathryn, leaning into her. "Oh, calm down, Kathryn. They're fine. So they get drunk and high. Big deal. Be cool."

"Rach—"

"Just come on."

She trailed them, feeling more and more out of place and aching to be back at her aunt and uncle's. Store after store, their conversations consisted of getting drunk and high and an obscene amount of swearing.

"It's not like you've been a perfect angel, you know, Kathryn," Rachael said as they left a clothing store.

"I don't pretend to be a perfect angel. But I'm trying to distance myself from that stuff. I...I don't want that life anymore."

"Since when?"

"Pretty much always. I know you like it, so fine. Whatever. But I don't. Being away from that house...it's making me see things differently."

"It wasn't *that* bad over there."

Kathryn stopped, spinning on her friend. "Seriously? You were on the phone when it happened, Rach."

"I'm not saying that wasn't awful. I'm just saying it wasn't all bad there. We had so much fun. You, me, and Val had a blast. Are you saying you didn't have fun with us?"

"I'm not saying that, but we can still have fun together. It'll just be different. Are you not going to want to be my friend if I'm not drinking with you?"

"Of course not. Stop. We've been friends forever, and nothing's going to change that."

"Val obviously doesn't feel that way. She hasn't even called me this whole past week." Kathryn picked up her pace again, her jaw tight.

"Really? Well, I don't know what her problem is, but I'm not her."

Kathryn felt the embarrassment of her outburst crawl up her cheeks. "I'm sorry. It's…it's all just been a lot."

"I know. And I'm sorry too. This all really sucks." Rachael stopped, looking around. "Ugh. Where are Steve and Caleb?" The girls sat on an iron bench facing a wishing pond in the middle of the wide hallway, complete with water fountain. "So, when do you think you'll go back home?"

"I don't know. Not any time soon." Kathryn flicked a penny off her thumb and watched it break through the water and sink to the silver and copper bottom.

"So not by next Friday?"

Kathryn snapped her head toward Rachael.

"Chill, Kathryn! I'm just kidding! Geez."

Silence.

Kathryn could feel Rachael's gaze as she watched the water droplets falling to the surface of the clear water, disturbing the pool lined with quarters, pennies, and wishes.

"You're different," Rachael said, her voice turning soft. "You just…don't seem to be the same since moving there."

"I'm not the same."

"Don't let them change you."

Kathryn broke her stare away from the fountain. "What? They're not changing me. I'm changing me. He changed me. I don't want…" She sighed harshly. "They're helping me."

"I know. I'd just hate to see you become someone you're not."

The irony almost brought Kathryn to hysterics, and she released a laugh laced with astonishment. How had she fooled Rachael so wholly, so completely? How could she not have seen through the farce this whole time?

"Someone I'm not? Rach, did it ever occur to you that this is who I am? Not that other person I was when I was with Val?"

"What? That doesn't make any—"

"Let's get out of here," Steve said, looking around hastily, Caleb at his heels.

"Where were you guys?" Rachael asked, coming to her feet.

"Just come on."

Kathryn followed them through the mall and back out the way they came in. As they walked into the parking lot, she heard the guys laughing, and Rachael jogged up behind them.

Rachael gasped. "You didn't." Her head snapped back in laughter.

"Oh, I sure as hell did," Steve said, pulling a black shirt out of his pants.

Kathryn's eyes widened at the stolen shirt, and heat shot through her. She braced herself for helicopters swarming the skies, descending upon them in a cloud of dust, for the police sirens surrounding the group, ready to slap the cuffs on them, for the SWAT team to charge the teens and take them down as they stood in the mall parking lot with the stolen eight-dollar shirt.

"Dude, that's awesome," said Caleb as he admired the shirt.

Kathryn fought to catch her breath. "I want to leave, Rachael."

She rolled her eyes. "Relax, Kathryn."

Kathryn looked at her friend, her blue eyes fierce. "Please."

"Ugh. Fine. Come on, guys. Kathryn wants to go back to her aunt and uncle's."

"Yeah, sure. Whatever," Steve said as he started walking to the car.

On the ten-minute drive back, Kathryn said nothing. She merely looked out the window and regretted ever answering Rachael's phone call. An uncomfortable twinge began building in her stomach, a severe disappointment thinking about their diverging paths—paths that were leading both girls from the same starting point but very different destinations.

Upon arriving back at the house, Kathryn was just thankful to not be in handcuffs. She followed Rachael out of the car and stomped past her and toward the house without looking back at Steve and Caleb.

Kathryn stepped onto the porch and turned to face her friend. "That was not okay, Rach."

"Oh, calm down, Kath."

"They stole something! What if we would have all gotten caught? Like I don't have enough to deal with right now?"

"That's just who they are."

"Well, I want nothing to do with them. I can't believe that you do. Don't bring them around me anymore." She swung open the purple front door. "See ya, Rachael." She let it close behind her without waiting for a response. Leaning against the door, her hand fluttered up to the ache in her chest.

"Hi, dear. How was your outing?" Aunt Hannah looked up from her knitting, her fingers still working.

"Um…fine. I'm kind of tired though. I'm going to go lie down."

She crashed on the blue comforter, and Mittens crawled out from under the bed and jumped up to see her.

"Hi, pretty girl."

Mittens pressed her nose to Kathryn's forehead.

"I can't believe Rachael did this to me, Mitters. She knows I wouldn't be comfortable with those guys. Why would she invite me along with them? I don't know what happened to her. We used to be so close. We were practically the same person. Now…" Kathryn caught a tear before it fell on Mittens' head. "She knows what he's done. She's seen it for years. She was even on the phone when he came in and…" She inhaled a ragged breath. "Rachael knows. Why would she…?"

Kathryn buried her face in the white tummy as Mittens kneaded the side of her head. After hiding herself away for hours, sleep came for her early that night, attempting to whisk away the anger, sadness, and betrayal, protecting her from even more loss.

Protect Me

Kathryn spent Sunday doing what she really loved—playing the cello. She needed to nail her part. As second chair, there were no excuses. After an hour, her fingers hurt, and her bowing arm was sore, but she had gotten it down. It was flawless.

As she raised the bow off the A string, holding her arm in the air as the tone reverberated through the small music room, the oak bifold doors parted slightly, and a set of thick lips puckered through the opening.

"Pssst...Kathryn."

She looked over, her arm still floating above her cello. "Uh...yeah?"

Jake held the knobs steady, his face smushed against the edge of the doors, altering his intelligibility. "Are you done?" he whispered.

"Yeah." She lowered her arm and stifled a laugh.

He swiftly swung the doors open in unison, the rush of wind ruffling his red plaid button down. "Then come play The Game of Life with us. I'm going to beat Sam this time. Mark my words." His eyes narrowed.

Kathryn's laugh broke through, and she placed her cello on its side next to her chair.

"And Mom's making popcorn!" Jake opened his mouth and stuck out his tongue, feigning drooling.

Her cousin's goofiness pulled at her lips, and she shook her head. "I'll go help her." Kathryn walked through the living room where Sam and Uncle Alex were rearranging the chairs around the coffee table.

"Do you need help, Aunt Hannah?"

She brushed her bangs off her forehead with the back of her wrist. "Can you ask the boys if they want butter?"

"Sure." She backtracked and peeked her head around the cased opening. "You want butter, right?"

"Obviously," said Jake and Sam in unison.

Kathryn returned to Aunt Hannah's side. "Obviously," she said, mimicking their voices with a chuckle.

"Silly us for even asking." Aunt Hannah placed the pad of butter in a small steel pan and began swirling it with a wooden spoon as it liquefied, spreading across the bottom. "So, sweetie, I don't want to push, but are you okay? You seemed upset when you got home from spending time with Rachael yesterday."

"She's just…not who she used to be. It feels like she's changing. She's actually more like Val, I guess, and I've been feeling more and more like I don't want to be friends with Val anymore. But Rachael is my oldest friend. We've been friends since we were kids. I don't think I can let that go."

"Well, you might not have to let it go. Maybe just get a bit of space. Rachael may be changing, but so are you, my dear." She tilted her head slightly, her hazel eyes soft and unblinking. "I see it. I've seen it for a while. Especially after everything that's happened. It would be impossible to not change. You just want to be careful you're changing into someone you like, someone you're happy with. Don't let him have too strong of an effect on who you become, though. Don't let him take that from you too. And as far as Rachael and Val, take some time to think about it. You can have as much or as little contact with them as you'd like. That's your choice. I'll pray for you, my dear. You'll find the path that has been set out for you."

The popcorn exploding and jumping around in the pan blurred through the tears welling up in Kathryn's eyes. "Thanks, Aunt Hannah."

Aunt Hannah leaned over and put her arm around Kathryn and gave her a squeeze. "Any time."

"The game is set up!" Sam called from the living room.

"Popcorn! Popcorn! Popcorn!" Jake and Sam's chants floated through the kitchen.

"All right, boys." Aunt Hannah carried in two big bowls of hot, freshly made popcorn drizzled with butter.

"Looks yummy," Sam said, snatching a handful. "Thanks, Mama."

Uncle Alex cleared his throat, rubbed his hands together, and started separating the colored car pieces. "Let's get this game started."

Everyone grabbed a spot around the small coffee table.

"Here's the yellow car," Sam said, passing the piece to Kathryn. "I'm blue!"

"Red!" shouted Jake.

"Here's the white car for you, my darling," Uncle Alex said, placing the piece in front of Aunt Hannah before kissing the top of her head. "I'll be green."

Every time Sam went to put a person peg in his car, it fell out, and Aunt Hannah shouted, "Roadkill!" It was silly, perhaps even corny, but it allowed Kathryn to escape into happiness if only for a little while as they huddled around the coffee table, the board game spread out before them, laughing as a real family.

By the time Wednesday night arrived, excitement pulsated through her fingertips twitching to dance along the neck of her cello on stage. With a quick wave to her family upon entering the high school, she set off through the halls.

The voices and tones of open strings grew louder as she came upon the orchestra room. All dressed in crisp black, her fellow students were scurrying around making sure their instruments were in tune. Kathryn made her way over to Lexie, who had her violin tucked under her arm and was swinging her bow around her finger.

"Hey, Kathryn! Are you ready?"

"Oh, I'm ready. Are you?"

"Meh." She laughed. "Is your mom coming tonight?"

"Yeah, she always comes. I don't think she's ever missed a single performance."

"Your dad?"

"Probably not."

"Aw…I'm sorry."

"I'm sure he'll call tonight and apologize. 'Hey, baby girl. I'm sorry I couldn't make it, but I bet you were perfect. I'll try to make the next one, okay?'" She shrugged. "It's fine. I'm used to it. I know he comes when he can. Your mom and dad are here?"

"Yup. And my sister."

"How's Anne doing?"

"Still has her rough days. Especially in school. Her first year of middle

31

school has been challenging. She gets so easily overwhelmed. I'm just hoping she can handle the concert. Loud sounds can be difficult for her. But you have to see how cute she looks in her new dress. She's so adorable. I *may* have put a pink highlighter streak in her hair to match the flowers." Lexie snickered.

"In your seats for warmups, people!" Mr. Darrow called out.

"I'd better get my cello."

"Good luck. You'll do great," Lexie said, giving her a quick hug.

"Thanks. You too."

By the time she got out her cello, the students were already sitting in their chairs for warmups. Mr. Darrow sang his A, and the students tuned their strings. After running through a few scales, it was time to go to the auditorium.

Kathryn took her cello by the neck and grabbed her bow, sheet music, and endpin rest and followed her stand partner, Cari, through the halls and to the side of the stage, the other cellists lining up behind them. Just hoping she wouldn't trip over her long, flowing, black skirt, she filed out to applause, and they all took their seats as the strong stage lights flooded down upon them. Vibrations filled the hall as the orchestra ceremoniously tuned as one, the notes resonating off the strings, blurring and mashing together, creating disharmony.

The crowd of family and friends clapped again as Mr. Darrow came out and took his place at the podium center stage, his tall, slender frame standing high above the seated musicians. He bowed and turned his suit-coated back to the audience. Holding his students within his amber gaze, he raised his baton. With the downbeat motion of his arm, they began.

As her fingers pressed into the neck of her cello and her bow glided across the strings, it was as if her mind shut off and her body took over. With a wave of relief, Kathryn was completely lost in the melody and harmonies as the violins and violas conversed, and the cellos answered with their low, deep voices, the basses creating a stable platform for the others upon which to dance. Her lips pulled up into a smile, the most genuine, true smile she had felt in far too long.

With her last down-bowed stroke, the concert was finished, and they all held their bows steady in the air. The auditorium erupted in applause, and as Mr. Darrow's baton dropped, their bows returned to their knees in resting position. He smiled as he scooped his hands up, signaling the orchestra to stand. They all rose to their feet, faced the audience, and graciously bowed as Mr. Darrow swept his hand up and toward the players, presenting them proudly.

After a final bow, they exited the stage and returned their instruments to their cases in the orchestra room as footsteps and chatter filled the halls. Lexie eyed Kathryn from across the room and gave her a nod. Kathryn took a deep breath and went to find her family.

She weaved in and out of the students receiving hugs and flowers from their families. Sam waved his long arms above the crowd, catching her attention, and she went to meet them.

"Fantastic concert, Kathryn!" Uncle Alex pulled her into a hug. "All that practicing sure paid off. The Brandenburg was flawless. Just wonderful."

"Oh, it was simply beautiful, my dear," Aunt Hannah said as she gave Kathryn a squeeze.

"Kathryn?"

She looked over slowly, her heart rate quickening. "Hi, Mom."

"Sweetie, that was just lovely. I love watching you play. You looked so grown up on that stage." She extended her arms and welcomed her daughter into an embrace.

Kathryn leaned into her and rested her head against her shoulder, her loose brown curls brushing against Kathryn's cheek. "Thanks, Mom. I'm so glad you came."

Jane broke away, and their blue eyes met. "I'm...*so* proud of you, Kathryn." Tears welled up in her eyes. "You look beautiful tonight."

She held her again, and Kathryn pulled her in tighter.

Lexie found Kathryn and her family through the heavy crowd and pulled her parents and little sister along behind her. "Hey, everyone!"

"The girls were really great tonight, weren't they?" asked Lexie's mom.

"They sure were, Dyann." Jane tucked Kathryn's hair behind her ear. "They were absolutely wonderful."

"Yeah, you were t-totally awesome," Jake said in Lexie's direction before inspecting the scuffed floor.

"Thanks," Lexie said, the corner of her mouth pulling upward.

"Oh dear, Jane." Dyann's fingertips floated to her mouth. "What did you do to your arm?"

Jane put her good hand on her swollen arm wrapped in a tan compression sleeve. "I have lymphedema. It's a side effect of my breast cancer surgery about five years ago. The sleeve keeps the swelling down and under control."

"Goodness. I apologize. I didn't mean to pry."

"It's perfectly fine. I don't always wear the sleeve, but when I do, I get asked a lot." Jane smiled. "We're going out for a celebratory dinner if you would like to join us."

Jake looked up from the intriguing tiles. "Yeah, you should totally come."

Kathryn stifled a giggle.

"Oh, thank you so much for the invitation, but I'm afraid we need to get Anne home. Tonight has been a bit overwhelming for her."

Dressed in yellow lace, the near replica of Lexie stood on her tiptoes, pressing her ear into her mom's arm, anxiety written on her young face.

Kathryn observed disappointment flash across Lexie's features as her shoulders slumped and her vision dropped to the floor.

Jane nodded. "Well, another time then."

"Absolutely." Dyann turned to Kathryn. "It was wonderful to see you again."

"You too, Mrs. Dabrowski."

"See you tomorrow, Kathryn," Lexie said over her shoulder as they turned to leave.

"Bye, Lex."

"Okay. Who's ready for some dinner?" asked Uncle Alex.

"Oh, I'm always ready," Sam said, rubbing his stomach.

Jane placed a soft hand on Kathryn's shoulder. "Sweetie, would you like to ride with me to the restaurant?"

"Sure, Mom."

She returned Kathryn's smile.

"We'll see you there then," Aunt Hannah said as she took Uncle Alex's hand.

Kathryn climbed into the front seat of her mom's car. Fidgeting with her Claddagh ring on her middle finger, she stared out the window, unsure of what to say. Feeling uncomfortable with her mom was unfamiliar, unsettling.

Jane was the one to finally break the silence. "So, how has everything been going?"

"Um...okay I guess."

"How's Mittens adjusting?"

"She's still mostly hiding out in the room. She's starting to kind of creep out just a little bit. She let Aunt Hannah pet her the other day."

"I'm glad." Her left hand rose into her hair, twisting the ends between her fingers. "I sent in the form and payment for orchestra camp just the other day. So you're all set there. I requested Grace as your preferred roommate."

"Perfect. Thanks, Mom."

"Are you excited to go back this summer?"

"Totally. I can't wait to see Grace again."

Silence once again held them in its awkward grasp. Kathryn sighed when her mom began again.

"I'll never forget the first year I dropped you off three years ago. It was

34

like dropping my twelve-year-old off at college. Such a strange feeling. But I'm so glad you love it there."

"I get to spend a week on a college campus with my friends and play my cello all day and night. What's not to love?" She smiled. "I'm also hoping this is finally my year for my quartet to make it into the Honors Recital."

"I bet you will."

"You're just saying that because you're my mom."

"Doesn't mean it's not true. You've worked so hard this year. I have to practically make you stop practicing."

Kathryn chuckled. "True."

After the first natural, somewhat comfortable conversation she had had with her mom since it all happened, the silence resumed. Her attention returned to the approaching nightfall blurring behind her translucent reflection as Kathryn focused on her image in the window. There beside her mom whom she missed so deeply, she couldn't suppress the memory of the last time they were together.

The fictional world into which Kathryn was trying to disappear simply couldn't compete tonight. Not tonight. The doorbell startled her, and she snapped her book shut and placed it on the bed. She closed her eyes and inhaled deeply, trying to calm her breathing and settle her stomach. It was pointless.

Kathryn walked into the hallway, tracing her finger along the wall. She glanced up at the framed pictures and caught the eyes of the little girl holding her baby doll. Wiping the tears off her warm cheek, she entered the living room.

Aunt Hannah sat on the flowered loveseat near the window, lemon water in hand. Uncle Alex cracked the door again to let Max, their tuxedo cat, outside to hunt for a special present. He closed the purple door and met Kathryn's eyes as she slowly stepped farther into the room.

Jane hunched near the door, leaning over to remove her soft flats, her amber pendant swinging from her neck. She straightened her long, dark skirt and looked up at her. "Oh, sweetie." Her mom swept her into an embrace as Kathryn's arms remained at her sides. Releasing her, she looked upon her daughter, a shaking hand softly resting upon her cheek. "Kathryn...I..." She tore her gaze from her daughter's face, shooting it toward the floor.

Kathryn remained silent, unmoving. Her mother's eyes met hers once more.

"I'm so...I'm so sorry. I can't believe that it's come to this. Sweetie, I...I want you to come home. Please. It's where you belong."

Kathryn took a step back. Her mind whirled with countless thoughts and emotions she couldn't hope to decipher.

"Why don't we all take a seat?" Uncle Alex calmly suggested. He sat down next to Aunt Hannah on the loveseat and took her hand.

Kathryn sat in the floral rocking chair across from the couch, facing her mother. Her left hand rested on her right, her poised fingers tapping as if skittering along the neck of her cello.

"Well, Jane, we wanted you to come over tonight to talk about what has happened and where we can go from here. Would you like to start?" Uncle Alex asked, his composure calm and gentle as though he mediated awkward gatherings for a living.

Jane turned her red-laced eyes upon her daughter. "Kathryn, honey, I love you, and I'm so sorry this has happened to you. I want you to come home. Please."

Kathryn couldn't find her voice. She simply stared at her mother—her sobbing, broken mother—and tried to no avail to find sympathy for her pain. In that moment, she simply had none to give. Her own agony was all she could see, all she could feel as it gripped her tightly around the neck and refused to surrender its hold. Its grasp was too strong, too consuming to let in anyone else's pain.

"Please come home with me. I can keep you safe. I won't let this happen again."

She fought for air, fought for her voice; she couldn't hold it in any longer. "You couldn't stop it the first time, Mom, or the second or third or any other time. You've never been able to stop it."

"I know, but I'm trying my best. If you just come back home, we can all sit down and talk about it. I'm sure we can sort all this out."

"Sit down and talk about it?" A laugh forced its way past her taut lips, starting quietly and building before her eyes hardened and her face fell flat. "I'm scared, Mom! I'm scared of him. Don't you get that? You're not home all the time. You can't always be there."

"I know, but I'll talk to him and make it clear—"

"What's talking to him going to do? He's going to do whatever he wants like he always does! He's going to do it again! Especially because he knows I ran over here and told someone." The reality of her words hit her like an all-too-familiar strike to the stomach. She told. It wasn't a secret anymore. "I'm scared for my life! This has been going on for too long. I can't live like this anymore!"

Aunt Hannah shifted uncomfortably, and Uncle Alex squeezed her hand.

Jane looked down at the beige carpet, her loose curls draping over her swollen face. "I...I guess I didn't realize just how bad it was."

"That's because he won't let me tell anyone! He threatens me! 'Don't you tell anyone or else you'll get it even worse.'" She was up on her feet without memory of her movements. "And don't act like you don't know about anything he does. You've seen it before."

"Kathryn, I...I don't know what to do. He's my son."

"And I'm your daughter! Why won't you protect me?" She stepped toward her, tears flowing down her reddened face. "Why won't you protect ME!"

Kathryn ran out of the room, hysterical and gasping as she flew down the hall and slammed the bedroom door. She threw herself on the bed and buried her face in the pillow, muffling her screams. The pain pulled at her chest and tightened around her throat, suffocating her.

When it felt as though she had no tears left, she pulled her face from her dampened pillow and sat up, trying to smooth her ragged breathing. Loud voices caught her attention, and she thought she heard someone crying.

She slid off the bed slowly. As she stood, brightness blurred into darkness as her head adjusted to its new upright position, and she gripped the bed to keep her balance. When her vision cleared, she cracked open the door and listened.

"I'm so sorry. Oh my God. I'm so sorry!" It was Jane talking through her sobs. "I didn't know he was there. I didn't see him. I didn't know he was under the car. I'm so sorry. I didn't know he was there."

Kathryn hurried over to the front window in the bedroom. The headlights flooded the driveway, and the car was parked in an awkward position. She surveyed the scene and gasped when she saw him. Their cat, Max, was lying under the car, lifeless.

"Oh my God. Max." Tears stung her sore eyes. "I caused this," she whispered. "Mom wouldn't have even been here if I hadn't run over here. She's here because of me." Then it came to her, boiling up from within. She stopped crying, and her eyes hardened, looking past her reflection in the window at poor Max on the ground, still, motionless, her sadness overtaken with anger. "No. Not because of me. We're not in this situation because of me. I'm here because of him. Because of my brother."

After a pleasant, albeit uncomfortable dinner, she said goodbye to her mom at the restaurant and went back with Uncle Alex and Aunt Hannah. Upon arriving at the house, she retreated into the bedroom and changed into her pajamas.

Curled up on the bed with Mittens, she was starting to drift off to sleep when there was a knock on the door. It opened with a gentle squeak, and Uncle Alex appeared around the edge.

"Kathryn, your dad is on the phone for you. Don't stay on too long, though. Please be done by nine thirty. You need to get to bed soon."

She nodded.

"Hello?"

"Hello, my baby girl."

Kathryn shook her head at the higher pitch of his voice—a clear indication he had been drinking.

"Hi, Dad."

"I called your house, and your mom said you were sleeping over at your aunt and uncle's."

"Um…yeah."

"I'm sorry I didn't make it to your concert tonight. I was working late at the bar, and you know how I don't like to drive at night."

"It's okay, Dad."

"I wish I could have been there. I bet you were great."

"Yeah, it went really well."

"Maybe you can come over and play your part for me."

"I could, but it won't sound right. I don't have the melody most of the time."

"That's okay. I'd like to hear it anyway. I really am sorry I wasn't there. I'll try to make the next one, okay?"

Silence.

"Well, it's late. I'll let you get back to your sleepover. I just wanted to tell you I was thinking about you and that I love you the mostest. But you already knew that, didn't you? See you later, alligator."

"After a while, crocodile."

He laughed. "I love you, Kathryn."

"I love you too, Dad."

"Thank you."

"You're welcome."

"Goodnight."

"Goodnight, Dad."

She clicked off the phone and laid her head on Mittens again.

"Do you think he'll ever stop thanking me for loving him, Mitter Bitters?"

A low grumbling purr sounded in Kathryn's ear as it pressed into the cat's stomach.

"Me neither."

Her eyes quickly grew heavy, and Mittens shifted under the increasing weight pressing on her as Kathryn started slipping away. She turned and crawled up to the head of the bed and rested upon her pillow, her thoughts swirling of her dad once more, picturing him hanging up the phone, sitting alone in his house—the house they once all shared as a family before everything went so terribly wrong.

Bridges

The last few weeks of school were a blur of tears, tests, and hiding away in the orchestra file room. Avoiding people started to feel more natural as she sought refuge any chance she could get. Every lunch and free period were spent concealed in that tiny box.

As she exited the double doors the last day of school with Lexie at her side, her face remained stoic in stark contrast to all the smiles, cheers, laughs, and high fives everywhere she looked.

She lowered her eyes in an attempt to block out the nauseating joy that surrounded her, but an elbow to her bicep made her snap her head to her left.

"Ouch. What?"

Lexie kept jabbing her and nodded forward.

Kathryn's breath seemed to escape her as she saw Liam coming toward her, that smile wide and those eyes crinkled.

"He's coming straight for—"

Kathryn's elbow fought with Lexie's. "Shh. Stop."

"Hey, Kathryn."

"Hey, Liam."

"Hi, Liam!" Lexie looked way too happy.

"Lexie," he said, nodding.

"Um...sooo, I'm gonna go find my bus, and ya know, get on it. So, uh, you call me later, okay, Kath?" Lexie walked past Liam and turned to face Kathryn, her smile wide as she viewed Liam from behind, giving a thumbs up and a wink, almost tripping over her feet walking backward. She slapped a

41

hand over her mouth as a laugh started to burst forth but held it together as she brought her other hand to her ear, mimicking a phone, and mouthed "call me" before turning and walking away with a little too much bounce in her step.

Trying to suppress a laugh, Kathryn set her attention on Liam, her heart pounding in her ears.

"Crazy that school is over already, huh?" Liam said.

"Yeah, crazy. Seems like it flew by."

"Yeah." His hand found the back of his head, running sideways through his short, raven hair and rubbing his neck. "So…uh…I had an awesome time in bio with you this year."

A smile upturned her lips as she tried not to let it overtake her face. "Yeah, me too. You were a great lab partner."

"Maybe we'll have a class together next year." He slid his fidgeting hands into his jeans pockets. "So…do you have any plans this summer?"

"Not really."

"Because I was thinking—"

"Li!" a deep voice shouted from behind her. Liam caught sight of someone over her shoulder. "Dude, come on. It's the last day of school! Woo! What are you still hanging around here for?" The blond with entirely too much product in his spiked hair eyed Kathryn with a flittering gaze.

"Just talking to—"

"Well, come on, man. The buses are starting to pull out." Liam's friend grabbed his arm and started dragging him away.

"Josh, hold up a sec." He pulled his arm from Josh's grip, righted his black backpack on his shoulders, and turned back toward Kathryn. "Have an awesome summer, Kathryn. I—"

"Liam!" Josh grabbed him by the arm and pushed him forward.

Liam looked back and offered a gentle wave and that smile again.

Kathryn waved back. "Bye, Liam." She watched him climb the stairs to his bus and steal one last look over his shoulder.

She stared after him, lost in thought until she saw the bus in front of his start moving. Snapped out of her reverie, she headed for her bus, picking up her pace as more buses started pulling forward. She made it just as her bus was next to leave and had to knock on the doors to get the driver's attention.

Spotting Val, she reluctantly made her way to the back and sat next to her.

"What the hell took you so long?"

"I was talking to someone. Remember Liam, the guy in my bio class? He stopped me and—"

"Whatever. I'm taking a magazine quiz."

Kathryn sighed as she rolled her eyes and grabbed her book from her bag.

Deeper into the small town, Val slapped her magazine shut. "So, I'm having a party at my house tonight. An end of the year bash. Lots of beer, obviously, and the whole gang is going to be there. They've been asking where you've been. You should come so they shut up about it."

"You know I can't. My aunt and uncle would never—"

"Oh my God! I'm sick of hearing about your aunt and uncle. They don't let you do anything fun! When are you going back home? They're such a drag! Fine. Don't come. I don't care anyway. Have fun playing your stupid board games."

Kathryn's brows scrunched. "They're not stupid. I've been having fun there."

Val rolled her eyes.

"Stop it. They took me in. I owe them a lot."

"Give me a break. You don't owe them a damn thing. All they're doing is keeping you from having any real fun. You shouldn't have even gone over there. My dad beat the crap out of my brother, and he didn't run away crying like a big baby."

"Val—"

"Whatever. I'm done fighting about this. You don't want to come over anymore? You and your new family are too good for us? Fine. Like I give a damn."

"What is your problem? If you were really my friend, you'd just be glad I'm safe. But all you care about is getting wasted, and you're just pissed that you can't come over and see all my brother's loser friends."

"They're a lot cooler than you. And basically, yeah."

"I'm so done with this. I'm done!"

"Good, bitch. Hey, look. There's your precious new home right there. Go run off to aunty and uncle and enjoy your boring summer."

Kathryn forcefully grabbed her bag off the floor as the bus came to a stop in front of her aunt and uncle's house and stomped off the bus without another word or look back.

She kicked at a loose stone in the driveway and screamed as it went flying toward the line of pine trees to her right. Anger overtook her, and tears began spilling onto her flushed cheeks. She fled to the side of the garage, hoping her aunt hadn't seen her get off the bus. Her fists balled, and her teeth clenched with rage as she paced along the side walkway. Kathryn repeatedly inhaled and exhaled deeply, smoothing out her breathing. She stopped and closed her eyes, her fingers releasing, and a smile parted her lips as the anger subsided and relief flowed in.

She brushed the wetness off her cheeks, took another deep breath, and went around to the front of the house, ready to begin her gloriously boring summer.

"I don't want you to go." Kathryn slumped into the couch.

Jake tilted his head, his kind blue eyes offering comfort. "I'll only be gone for a few weeks. I signed up to be a camp counselor before...everything happened. I can't back out. Plus, your week at camp lines up with my last week. So we'll come home together and have the rest of the summer."

"Will you be back in time to come to my final concert?"

"Yeah. Mama and Papa will pick me up Saturday morning with plenty of time, so I'll be there. I promise."

Kathryn looked down at her ring, the crown of the Claddagh digging into her knuckle. "Well, that's something, I guess."

"Oh, don't be like that. Let's just have an awesome last day together. Um...what time is Lexie coming over?"

Kathryn observed his pale skin redden, and she fought a smile. "In about an hour. What should we do?"

"Maybe a walk down the bike path?"

"Perfect."

"I'm going to go change."

"But you look..."

He was already in the hallway, heading back to his room.

Kathryn laughed and shook her head. As she walked into the kitchen for a quick snack, the phone rang.

"Jake? Sam? Kathryn?" Aunt Hannah called from the basement.

"I'm here, Aunt Hannah."

"Can you grab the phone, dear? I'm switching the laundry."

"Um...okay." She hustled over to the phone, dragging her feet along the linoleum. "Hello?"

"Hey, Kathryn."

"Hey, Rach."

Silence.

"I...I'm sorry about what happened at the mall. I just wanted to spend some time with you. You have to know I had no idea he was going to steal that shirt. I really am sorry."

"Thanks, Rach. Let's just move on, okay? I have enough going on, and I certainly don't want to lose you."

"Me neither." She paused. "I talked to Val, and she told me what happened on the bus."

"Oh, did she? I'd love to hear her side of the story."

"She said you just got all pissy with her and didn't want to come to her house for the party the other night."

"Oh, come on. I told her I *couldn't* come. My aunt and uncle would never let me, not that I wanted to go anyway. And then she got all mean and bitchy. I snapped. I'm done with her."

"You don't mean that."

"Yes, I do," Kathryn said, her volume increasing.

"But you've been friends for years."

"And she's been awful to me for years. I don't even know why I put up with it."

"Well...I still want to hang out with her."

"No one's saying you can't. I just won't be there."

"That sucks though. You're the one who introduced us."

"I can't, Rach. Please just let it go."

"All right."

Silence.

"I should go," Kathryn said. "I have some stuff to do today."

"Okay. I really am sorry."

"Like I said, let's just move past it. I'll talk to you later. Bye."

"Bye."

"It's so beautiful here. Why haven't you brought me back here before?" Lexie's blond head bent back toward the clear sky partially blocked by towering trees lining the five-foot-wide blacktop path, their branches draping over them like innocent, joyful hands interlocking to create a tunnel for little feet to scurry under.

Kathryn shrugged. "No clue. It was actually Jake's idea."

"Well, it certainly was a good one," she said, nudging Jake's shoulder with her slender forearm.

"Oh...uh...thanks. Yeah, I love it back here. Just wait until we get to the bridge."

Kathryn halted, movement to her left catching her attention. She watched as a light breeze rustled the tall grasses and twirled a patch of daisies. A hushed gasp escaped her lips as a gray bunny bounded out from the flowers and scam-

45

pered away through the thick weeds. Looking ahead on the path, she noticed Lexie and Jake a few yards ahead of her. Jake twisted the right edge of his shirt with his finger, coinciding with Lexie's hand that kept brushing her hair off her shoulder. Her head snapped back in one of her dramatic laughing fits, and she softly pushed his arm, yo-yoing him a few feet away before drawing him back.

Lexie caught sight of Kathryn over her shoulder mid hair flip. "Keep up, Kath!"

Kathryn smiled and quickened her pace, falling in step at Lexie's side. The three of them continued, their flittering shadows slicing through the lattice pattern lit on the ground from the hot July sun sneaking through the breaks in the canopy of protection.

They approached the quaint bridge, and the black pavement gave way to thick railroad ties clearly patched with new wood to solidify the weak spots speckled throughout the long-standing structure from years of wear. The three teenagers stopped and leaned their elbows on the corroding railing, gazing out over the landscape.

"Wow. This is amazing, guys," Lexie said in wonderment.

The whispering stream wound and curved before them, creeping between the trees and slowly wearing down the rocky soil as it turned sharply out of view behind a small field peppered with black-eyed Susans.

Kathryn drew in the clean air. "I'm not sure I've taken the time to actually appreciate this before."

A splash behind them made them turn and dash to the other side of the bridge where the stream continued, weaving through larger rocks and higher banks than the other side.

"Look! There's a piece of land that juts out a bit over there. Let's get closer," Lexie said, grabbing Kathryn by the arm.

They walked back onto the pavement and found a narrow dirt path sloping toward the banks. Lexie went first, reaching behind her and taking Kathryn's hand as she bent back for balance on the steep decline. They stepped out onto the small peninsula barely big enough to hold all three.

Lexie put her arms around their shoulders as they stood among the beauty, following the ebbing of the water as it came to a point in the distance, kissing the horizon.

"Thanks for getting me out of the house and keeping my mind off everything, guys," Kathryn said.

Lexie rested her head against Kathryn's shoulder. "We're always here for you. You know that. No matter what. Right, Jake?"

"Of course."

Kathryn found herself smiling, unshed tears gleaming in her blue eyes.

"You guys are the best friends anyone could have." She leaned her head against Lexie's. "Thank you."

Kathryn stood in the doorway the next morning, waving at Jake and Uncle Alex as they pulled away, feeling herself sink deeper. Unsure of how to cope without him around, she buried herself in her cello, her only true source of purpose. She lost herself in the music flowing from her hands and attempted to block out the demons that usually found their way to the surface any time she even slightly let the darkness descend upon her.

Enveloped in the music, she was startled by the deep tones intertwining harmoniously with her cello. She stopped and looked back to find Sam clutching his double bass.

"Keep going," he said with a smile.

She continued the piece through to the end as Sam played right along, offering a smooth platform for her melody.

At its conclusion, she turned again to face him. "How do you do that?"

"Do what?"

"Just know what to play even if you don't know the piece."

"I could tell what key it was in, so I just kind of winged it. We clashed here and there a bit."

"Well, I barely noticed. That's amazing. I could never do that without the music."

"Just have an ear for it, I guess." He placed his bass against a stool. "That was really fun. We should definitely do that again before you leave for camp."

Kathryn nodded gently. "I'd like that."

Sam exited through the wooden bifold doors of the music room and into the living room, disappearing from sight as he turned toward the kitchen.

Kathryn considered her younger cousin for a moment, her hand sliding down to the shoulder of her cello. After pushing in the endpin, she put her instrument in its case and went to the kitchen, finding Sam at the table, having some yogurt.

"Hey, Sam, we found this cool spot down on the bike path yesterday. I feel like getting out of the house. Wanna go check it out?"

"Sure," he said with a glint of surprise in his voice.

"That sounds lovely," Aunt Hannah said, her hands deep in soapy water at the kitchen sink. "Kathryn, when you get back, if you'd like, I was thinking I'd take you out for a new dress for the dance at camp. I overheard you talking with your friend Lexie about it yesterday. I don't get to take girls shopping often…or ever"—she giggled—"so I thought it might be a fun outing for the two of us."

Kathryn smiled. "I'd love that. Thank you."

"Wonderful. Now you two have a nice time and enjoy this beautiful day."

The early July sun greeted them as they started on the sidewalk that would lead them to the bike path. She tried to keep her eyes forward when they passed her house across the street to their left, but they drifted slightly, catching a fleeting view of the dark wood siding and slate blue shutters. Sam's long strides brought him in between Kathryn and her home, and she instantly found the concrete sidewalk again, observing the pavement darken as the passing clouds eclipsed the sun briefly before allowing the beams of light to shine upon them once more. Her sandaled foot kicked a small stone, launching it into the grass.

"So, how are you doing with everything?" asked Sam.

She shrugged. "Good days and bad, I guess."

"Do you miss being home?"

"Yes and no. I don't miss being scared all the time."

He shook his head. "I can't even imagine that."

"But obviously, I miss my mom. That's the hardest part."

"I'm sorry." Despite their age difference, Sam was almost as tall as Kathryn, his long arm easily reaching around her shoulders to give her a little squeeze.

As they advanced on the bridge, their conversation had spanned from music to cartoon characters, but Sam seemed to avoid any more mention of her brother. They stopped on the bridge and rested against the railing.

"Wow," Sam said. "I'm not sure I ever stopped here to look around."

"That's what I said too. I always just fly through here on my rollerblades." She pointed down below. "That's the spot we found yesterday. It feels like you're in the water when you stand on it."

"Awesome. I'm going to head down. You coming?"

"Nah. I'll watch from here."

Sam started down the dirt path as Kathryn leaned deeper into the railing, putting her face in her hands. The image of her home flashed across her fragile mind, and it drifted, the darkness sneaking up on her.

"No really, Rach. I'm telling you. He's so sweet."

"Well, do you think he likes you?"

48

"I don't know. He's sort of popular. I can't really see him being into me. But he's nice and fun to talk to, so for now, I'm happy just being his friend."

"But you'd want more?"

"If he liked me, yeah, I would."

"You don't give yourself enough credit, Kathryn. You're awesome, and he'd be lucky to be with you."

"We've been friends since we were babies, so you have to say that."

Rachael laughed. "Doesn't mean it's not true."

Kathryn switched the phone to her other ear and shook out her stiff hand.

"Oh, I have to tell you about something Val said."

Kathryn's attention was pulled away from Rachael's voice as a slight rattling sound met her senses. Her gaze snapped to her door. The doorknob was shaking.

"What the...?" Kathryn said, cutting Rachael off.

"What? What is it?"

"It looks like someone is trying to get into my room. The doorknob is moving. It's probably Brandon."

"Why would Brandon be trying to get into your room?"

"No idea." She scooted herself out of bed and approached the door. "Brandon? What are you doing?"

The doorknob continued to shake.

"Brandon? What do you want?" Kathryn leaned her head to the side, holding the phone in between her chin and her shoulder, and she grasped the doorknob as it jiggled in her panicked grip.

"What's going on?" Rachael asked, her voice laced with unease.

"He won't answer me. Brandon! What are you doing?"

The doorknob shook rapidly.

Kathryn's feet slid on the plush carpet as the door began opening in sharp jabs. "Stop!" She pressed her shoulder against it, digging her bare feet into the floor, pushing her weight against the door. "What are you doing! Leave me alone!"

"Kathryn! What's happening!"

The door flung open with such force Kathryn stumbled back, nearly losing her balance. The phone slipped from her shoulder, but she caught it and held it in her trembling hand. Brandon stood before her, draped in black, barely out of breath, rage seething beneath his dark, calm stare.

"Kathryn!"

She snapped her head up, sweeping a tear across her warm cheek.

49

"Come on down here! There's some kind of awesome, gross creature on the bank."

"Um...I'm good here."

He shrugged and knelt to observe it further.

She turned her back to him and leaned against the rusted railing, rubbing her bare arms harshly, suddenly feeling cool in the humid summer heat. Her eyelids fell in an attempt to calm herself, but he was there, always there, ready and waiting to pull her into the darkness he created. Kathryn's eyes fluttered open to the beauty before her, the trees surrounding her with comforting familiarity, voices resonating through her mind.

"Up and over."

"You ready?"

She blinked hard, turning toward Sam's voice. "What?"

"You ready to go?"

"Oh...sure."

"You okay?"

"I'm fine." Her lips fought to feign a smile to no avail.

"Kathryn..."

"I'm fine, Sam." She started down the trail.

Sam caught up and fell in step with her as they headed back to the house, not a word spoken between them.

Kathryn knocked lightly on the door across from hers, and Sam appeared behind it.

"Hey, Sam. Can I come in?"

"Sure." He moved aside as she walked in and pulled out the desk chair.

She surveyed the room as she sat at the red-painted desk. A collage of Jake and his band friends hung above his headboard, and a worn, plush Mickey Mouse sat next to a miniature drum replica atop the dresser. A few of Sam's clothes hung on the closet doorknob, and his favorite stuffed raccoon, ratty with years of love, sat on a pile of folded blankets stacked against the wall next to Jake's bed.

"You can stay in my room," Sam said without a speck of hesitation in his voice. *"I'll bunk with Jake."*

Kathryn shook her head. "I can't ask you to do that."

"You didn't."

50

The kindness in his eyes in that selfless moment mirrored his gaze as she looked upon him. "I bet it's nice to get Jake's bed while he's away. The floor can't be too comfortable."

"It's not so bad. Papa helped me make it softer with a bunch of blankets and pillows."

Kathryn nodded and inhaled deeply. "I'm sorry I snapped earlier."

"It's okay."

"It's not. You've been nothing but kind and welcoming. You gave up your room for me. You...you didn't deserve me taking my crap out on you. I'm sorry, Sam."

"Really, Kathryn, it's okay. I know you're going through a lot. I can't even imagine what you're really going through. To grow up like that. To be scared in your own house. I... Really, it's okay."

"I won't do it again. I just...shut down sometimes. It all keeps flooding back, and...I...get taken back there. It's as if I'm there all over again. I can't really explain it. I just wish it would stop."

"I suspect it will...in time. Maybe if you talked about it?"

"I'm not ready yet." She shook her head. "It's too hard."

"Well, I'm here when and if you need to talk."

"Thanks. I really appreciate that."

Their eyes held for a moment longer.

"Wanna jam?"

She laughed through the tears trickling down her face. "Sure."

Kathryn sifted through the racks of dresses, scrunching her nose at them.

"Doesn't look like this place has what you want either. Let's go check out another one," said Aunt Hannah.

They strode out into the open hallway of the mall, making their way to the third store.

"What usually happens at these dances?" Aunt Hannah asked.

"They're usually pretty low key. I just hang out with Grace and my other friends."

"There are no boys there that you'd like to dance with?"

Kathryn giggled. "No. Not at camp."

"So, there's one *not* at camp?"

Kathryn blushed. "Kinda."

"Oh, do tell. I don't get girl talk very often," she said, hooking Kathryn's arm.

51

"His name is Liam. He's in one of my classes. I like spending time with him. That's all it is for now."

"Aw. That's really nice. Crushes are so fun. I remember when I first started dating your uncle—all butterflies and giggles." They turned left at the fountain, heading down another long hallway. "Oh, how fun is this? I always wanted a girl to do stuff like this with. It just wasn't in the stars for us, though."

"But you've got me."

Aunt Hannah placed a soft hand on her niece's arm. "Yes, dear. I've got you. And how blessed I am."

"Did you ever think about having more kids and maybe getting a girl?"

"We did actually want more, but there were complications after Sam was born, and...well...like I said—it was not God's plan. Do you picture yourself as a mother someday?"

"I'd love to be a mom. It's been the one constant thing I've always wanted to be when the time is right. It's just..."

"What is it?"

Kathryn's breath slowly glided past her lips. "What if I have a boy first? What if my kids are like Brandon and me?"

"Oh, honey. They don't have to be. You won't let them be. My brother and sisters and I have not always gotten along. It never escalated to physical violence, but we had many issues. There's a lot of pain and anger there even to this day. We're not close, and it still hurts. I knew when I became a mom that I wanted to raise my children differently. I wanted to specifically nurture their relationship, help them to build a strong bond. I know it's not always that easy, but I was determined to make that a priority with my boys. And look at them. Sure, they have their moments as all siblings do, but they are good to each other. They care for one another and watch out for each other. I know you can and will be that mom to your children. You won't let the cycle repeat itself. I know you won't."

Kathryn nodded, a small smile spreading across her mouth. "I hope you're right."

"Oh, I know I am." She softly rubbed her niece's back. "This store looks promising. Let's give it a shot."

Kathryn immediately zeroed in on a soft pink dress displayed on a mannequin in the junior's section.

"That one is lovely," Aunt Hannah sang next to her. "Here they are." She bustled over to the rack and snatched Kathryn's size, holding it up to her.

Kathryn ran her fingers down the silhouette, fanning out the flowing, knee-length skirt. "It's so pretty. I love it."

"Go try it on."

A few minutes passed, and Kathryn emerged from the dressing room. "It's perfect!"

"Then I believe we have found the dress." She smiled, her hazel eyes soft.

"Thank you so much, Aunt Hannah. Not even just for the dress...for everything." She reached for her aunt and embraced her.

"You are so very welcome, my dear," Aunt Hannah said, rubbing Kathryn's back. "Let's go pay for this, and then maybe we can grab dinner. I'll give Uncle Alex a call and tell him they need to fend for themselves tonight."

"So, they'll order pizza?"

She nodded. "Without a doubt."

"Sorry, Mitter Bitters. You can't come with me this time." Mittens stared at her, looking entirely too comfortable sitting tall in her suitcase on the bed. She leaned down, and Mittens pressed her black nose to her forehead. "I'm going to miss you, baby girl. Aunt Hannah will take good care of you. I promise."

Mittens mewed and turned in a circle before flopping down, curling up in a ball, and closing her eyes. Kathryn folded her clothes and piled them next to the suitcase.

The first two weeks of July had passed, and Kathryn was set to leave for orchestra camp the next morning. As she opened the drawers to grab her shorts, a door slamming outside brought her attention out the front window. She parted the blinds and spotted her grandfather walking toward the house. Smiling, she headed out to the living room, excited to see him for the first time in weeks.

Kathryn stopped halfway down the hall at the sound of Uncle Alex's unfamiliar, stern tone.

"Not here, Dad. Let's go out back."

Kathryn stayed still until she heard the front door close and turned back to go into the bathroom at the rear of the house. She shimmied the small window open as it squeaked in protest. Cautiously dividing the lace curtains, she peeked out to see Uncle Alex and her grandpa standing a few feet away from each other, arms folded in front of them. Gray clouds cast their serious faces in shadow—mirror images separated by thirty years.

"Why are you doing this to our family, Alexander?"

"Dad, we're protecting Kathryn."

"She should be home with her mother."

53

"You're right. She should be. But we don't believe she's safe there right now."

Grandpa's hand raised to his grooved forehead, stretching and scrunching the skin with his thumb and fingers as he looked down and away from his son. "We don't believe she's in any danger there." He looked up again, his arms flailing out to the side. "Goodness, Alex. They're kids. Kids fight sometimes. You fought with your brother and sister, too."

"I never once feared for my safety in our house. I never once feared that Jane or Tom would ever purposefully cause me physical harm. Yes, siblings argue and bicker, but that's not what this was. This was planned and orchestrated through an intense, irrational anger toward her that has been building for too many years."

"Your mother has seen Kathryn do things to get under his skin too."

Uncle Alex looked down, his fingers pressing the bridge of his nose. "Oh, Dad. Please." He met his father's eyes, straightening his glasses. "Please stop this. We're not talking about little kids here. They're teenagers. Brandon is practically an adult. I don't care what she's done. No one deserves to be abused."

An unfamiliar expression formed across the lines of her grandpa's face as anger pinched his mouth and hardened his eyes, a look Kathryn had never seen on her mild-mannered grandfather. "Abused?" he said just above a whisper. "Alex, one incident doesn't equal abuse."

"One incident? Dad, you don't understand what's been going on over there. One incident...?" He shook his head and inhaled deeply. "This is not an isolated incident."

"Jane said—"

"You've been misinformed. She may not even know the full story. This one time may have escalated to a new level, but this is by no means the only time something like this has happened."

Another rare look graced her grandpa's face: despair. "Alex, I don't know what to believe. I just know she should be with her mother. Jane is devastated."

"I know she is. This is a terrible situation for everyone involved. You have to understand that she came to us. We didn't take her out of her home. We have to believe Kathryn's side of the story though. Anything else is risking her safety. She will go back when she's ready and feels safe, and we will keep her and take care of her until she decides that for herself."

Grandpa released an audible sigh. "I just hope you know what you're doing. This is not good for our family."

"I'm sorry you feel that way, Dad, but this is what we have to do."

Her grandfather's head hung low as he turned from his son's firm gaze and hard stance, and Uncle Alex's arms fell to his side, spinning toward the house. Kathryn quickly ducked, holding her breath, hoping he hadn't seen her. She slid to the yellow tiled floor, grasping at the side of the bathtub for stability.

She heard the front door close and used the edge of the bathtub to push herself up on her shaking legs, forcing herself to get back into the bedroom before Uncle Alex spotted her. Without looking, she ran out of the bathroom and into her temporary room across the hall, closing the door swiftly and as quietly as possible. She leaned against the door, her breathing heavy and hastened.

Mittens poked a sleepy head up over the rim of the suitcase and meowed at her best friend.

"I had no idea the family felt like that, Mittens." She lay on the bed, and Mittens crawled over to her, pushing her face into Kathryn's outstretched hand. "Grandma and Grandpa think this only happened once?" She turned over on her side, bunching the pillow beneath her head. "They have no idea about any of it, do they?"

Understory

A knock came to the front door as Kathryn lugged her suitcase down the long hallway to the living room. Aunt Hannah bustled over to the door, her white apron flittering about, a wooden, batter-covered spoon still in her hand.

"Good morning, Jane. Please come in," she said, stepping to the side.

"Morning, Hannah. I hope I'm not late."

"Not at all. I think she's just about ready."

With a sharp intake of breath, Kathryn stepped out into the living room. "Hi, Mom. I just have to grab one more bag from my...the room. Can you grab my cello from the music room?"

"I'll get it," Sam said, walking in from the kitchen.

Back in the room, Kathryn knelt down next to the bed and extended a hand toward Mittens, whose head popped up with a start and a gentle moan. "I have to go, baby girl. I'm going to miss you so much." Mittens purred and arched her back against her touch. "I'll be back in a week. I promise." She buried her face into her best friend's soft side, her black fur tickling her nose. Mittens spun around and pushed her dark head into her damp cheek. Kathryn moved back, and Mittens pressed her nose into her forehead. "I love you too."

Kathryn gave Mittens a kiss and a rub on the nose before slinging her bag over her shoulder. With one last look back, she gently closed the door.

"If her quartet makes Honors, the recital will be Saturday before the final concert. I'm sure we'll hear as soon as she knows." Her mother looked up at Kathryn as she walked into the room. "Right, sweetie?"

"Yup. Are you all going to come?"

"Of course, my dear. We wouldn't miss it. We'll be picking up Jake that morning from his camp, but we'll make it in plenty of time." Aunt Hannah pulled her into a hug.

"Take good care of Mittens. She's still a bit scared."

Aunt Hannah tightened her hold. "She's in good hands. You take good care of you, darling." She pulled back and tucked Kathryn's ashy locks behind her ear. "We'll see you soon. Play your heart out."

They all snapped toward the bang of Sam's sneaker against the wooden threshold as he tripped coming in the front door. He laughed and righted himself, straightening out his yellow-striped T-shirt. "Glad I didn't do that when I was carrying out your cello."

Kathryn giggled and embraced her cousin. "See you in a week."

"See you in a week." Sam offered her a smile and a nudge on her arm as he took a pace back.

Uncle Alex stepped between them, and she lifted herself onto her toes to give him a squeeze.

"Make beautiful music and have a wonderful time. You deserve it."

Mother and daughter set out on the main road, the trees casting long shadows on the blacktop as the morning sun continued its ascent. About twenty minutes into the hour drive to the college campus that held the orchestra camp, Kathryn had barely said a word. The awkwardness between them erected an invisible barrier, a divide so firm Kathryn feared nothing could ever bring it down. She leaned her head against the window, remembering what it felt like before he did this to them.

They sang loudly, carelessly, freely as they drove onward. Kathryn's soprano carried the melody as Jane's alto took the lower harmony. She looked over at her mom, her words slurring a bit as a grin broke her form. Jane glanced back quickly, holding the lower tone as her daughter held out the high note that ended the song they sang so often.

"You're nailing that part, Mom."

"Why, thank you. Only because you sing your part so well."

Kathryn smiled and reached forward to turn up the next song, but Jane's hand landed on top of hers before it could spin the knob.

"Kathryn, don't ever marry someone you can't sing that song to."

"Marry someone? Mom, I just turned fifteen."

"I know...but you won't always be. When the time comes, don't marry

someone who doesn't make you feel like that—someone who strengthens you, loves you for exactly who you are, someone who shows you beauty you never knew was there before. If you can't look him in the eyes and sing that song to him and mean every word, he's not the one for you."

"Can you sing this to Mitch?"

"Yes, I can," she said as her thin lips turned up.

"So you think you'll marry him someday?"

"We've talked about it, but neither of us is ready for all that entails. He doesn't want to leave New Jersey, and I would never uproot you guys, taking you away from your family and friends here. But when the time is right, yes, we'd like to get married. He makes me happy."

"I'm glad. It took me a few years, like ten, but I guess he's growing on me...a little. But having a few states between us is still probably a good thing for now."

Jane chuckled. "Even long distance, he's been a great support for me, especially throughout my cancer treatments years ago, helping me out with you guys when he could travel up and taking time off to care for me when my treatments kept me home from school for two weeks at a time."

"I know. Not sure I'll ever find that though. That would require someone actually wanting to be with me."

"Don't do that, Kathryn. Don't doubt your self-worth. You're a kind, intelligent, caring, compassionate, talented, beautiful young woman." Her voice was laced with a stern tone Kathryn wasn't used to. "Don't you settle for anyone who doesn't see that and appreciate you for exactly who you are."

"Okay, Mom. Settle down." She laughed. "I'll make sure I can sing that song to a guy before I marry him. His love shall be the music of my heart. Promise."

"Good. So, anyone on the radar at the moment?" she asked with a sidelong glance at her daughter's blushing face.

"Kinda. But I'm certainly not ready to sing to him yet," she said, laughing. "Now turn it back, and let's belt it out again."

Kathryn started her part as her mom swooped in from down low to carry her.

"Your fourth year already."

Kathryn lifted her head off the window, bringing herself out of her memory, and turned to face her mom.

She shook her head. "Time really does fly, doesn't it? Doesn't seem like that long since I was helping you set up your dorm room. Setting up a dorm with my twelve-year-old. What an odd feeling that was."

59

Kathryn smiled. "I was ridiculously scared that first year."

"I was so proud of you for taking a step like that and amazed at your bravery. So young, staying overnight for a week at a college campus, not knowing anyone. I don't think I could have done that at your age."

"Oh, and do you remember that my roommate never showed up? I had the room all to myself. That was actually pretty awesome."

"That's right. I do remember that."

"Luckily, I was in the same group as Grace. I'm not sure what I would have done without her that first year, making me feel welcome and comfortable. Although, she did almost get me into trouble. She talked me into sneaking into her room in the middle of the night. One of the counselors came through and must have heard us and knocked on the door and wanted to come in. I freaked out and hid in her closet. I was so scared I was going to get caught."

Jane laughed. "My little rebel."

Mile by mile, mother and daughter talked, each smile, each laugh chipping away at the barrier, slowly breaking it down and mending what was damaged between them.

Jane pulled from happy memories, painting a rosy picture for her daughter. The images flashed through Kathryn's mind: watching movies while snuggled on her mom's bed, shopping at the mall for school clothes, taking walks down the bike path, hanging out together in the living room and talking, singing in the car. Those times felt distant, as if they were from a different lifetime.

"And when you two were little, when we lived at our first apartment after moving out of Grandma and Grandpa's, we used to unfold the pullout couch and pile it high with pillows and blankets and watch movies together."

"Really? I don't remember that."

"You don't?" She frowned. "We did that a lot. We called it camping. You both loved it."

"And we did that without fighting?"

"Believe it or not, you did. It wasn't always bad, you know."

Silence.

Jane's hand shifted down slightly on the steering wheel. "I suppose that was a long time ago, though."

"Can't see that happening again any time soon."

"No. I guess not."

More silence.

"Wasn't always bad…" Kathryn pondered that statement as she once again observed the trees blur past her on the highway. If she and Brandon had good

times, they were hiding in the far reaches of her subconscious. At the forefront was only anger—more anger than anyone knew how to handle.

"Go fish!"

"Oh no! Not again!" he said.

Kathryn laughed as her grandpa's hand dramatically landed on his heart.

The toys scattered about her grandparents' living room looked out of place among the strategically placed crystal vases, floral embellishments, family pictures, and expansive travel memorabilia. The yellowed curtains drawn tightly across the front picture window dimmed the daylight, sheltering Kathryn as she swung her short legs above the floor. Her grandfather leaned his elbows on the table as his hand hit the pile of cards on the rose-patterned fabric draping the round wooden surface.

Kathryn peeked over her deck of cards spread out like peacock feathers in her small hands. "Do you have any fives?"

"Nope," Grandpa answered with a popping sound.

She snickered. "Grandpa, I just saw you pick one up."

He held his cards to his chest and feigned a gasp. "How did you see that?"

"I accitentilly saw your card when you picked it up."

He slid the card over to her. "Oh, well, I guess I'll have to be more careful then."

"Do you have any twos?" the little girl asked.

Her Grandpa slapped the card down. "I'm losing to a four-year-old! Are you cheating? You have to be cheating."

She broke into a fit of giggles. "No, silly goose."

"Well, then I guess you're just that good." He placed a gentle hand on her shoulder. "Let's play War after this. Maybe I'll finally beat you at that."

"Okay, but I—"

"No! I don't want to go!" he screamed from the back hallway. Brandon clomped out into the kitchen, his thin arms crossed over his chest.

"I'm sorry, Brandon, but you have to. Doctor Joe wants to talk to you," his mom said, trailing behind him.

"No! I'm not going!" he shouted as he pushed her hands away. He swung around and knocked a box of crackers on the floor, the white squares sliding across the faded linoleum.

Kathryn hopped off her chair and climbed into her grandpa's lap. He wrapped his arms around her as she laid her head on his shoulder.

"Grandpa, why doesn't Brandon want to see Doctor Joe? I like talking to

him. We play games, and we talk about Mommy, Daddy, and Brandon. I tell him how much I miss Daddy."

"I'm not sure, Kathryn. Things are…hard for your brother."

"He's always so mad." She pushed her head into the side of his neck.

"I know, honey."

Brandon stomped his feet on the kitchen floor, smashing the crackers to a fine powder. "I'm not going, and you can't make me!"

"Bill, we should go help her," Kathryn's grandma said, putting down her crossword puzzle.

"You're right, Lorraine. I need to go help your mom." He stood with his young granddaughter still in his arms and placed her back down on the chair. "Stay right here."

Kathryn watched him walk into the kitchen, his arms slightly outstretched as he cautiously approached the young boy of only seven, her grandma hanging back a bit.

"Leave me alone!" Brandon slapped his grandpa's hands away, balled his fists, and screamed at the ceiling.

Kathryn slipped out of her chair and crawled under the table. Brandon ran back into the hallway toward the rear bedrooms, and his mom and grandparents followed. The frightened girl lifted the edge of the tablecloth, her blue eyes watering, and scooted out from under the table, dashing for the front door. Looking to her right, she grabbed the familiar handles of two tennis rackets and pried open the front door as it squeaked in complaint. With a short glance back, she scurried out onto the front porch and carefully closed the door behind her.

The young child took a deep breath in the calming silence. Flipping the rackets over so the taped handles rested on the black driveway, she slipped her thumbs and index fingers through the laced holes at the top of each racket, pinching them tightly together. A soft hum resonated from her throat as she began walking, swinging the rackets as she made her way down the driveway and onto the sidewalk.

A gentle gust of wind tousled her lemony brown hair hanging down her back and rustled the fallen crimson maple leaves at her feet. She twitched her small head to the side, swishing her thick bangs off her forehead as she risked a glance toward the house, the curtains still closed. With a sigh, she continued on, crunching the dried leaves with every step she took away from chaos.

Kathryn pulled her gaze away from the passing nature and turned to her mom. "That's just not how I remember it. When we were living with Grandma and Grandpa after leaving Dad, he was always so mad."

"Yes, he was. He's...always been an angry boy. Well, since we left anyway. He... Kathryn, he didn't handle us leaving very well. It was...especially hard on him."

Kathryn rolled her eyes. "I've heard this all before. It's not like it was easy on me."

"I know that. I don't mean to say it was. But he was older, and he understood more of what was going on. He saw things your dad did. He heard some scary things he said, and it...affected him deeply."

"And leaving my dad alone in his house to live somewhere else didn't affect me?" she asked, an edge to her voice.

"Kathryn, that's not what I'm saying. I'm just saying you both reacted differently to us leaving. He was angry. You were more sad, I think. You were worried about your dad and sad you couldn't be with him. That's how you dealt with your grief. You got sad while he got angry. Of course leaving affected you, but it just didn't affect you the same way it did your brother."

"The way it affected him affected me."

Silence.

Jane reached a hand over to her right and placed it softly on her daughter's knee. "I know that. I truly do."

"When he used to go off on those rages, I remember taking walks outside Grandma and Grandpa's house. I'd take the tennis rackets and—"

"Swing them between your fingers."

Kathryn's eyes widened. "You knew about that?"

"Of course I did."

"I didn't think you noticed me leaving."

"Sweetie, I may have been overwhelmed with having to tend to Brandon, but I certainly knew where you were. Your grandpa would often take over, and I would go into the living room to take a breath and calm myself. I'd see you walking on the sidewalk, swinging those rackets, finding a way to escape a situation you should never have been placed in. I'm sorry you didn't think I saw you."

Kathryn shrugged. "It's okay."

"No, it's not. It's one of my biggest regrets, the way I handled things with you after we left. I was...so broken, on my own, trying to keep Brandon from losing control, and I... Kathryn, you were so good, so quiet, so well-behaved. You were just this little girl standing there in the midst of all this chaos. I was just so thankful that you were good and not giving me a hard time like Brandon was, because...after I taught all day and had to give so much energy and attention to Brandon...there were times I didn't have anything left to give."

Kathryn's hand found her stomach, and she drew a sharp intake of breath as she felt her throat fight to stay open and her eyes moisten. "You didn't have anything left to give me? I'm your child too. I was just a little girl," she said, her voice breaking.

Jane flicked her turn signal up and pulled over on the side of the road. She turned to face her daughter. "Honey, I know, and I'm sorry. I'm not excusing it. I'm not saying it's okay. That's just how I felt at that time. I saw you hiding. I saw you not wanting to be a problem for me. I saw you go inside yourself almost—almost as if you were trying to disappear." She reached toward Kathryn and caught a tear as it cascaded down her pink cheek. "It's not okay. It's not what I wanted to be for you. None of this is what I wanted for you. This is not what you deserve. I'm so sorry. I'm so sorry for all of it. For everything."

Jane leaned in and embraced her daughter. Kathryn's arms remained at her side as she fought the urge to pull away while simultaneously fighting the desire to sink into her mother's arms and never leave. She laid her head against her shoulder and raised a hand to her mom's back, her eyes closing tightly, releasing tears concocted of a plethora of emotions.

Her mom pulled away and took Kathryn's face in her hands, her right swollen—a never-ending reminder of her fight to live. "My girl. My sweet, precious girl. I love you so much."

"I love you too, Mom. It's never been about you. It's him."

Jane's vision fell to her lap, her hand finding her amber pendant. "I know. I...I don't know what to do."

"And I can't come back until you do."

"I'm going to figure this out. I promise." She took Kathryn's hand and gave it a squeeze. "Goodness, look at the time. We have to get back on the road if we're going to make it in time for check-in. You ready?"

Kathryn offered a weak smile. "Ready."

The sun reflected brilliantly off the Western New York University sign as they pulled into campus. Kathryn couldn't repress the excitement of being back again. With her nose practically against the window, she took in the familiar scenery. The miniature city towered before them, the deep red brick buildings standing out against the gray clouds lurking ominously in the distance, a stark contrast to the brightness overhead.

The twisting inner road led them past the practice building, the cafeteria, and King Concert Hall, which would hold the finale recital at the end of the week. Pulling up to the five-story dormitory, Kathryn opened her door before the car had come to a complete stop. She slung her cello strap over her shoulder and grabbed her smaller bag as her mom carried her suitcase.

The lobby looked just as it had the past few years save for the current flyers on the bulletin board next to the pay phone. To their left, the tan couch still stood in the center of the room, facing an old TV atop an oak cabinet pushed against the side wall. Between them and the couch, girls were already facing off at the air hockey table. Two large windows set into opposite walls on either side of the couch were dressed in maroon curtains tied to the side with string, allowing the gradually dissipating glow of the late morning to filter in and offer natural light to assist the florescent fixtures buzzing over-head. To their right, inspirational sayings held in wooden frames adorned the bruised ivory walls that led up the stairway to the dorm rooms. Before them, long tables were placed, and the college-aged counselors sat ready to check in the young orchestra players and supply them with their assigned dorm rooms.

A dark-haired teenage girl smiled as they stepped up to the table. "Hey there. Welcome! What's your name, hon?"

"Kathryn Lucas."

She slid the tip of her pen down the long list of names. "Lucas... Lucas... Luucaasss... Yes. Here you are. Your group counselor is Isabel Taylor. You are paired up with Grace Crawford in room three ten. Up two flights of stairs and make a left. Everyone is expected to meet in King Concert Hall at eleven for a brief welcome concert and some information before it's time for parents to depart. So that gives you about"—she looked at her watch—"thirty minutes. There's a map of the campus included in your packet here along with the names of the other two girls in your group and your schedule. Your quartet assignment can be found posted on the wall just inside the concert hall. I think that's it. Have a great week!"

"Thanks," Kathryn said, reaching out for her packet. She hoisted her cello case back on her shoulder and started up the stairs to her dorm room. Her heart felt as though it might explode with excitement as every step took her closer to Grace and a week away from everything.

She heard music blasting from a room to the left as she came to the top of the second flight of stairs. Without even looking at the numbers, she followed the singing and found Grace hopping around their dorm room, whipping her ashy brown curls through the air and flailing her arms around her body.

"Ah! Kat! You're heeere!" Grace bounded over to Kathryn and flung her arms around her, pulling the neck of her cello into the hug as well. "Come on! Let's get you unpacked. We only have a little bit before we have to meet in Ka-cha."

"Ka-cha?" Jane said with a raised brow.

Kathryn laughed. "King Concert Hall is shortened to KCH on our schedules. Ka-cha."

"I see."

"I can hardly follow all of it either," said Grace's mom, extending a hand toward Jane.

"Glad I'm not alone then," she replied, shaking her mom's hand. "Good to see you again."

"I took this bed." Grace gestured to the left side of the small room. "I hope that's okay. Do you mind taking that one?"

"No. This one is fine."

"Okay, good! I already put my clothes in the drawers and hung up my shirts and dresses."

The song changed on the radio, and Grace started swaying her hips. "Oh! My jam! Unpacking can wait!" She took Kathryn's shirt from her fingertips and threw it on the bed, grabbing her hands and bouncing to the music.

Kathryn danced with her friend, singing along to the song in between laughing fits, joy spreading through her, the taste of freedom overtaking her senses.

"And he popped the string right in his face! He had a line going down right here," Grace said, tracing her finger down her cheek. "I've never seen a string snap like that. It was crazy. But luckily, he had a spare in his cello case, so we were able to continue with the recital. Our quartet rocked it."

"My dad popped a string in his face once," Kathryn said with a chuckle. "He just grabbed the A peg and turned it way too hard and fast, and it snapped."

"Ha! Parents should never be trusted with the pegs."

"When did you have your cello at your dad's?" Jane asked.

"One of the times he missed my concert and wanted to hear my part. Didn't exactly work out."

"Oh! There's Kelcee!" shouted Grace, pulling at Kathryn's arm. "Kelcee! Hey!"

With remarkably thick blond hair nearly brushing against her full hips, Kelcee pranced over to them, with another girl at her side, their parents trailing along behind them. "Hey, ladies! We're in the same group! Ah! This is Virginia, my roommate," Kelcee said with a nod to the auburn-haired girl on her right.

Virginia pushed her dark glasses up the bridge of her thin nose with a slender, shaky hand. "Hi," she said just above a whisper. "You can actually just call me Ginny."

"Hey, Ginny!" Grace leapt forward and pulled her into a quick hug. "I'm Grace, and this is Kat. You're new, huh? Don't worry. We've got you. We're the best ones here." She winked.

"Yeah, we are. We'll show you everything you need to know," said Kathryn, feeling compelled to help Grace make Ginny feel welcome.

Ginny's lips turned up slightly, and her quivering hand stilled as she released the comfort of her elbow-length hair.

"Let's head over to Ka-cha, ladies." Grace extended her arm, guiding Ginny forward toward the concert hall.

The magnificence of King Concert Hall reflected in Kathryn's wide eyes lit by wonderment and heavy lighting as the girls entered through the double doors revealing the vast, eloquent interior. Her sandaled feet shuffled along the plush maroon carpeting that flowed up four stairways woven through matching suede-covered seats cascading from up high. At their final descent, an amber-stained stage held a copper pipe organ at the back that nearly kissed the grand height of the ceiling.

The girls walked farther into the building as chatter and clicking shoes up on the wooden stage echoed around them. Metal stands scraped against the surface, and chairs slid into place as the gathering of college string players and adult coaches prepared for their upcoming performance.

After placing their instruments in the lockers in the back room off the stage, the young teenagers and their parents found seats on the aisle just as the conductor flicked her music stand with the wooden end of her baton, signaling the musicians to tune their open strings, silencing the crowd. With a flourished wave of her hand, they stopped, and she leaned into the microphone.

"Welcome, young musicians and dedicated parents who encourage and support them. I am Elizabeth Gail, and we're honored to have you here with us this year—this our fifteenth annual WNYU Young Musicians String Camp. I just know this is going to be our best year yet." She paused for the hoots and hollers from the excited teens. "We hope you enjoy our short performance."

She spun back on the instrumentalists, her arms raised into the air, and the orchestra began at her downbeat. Kathryn's attention was ripped from the music as Grace elbowed her arm.

"I'm sooo hungry. Come on, people. Finish up so the parents can leave and we can go to lunch." She dramatically leaned her head on Kathryn's shoulder and let her tongue hang out.

Kathryn stifled a laugh as Grace's mom gave her a light slap on her thigh. Grace rolled her eyes at Kathryn and returned upright.

As the piece crescendoed to its final note, Kathryn's heart rate increased at the thought of how close she was to freedom. In years past, part of her dreaded her mom leaving, but this year, she could not have needed this escape more.

Ms. Gail turned toward the audience's booming applause and offered a low bow before looking out over the seats below. "Thank you. Thank you. Your children will have the privilege of attending nightly concerts like this their whole week here, and they will be learning from accomplished, talented musicians. We look forward to showing you everything we've learned over the next week. Students, it's that time again. After bidding a fond farewell to your parents, please head over to the dining hall for lunch. If you're in the Brahms orchestra, you will proceed to your technique classes afterword. If you are in the Beethoven orchestra, you will meet back here for your first orchestra rehearsal to be held at one o'clock sharp. You're expected to be in your seats, instruments out, bows rosined, and ready to start at one, so please get here in plenty of time to find your assigned chairs. Parents, thank you for entrusting us with your children. See you at the finale concert next Saturday. Safe travels home."

Jane stood and turned toward her daughter. "I guess this is it then." She swept Kathryn's hair behind her ear. "Have an absolutely amazing time this week. I'll see you Saturday at your recital."

"Thanks, Mom." She leaned forward and hugged her mom around her waist, hesitating before releasing her. "I'll call you soon."

Jane took a small step back, surveying her daughter. "I love you, Kathryn," she said with a firm tone.

"I love you too, Mom."

Jane slowly turned and walked away, stealing one last glance back over her shoulder. Kathryn could have sworn she saw tears gathering in her eyes before she continued on through the double doors without looking back again.

Kathryn spread an unexpected tear across her cheek and took a deep breath as her attention was pulled to the excited shriek coming from near the entryway. She looked over to see Grace slap her hand over her mouth and duck her head. She met Kathryn's eyes and mouthed a silent scream. Kathryn tilted her head quizzically and started toward her friend, meeting her halfway.

"We're in the same quartet!" Grace said, jumping on the balls of her feet.

"What? Seriously?"

"Yes! Ah! So cool!"

"How am I in your quartet? You're always grouped with the best players."

"Yup."

Kathryn's smile widened with realization.

Grace squealed. "This is going to be so much fun! And we have Mr. Corrigan as our coach. He's awesome. And not bad on the eyes either," she said, leaning in closer with a toothy grin. "Come on. Let's go eat lunch. Oh my God. This is going to be the best year ever!" She threw an arm around Kathryn, whose mouth still hung agape at the shock of being chosen to be in Grace's quartet.

Kathryn felt her feet start moving, and she let Grace lead her out of the hall. The unexpected chill in the air snapped her back to reality, and she spotted her mom getting in her car. Grace turned her toward the dining hall, and Kathryn watched over her shoulder as her mom drove away.

Freedom.

The Calm Before

A light drizzle had begun to coat the campus by the time the girls left the dining hall and set back toward King Concert Hall. Kathryn's cheeks were sore from smiling, a welcome discomfort she hadn't felt in far too long.

"I'm sure you'll be up front in the first violins, Grace. You always are," Kelcee said. "Between your obviously glowing teacher recommendations and your perfect All County Orchestra scores, you're sure to be first or second."

"I was third chair last year, but I did rock my All County audition this year. What about you, Kat? How'd you do on All County?"

Kathryn's mind flashed to the morning of All County auditions. Yelling. Screaming. Crying. A sharp pain in her right shoulder as she was knocked into the kitchen doorway. "I...didn't do as well as I had hoped. I got a ninety-six. Messed up my sight reading."

"That sucks. Sorry, Kat. So you didn't make it?"

"No. My orchestra teacher said he's never seen anyone get in with less than a ninety-eight. That's why I was so surprised we were placed in the same quartet."

"All County scores aren't everything," Kelcee said. "I bet your orchestra teacher gave you a great write-up. It may also have a really difficult violin part, but the cello part may be a level or so below. Wait. That didn't sound right. I just meant—"

"I know, Kelc." Kathryn laughed. "It's fine. Grace is in her own league. I guess we'll see how it all affected my placement in orchestra."

The girls pushed open the double doors to the hall and followed the maroon carpeting to the stage. They split off in search of their seats in their own sections. Kathryn weaved her way through the viola section and began looking for her name toward the back of the cello section. Chair after chair, name after name, she continued searching. As she moved closer to the conductor's podium, annoyance furrowed her brow. She took a step to the left, ready to turn back, convinced she missed her name, but with a quick glance down, she saw it, and a slight gasp escaped.

Kathryn looked at Grace and held up her hand, all five fingers extended. "*Fifth*!" she mouthed.

Grace air clapped before holding up two fingers.

Kathryn's hand closed into a fist, and she punched the air. "Yes!" she said louder than she had intended.

Grace laughed and bounced on the balls of her feet.

After retrieving her cello from the lockers behind the stage, Kathryn took her seat as fifth chair. She tuned up and started sifting through the sheet music on the stand—some Haydn, Bach, Schubert, Beethoven, and Rossini's William Tell Overture as a grand finale. A small blond swished her skirt to the side as she sat down next to Kathryn in the sixth chair.

"Hi. I'm Nicole," she said with a shy smile.

"Hi. I'm Kathryn, but people here call me Kat. Do you want to see the music?"

"Sure."

Nicole moved to take the music when a familiar figure stepped onto the podium and raised a delicate hand.

"Good afternoon, students. As you hopefully remember, I am Ms. Gail, and I will be your conductor this week. You all have been selected to be a part of this, the Beethoven Orchestra, which is reserved for the top performing students. As such, I expect professionalism, dedication to your craft, and your very best effort this week. Show me I was right to trust your scores and your recommendations." She licked her thumb and leafed through the music on her black metal stand. "Now then, let's get right to it, shall we? We'll be starting with the Haydn symphony." She raised her baton in the air, and bowing arms followed, gently touching the strings without a sound. With the downbeat, Ms. Gail's curved hands danced to four-four time while the string instruments provided accompaniment.

After two hours, Kathryn let her bowing arm fall and shook it out as she stood, stretching her legs. Space in the back room was scarce as everyone packed up their instruments for their next class.

"Great music this year, huh?" said Grace as she zipped up her violin case.

Kathryn nodded. "I love every piece," she said, loosening her bow before slipping it into the pocket in her case. "Hopefully we'll have good luck with our quartet piece, too."

"We're about to find out. Let's head over. I hope we end up with a good second violin and viola. Some girl named Sarah and a guy named Chad...or Brad. Something like that."

The mist had increased to a steady rainfall, and the girls held tight to the sides of the campus buildings, dodging around the lush bushes decorating the exteriors as they made their way to the practice rooms of Douglas Hall.

"It's room three twenty-eight, I think." Grace glanced in the window to their right and gasped. She dropped her violin, and her hands immediately found her hair, smoothing out the rain-soaked strands. "This Chad or Brad better not be hot. I'm a freaking mess." She attempted to fluff and scrunch her curls but gave up and tied her hair back. With an annoyed moan, she slumped her shoulders. "Let's just find the room."

They followed the numbers down the hallway, weaving through the other students trying to find their practice rooms.

Kathryn watched the numbers increase. "Three twenty-four...three twenty-six..."

"Please don't be hot. Please don't be hot."

"Here it is."

"Please don't be hot. Please don't..." She turned the corner. "Oh, crap." She ducked behind Kathryn.

"Hello there. My cello and first violin have arrived." The handsome man smiled broadly, the corners of his eyes creasing his fair skin near his graying temples as he ushered them in with haste. "Welcome. Welcome. I am Mr. Corrigan."

"I'm Kat, and this is Grace," she said, moving to the side.

Grace stood up tall, casually flittering her fingers. "Hi."

A bespectacled brunette stepped forward, flipping a long braid off her shoulder, viola clutched under her arm. "Hi. I'm Sarah."

The boy to her left swished his dark bangs off his forehead, his green eyes striking as he smiled. "I'm Craig."

"Craig?" Grace whispered, halfway behind Kathryn. "Close enough."

Kathryn stifled a laugh. "Hey, guys. Nice to meet you."

"Well, with introductions out of the way, let's get down to it." Mr. Corrigan gestured toward the four chairs bunched together in the center of the small room. "We will be performing the third movement of Beethoven's Opus eighteen, number one, Scherzo and Trio. Excellent violin part for you, Grace. You're going to love it. I hope you're up for a challenge. Instruments out, in your seats please, and we're diving in. We only have five days before we perform for the panel of judges. My quartet has been one of the five chosen for the Honors Recital every year I've been here."

"So, no pressure," said Craig.

The girls giggled, Grace louder than the others. Her cheeks flushed as she rosined her bow.

An hour and a half of practicing flew by, and Kathryn was impressed by Sarah and Craig's playing. While her cello part did little to challenge her, she dug into the notes, her rich tone supporting Grace as her fingers danced along the neck of her violin, mastering the extensive sixteenth note triplet runs on her first try. Feeling quite confident about their chances of making Honors after just the first practice, Kathryn packed up her cello. She looked over at Grace, who had finished putting away her violin and was staring over at Craig.

"Go talk to him," Kathryn whispered, nudging Grace in the back.

"Now? Looking like this? Oh, no, no, no. Tomorrow. When I don't look like a drowned cat. Sarah better watch those flirty eyes though."

Kathryn laughed. "That's why you gotta get in there. You really do look fine."

"With this frizzy mess? Nope. Tomorrow. I'll meet you at Ka-cha after technique. We'll drop off our instruments and head to dinner. I'm already starving." Grace groaned.

"What's wrong?"

"Craig's probably in technique with me too. Why did it have to rain today?" she asked, whining, harshly flicking her hair.

Kathryn giggled and shook her head as she playfully shoved her friend into the hallway before heading off to her technique class.

Kathryn and Grace met up with Kelcee and Ginny, and after dinner, they returned to King Concert Hall for evening orchestra practice. Another hour and a half of practicing pushed even Kathryn to her limit, and the students spread throughout the soft maroon chairs for the customary nightly concert put on by some of the camp counselors and coaches.

During the second movement, Grace leaned into Kathryn's side. "Do you think I have a shot with Craig?"

"Of course," Kathryn whispered back. "If you stop hiding behind me."

Grace clapped a hand over her mouth and tried to hide a laugh a little too late. Their group counselor, Isabel, eyed them from down the row and brought her finger up to her pursed lips before turning back toward the concert.

"After the storm tonight, it's supposed to be a nice day tomorrow, so no hiding will be necessary."

"Oh, thank goodness," she replied with feigned seriousness.

Grace jabbed Kathryn with her elbow, and it was her turn to poorly attempt to stifle a laugh. Isabel turned again, her eyes narrowed and lips tight.

"Sorry," Kathryn mouthed.

Grace pretended to zip her lips shut, and Isabel turned to the stage again.

The friends looked at each other, and Grace rolled her eyes. Kathryn smiled and set her attention back on the concert for the final piece.

The approaching darkness of night enveloped the girls as they entered the cool summer air, the stars blocked out by a thick blanket of clouds looming ominously above. Kathryn's sandaled foot disturbed a still puddle on the sidewalk left in the aftermath of the day's miserable weather.

Grace looked up into the moonless sky. "I hope we make it back before it starts again. My mom said it's supposed to get bad." She picked up her pace, and Kathryn kept up with her, Kelcee and Ginny lagging behind. "So, what's been going on with you? I've been blabbing so much about myself I've barely let you talk."

Kathryn looked down, entirely too entranced by her wet foot. "Um...not much."

"How's your mom doing? I noticed her sleeve earlier. She's still in remission, right?"

"Oh, yeah. Almost...five years now." She paused. "That would mean she has another mammogram coming up."

"She hasn't said anything to you about it?"

"No. We...haven't really talked a whole lot lately."

"Why not?"

"Kind of a long story."

"I have time," Grace said, nudging Kathryn's arm.

"Um—"

"Hey, ladies," a deep voice said from behind.

The girls turned to see Craig strolling up, another boy at his side.

"Hey," Kathryn said, nodding.

Grace giggled before clearing her throat. "Hey, Craig. Great job in quartet today."

"Right back at ya, Grace. I think we have a real shot."

"We do?" Grace gripped Kathryn's arm.

"Oh, yeah. We've already got it down after just one practice. The Honors Recital is in the bag."

Kathryn's eyes jumped back and forth between the teenagers as they stared at each other for a moment longer. Craig startled when the other boy elbowed his side.

"Oh. Sorry, man. Grace, Kathryn, this is Zac, my roommate. He's a first year. Bass player."

"Hey," he said with a nod more in Kathryn's direction.

"Nice to meet you, Zac," Kathryn said.

"You too."

His attention lingered on her, and Grace squeezed her arm again.

"Well, night, ladies," Craig said, flipping his hand. "See you tomorrow." He clapped Zac on the shoulder as he guided him forward, catching up to a group of guys just ahead of them.

Kathryn chuckled. "Breathe, Grace. Just breathe."

Grace pulled down on Kathryn's arm, pretending to stumble and need her support to stay upright. "He's so darn cute. If I play it right, maybe I'll get a dance at the party Thursday night. And if the look on Zac's face was any indication, you might too."

"Huh?"

"Don't tell me you didn't notice that."

"Notice what?"

"Zac's totally into you."

"He doesn't even know me."

"Well, he wants to. Trust me." The girls made their way past the brightly lit courtyard, not stopping to admire its beauty in their rush to get back to the dorms. "So, any guys at home you have your eye on?"

"Um…yeah. There's this guy. Liam."

"Oooh, Liiaamm. I like that name. He sounds hot."

Kathryn laughed. "You don't even know what he looks like."

"Well, you're going to tell me."

"He's tall. Dark hair, almost black. Brown eyes and tanned skin. Olive, I guess you'd call it. He's really sweet. He was in my bio class last year."

"See, he sounds hot. Anything happen between you two?"

"No. Nothing more than just being friends. I don't think he'd like me that way."

"Why not?"

"I just don't think he would." Kathryn's gaze returned to her sopping foot.

"You're sweet, talented, and pretty. What's not to like?"

"That's really nice of you to say, but I just don't know if he sees me like that. You should see the other girls at my school."

"I don't even have to see them to know he's probably into you."

"My friend Lexie thinks he is too."

Grace gave a swift nod. "Smart girl."

"I don't know. I guess we'll see how next year goes. Hopefully we'll have another class togeth..." Kathryn held out her hand, and a heavy raindrop splattered against her skin. "Uh oh. Run."

Grace screamed as almost instantly rain unleashed from the sky, pelting them with thick drops, soaking through their clothes and plastering their hair to their makeup-tracked faces.

A horde of students raced for the dorms as Kathryn and Grace followed behind a group of shrieking girls.

"Geez! I guess my mom was right," Grace said, dripping water onto the tiled lobby floor.

The girls headed upstairs to their dorm room.

Kathryn grabbed a bag from her closet. "I think I'm going to take a shower tonight. What about you?"

"Nah. I want my hair to be perfect for tomorrow, so I'll take one in the morning."

"Okay. See you in a bit."

The showers were deserted, a welcome change from mornings when most girls were showering before breakfast. Kathryn stepped into the steaming stall as it rinsed the cold rainwater from her hair. She closed her eyes against the pressure, letting it wash over her, attempting to clear her mind. Once again alone, she couldn't continue to force it down; it was always there, waiting just below the surface. She knew she'd have to tell Grace.

After wrapping herself in a towel, she cleared the steam off the mirror, revealing her reflection. She wet her washcloth and cleared away the smeared black makeup shadowing her face. Looking into her bare eyes, an unsettling likeness of her brother stared back at her, and she shuddered, reaching for her eyeliner in her bag, quickly masking the resemblance.

After dressing and combing through her hair, she returned to the dorm room to find Grace asleep. She grabbed some quarters from her purse and left the room, taking the stairs down to the lobby. A small group of girls were still up, some watching TV or playing on the air hockey table.

"Fifteen minutes until lights out, ladies," Isabel announced.

"Is it okay if I make a phone call?" Kathryn asked her.

"Of course. Just make sure you're upstairs and in bed in fifteen minutes."

Kathryn slipped the quarters into the pay phone and dialed her number, hoping with all her being Brandon wouldn't answer.

"Hello?"

Kathryn breathed a sigh of relief. "Hi, Mom."

"Oh, hi, Kathryn! It's so great to hear from you. How's everything going? Are you having a nice time?"

"Yeah. Everything's fine. I'm having a lot of fun with Grace. And I made fifth chair in the orchestra."

"You did? That's wonderful! I'm so proud of you."

"We're also in the same quartet this year. I'm still kind of in shock."

"That's so exciting. How are the other players?"

"They're both really good. I have a good feeling about this year."

"Wonderful, sweetie. Well, if you make it to Honors, you can count on me to be there."

"Thanks, Mom." She drummed her fingers atop the metal counter. "Um... I was thinking about something. Is your five-year mammogram coming up soon?"

Silence.

"Mom?"

Jane inhaled sharply. "Yes, honey. I have a mammogram in about a month, the last week of August."

"Why didn't you tell me?"

"You have enough going on right now. I didn't want to weigh you down with anything else. I wanted you to have a great time at camp and not have to worry about me."

"You could have told me. I'm not ten anymore."

"I know, and maybe I should have. I'm sure everything is going to be just fine."

Silence.

"Sweetie, I don't want you to worry. Joke around and have fun with Grace. Make beautiful music. Don't worry about anything else. Just have the time of your life."

"Okay. I love you."

"I love you too, Kathryn. I'll talk to you soon. Bye."

"Bye, Mom." She placed the phone on the hook, her hand lingering on the handpiece for a moment. She glanced behind her at the clock and picked it back up, threw in another quarter, and dialed a different number.

"Hello?"

"Hi, Dad."

"Hi, Kathryn. I'm so happy to hear your voice."

"I don't have much time before lights out, but I just wanted to give you a quick call. I'm having a lot of fun at camp, and I made fifth chair."

"You did?" He laughed. "Good for you, baby girl. I'm so happy you're happy."

"Thanks, Dad. Everything okay with you?"

"Oh, you know, the usual. Cleaning the bar in the mornings, dealing with the morons at night, but I'm getting a few hours working at physical therapy lately, so that's been helpful. Busted knee or not, I can still pitch in there and help others with their injuries. My gardens are coming along nicely this year too. Maybe I can bring you a hanging basket of your favorite pink flowers when you get home."

She shifted to her other leg and ran her fingernail along the thick phone cord. "Um...sure."

"Three minutes, ladies!"

"I gotta go, Dad."

"Okay, my sweetest. Try to sneak in another call for your old dad before the week is over, huh?"

"I will."

"I love you."

"Love you too, Dad."

"Thank you, baby girl."

"You're welcome."

He chuckled lightly. "Bye."

"Bye."

Just as she opened the door, a lightning strike lit the night outside their third-story window. In the brief flash of illumination, Kathryn could make out the thick sheets of rain slamming against the glass. The crash of thunder followed, disturbing Grace, and she rolled over and lay still.

Kathryn climbed into bed and stared up at the ceiling, her mom overtaking her thoughts, sleep seeming like a distant destination too far out of her reach.

She hopped out of her mom's car with a burst of energy, running into the house through the garage door.

"Hi, Otis!" she said, patting the black lab's back as he trotted up to greet her.

79

Throwing her backpack on the kitchen floor, she went straight to the refrigerator. Her mom came in behind her, nearly tripping on the backpack.

"Kathryn, please move this!" Jane said sharply.

Kathryn looked up from the fridge, her young eyes wide. "Oh, I'm sorry, Mommy." She quickly picked up the bag and took it into the living room, placing it on the couch. She went back into the kitchen, eyeing her mom. When she didn't look up at her, Kathryn dove back into the fridge.

Jane walked past her daughter and opened the basement door. "Brandon, can you please come up here?"

"For what?" he shouted from below.

"Brandon! I said to come up here!"

Within seconds, footsteps came trudging up the basement stairs.

Kathryn peeked over the refrigerator door and watched her mom take a long, deep breath with her eyes closed. When she opened them, Kathryn saw a bit more of their usual calmness.

"Kathryn, can you come into the living room please?"

The little girl frowned. "But I want a sandwich."

"I know, sweetie. I just need to talk to you both about something first."

She groaned. "Okay." Kathryn closed the refrigerator door and skipped at her mom's heels, quickly passing her and leaping onto the couch, her knees rebounding off the cushion. She flung herself around and settled in the seat as the padding below sank with each bounce. Brandon giggled, and Kathryn reciprocated until they turned from each other and saw their mom's solemn expression and pallor as she sat on the loveseat, facing them.

Jane blinked slowly and drew another deep breath. "So, Brandon, how was school today?"

"Um…fine, I guess."

"Just fine?"

"Yeah," he answered plainly with a slight shrug.

She chuckled to herself and turned her attention to her daughter. "Kathryn, how was your day?"

"It was good! I had a lot of fun playing with Alicia after school on the playground. Mr. Avery told me I'm doing really good on my cello. He said he was impressed by how good I'm doing. I'm not as good as the other fifth graders because I just started. They've been playing for a year already, but I think I might be able to catch up! I hope so because then I can be in the orchestra next year. And you can come see me perform! That would be so cool!"

She smiled weakly. "I'm glad you had such a good day, sweetie."

Kathryn noticed her mom's eyes quickly looking down to her lap, and her young smile faded.

"Mom, what's going on?" asked Brandon.

She looked up at her children, her sad eyes sparkling with tears.

Kathryn shifted, leaning forward. "Mommy, what is it?"

Jane placed a hand on each of her children's. "I went to see the doctor today, and I had some tests done. The doctor looked at the tests and told me she thinks I might be sick."

"You're sick? Sick with what?" asked Brandon.

"The doctor thinks I might...I might have cancer."

Brandon was quick to his feet. "Cancer? You have cancer?"

"Sit down, honey," she said, pulling at his hand. "The doctor thinks that I might have cancer in my breast. I'm going to have to go see her again for what's called a biopsy. They will take some tissue from my breast, look at it closely, and see if there is cancer in it."

"Mommy, I don't know what cancer is."

"People die when they get cancer!" yelled Brandon.

Kathryn gasped. "What? Mom, are you going to die?"

"No. No, I'm not going to die," she said sternly, her eyes flitting between them. "If they find cancer in my breast, there are things they can do to help me and make me better."

"Oh." Kathryn's shoulders relaxed. "Well, then why are you so upset? They'll just make you better."

Jane leaned forward and took her children, one in each arm, and pulled them toward her, hugging them tightly. She rested her head against her son, and Kathryn heard her whisper something unintelligible to him. When she pulled away, she stared at her son and daughter for a moment longer.

"Um...can I go make my sandwich now?"

"Sure, Kathryn. Go ahead," her mom said with a slight upturn of her lips.

A deafening crash outside the window startled her, and Grace shook awake.

"What the hell?" She held herself up on shaky arms, panting.

Kathryn laughed. "Just a thunderstorm."

"Oh, okay." Her head hit the pillow, and she was out again as quickly as she awoke.

The voice of that little girl in her memory resounded in her mind once more. *"Then why are you so upset? They'll just make you better."* It occurred to Kathryn as she replayed the scene that she couldn't possibly have comprehended at that moment that her mom was going to be fighting for her life. She couldn't have known that when her mom hugged them, she may have wondered how many more hugs she'd be able to give them. She didn't recognize that when she paused to look at them, she probably worried she may not be around to watch them grow up. And such a young, innocent little girl wouldn't have been able to understand that in that moment, her mom was afraid she was going to die. But she wasn't that naïve little girl anymore.

She shook her head, refusing to let her mind wander to that dark, terrifying place. This was only a routine five-year mammogram. There was no need to worry before there was a reason to. She didn't know how she would be able to deal with one more complication right now. It was just too much. Would she be back home when her mom went for her mammogram? Would she have to watch her fight again, this time from afar? The thought of not being home with her mom if she had to go through this all again tore at her soul. Is this one more thing her brother would take from her? As if he hadn't taken enough? As if he hadn't done enough to her! Her hand drifted up to her temple.

With every strike that illuminated the room, she saw him. With every crash, she heard him. Kathryn turned on her side and curled up, bunching the pillow beneath her head. There, alone in the darkness, her strength frail and splintered, she couldn't fight it anymore. She let her mind give in.

The Storm

Kathryn shoveled another handful of popcorn into her mouth, her eyes reflecting the flicker of the television. She joined in with the laugh track at the silly antics on the screen. Readjusting her pillow, she sank farther into her bed and turned up the volume. When the phone rang, she sighed and rolled her eyes. Hoping it wasn't one of Brandon's jerky friends, she hesitantly reached for the cordless phone next to her and brought it to her ear.

"Hello?"

"Hey, Kathryn!"

Kathryn sighed again. "Rachael…goodness. I'm so glad it's you."

"And not one of the assholes?"

"Exactly."

Rachael giggled lightly. "Nope. Just little old me. What's up, girl?"

"Nothing much. Just watching TV. You?"

"Eh, not a whole lot here either. Met a few guys in the neighborhood. I've only been here for a week, and my dad is already driving me crazy, though. Not that that's anything new."

"How's Pete doing? Is your dad driving him crazy too?"

"Nah. They get along better. But I don't want to talk about my brother. Weren't you going to try to talk to Liam today? What happened?"

Kathryn scratched Mittens under her chin as she purred. "I didn't really get a chance to talk to him in biology. We had a pop quiz. But I did talk to him at lunch. Lexie and I sat at the table next to his. The tables were close together, so he kind of just leaned over to talk to me."

83

"I need to see a picture of this guy!"

"I'll show you his yearbook picture from last year. He's so cute. Well, I think so, but we like different kinds of guys. Not sure he'll be your type. You always go for the bad guys."

"Ha! Yeah, that's true, and you always go for the good guys! So, this Liam, he's a good guy? Really?"

"No really, Rach. I'm telling you. He's so sweet."

"Well, do you think he likes you?"

"I don't know. He's sort of popular. I can't really see him being into me. But he's nice and fun to talk to, so for now, I'm happy just being his friend."

"But you'd want more?"

"If he liked me, yeah, I would."

"You don't give yourself enough credit, Kathryn. You're awesome, and he'd be lucky to be with you."

"We've been friends since we were babies, so you have to say that."

Rachael laughed. "Doesn't mean it's not true."

Kathryn switched the phone to her other ear and shook out her stiff hand.

"Oh, I have to tell you about something Val said."

Kathryn's attention was pulled away from Rachael's voice as a slight rattling sound met her senses. Her gaze snapped to her door. The doorknob was shaking.

Mittens jumped off the bed and sprinted under the nightstand.

"What the...?" Kathryn said, cutting Rachael off.

"What? What is it?"

"It looks like someone is trying to get into my room. The doorknob is moving. It's probably Brandon."

"Why would Brandon be trying to get into your room?"

"No idea." She scooted herself out of bed and approached the door. "Brandon? What are you doing?"

The doorknob continued to shake.

"Brandon? What do you want?" Kathryn leaned her head to the side, holding the phone in between her chin and her shoulder, and she grasped the doorknob as it jiggled in her panicked grip.

"What's going on?" Rachael asked, her voice laced with unease.

"He won't answer me. Brandon! What are you doing?"

The doorknob shook rapidly.

Kathryn's feet slid on the plush carpet as the door began opening in sharp jabs. "Stop!" She pressed her shoulder against it, digging her bare feet into the floor, pushing her weight against the door. "What are you doing! Leave me alone!"

"Kathryn! What's happening!"

The door flung open with such force Kathryn stumbled back, nearly losing her balance. The phone slipped from her shoulder, but she caught it and held it in her unsteady hand. Brandon stood before her, draped in black, barely out of breath, rage seething beneath his dark, calm stare.

Kathryn stood frozen, looking into the face of the young man whom she feared above all. That look—she knew it all too well. Her heart pounded in her ears, her breathing rapid and labored. She couldn't move, held firmly in place by too many years of abuse at his hand. "Get out," she said, her voice a raspy whisper.

His lips parted into a smirk, his eyes wide and unblinking. "Oh, I can't do that. See, tomorrow is my eighteenth birthday." He took a slow step toward her. "If I beat the shit out of you the day before I turn eighteen, they can't do anything to me."

She was thrown back on her bed without even registering his right fist shooting at her head. Her vision blurred under the impact, the throbbing pain in her left temple searing through her whole body. She slid off the side of the bed, gasping, tears streaming down her face as she attempted to see through the bright, wavy glare clouding her sight. Pulling herself up, Kathryn dashed forward, slipping past her brother and knocking into the door that still remained open. His open hand came toward her, but she managed to escape its hate-filled grasp.

Kathryn took off down the stairs. Her feet slipped out from under her, and she tumbled down the last half, falling forward into the front door. He stampeded behind her as she ripped the front door open and fled into the mild spring air. Without risking a glance back, she sped along the grass to the street. A car rushed past her, whipping her hair back, and she screamed as its horn sounded. Without hesitation, she ran across the street and into the road adjacent to her house, sharp pebbles along the shoulder piercing her bare soles.

She snapped her head back to the house. He stood at the end of the driveway, his fists tightly clenched at his side, his face remaining eerily stoic among the chaos. He glowered at her and feigned a threatening step forward. Kathryn took a stumbling pace back despite the distance between them.

Through her gasps and whimpering cries, she heard Rachael's voice frantically calling to her in the phone still clutched in her hand. She lifted it to her ear.

"Kathryn! Kathryn! What's happening! Answer me!"

"I-I'm here."

"Oh my God. What the hell is going on!"

"He attacked me. He...he broke in. I don't know...what—"

"Where is he?"

"Across...the street."

"I'll call Val! Her mom can come get you. Stay right there. If he comes after you, run to the closest house and call me. I'll call you right back."

The phone clicked off, but Kathryn didn't move—couldn't move. She stared back at Brandon on the other side of the street, the view of his disturbing image flickering as cars passed between them. Kathryn slightly turned her head, looking down the road toward her aunt and uncle's house before her eyes snapped back to him. Brandon lowered his head, keeping his unmoving glare upon her, a hint of some form of emotion finally cracking along his tightened lips. He shook his head slowly, a movement barely perceivable from the distance. Her body flushed with heat, knowing she wouldn't make it—not before he caught her.

She managed to turn the portable phone off with her thumb, still not moving it from the side of her face. Seconds seemed like hours as her body quaked with panic, her breathing sharp and raspy.

The phone rang in her ear, and she clicked it on without looking at the keypad.

"They're on their way—Val and her mom. They're coming to get you. I'll stay on the phone with you until they get there."

"Okay."

She stood rooted in place, refusing to allow herself to crack and fall to the ground, not with him watching. Unable to stifle her sobs completely, her tears trickled onto the phone before gliding off and dripping to the ground at her cut feet. Rachael continued to speak in an attempt to calm her, but it merely fused with her gasps, the swoosh of passing cars, and the click of the quivering phone against her earring, creating a mess of incomprehensible noise as Kathryn's mind drifted in and out.

A car advanced from her left and slowed down. It took her a moment to realize it was Val's mom's car.

"She's here, Rach."

"Oh, thank God. My dad's going to drive me over to Val's. I'll see you in a bit, okay?"

Without answering, Kathryn hung up the phone. Val pushed the rear door open, and Kathryn got in without looking at Brandon. Val's mom did a three-point turn and started back toward their place. With a last glance back, Kathryn saw Brandon retreating into the house.

Kathryn exhaled deeply, closing her eyes and leaning her head against the headrest.

"What the hell happened?" Val asked. "Rachael said Brandon attacked you?"

Kathryn inhaled deeply, trying to calm her ragged breathing, but as the fear subsided and relief took over, her cries broke forth, and she doubled over. She felt a light hand on her back, and it stayed there until they returned to Val's house.

Kathryn sat in silence at the kitchen table. Val's mom placed a tall glass of water in front of her and left the girls alone. She wrapped her hands around the glass, the cold stinging her skin, but she only gripped it harder. An indeterminate amount of time blurred past before Rachael flew through the side door and into the kitchen.

Rachael flung her arms around Kathryn from behind and leaned her blond head into hers. "Kathryn, oh my God. I'm so glad you're okay." She released her and sat down in the wooden chair next to her.

"Rach," Val said just above a whisper, "she hasn't spoken yet. She won't tell me what happened."

"Her damn brother is a stupid asshole—that's what happened. I was on the phone with her the whole time. He broke into her room and attacked her. That's the best I could make out. She ran away and out of the house. That's when I called you." She turned to Kathryn and placed a gentle hand on her forearm. Kathryn flinched, but Rachael's hand remained. "What exactly happened?"

The recounting of what Brandon did, of what he said, trembled out past her chapped lips. She found her hand involuntarily raising up to her left temple where his fist met her with an anger and violence that, despite the litany of prior attacks, she had not witnessed from him before. There was something different about this one—a darkness...malice behind his rage. A chill coursed through her body.

"Damn. And he actually said that? 'They' can't do anything to him? Who's 'they' anyway?" Val asked.

Rachael shook her head. "The police? Like before he turns eighteen so he can't be charged as an adult? That's messed up."

"Did you guys fight at all today? Did you do anything to piss him off?"

"No. I barely even saw him today. I don't know what I did."

Rachael squeezed her arm. "You didn't do anything. You didn't do anything to deserve this. Okay?"

Kathryn nodded and took another sip of ice water.

"So what now?" Val asked. "We have school tomorrow."

"Well, she's not going back. You're not going back."

"I don't even have shoes. Or clothes for tomorrow. Or my backpack and homework."

"Maybe call your mom and tell her what happened and have her bring your stuff over here," Val said. "I'm sure my mom will let you spend the night. You can take the bus with me tomorrow morning."

"I...I don't know if I should tell her."

Rachael furrowed her brow. "What? Why?"

"I don't know what else he might do. He never meant for me to get away. I don't think he finished what he started. She...she's not home all the time. I don't know what he'll do to me if I tell her."

"Then just call her and have her bring your stuff, and we'll figure it out," Rachael said. "Do you think she'd be home by now?"

Kathryn nodded.

Val put the cordless phone in Rachael's outstretched hand, and she dialed Kathryn's house. After a moment, she handed it to Kathryn. "She answered."

"Mom?"

"Kathryn? I thought you were upstairs in your room. I heard the TV on from downstairs. Where are you?"

"At Val's. Her mom picked me up after school."

"Oh, okay. When will you be home?"

"Actually, I was thinking of spending the night if it's okay."

"It's a school night, sweetie."

"I know, but we have...a history test tomorrow, and we were going to study together tonight."

"Well, I guess that's okay."

"The thing is, I don't have any of my stuff. I hadn't planned on spending the night. Could you maybe bring me my stuff for tonight and for school tomorrow? A change of clothes, my contact solution, my backpack. And... um...my blue sneakers. I just grabbed my flats on my way out. I'd rather not wear them to school tomorrow."

"You didn't even bring your backpack? How did you plan to study?"

"Um...I forgot about it. Val just reminded me. That's why we need to study."

"Kathryn, is everything okay?"

She swallowed hard, her cheeks flushing. "Yeah, Mom. Everything's fine. I've just been a little...off lately, I guess."

"Well, if you're sure. I'll bring the stuff in a little while."

"Thanks. See you soon."

Kathryn clicked off the phone. "I hate lying to her."

Rachael laid a soft hand on her shoulder. "I know."

Within the hour, Jane arrived at the house. Kathryn had borrowed some of Val's makeup to cover the evidence of too many tears. She went out to meet her mom, pasting a smile on her face and trying to act normally.

"Here's everything. I think I got everything, anyway."

"Thanks, Mom."

Jane leaned in for a hug, placing her hand on the back of her daughter's head. "Are you sure everything is okay? You know you can talk to me about anything."

"It's fine, Mom. Really."

Jane pulled away and surveyed her daughter. "Okay. I'll see you tomorrow when I get home from work. I shouldn't be late. I don't have any kids staying after school." She embraced Kathryn again. "I love you."

"Love you too, Mom." She squeezed a little tighter.

Kathryn watched as her mom pulled away, the angst in her throat threatening to choke her. She turned on her heel, having to try a little too hard to keep Val's two-sizes-too-small flip-flops on her sore feet as she took the stone path back to the house.

Kathryn gripped the side of the seat with her right hand as the bus began moving again after picking up another student on the way to school the next morning. "What am I going to do if he's home when I get home? Sometimes he is, sometimes not. I don't know what I'm going to do if he is. I—"

Val's hand hit her knee with a slap. "Kathryn, um...the bus ride before we get to your stop is kind of my time to...prepare for when you get on, so can we just sit quietly and not talk about this anymore? It's like all we've talked about. Like, enough already." Her stare dropped to the magazine in her lap, and her thick, dark hair fell, blocking her face.

Val's words ripped the breath from Kathryn's lungs. Her eyes burned with tears, and she inhaled deeply, trying to stave off another wave of crying. A burst of heat spread throughout Kathryn's body as the anger rose from within. She crossed her arms over her chest, staying completely silent as she blinked a single tear from her azure eyes, so sick and tired of crying, of being around people who made her cry.

When the bus stopped at school, Kathryn grabbed her bag and exited the bus without a word or a glance back at Val. As she turned the corner into the

89

red locker-lined hallway, she attempted to steady her breathing, willing her tears not to pour forth.

She spotted Lexie loading her bag for her morning classes. Trying to avoid looking at her, Kathryn turned her lock combination and buried her head in the metal cavity. Her useless attempt at holding in the sadness, the rage, the devastation, finally gave way. The pain pulled at her chest, spidering out to her limbs until she could barely stand any longer. Her knees buckled, and the stabbing agony pitched her forward, her knees hitting the tiled floor. She instantly felt someone at her side, a hand around her shoulder and one on the back of her head. Tender fingers cleared her hair from her face, and she wailed, surrounded by a swarm of ninth-grade onlookers. A familiar voice called her name from her right, and as the physical pain lessoned slightly at the forceful release of emotion, the voice became clearer.

"Kathryn! Oh my God. Talk to me, please. Shh... It's okay. It's okay. Back up, guys. Give her some room. I've got this. Kathryn, please. What happened?"

"He...he did it again." She brought in a long, shaking breath. "This time...he broke into...my room and...punched me...in the head."

"He what?" She leaned against her and wrapped her arms around her friend. "Oh my God. I'm taking you to the counselor. Come on."

Kathryn felt Lexie's arms pull at her shoulders, gently guiding her to her feet.

"But...he'll be...so mad if I tell," she said through her gasps.

Lexie put her arm around Kathryn's back, supporting her unsteady gait. "You have to tell someone. He can't keep doing this to you. He's gone way too far this time."

Mr. Denham tilted his head, all the while keeping a gentle yet unrelenting gaze upon the weeping teenage girl on the other side of his desk. After Kathryn forced her way through the ordeal, she looked from Mr. Denham to her best friend sitting next to her, her hand clutched tightly while lying on the armrest. Kathryn took in the expression on Lexie's face—shock, sadness, helplessness.

Mr. Denham leaned forward, placing his arms flat on his desk. "Kathryn, I'm so glad you came to me about this. Lexie, thank you for bringing her. You did the right thing. I am so sorry this has happened to you, Kathryn. This is absolutely unacceptable. He had no right to lay a hand on you. I'd like to call your mother and discuss this matter with her."

"But I haven't even told her yet."

"Why not?" Mr. Denham asked, his brow furrowed above his round glasses.

Kathryn hesitated and looked to her left. Lexie nodded, and Kathryn exhaled forcefully. "Because I don't know what he'll do if he finds out I told someone."

"How long have incidences like this been happening?"

"This is the worst it's gotten, but he's been...hurting me for years."

"And your mom doesn't know?"

"She knows some of it. I don't tell her everything though. He threatens me."

He stood from his rolling office chair and stepped around his desk, leaning against it in front of the girls. "Kathryn, it's time to tell her. This can't continue. You shouldn't have to live like this."

"That's what I told her." Lexie turned to her friend. "She needs to know. I'm scared for you," she said, her voice breaking, her emerald eyes wet with unshed tears.

Kathryn's hand swept across her cheek—the cheek stained with too many tears, too much fear, too much pain, too many years of victimization. She nodded.

Kathryn stared silently out the other side of the bus on the way home, the trees becoming more familiar as they drew closer. She risked a sidelong glance at Val sitting beside her, still with her face turned away, ignoring Kathryn completely.

As the bus pulled up to her house, she peered out the window again, and her breath caught, a rush of heat coursing through her body. She raised up on quivering legs, gripping the backs of the seats as she hesitantly made her way to the front of the bus and descended the stairs onto the driveway.

Kathryn stood frozen, struggling for breath, her eyes unblinking.

He was there. He was waiting for her. His sinister glare bore through her as he knelt on the loveseat in front of the picture window, his elbows resting on the back. He raised one hand and extended his index finger, hooking it toward himself, motioning her to him.

Without further thought, she bolted. Pebbles and dust kicked up behind her as she dug her blue sneakers into the shoulder of the road, her backpack slamming against her. She didn't dare look back. She simply ran—ran for her life, ran for her safety, ran for her freedom.

The long, blue ranch-style house came into view, and the purple door drew closer as she fought through the burning in her legs and lungs, only pushing harder. She leapt up the stairs two at a time, landing on the porch, and frantically banged on the front door. Peeking around into the window, she saw her aunt walking to the door, and she whipped her head back toward her house.

No one.

She looked back into her aunt's eyes.

"Kathryn? Honey, what's wrong?"

"I...I can't go home. I can't." Her trembling hand found her midsection, and she bent forward, bracing her other hand on the door frame as she fought for her words through gasps. "Please. I can't go back there."

"Come in. Come in." Aunt Hannah stepped aside and put her arm around Kathryn, gripping her bicep and assisting her over to the flowered living room couch. She sat next to her niece and took her hand. "My dear, what happened? Why can't you go home?"

Years of holding it all in...years of secrets kept...years of lies... No more. It all burst forth, pouring out of her like a river that broke through a dam that centered its existence around suppressing the flow of something meant to be beautiful.

Aunt Hannah's eyes grew larger and larger until they fell closed and over-flowed with anguish.

With one last sharp intake of air and one final word, Kathryn sobbed uncontrollably, giving in again to too much. It was all just too much.

Aunt Hannah slid closer to Kathryn and pulled her into her shoulder, holding her as she wept, rubbing her back. "Oh, my dear. I'm so sorry. I'm so glad you came to us. You're safe now."

Her tears had dried up as if she had nothing left to give. Her red-laced eyes stared forward at nothing, and sudden bursts of inhalations assaulted her body every few seconds. She twitched at the soft pressure on her ankle. "Hey, Max," she said, offering her hand for the tuxedo cat to rub against. She scratched under his chin, and his throat rumbled with affection. Max pushed his back into her touch as she pet him, sliding to the tip of his black tail.

Aunt Hannah came into the living room and placed a ham sandwich on the coffee table in front of her niece. "Just in case you're hungry." She handed her a glass of iced tea. "Take a sip. It'll calm your breathing."

Kathryn took the iced tea and swallowed a big gulp through her swollen throat.

"Honey," Aunt Hannah said, sitting next to her, "I just spoke with Uncle

Alex. I had to tell him everything." She placed a gentle hand on her shoulder as Kathryn forced herself to blink and turned toward her aunt. "We'd like you to come stay with us for a little while. Just until all this is sorted out. We don't feel comfortable with you being there. It's your decision, of course, but we truly want you to stay with us. Your safety is the most important thing to us."

Kathryn blinked again. "I could really stay? You don't mind?"

"Mind? Oh, Kathryn. I couldn't love you more if you were my own daughter."

Kathryn looked down at the iced tea in her hands as it rested on her lap, observing the beads of condensation cascading over her fingers. "Why does he hate me?"

Aunt Hannah tilted her head. "He's not well, Kathryn. He hasn't been for a long time. This is not your fault."

"He planned it all. He planned to come into my room. He planned to attack me. Then...he was waiting for me. He was actually there waiting for me. I don't know what I did," she said steadily, her eyes and face now dry.

"You didn't do anything. He did. He's...an angry person. He takes that anger out on you. It's irrational. None of this is on you." She took Kathryn's hand. "Please say you'll stay."

Kathryn nodded. "Thank you." She reached out and hugged her aunt again.

"Of course," Aunt Hannah said into her hair, stroking it. "I'm going to give Alex a quick call. He's very worried. It'll give him some peace to know you'll be with us."

Kathryn stood as Aunt Hannah bustled from the room. Her legs once again stable, she approached the bay window at the front of the house. She leaned her forehead against the cool glass, comforting on her warm skin. Her breath washed out, dispersing along the surface, and she drew her fingers across the fogged glass, slicing it into fragments. Her eyes fell shut under the weight of her situation. Leave her home? Leave her mom? Mom... But she wasn't safe. She couldn't stay. She would leave her home, leave her mom. He would stay, and she would leave. He won.

She opened her eyes again, crystalline and hardened, anger boiling from within, staring past her reflection at the beauty of the birch-lined yard.

"Congratulations, you son of a bitch."

Singed

The pillow lay damp beneath her cheek as the theater in her mind concluded the painful scene that brought her to this moment of devastation that felt as though it would never relinquish its hold. The release of finally letting her mind play through the events of those days allowed her to exhale a breath of great relief while it simultaneously strangled her.

"Kat? What's wrong?"

"Um…nothing. I'm fine."

"It sounded like you were crying. What's going on? Are you okay?"

Kathryn shifted her body weight and rolled to face her friend as she pushed herself up and swung her legs over the side of the bed. "No, I'm not okay."

Grace reached forward and turned on the lamp atop the nightstand, spreading a hazy dose of light around the small dorm room. "Talk to me."

After blocking her mind from recalling the trauma of that day for weeks, she relived it twice in one night. The tears streamed down her tracked cheeks as the words spilled forth, leaving her lips in between gasps and sobs. Saying the words aloud brought a new reality to each syllable. She hadn't spoken about it since that day she sat crying on her aunt's couch, the day she took her in, the day she protected her.

Grace flipped her covers off and scampered over to Kathryn's bed, sitting beside her and throwing her arm around her friend's shoulders. "I'm so sorry you had to go through that. I mean, I fight with my sisters, and we mess with each other, but we never go at each other like that. Is this the worst thing he's done?"

"It's mainly random, out-of-anger punches or pushes. He's grabbed me by my hair and slammed me into the wall. He...stabbed me in the ankle with a pen once."

Her eyes widened. "He what?"

Kathryn brought her left foot onto the bed and brushed her finger along the scar on the inside of her ankle. "When I was twelve, he called me an idiot when I was sitting on the couch doing homework, and I said, 'takes one to know one,' and he grabbed my pen from my hand and stabbed me with it."

"That's freaking insane. I... That's messed up."

"Well, he's pretty messed up."

"God, Kathryn. Does your mom know?"

"Oh, she was there for that one. She saw it happen. She screamed at him, but nothing phases him. He doesn't care."

"That kid needs serious help."

"I don't know what I did. I don't know why he hates me so much. Sure that comment back to him was bratty, and I guess I should have known not to say it, but—"

"Don't put this on yourself. He sounds deranged or something. If my little sisters came back at me with that line, I may have tossed a pillow at them or something. Not freaking stab them. That's not normal. You can't blame yourself."

Kathryn yawned through trickling tears and brushed her dampened strands of hair from her cheeks.

"Try and get some sleep, Kat. We have such an awesome day ahead of us tomorrow, an amazing week. We're going to help you forget all about him."

A slight smile broke through on Kathryn's somber face, and she nodded as she yawned again. Grace went back into her own bed, and Kathryn rolled over and pulled the thin blanket up over her shoulder. With the trauma flashing continuously through her exhausted mind, Kathryn feared she'd be awake all night. Sleep eventually found her, though, whisking her away from her brother and throwing her into sweet dreams of the tall elm tucked into the back corner of the lot sprinkled with patches of golden tulips, encasing a house of far too much sadness dusted with happy moments with her dad.

The sun shone harshly against her young, pale skin as they walked along the garden lining his garage, Kathryn's small fingers trailing the cedar siding.

"Let's go this way, Daddy. I want to lift our hands over the tree again,"

the little girl said, tugging at his hand. But with a blink of her blue eyes, she pulled on air, and her hand fell to her side. "Daddy?"

She ran across the grass to the driveway, kicking up pebbles as she sprinted toward the street, scanning the yard. The girl jumped up onto the thick railroad ties that lined the driveway and bordered yet another patch of precisely designed flower arrangements. "Daddy? Daddy! Where are you!"

"Kathryn? Kathryn, where did you go?" his rough voice called.

"I'm here, Daddy! I'm over here!"

"Kathryn! Kathryn!"

"Daddy!"

She spun back to the house, and her flaxen hair twirled and whipped in the burst of flames that erupted in front of her. She fell into the bed of pebbles and cowered before the fire as it spread wildly along the railroad ties and grew upward and across the stone driveway, creating a wall between her and the house, fueled by an invisible element.

Through the dancing reds and oranges, the images of her dad, mom, and brother swirled behind the heat-streaked air as sparkling embers drifted into the sky suddenly overtaken by darkness. The hem of her yellow dress got caught up in the churning wind, and she jumped back, screaming and flailing on the ground. At a safe distance from the inferno, her tiny fingers trailed along the blackened hem, the soft, innocent yellow singed and damaged beyond repair. She pulled her hand away, inspecting her soot-covered fingertips before stumbling to her feet.

"Mommy! Daddy! Help me!"

"Kathryn," her dad said with unnatural calmness, his stoic expression illuminated by the blaze. "Come on, baby girl. Come to us."

"I can't get through! It's too hot!"

"You can do it, sweetie," her mom said, echoing the serenity of her dad's tone.

Kathryn stepped forward, reaching a hand toward the flames but recoiled at the intense heat. She knelt on the stone driveway, the pebbles digging into her bare knees. "I can't," she said through her tears drying instantly upon her overheated cheeks. "I don't know how."

She snapped up in bed, scanning the dorm room with her naturally blurred vision, gasping through the blackened air. But as her eyes adjusted to her dark surroundings, the storm out her window still rampant, she continued to draw in rapid breaths of clean, smoke-free air and lay back down in a rushing wave of relief. Kathryn looked over to Grace sound asleep in her bed. She pulled the alarm clock closer to her face—4:04.

That childhood nightmare had returned, infiltrating her subconscious for the past few weeks. Always the same. No matter how many times she awoke choking on coal-black, nonexistent smoke, the realness never lessened. The terror never faltered. This time, though, the thunderstorm raging outside woke her up before it finished.

She closed her eyes, the image of her family behind a wall of fire painted under her eyelids. She squeezed her eyes tighter, trying to force it away. As they faded from view, they were replaced with pure darkness, and Kathryn once again drifted into unconsciousness.

Determined not to let him ruin her week, she poured herself into her cello like never before. Over the next several days, Grace and her other friends were a welcome distraction as well, and the days passed with more music and laughter than she could recall in recent weeks. Not being the girl who cries in the hallway allowed her a much-needed freedom from her life back home. Kathryn could be anyone she wanted to be. She could be silly and stupid and laugh hysterically as Grace found out how absorbent the pancakes were. They soaked up almost half a glass of Grace's orange juice. She was about to test how much milk it could absorb before Isabel put a stop to her experiment. Not being the girl with the troubled brother meant she was just Kathryn, and every person she met knew only what she chose to tell them.

"I'm not sure what to do with my hair for the dance tonight. Up? Down? Should I straighten my curls?" Grace softly tugged at a section of her hair, pulling it straight.

Kathryn skimmed a handful of Grace's curls off her shoulder. "They're so pretty though. Up would be fun, but your natural hair is beautiful as it is."

"I guess I'll put my dress on, and we can play around with it a bit. Which dress did you bring?"

"My aunt actually took me shopping for a new one."

"How sweet. Eeek! I can't wait!" Grace squealed.

"Just one more quartet rehearsal and we can start getting you ready."

"Not just me. You too! There has to be someone here who's caught your eye. Maybe someone you'd like to dance with?"

Liam's smiling chocolate eyes flashed in her mind. "No one here."

"Well, I know Liam isn't here, but that doesn't mean you can't have fun dancing and hanging out with another guy. What about Zac? I've seen you talking to him this week. He seems really nice, and I think he's into you."

"He is nice. I just...don't really see it going anywhere."

"Why not?"

"He lives like an hour from me, and I'm just in a messed-up place right now."

"Doesn't mean you can't have fun with him. It doesn't have to go beyond that. Besides, I know you're crazy hung up on Liam, so I get it."

Kathryn felt a rush spread through her as her heart sped at the image of Liam flashing behind her eyes. Music had overtaken her thoughts lately, and Liam had only snuck into her mind in the rare quiet moments right before she fell asleep each night.

Grace popped her newly glossed lips and fluffed her hair one last time. "Okay. Let's get to the practice hall."

Kathryn watched Grace smile and attempt to tuck her mess of curls behind her ear as they entered the practice room and saw Craig rosining his bow.

"Okay, ladies and gent, let's run through it, top to bottom. Tomorrow is the day we've been working so hard for. We make Honors or…we make Honors. There's no other option."

"Awesome pep talk, Mr. C," Craig said with a wink.

The girls laughed, Grace a little too much as usual. Kathryn met her eyes, and Grace reined it in.

Grace cleared her throat, met their eyes one at a time, raised her violin, and hovered her bow just above the strings. The quartet mirrored her movements. A sharp intake of breath through her nose acted as a signal, and she swept her bow across her instrument, the others following suit.

With a final down-bow, Kathryn's C string resounded through the small practice room, blending perfectly with the other instruments.

"Yes!" Mr. Corrigan shouted, jumping up from his seat. "Gorgeous. Just gorgeous. Grace, the triplet runs in the Trio are magnificent. Craig and Sarah, that was terrific. And Kathryn"—he placed his hand over his heart—"your tone. So rich and full. Fantastic job, everyone. Fantastic. We've done all we can. Just play your best. The rest is up to the judges."

The string players beamed in the glow of their coach's praise. They looked around at each other, matching smiles on all their faces.

Kathryn slid in her endpin and pried open her case, carefully placing her beloved inside. In the small room, it was hard not to overhear the deep voice behind her.

"So…uh…Grace, are you planning on going to the dance tonight?" Craig asked.

99

"Oh, yeah, I am. Kat and I were just talking about it before practice. It should be fun."

"Well, I guess I'll see you there then."

Kathryn turned to see Craig's back as he walked out, and she locked eyes with Grace as her pink cheeks pinched up, forming a smile that overtook her whole face.

"Well, we better get to planning what to do with that hair," Kathryn sang.

"Zip me up and tell me more about Liam," Grace said, turning her back to Kathryn.

She grasped the zipper of the flowing, gold, glittering dress and drew it up as Grace held her hair off her neck. "What do you want to know?"

"Oh, just everything."

Kathryn giggled. "Um…like I said, we had bio together. We were lab partners. He's so sweet, cute, funny, and smart. He plays baseball."

"So he's a jock? Nice." Grace turned, sweeping her hair into a loose pile on her head. "How's this?"

Kathryn hooked her finger into the front of her friend's hair, loosening tendrils on either side of Grace's made-up face, twirling them into smooth, bouncy curls. "Perfect." She grabbed the clip on the dresser and turned Grace toward the mirror. "I guess he's a jock, but he doesn't act like one. He takes baseball really seriously. He's kind and approachable. Lots of the other jocks are all jerks and stick with their own crowd. They wouldn't look twice at someone like me. He's not like that." Kathryn placed the clip, and it disappeared within the mop of caramel curls. "You look stunning."

"Aw. Thanks, Kat. Now it's your turn," Grace said, spinning her finger, gesturing Kathryn to turn around.

Her soft pink, knee-length dress twirled lightly as she spun.

"This dress is so gorgeous." Grace began to fasten the row of clasps climbing her back. "And he doesn't seem to mind that you're a music nerd?" Grace snickered.

"He knows I play and even asked me about it before. I think it seems like he wants to get to know me."

"Sit. It's makeup time."

"It's okay. I can do it."

Grace shook her head. "Nope. I'm going to work my magic."

Resigned, Kathryn sat with her back toward the mirror, and Grace set to work, starting with liquid foundation followed by inky eyeliner darker than Kathryn typically used.

"Do you think he likes you likes you?" Grace asked as she swept gray eyeshadow across Kathryn's deep-set eyelids.

"I don't know. He's just so adorable and kind of popular. I see other girls looking at him, so I really don't know if he's interested in me like that. I'm not sure why he would be with cheerleaders eyeing him."

Grace drew a large brush along Kathryn's cheekbones. "Maybe he doesn't even see them because he's too busy eyeing you. Pucker for me." She dabbed Kathryn's full lips with a rosy lip gloss, fragrant with raspberries.

"He's just so...him. And I'm so me."

"Which is why he probably likes you. Blink." She brought black mascara through Kathryn's eyelashes. "Does he try to make you laugh?"

Kathryn saw an image of the elodea leaf and a vision of old-fashioned wallpaper. "Yeah."

"Does he flirt with you?"

"I'm so clueless when it comes to flirting."

Grace laughed. "Does he try to be near you when he doesn't have to be? Or go out of his way to talk to you?"

"I guess so. This one time, he was walking behind me coming off the bus. I didn't know he was there, and he gently pulled on my hair."

"Oh my God. He's practically pulling your pigtails on the playground."

The girls giggled.

"But why me?"

Grace turned her friend to face the mirror. "Kat, why not you?"

The corners of Kathryn's painted lips pulled up slightly as she gazed at her reflection, at the girl—the young woman—staring back at her.

Grace bunched her friend's locks, twisting upward, and clipped it in place. Kathryn reached up and brought a small slice of hair down on one side, and it swung loosely along her jaw.

"This is just what's on the outside," Grace said, adding a touch more gloss to her lips. "Sure, it's what's going to get his attention first. But if he's trying to get to know you, there's no doubt in my mind that he's a smitten kitten. I bet he'll come right up to you the first day back to school, and you'll pick up right where you left off."

A rush of excitement swelled up within Kathryn, and she wished so badly Liam would be at the dance. Just another chance to see him and be near him, to look into those brown eyes as they smiled at her, to hear his deep voice, and breathe in his clean scent.

"On the last day of school right before we boarded the buses to go home for summer, he came up and talked to me, and it seemed like he wanted to say something or ask me something. His friend, one of the jerky jock guys who ignores anyone not in their little circle, showed up and pulled him away before he could finish what he was going to say."

"No. Ugh. That sucks. I bet anything he was going to ask for your number or ask to get together over summer or something."

The thought brought that wave back up through Kathryn's body, and her glossed lips parted in a smile. She turned to Grace. "I certainly hope you're right, but he's not here now. Craig's here. And we have a dance to get to. He's going to be floored when he sees you. Come on."

The dining hall looked completely different as the girls walked through the curtain of crimson streamers draped across the doorway. The dimly lit room sparked with flashes of strobe lights, and colored beams jutting into the air near the DJ flared to the beat. Specks of silver sparkles webbed out over the dance floor, reflecting off the oversized disco ball strung up on the ceiling. Red and purple streamers and balloons overtook the space, and the tables that usually sat in the middle of the room now bordered the circumference of the large dining hall.

"Yikes," Grace said with a chuckle. "They really went all out this year."

Kathryn scanned the room, taking it all in. "It's a bit much."

"Just a bit."

They walked farther into the hall, flanked by Kelcee and Ginny.

"There's an open table over there," Grace said, pointing in the back corner.

Kathryn nudged Grace's arm with her elbow. "That one near Craig and his friends is open too."

Grace grabbed Kathryn's hand and led her to the table along the side wall near the DJ, the other girls trailing close behind.

They set their clutches down on the table and stepped onto the floor, dancing as a group to the up-tempo number. The long string of fast songs broke for a ballad, and the girls went back to the table to catch their breath.

Grace sat facing Craig's table and leaned her chin on her hand, staring dreamily at the tall, dark-haired violinist as one ballad wrapped up and another began.

Kathryn looked over her shoulder and back at her ogling friend. "Too obvious, Grace."

"What? Oh, crap. Yeah. I need to play it cool." She lifted her hand to her forehead and continued to peek through her fingers. "Oh my God. Oh my God. He's coming over here. Quick, say something funny."

"What?"

Grace burst out into a fit of laughter. "Oh, Kat, you're hilarious!"

"Hey, ladies. What's so funny?" Craig asked with a swish of his hair.

"Oh, just something Kat said. She's a riot."

Kathryn flushed and attempted to hold in a chuckle. "Yup. That's me. Hey, Zac."

Zac nodded from his roommate's right. "Hey."

Craig fiddled with his maroon and gold striped tie while keeping his focus on Grace. "So, uh...Grace, would you like to dance?"

"Me?" Her hand fluttered to her chest. "Oh, I'd love to." She took his outstretched hand.

Kathryn noticed Craig nudge his friend who remained at the table.

Zac raked his fingers through his brown hair. "Kat, would you like to dance?"

Kathryn's eyes widened as she processed the words that left his mouth. "Um...okay. Sure."

He exhaled deeply and grinned.

She followed him out onto the dance floor centered beneath the spinning disco ball, her legs slightly weak. He turned to face her and held his arms out. Kathryn looked at them, completely clueless as to what to do with them. Zac laughed at her hesitation and placed his hands lightly on her hips. Stealing a glance at Grace and Craig, she put her hands on his tall shoulders, feeling the crispness of his dress shirt under her palms. She felt her feet moving and let him guide her.

"How are you liking your first year?" she asked, practically screaming over the blaring music.

"I like it a lot. Craig's cool, and I'm learning tons. I'll probably come back again next year."

"That's awesome. The people make all the difference. I met Grace my first year."

"How many years have you been coming here?"

"This is my fourth."

"Ah, so you're an old pro then."

She looked up into his eyes and felt her cheeks stain pink noticing the cute way his nose crinkled when he smiled at her.

"So, do they always go a bit overboard with these dances?"

"Not really. This is the first year I've been here where they went crazy with the decorations. Not sure we've had a disco ball before either," she said, flicking her vision up.

He chuckled. "Lucky me."

The slow song ran into the next, followed by a random slew of strong beats and soft ballads. Craig rarely left Grace's side, and Zac's confidence seemed to increase every time Kathryn agreed to dance with him.

As the night wound down, Kathryn once again rocked to the slow tempo with Zac, a genuine smile on her face as she recalled the year she and Grace locked themselves out of their dorm room, Grace only in a towel after showering, thinking the other had the keys. His eyes intently focused in on hers as she spoke, the darkness lit only by flashes of colored light and reflections from the mirrored surface above them, she was taken in for a moment by the deep blue shading in his kind stare. His hands moved on her waist, his fingers inching closer together along the small of her back.

She felt a knock to her shoulder and stumbled before whipping her head around to see Grace and Craig.

"Hey, you two," Craig said with a wink. "Glad to see you're hitting it off. Zacky here's been talking about you for days."

"Dude!" Even in the dim room, Kathryn saw the color creep across his cheeks.

Craig laughed, and Grace's eyes widened upon Kathryn.

Zac punched Craig in the arm, and the couple spun away.

"Um…sorry about that." He looked away for a moment. "So, uh…some of the guys were going to go hang out behind the practice hall. There's a patch of tall bushes there where they won't be seen. I guess one of the guys snuck in a flask of something."

"He snuck in alcohol?"

"Apparently. I thought I might head over there. The dance is almost over, and if nothing else, it'll be a break from these seizure-inducing lights. You and Grace want to tag along?"

Kathryn stiffened, and a shiver crawled down her spine. "That's not really my scene."

"That's cool."

The final chord of the ballad strummed, and she broke apart from Zac, sliding her hand over her ear, forgetting her hair was swept back.

"Well, thanks for the dances, Kat. If you change your mind, you know where we'll be. See you in rehearsal tomorrow morning."

Kathryn watched him walk over to his group of friends at the next table. She turned to head back to where Ginny was sitting with her chin resting in her hand, and she flopped in the chair opposite her and huffed.

"What's wrong?" asked Ginny, looking up.

"I'm just ready for the night to be over."

Ginny nodded. "Me too."

"You're not having fun either?"

"Not really. Too many…people." She released a light giggle, and Kathryn joined in.

Kelcee hurried over to the table as her deep purple dress rustled in her haste, and she grabbed her cup of water, holding her heavy hair off the nape of her neck. "The guy I just danced with was a total jerk. After the second time I had to slap his hand, I just walked off." She rolled her eyes as she took a gulp. "Your guy is cute, Kat."

"Maybe, but he's so not my type."

"Kat!" Grace's voice shrieked in her ear. "Best. Night. Ever! Oh my God. Craig is so amazing."

"That's awesome. I'm so glad you had such a nice time with him."

"And how'd things go with Zac?"

"Fine until he invited me to go drinking behind the practice hall."

"What?"

"Someone snuck in alcohol, and he wanted us to join them."

"Seriously? They're going to get in huge trouble if they're caught." She let one hip fall and crinkled her nose. "That sucks. He's so cute, and Craig said he really likes you."

"He doesn't even know me. If he did, he'd know not to ask me to go drinking with him."

"Sorry, Kat."

"It's really no big deal."

"And you have Liam to go home to."

Kathryn rolled her eyes and chuckled.

"Come on. I love this song," Grace said, bouncing to the faster rhythm. "Let's go dance, girls!"

The four young ladies made their way to the dance floor, raising their hands and shaking their hips to the upbeat tune. Craig stole Grace away for the remaining slow songs, and Kathryn held tight to Kelcee and Ginny for the rest of the night. She scanned the hall for Zac, but she couldn't find him. The image of Zac and a group of guys crouched on the ground throwing their heads back with each swig churned her stomach, and she shook her head, determined not to let the vision morph into what her back yard looked like on a Friday night, Val at the epicenter.

Grace was once again with Craig as the last song ended, and the lights went up, forcing the group of teenagers to squint in the rapid contrast.

Kathryn grabbed her purse from the table, turning to see Grace skittering up to her.

"Craig asked if he could walk me back to my dorm." She squealed, a smile overtaking her face.

"Aw. That's so sweet. I'll walk back with the girls. You go. Have fun. I'll see you back in the room, and then I want to hear all about it."

"Oh, you're getting every detail."

Kathryn watched Grace skip off to Craig's side and saw her hand interlace with his. Her lips upturned at the end to her friend's amazing night.

She closed her eyes and could almost imagine what Liam's strong hand would feel like, his tanned fingers intertwined with hers, complementing her porcelain skin. She felt a pinch in her chest; she missed him. He was constantly there with her in the back of her mind. He, unlike her brother, was a welcome inhabitant in her thoughts. She found herself opening up more to the possibility he might actually care for her. If Zac could like her without even knowing her that well, maybe Liam could too. She wondered if perhaps she let the thoughts and fantasies of him in more, they would chase out the unwelcome thoughts of her disastrous life at the moment. He always had a way of making her forget. *Sure, you can walk me back to my dorm,* she thought, imagining his deep voice and picturing his sparkling smile. She giggled and set off behind Kelcee and Ginny back to the dorms, holding on to his image and the fanciful touch of his hand.

Kathryn flopped onto her bed without even bothering to take off her shoes, her dress fanning around her thighs. She closed her eyes and felt sleep swiftly coming for her, but she jolted upright when the door slammed.

Grace squealed. "Oh my God, Kat. He kissed me!" She bounced on the balls of her feet, her updo loosening with every bound, more tendrils falling to her cheeks.

"Really? Ah!" Kathryn sprung up and grabbed her friend's hands, joining in with her giddy, gleeful celebration.

"He was so sweet. He walked me to the front doors, and a few girls passed us, so we just talked for a few minutes. Then when there was no one around, he asked if he could kiss me."

"Wow. What a gentleman."

"Right? I am so falling for him." She floated over to her bed and collapsed, the back of her hand draped across her forehead.

Kathryn sat next to her. "Was that your first kiss?"

"Yeah. I'm so glad it was with him."

"What was it like?"

Grace pulled herself up. "You've never kissed a boy either?"

Kathryn shook her head.

"It was short and sweet. He didn't like ram his tongue down my throat or anything, thank God. He just leaned in slowly and kissed me."

"That sounds really sweet. I'm so happy for you."

"I'm happy for me too!"

The two friends laughed in unison, and Kathryn listened intently as Grace gave her a detailed description of her wonderful night.

Between

After a long night of girl talk, Kathryn's alarm clock buzzed in her ear way too early. She flung her arm over and pressed the snooze button before rolling back on her side. She was drifting off again when the door closed, and she sat up, startled, and saw Grace wearing her black concert dress and a towel wrapped around her head.

"You're up already?" Kathryn asked with a yawn.

"Oh, I've been up since, like, five thirty. I woke up and couldn't fall back asleep, so I thought I'd jump in the shower before it got crazy. There aren't any lines yet if you want to hop in."

"Yeah, I probably should."

She hoisted herself up and put on her glasses. After grabbing her shower basket and concert dress, she rushed to the showers, hoping a line hadn't formed out the door yet. Luckily, she was able to get right into a shower stall. Forcing herself to stay awake as the hot water poured down on her, she completed her routine, dressed, and exited the shower to see the typical long line wrapping around the bathroom. A girl quickly slipped into the shower stall as soon as Kathryn stepped out, and she headed back to her dorm room.

With her hair held out of her face by the towel spun around her head, Kathryn stood beside Grace at the mirror and began her makeup.

"Why do you do your eyeliner first?" Grace asked as Kathryn drew the black line along her eyelid.

"Oh, um…"

109

"I've just never seen someone do their eyes first. I noticed you do every time, so I was just wondering if there's some tip I don't know about."

Kathryn hesitated. "We have similar eyes, Brandon and I. Similar color, similar shape. When I'm not wearing eye makeup, I see the resemblance. I can't stand to even look at myself without it, so I always put eyeliner on first."

"Geez. It's like you can't get away from him."

"Sure feels like that sometimes."

"Another reason to be thankful for makeup." She held up her eyeshadow brush and clinked it to Kathryn's eyeliner pen.

With her eyes lined, Kathryn moved on to her next step. "Can I borrow that lip gloss you used on me last night?" she asked as she smoothed her foundation along her jawline.

"Of course. You know what? You can have it. It's totally your color."

"Really? Aw. Thanks."

"I'm sure Liam will like it too," Grace said, winking dramatically.

After Kathryn finished drying her hair, she looked over at Grace studying herself in the mirror and stepped up to her side. "You look beautiful. Don't be nervous to see him again. He spent the whole evening with you. He clearly really likes you." She spun her friend to face her. "We're going to rock this piece today and get into Honors. We don't need your nerves on hyperdrive any more than they already are."

Grace laughed. "True. We've got this."

"Okay, ladies and gent, this is it." Mr. Corrigan paced offstage as the string quartet gathered, waiting for their turn coming up next. "Kathryn, make sure you're digging in and making the best of that tone of yours. Draw it out and create that stable foundation for everyone. Sarah, you've really strengthened your part the past few days. It's solid. Well done. Craig, follow Grace. Watch her closely."

"Oh, I will."

Kathryn nearly choked on a laugh.

"And, Grace"—he stopped pacing in front of her—"well, you know exactly what to do and do it so darn well." He scanned his students. "You're a talented group of young musicians. I believe you have a real chance. If you don't screw it up, that is."

The quartet chuckled, and Mr. Corrigan began pacing once more.

"Wait. Was that sarcasm or a warning?" Craig whispered to the girls, his hand cupped around his mouth.

It was too late to ponder the question because the quartet on stage had completed their piece and was filing off, offering polite smiles as they passed. Grace led the group onto the stage, and they turned in unison toward the judges and the small gathering scattered among the maroon seats of King Concert Hall. With a short bow, they took their respective seats. As Grace brought her violin to her chin and suspended her bow above the strings, a sharp intake of breath signaled their down-bows.

Kathryn dove in with all she had in her, refusing to let her quartet down. Any thoughts of Brandon, her mom, or Liam vanished as her body took over. Digging deep into the strings, her left hand danced along the neck of the cello as her strong vibrato rang throughout the hall.

With a firmly drawn down-bow, the four instrumentalists held their arms in the air, allowing their strings to resonate for a few seconds before standing to make their final bow for the judges. The spectators applauded the group, but the judges' faces stayed flat as they nodded and began scribbling on their pads of paper.

Kathryn led them off to the right of the stage where Mr. Corrigan was waiting for them.

"Guys…" he said, pausing as tension held in the air, "that was perfect!"

The girls beamed.

"Thanks, Mr. C. Having a great coach certainly helped."

Mr. Corrigan waved off Craig's comment. "Oh, please. All I did was listen and nag you to do what you already knew how to do. Now let's just hope the judges agree. Results will be posted around two. It usually doesn't take them long to decide after all quartets have played. I'll meet you all back here then."

The group retreated farther behind the stage to pack up their instruments.

"So, now what do we do?" Sarah asked. "We don't have orchestra rehearsal until three, and lunch isn't for another two hours."

"Just drive ourselves crazy waiting, I guess," Grace responded.

"I have a better idea of how we can spend our time," Craig said, taking Grace's hand.

Grace giggled and looked over to Kathryn.

"Go have fun, you guys. I'll head back to the dorm and start packing. I'll see you later, Grace." Kathryn nodded to Craig and waved to Sarah before starting back to the dorms.

Pack… It was time to start packing already. The thought of tomorrow being her last day there stabbed at Kathryn's chest. Tomorrow, she'd have to go home. Home… What did that even mean? What home? Back to her aunt and uncle's? Back to her real house? She couldn't, could she? After the first night when she melted down, she had been able to push reality to the back of

111

her mind and keep it there with endless hours of playing and having fun with her friends. Now, with the end of camp looming, the reality started to sink in and pull her back to the real world where she feared her brother and lacked a real home.

The tears that usually accompanied the sadness were absent as anger started to build within. Her pace quickened along the sidewalks of the campus, her shoes scraping along the concrete.

Kathryn's mind elsewhere, her shoulder slammed into someone on the sidewalk. "Sorry," she said without looking up.

"Where's the fire?" a familiar voice asked with a chuckle.

She turned to see Zac, his hand rubbing his shoulder. "Oh, hey. Sorry. I was…" She blinked hard and shook her head. "I'm sorry."

"No biggie. I think I'll make it." Zac tilted his head and leaned down, trying to catch Kathryn's eyes as they stared at the pavement. "You okay?"

"No. Not really. But I'm sure you don't want to hear about my problems."

"Try me."

"Wouldn't you rather be with your drinking buddies?"

"Nope. I left that to them last night, and I'll let them waste what time they have left here. I'd rather talk to you."

"You didn't drink with them?"

"Nah," he said, shaking his head. "It was stupid. I just wanted to hang out with friends. I didn't care about the drinking. They were already drunk when I got there. Looked like they snuck a lot more than just a flask. They were being idiots. I stayed for a few minutes and just went back to the dorms."

"Oh…"

"So, really. What's wrong?" He gently took her by the arm and led her to the courtyard and a nearby bench sitting among a small garden of daffodils so golden yellow the sun would be jealous of their brilliance.

"I don't even know where to begin." She inhaled deeply. "My brother is an abusive ass, and I had to move out of my house."

Zac's eyes widened.

"Told ya."

"Geez. Go on."

"I had to move in with my aunt and uncle because I couldn't live at home anymore. That's the short version. Now I have to leave here, a place that I love, and go back to a mess. I don't know if I want to stay with my aunt and uncle or try to go home. I love my aunt and uncle, and they've done so much for me, but it's not my home. But how can I go home when I never know what my brother is going to do next? And it's not even just him. His friends come in and out of the house at all hours. They're drunks and druggies, and I hate every single one of them."

"Your reaction to drinking last night is making more sense right now."

"I can't be around it. And I can't be friends with someone who will bring it into my life in any way. I just can't."

"Lucky for me, I honestly have no interest in it either." He swayed into her playfully.

A faint smile broke through her taut face, and her shoulders relaxed slightly at his kind grin.

"What do you want?" Zac asked, any hint of joking gone.

"It's not that easy."

"What do you want?" he repeated with a slight stress on each syllable.

"I want my brother to not be such a jackass."

"That's fair," he said, nodding his head on a tilt. "But if you can't get that, what do you want to happen when you go back?"

Kathryn turned from him and surveyed the campus, the miniature city of red brick buildings laid out before her. She exhaled and slumped down at the thought of not seeing this view for a whole year. Leaning against the back of the bench, she rolled her head to the side to face him again, a lone tear escaping down her cheek. "I want to go home. I want to get back to my normal life, minus the violence, preferably."

"But how can you be sure you'll be safe?"

"I don't know. But how can I keep letting him upend my life? He has too much control over me. I don't want him to have control over me anymore."

Where the single tear had once been, a steady flow now followed along the same track. Zac slid closer to her and lifted his arm, placing it around her shoulders. Silent tears fell as they sat there on the bench in the middle of the other string players bustling around them. But they simply sat—Kathryn's head sinking into Zac's shoulder, her eyes closed as he stroked her arm with his fingertips.

As she calmed her crying, Kathryn could hear footsteps shuffling along concrete as groups passed by them, talking and laughing, and the slap of leather hitting outstretched palms struck behind them as a small group of boys tossed a football around in the courtyard.

"Kat? What's wrong?"

She opened her eyes to see Grace, concern etched in the lines of her face.

"Zac, dude, what's going on?" Craig said with a smirk.

Kathryn sat up, and Zac withdrew his arm.

"I rammed into him on accident and then burdened him with all my crap." She turned to him. "You're welcome."

Zac laughed. "Oh, stop. You did not. She was having a tough time. I was just being a sounding board."

"Looks like more than that to me," Grace said, her eyebrows raised. "Come on, Kat. Let's go back to the dorms and talk."

"I don't want to take you away from your time with Craig."

"Stop. I'll see him later. Come on."

Kathryn and Zac stood and faced each other.

"Thanks, Zac. I appreciate you listening. Truly. Sorry I unloaded all that on you."

"I'm glad I could be here for you. Good thing you ran into me...literally." He breathed a laugh, his sweet smile wide. "See you at lunch?"

"Sure. Save us a seat."

Zac gave a half-smile and nodded, and she turned to walk back to the dorms with Grace.

"I thought he was a total jerk and that you didn't want anything to do with him. Then I find you snuggling with him?"

"We weren't snuggling."

"Does he know that? 'Cause he likes you and you know that. You might be giving him...mixed signals."

"He caught me at a rough moment and asked me what was wrong. I told him he didn't want to hear it, but he pushed a bit more, and it all just came out. He was comforting me. That's it. Zac's not so bad after all. He said he didn't even drink last night with those guys. Said they were just idiots and he ended up going back to the dorms early."

"Oh, really? Hmm..."

"So, yeah, he's not so bad."

"Does this mean you like him back?"

Kathryn shook her head. "He's really sweet, but I only see him as a friend."

"Okay, but just...be careful with him. You two looked really close."

"Just friends. He does smell really good though."

Grace shrieked with laughter. "So does Craig. Maybe they share the same cologne."

The girls giggled as they approached the doors to the dorm building.

"So back on topic, what's going on? Why were you so upset that cutie Zac had to swoop in and comfort you?"

"It just hit me that we have to go home tomorrow, and I don't have a home to go to."

"You don't want to go back to your aunt and uncle's?"

Kathryn reached for the stair railing as she took the first step upward. "I love them both so much for what they've done for me, and I'll never be able to repay them for it. But it's not my home. Zac asked me what I want, and I want to go home. I just don't know how to feel safe there. But I'm so sick and tired of letting Brandon control my life! So damn sick and tired of it."

"It makes me nervous to think of you back there, but I completely understand. Maybe talk to your mom about it?"

Kathryn pushed their dorm door open. "I don't even know how to talk about it with her. There's still so much hurt and anger there. I feel so stuck. How is this even my life?" She plopped herself on her bed.

Grace sat beside her and put her arm around her. "It's not fair. Plain and simple. It's not. And I so hate that you're going through this. I want you to be happy, but I also want you to be safe. I'm not even sure what to advise you to do."

"It's a decision I have to make on my own, but I appreciate you listening and being here for me."

"No thanks necessary. Of course I'm here."

"My mom's going to drive me home, and I can't imagine she won't bring it up, so I guess I'll just see what happens. I don't know what else to do. I'm too torn."

"That sounds good." Grace gave her a quick squeeze and brought her arm back to her side. "I guess we should pack up a bit. Not leave all of it to tomorrow. I'm going to miss the hell out of you, girl."

"Me too."

"Ugh... No more tears today! We still have the rest of today and tomorrow together. And we'll find out Honors in a couple hours. Let's blast some music and dance our troubles away before lunch."

Kathryn smiled. "Let's do it."

"I can't look. I can't look. Nope. You do it," Grace said with her hands over her eyes.

Kathryn laughed. "What makes you think I can?"

They turned to Sarah.

"Don't look at me!"

"Oh, for goodness' sake, girls," Craig said with an eye roll and a chuckle. "I'll do it."

Grace peeked through her fingers, and Kathryn rocked on the balls of her feet as Craig casually strolled over to the paper taped to the front hallway of King Concert Hall. As if forcing his way through water, he took dramatically sluggish steps up to the wall, skirting around the small group that had gathered.

"Oh, come on!" Grace yelled, stifling a giggle.

Craig let out a roaring laugh and turned to face the girls. "We're in!"

"What? Really! Ah!"

Craig mimicked Grace's screeching and goofily bounced toward the girls, pulling them into a group hug.

"You're acting surprised?" a voice sang from behind them.

Craig looked up from the bouncing huddle. "We did it, Mr. C!"

"Just like I knew you would. Congratulations, guys. I want to run through it one more time tomorrow before the recital. Make sure you tell your parents to come an hour early so they can see you perform before the big finale concert. Well done, my fabulous students."

Grace pulled apart from the group and motioned with her hand over her shoulder, still bouncing away. "Come on! Let's go call our parents!"

"You made it? Oh, Kathryn, how exciting! I'm so proud of you, sweetie."

"Thanks, Mom. I can't wait for you to see the performance. It's such a beautiful piece. So make sure you come an hour early. We perform before the first orchestra does."

"I'll be there. And I'll let Alex and Hannah know as well. I'm sure they'll want to be there too. Are you going to call your dad?"

"Yeah, I'll call Dad. But Sarah still has to call her parents, so I need to let her use the phone. I'll see you tomorrow, Mom."

"I can't wait. I love you."

"Love you too. Bye."

"Bye."

Kathryn hung up the phone and turned to Sarah. "All yours."

"Thanks, Kat. You're not going to call your dad?"

"Nah. He won't drive all this way, and I talked to him the other day. I'll tell him all about it after I get home."

Kathryn spotted Grace and Craig on the couch in the common room off the lobby and started toward them when she caught sight of Zac leaning against the air hockey table, strikers in hand. "Care for a quick game before orchestra rehearsal?"

She smiled. "Sure."

That night, Kathryn lay awake staring at the ceiling, the uncertainty of what tomorrow would bring lying heavily on her chest. She tossed and turned for what felt like hours before she resigned herself to what would be a late night. Reaching over, she grabbed her diary and pen off the side table. She propped up her pillows and pulled her knees to her chest, resting the open diary on her legs and tapping the pen against the blank page. She retraced the thick heart around Liam's initials a few times before her breath washed out through her full lips, and she capped the pen.

Flipping through the pages that spanned almost five years of her life was anything but comforting. She flicked to the first page.

Dear Diary, August 3, 1993

You're a present from my mom. She thought it would be good for me to have a place to write down my feelings. I guess it could be fun. So hi there. My name is Kathryn Lorraine Lucas. I'm 10 years old. I like kitties, pink, and playing my cello. I just started last year and I love it so much. I have a brother named Brandon. He's mean so I try to stay away from him. I live with my mom. My dad doesn't live with us. They got divorsed when I was 3. So I live with my mom, stupid brother and my cat Mittens. She's my best friend in the whole world.

My mom thinks I need to write down my feelings because she's really sick. She has brest cancer. She said she's going to be ok though. I hope so. I really love her. I'm scared and sad about it. Those are my feelings about it. I'll write back soon. Bye!

From,

Kathryn Lucas

She grabbed a handful of pages and flipped through them, catching only glances of her sloppy handwriting scratched on the flowered pages with a shiny pink pen. The sparkly ink made each page of sadness, fear, and juvenescence appear pretty and sweet at first glance. But confessions of violence laced too many pages, and too many words were smeared with young tears.

She snapped the book shut and tossed it on the floor, watching as it slid across the tile and bumped into the closet doors. Bunching her pillow beneath her head, she forced her eyes shut and waited desperately for sleep to take her.

Kathryn folded the last shirt that had been hanging in the closet and placed it in her suitcase, smoothing the pink fabric under her fingertips.

"How's this look?" Grace asked as she spun in her knee-length black dress.

"Perfect. You're so lucky you can wear something that short. Mine always go to the floor," Kathryn said, ruffling her flowing, black skirt.

"Curse of the cellist," she said, giggling.

"At least I don't have a permanent hickey from the violin digging into my neck," Kathryn said, stifling a laugh.

"All the better to hide real ones, my dear."

Kathryn gasped before roaring with laughter. After a few moments, their hysterics gave way to their somber expressions.

"It can't be another year before we see each other, Kat. Not again."

"Not again. I promise. I'm not sure where you'll be coming if you visit me, but we'll get together soon. You have to meet my friend Lexie. She's so awesome and has really been there for me through all this. You two will get along really well."

"The violinist, right?"

"Yup. She's no Grace Crawford, though, of course."

"Well, no one is," she responded with a flip of her hair. Glancing at her watch, she sighed. "It's about that time. We better head over to Ka-Cha. If we forgot to pack anything, we can grab it when we come back with our parents."

Grace started toward the door, but Kathryn didn't move.

"I don't want to be sad today. I want to be excited about our performance. But what comes after…"

"I know. Just try to focus on playing for now."

Kathryn nodded. Brandon had taken enough from her. He would not taint the honor of being chosen to perform in this recital with her friends.

Grace linked her arm with Kathryn's, and the girls set off for the recital.

With the bow on the C string and her left hand upon the neck of her cello, Kathryn watched Grace as she quickly scanned the eyes of her fellow quartet members for the final time. A short inhale and a barely perceivable lift of her violin signaled the upbeat, and the string players began. The music flowed effortlessly from their instruments as their bows skated along the strings, their fingers moving rapidly and trembling with vibrato. The tones bounded and ricocheted around them as spectators sat silently, taking in the splendor of classical music.

As always when Kathryn played, it was over all too quickly, and her bow slashed across the string, rising into the air as the final notes vibrated through the great hall. Before the resonating instruments could still, the hall filled with applause and cheers for the young man and women, the final quartet to perform. In unison, they stood, turned, bowed, and exited the stage.

After a short intermission and the Brahms Orchestra's performance, the Beethoven Orchestra filed out. Kathryn took her place in fifth chair on the rim of the stage. The students tuned their instruments ceremoniously, the hall bursting with dissonance—one of Kathryn's favorite sounds.

Ms. Gail walked onto the stage to applause and bowed deeply before stepping onto the podium. Her baton danced to the rhythm and tempo of the first piece for just a moment before signaling the string players to bring their instruments into starting position. After one measure of counting, Ms. Gail beckoned them to draw sixty bows across their strings, the room erupting with rare beauty.

As the concert came to a close, one of the guest percussionists crashed his symbols together as the finale of the William Tell Overture raged on, building, crescendoing. The music rose to the high-reaching ceiling, spreading up the ascending seats and flowing back over the string players to the two-story pipe organ towering at the rear of the stage. Ms. Gail's conducting hands held strong in the air as bows whipped off their strings for the final time, and the crowd of proud families rose to their feet in admiration.

A wide smile spread across the conductor's face, and her hands scooped up, signaling the young musicians to rise before their adoring audience. Kathryn stood, pride swelling up from within as she looked out over the hall, scanning the room, but her mom was lost within the masses. She knew she was there though. She was always there. Now, Kathryn just had to face her and confront what lay ahead.

The high of the performance fell away, absconding with every shred of happiness she had felt prior to this moment, uncertainty overwhelming her senses. In front of the entire hall packed with people, she felt herself breathing heavily, gaining speed as the seconds ticked on and the clapping started to wane, her chest constricting as though the concert hall were caving in on her. As the other students started exiting to the sides, she gripped her cello with shaking hands and forced her weak legs to carry her offstage and into the unknown.

Kathryn walked out into the July heat, the double doors of King Concert Hall banging closed behind her. A gentle wind ruffled the lush landscape of the campus and carried the buzz of chatter, laughter, I missed yous, and I'm so happy to see yous while wafting the faint scent of colorful bouquets held excitedly in string players' callused hands. She blinked hard against the smiles, cheek kisses, and hugs all laced with a slight air of sorrow yet acceptance of the end of another year at orchestra camp—acceptance that they all must leave their friends and go home once more.

Kathryn spun on her toes, her black flats slipping off her heels as she scanned the gathering of happiness that ensnared her. Each face she spotted lit with joy and toothy smiles, arms wrapping one another in warming comfort, and each moment, each speck of glee felt like needles piercing her chest. Each ring of laughter brought weight down upon her shoulders, threatening to crush her. She gasped for air, and while she was no longer spinning, the world continued to swirl as she stumbled over to a tree and grasped at the trunk for stability. The deafening commotion began to close in on her, suffocating her as she continued to struggle for breath.

As she risked a glance up, she spotted her mom within the clustering of people. Kathryn turned from her, blinking away tears and forcing herself to inhale and exhale deeply, steadying her ragged breathing and drying her face with her palms.

"Kathryn!"

With every ounce of composure she could possibly gather in that moment, Kathryn turned toward her family as they wove through the crowd. She inhaled and forced a smile, belying the anguish beneath. "Hey, you guys."

"Oh, Kathryn, that was wonderful!" Jane pulled her daughter into an embrace. "Your quartet, the orchestra, all of it was just wonderful. You were amazing." She pulled back and took Kathryn's face in her hands. "I'm so proud of you."

Kathryn's false smile slowly morphed into one that resembled sincerity as she took in her mom's prideful expression. "Thanks, Mom."

"Hey, there she is!" Uncle Alex said with that chuckle. "Kathryn, what an amazing concert! The Haydn and Rossini were killer. What an impressive program they have here. Quite an experience."

"The percussion was awesome!" Jake shouted a little too loudly before giving Kathryn a quick hug. "I mean, the strings too, but the percussion was on point. I wish I could have been back there with them."

"I didn't realize what a production this would be," Sam said, his eyes bright. "I might look into coming here next year. They seem to have a good number of basses. I'm not used to seeing so many. And congrats on fifth chair."

"Thanks, Sam."

Aunt Hannah stepped around her boys and approached Kathryn, her face bright with joy and her hazel eyes graced with their usual kindness. "My dear, that was immaculate, exemplary, pure beauty from our beauty." She leaned in softly, placing her hand on the back of Kathryn's head. She held there a moment longer before releasing her niece.

"Thank you so much, everyone." She looked down at her ring, unsure of what to say. To reply she was happy to see everyone wasn't a lie, but the layers of multifaceted emotions she was feeling as she looked upon their delighted faces were too complicated to process.

A few moments of silence slipped by before Kathryn spoke again.

"I have to go back to my dorm and get the rest of my stuff."

"Can I come?" Jake asked.

"Um…okay. Sam, would you mind taking my cello so I don't have to lug it the whole way?"

Sam nodded. "Sure. I'll carry it to the car."

"I'll walk him over there and meet you at your room to help get it all to the car," Jane said, pulling her keys from her black leather purse.

Kathryn turned from her family and started back to the dorms, taking the cement pathways she came to know so well.

She heard Jake catching up to her, and he fell in step alongside her.

"You okay, Kathryn?"

"I'm fine."

"You look upset."

"I just…don't want to leave."

"Aw. I get it. I didn't want to leave my camp either."

"You don't get it," she said barely above a whisper, tears starting to gather in her eyes.

"Sure, I do. I had such a wonderful time at camp—the people, singing around the campfire, the prayer groups, kayaking, hiking, staying up late and talking with friends. It was hard for me to leave too. I like to think of it as great experiences I get to hold on to. I left feeling grateful for my time there and for happy memories that I'll always cherish."

Kathryn's fists clenched. "Well, I'm just feeling sad right now about having to leave, okay?" she said through gritted teeth.

"Okay. But try to think about all the good memories you made this week."

Heat was rising through her body, flowing through her veins, burning, painfully scorching every nerve.

"Focus on that and be grateful for your time here and that you had so much fun. That's how I like to think of it anyway. I was excited to share my experiences with everyone, so I was actually happy to go home."

Kathryn halted and snapped toward her cousin, unable to control the rage within. "Yeah, well, you had a home to go back to, didn't you!"

Jake's eyes widened while the outer corners simultaneously slouched, his brows dipping inward, sympathy pouring forth. He decreased his pace as Kathryn quickened hers, and the space between them expanded with every desperate step she took.

Hurrying past the courtyard, she weaved between families on the sidewalks.

"Kathryn!" a deep voice called from behind her.

She continued on.

"Kathryn!"

Continued still.

"Hey, Kathryn!"

She spun back. "Leave me alone!"

Zac stopped chasing her and stood silent.

"Zac…I didn't know it was you. Sorry."

"Nah. It's fine."

"No, really. I thought you were my cousin. I just snapped at him and took off."

"I know how he feels."

In spite of herself, she felt the corner of her lips twitch upward.

He started toward her. "I just wanted to say goodbye. I really enjoyed getting to know you this week."

Kathryn scoffed. "You enjoyed getting to know me? What's to enjoy? I'm a mess."

Zac shook his head. "You're just going through a tough time." He took a step forward.

She lowered her head, still eyeing him. "I'm a complete and utter mess."

"Mess or not, I still liked getting to know you." He took another step.

"I'm sorry. I'm being awful. I'm just not handling this well," Kathryn said, slumping her shoulders.

Another step. "That's one reason why I wanted to come find you. I wanted to check on you. I was worried about you."

A slight smile broke through her hardened expression. "Thanks, Zac. You're really sweet. I appreciate that."

"Of course. I'm so glad we met this year. Our dances"—he inched closer—"talking on the bench"—closer—"making you smile…" He closed the gap between them with one final step.

Kathryn looked up into his blue eyes as they slowly moved closer, heat radiating from his body held within his black suit. She took in the soft scent of his hair as he leaned in toward her, the spearmint on his breath touching her nose as he came within inches of her face. Her heart caught and instantly sped up uncomfortably as she attempted to process what was happening. Her lips parted.

"Zac..." She stepped back.

"I...I'm sorry. I..." He swung back, shaking his head, his hand finding the nape of his neck. "That was stupid of me."

"No, it's fine. I just—"

"You don't have to say anything. I shouldn't have done that."

"I'm really sorry."

"Don't be sorry. I...I really like you. But this wasn't the time." He looked down at the sidewalk.

She inched closer to him. "I'm just such a mess right now."

"Which is why I shouldn't have done that. I really am sorry."

She dipped her head, finding his eyes and pulling them away from the ground. "I appreciate you being such a good friend to me. I truly do. You really helped me the other night. You were there for me when I needed it."

"Then I had to go and be an ass."

"You weren't. Really."

The two teenagers stared silently at each other in the midst of the bustle of people dragging their instruments and suitcases to their cars.

"Can I maybe call you sometime?" Zac asked.

Kathryn smiled. "Sure. I'd like that. Actually, I'll call you. I'm not sure where I'll be, and if I am home, I don't like answering the phone."

Zac exhaled deeply and took a hesitant step forward. She met him, lifting up on her tiptoes to wrap her arms around his neck. He hugged her around the waist and pulled her in closer.

She stepped back as he released her, and her eyes drifted from his and spotted her family closing in. He followed her gaze behind him and turned back to her.

"I guess you have to get going."

"Yeah, guess so."

"Bye, Kat."

"Bye, Zac."

He slipped his hand into his dress pants pocket and walked past her, light-heartedly nudging her shoulder with his arm as he went by.

She wanted to run. She didn't want to face them. With every step they took, the needles piercing her chest pressed deeper and deeper. Jake broke away from the group, speeding ahead of them and getting to her first.

"Kathryn, I'm sorry. I was trying to make you feel better, but I guess I just made you feel worse. I wasn't thinking. I'm really sorry."

"It's okay," she said, lightly shaking her head. "I'm sorry I snapped. I'm not exactly holding myself together very well at the moment in case you couldn't tell."

He smirked. "I know my house isn't really your home, but we love having you there, and I know my parents will let you stay as long as you want to."

"I appreciate that more than I can say. I honestly don't know what I'm going to do."

"You mean…you might not come back to our house?"

"I don't know. I'm so all over the place right now."

As the group got closer, they turned and started toward her dorm.

"So," Jake said, quelling the conversation, "who was that guy you were talking to?"

"That was Zac, a new friend I made this year."

"Just a friend? Looked like more from where I was," he said with a chuckle.

She playfully elbowed him in the chest. "Just a friend."

Kathryn pushed her dorm room door open, her mother at her heels, and Grace swung around to face her, suitcase in hand.

"There you are. I was worried I wouldn't get to say goodbye."

Kathryn nodded her head toward the door, and Grace followed her out into the hall.

"What's going on?"

"Zac just tried to kiss me."

"What? Tried?"

"I didn't let him."

Grace frowned. "Why? It sure seemed like you liked him any time I saw you with him."

"I don't know."

"How can you not know? You do or you don't."

Kathryn's hands raised in the air and slapped down to her sides. "I'm not sure of anything right now. I can't even think straight." She turned and took a few steps before coming back. "And you only get one first kiss. To have it be now, tainted with everything going on… I don't want that."

Grace tilted her head. "You want it to be Liam."

124

"I don't even know if I'd say yes to Liam right now. This is all just too much. It's all too damn much."

Grace took her hand as Kathryn's eyes welled with tears, and she pulled her friend into a hug. "I just know you're going to figure this out, Kat. You have to believe it's all going to work out."

Kathryn pulled away. "I don't know if I can believe that," she said, smoothing the wetness across her cheek.

"I do," she said, offering a reassuring smile. "Call me soon, okay? I need to know you're all right and what you've decided to do. I'm nervous about you going back home, but if that's what you choose, I'll be behind you." She stepped forward and embraced her friend again.

"Thank you so much for everything, Grace. I don't know what I would have done without you this week."

The dorm room door opened, and the girls' parents emerged, struggling to hold all their things.

Kathryn reached for her pillow and one of her bags. "Sorry, Mom." She took one last look around the dorm room and shut the door.

Kathryn watched out the back window as the WNYU campus got smaller until her mom turned right, and the red brick buildings disappeared from view. She turned around and slumped in her seat, a heavy mix of seething anger and all-consuming despair pulsing through her and continuously escaping down her cheeks.

"Mom...if I were to come back...what would change?"

She observed her mom's eyes grow larger, and Jane began to stumble over her words before taking a breath and forming a coherent sentence.

"Tell me what you want to change, and I'll make it happen."

"I need to feel safe."

"Of course."

"I want a new lock on my door. One that he can't pick. Maybe a key lock for outside doors."

"Absolutely. I can pick one up right away and install it immediately." Jane gripped the wheel, wringing the black leather. "I was also thinking, when you're ready, whether that's now or not, maybe we could redo your room. You could pick out new carpet, a new paint color, maybe new bedding, whatever you'd like. But when you're ready."

"Really?"

"Of course. The offer doesn't expire though. Whenever you're ready, we can do it."

Kathryn nodded, far too many thoughts overwhelming her fatigued mind.

"I...I also wanted to tell you something earlier, but it never felt like the right time. Uncle Alex talked to a friend of his whose son is a police officer. He sent him over to the house to talk to Brandon. He didn't tell us he knew Alex at first, just that he was called to the house for...domestic...violence. He impressed upon him the seriousness of what he did to you and how much trouble he would get in if he were to do it again. He told him he's on their radar, and one call from you would lead to serious repercussions. You're a minor, and he's not. He knows he would be in huge trouble if he were to do anything to you again."

"Do anything? Punch me, kick me, stab me with a pen, beat me in the stomach with Otis's dog rope, throw me into a wall? Those kinds of things?" Kathryn asked, malice tinting her tone. She noticed a small shiver spread through her mom as she flinched at her words, but she had no regrets finally saying it out loud.

"Yes. Any of those things. One call to the police and he'll be in major trouble. Our house has been flagged with a previous call for domestic violence."

Kathryn sat in silence, taking in this new revelation. "When did this happen?"

"About a week after you first left."

Kathryn gasped. "A week? This happened almost a month ago? Why didn't anyone tell me?"

"You weren't ready yet, sweetie. It was all too fresh. You needed more time. Would you have actually come back home a week after you left, knowing this?"

Kathryn pondered the question. "No, I wouldn't have."

"Whether you see it or not, I've been trying to give you what you needed throughout all this."

"What I needed was to be protected. I needed my brother not to abuse me. I needed to feel safe in my house."

Jane pulled off the highway onto the shoulder and threw the car in park, turning to her daughter. "I can't go back, Kathryn. I can't undo what he did. I'm trying here. This has been hard on all of us."

"Oh, has it? I'm so sorry if this has been so tough," she snapped, her words dripping with sarcasm. "I'm the one who had to move out of my house! I'm the one who doesn't know if a single word or wrong look will end with me curled up on the floor crying!"

126

"That's not what I meant." She held her head in her hands, rubbing her temples with her palms. "This is coming out all wrong." Jane took a deep breath as she looked upon her daughter. "I know this has been incredibly difficult for you. Those words aren't even enough. I couldn't come up with adequate words if I tried. And I can't truly know what you've been feeling. If I could go back and stop this from happening, I would. But all I can do is move forward. That's all any of us can do. I want you to feel safe in our home. I want you to be comfortable and not live in fear. I will do anything to make that happen. I will get you a new lock for your door. I will make sure I'm home more often. I'll do anything." She started to choke on her words, and sobs spilled forth. "I'll do anything." She took her daughter's tearful face in her hands. "You're my baby, my sweet little girl. I'll do...*anything—anything* to have you back home with me."

She leaned her forehead against Kathryn's, and mother and daughter wept together.

Kathryn inhaled a ragged breath. "Mom...I want to come home."

Home Sweet

They pulled into the driveway of the long, blue ranch, and Kathryn noticed the drapes sway closed. The purple door opened moments later, and her aunt stood behind the glass.

Kathryn had been trying to think of something to say the whole way home, and nothing seemed adequate. Nothing felt anywhere near close enough to express the gratitude and adoration she felt for her family who took her in and gave her a loving, safe home when she had none.

"Mom, can you wait in the car? I want to say goodbye to everyone."

"Sure. Take your time."

As Kathryn entered the house, Aunt Hannah stepped aside, and she saw Jake, Sam, and Uncle Alex spread around the living room. Kathryn focused in on Jake, and his gaze fell to his twisting hands in his lap, breaking eye contact, and she knew he had told them what they had talked about. They knew she was leaving.

"Aunt Hannah—"

"You don't have to say anything, my dear. It's your home. We knew you'd go back when you were ready."

"I can't begin to thank all of you, to tell you what you all mean to me," she said, her voice breaking as she scanned the room.

Uncle Alex stood. "No need to thank us. We're family. It's what family does for each other." He took his niece's hands. "And we'll always be here, no matter what, for anything you may need."

Leaning in for a hug, she laid her head on his chest, closing her eyes. "Thank you."

She ambled over to Sam. "You get your room back," she said with a forced chuckle.

"I would have kept staying in Jake's room as long as you needed me to."

Kathryn paused, gathering her voice, looking into his hazel eyes that mirrored his mom's. "I know." She embraced him, slightly surprised by how far up she had to reach. "Thank you."

"You're welcome. I'm going to miss you."

"I'll miss you too. We'll take another walk down to the bridge before the summer's over, okay?"

He nodded. "Sounds good. And maybe a jam session?"

She released a light laugh through her tears. "Absolutely."

Turning, she met Jake's watery eyes and slowly approached him.

"It's not because of what I said earlier, is it?"

"No. No, I swear it's not. This was coming sooner or later. It's my home. I'm not leaving because of any of you. You all made me feel so welcome. I never..." Her voice broke, and she paused, hoping she could find enough strength. "I never felt like I didn't belong, like I wasn't an immediate part of this family."

"You *are* part of this family. I don't care what genetics say. You're my sister."

Kathryn held him, squeezing him tightly as her sobbing increased, wetting the shoulder of his shirt.

She spun around to her left to see Aunt Hannah, her hands folded in front of her, her face peaceful and tender. Kathryn walked up to her, tears still dripping off her chin. "I don't even know what to say."

"You don't have to say anything, my dear."

"But I do. When I came to you, you took me in without a moment's hesitation. You invited me into your home, and you made me feel safe...something I hadn't felt in a long time. I can't fully explain what that means to me. Thank you doesn't seem like enough."

"It is, Kathryn. You don't owe us anything. Like Uncle Alex said, we're family. We'll always be here for you. No questions asked. No matter what." She extended her arms and pulled Kathryn close.

Kathryn rested her cheek on her aunt's shoulder, closing her eyes, unable to hold in her devastation at the whole situation.

After a few moments, she broke away. "I'm going to go get my stuff."

Kathryn ambled back to the room she had stayed in for a month, closing the door behind her. "Mittens?" She heard her best friend meow and saw her crawl out from under the bed. Kathryn knelt down and scooped Mittens up in her arms as the cat pressed her nose into her forehead. "My sweet baby girl. I missed you so much. Do you want to go home?"

Mittens hopped out of her arms and went to the door and sat down expectantly.

"Oh, so now you're comfortable here?"

Mittens merely stared at her friend, her bright green eyes blinking sluggishly with weariness.

Kathryn gathered her few remaining belongings and stuffed them in a canvas bag. Before picking up Mittens, she surveyed the room one last time, tears once again filling her eyes. She thought about the first night she spent there—the night she escaped. Despite the circumstances, she slept soundly that night, unburdened of fear.

Her legs suddenly became weak as reality washed over her. Before she could catch herself, her knees hit the wooden floor, and she pitched forward under the agony ripping at her chest. Her forehead met the cool surface, and sadness released from her eyes as anger brought her fists down hard onto the floor over and over again.

The uncertainty of whether she was making the right decision overwhelmed her as the hope in her mom's eyes versus the sadness in her aunt's flashed through her mind. No matter what, she was hurting someone she loved dearly. There was no way to avoid it. And she was stuck in the middle between these two women she loved, forced to make decisions a fifteen-year-old girl should never have to make.

The most traumatic moment of her young life had thrown her into this family—a family she never knew she always wanted. These wonderful people, they were a true family. Family didn't abuse. Family didn't make one cower. But he wouldn't win. No more.

As though she had no tears left behind her exhausted eyes, she calmed her breathing and stood, lifting Mittens into her shaking arms. Beads of despair still clung to her eyelashes as she grabbed her bag and closed the door behind her.

Mittens started wiggling to get free as she walked out to the living room.

"It's okay, baby girl." Kathryn dropped her bag to keep a grip on the frightened cat. She looked up at the guys standing around the room. "I'll see you soon, okay? Just a few weeks until school starts, and then you'll be on my bus, Jake. And Sam, I'll call you, and we can take that walk."

They nodded and offered weak smiles.

Kathryn couldn't bear to drag this out any longer.

"I'll walk you out," Aunt Hannah said, picking up Kathryn's bag and motioning to the door with a sweep of her arm.

Jane got out of the car as they came outside and stepped toward Aunt Hannah. She took a deep breath as her hand found her hair, twirling it with her fingertips. "Hannah…thank you for all you've done for her. Through all this, I was grateful to know she was being well cared for."

"It was my pleasure."

Kathryn got in the car, still holding Mittens tightly so she wouldn't escape. As they pulled away, she risked releasing a hand to wave goodbye to her aunt. She noticed Aunt Hannah's hand flutter up to her cheek and brush away what she assumed to be a tear.

They pulled into the driveway only moments later, and Kathryn got out of the car, grimacing slightly at the sight of her house. "Did you paint the shutters? And the siding on the garage?"

"Yeah. I needed a little project for myself this past week. The blue on the shutters was a bit worn anyway, and the siding needed to be freshened up. What do you think?"

Kathryn cocked her head to the side. "The blue is okay, a little pastel-y. But the siding…it's kind of…pink."

"It's supposed to be peach."

"It's pink."

"I thought you like pink."

"Not on my house," Kathryn said, laughing.

"It's a bit brighter than I thought it would be. I think the dark wood on the face of the house tones it down a bit though."

"It…looks…like a dollhouse."

Her mom laughed. "You want to repaint it?"

Kathryn stifled a giggle. "Nope."

"Then I guess we live in a dollhouse."

Her mom threw her arm around her daughter and led her toward their pink dollhouse.

"I'm not ready to see him," Kathryn said, slowing her pace.

"I'll go in first and make sure he's in the basement."

Kathryn nodded.

After her mom gave the all clear, she walked through the front door for the first time since she fled out of it. "Hey, boy," she said as Otis trotted up to her. The black lab mix wagged his tail and sniffed her hand before it swept over his head and scratched behind his ear.

Mittens spasmed in Kathryn's arms as they went up the stairs off the front entryway. It was impossible not to think of the last time she was on these stairs, running away from him after he had attacked her. That step there, it occurred to her, was where she had fallen before tumbling into the front door.

She shook her head and turned left to go into her room. Mittens immediately fought to get down, and Kathryn released her. As if the past month hadn't even happened, Mittens dashed to her usual spot under the nightstand next to Kathryn's bed, hidden behind a flowing tablecloth. Kathryn peeked into her guinea pig's cage and wiggled her fingertip at the gray mop of hair. "Hi ya, Harry." The guinea pig looked up, his beady eyes barely visible through his long hair. He wiggled his nose and resumed nibbling on his alfalfa. "Good to see you again too, little guy."

Kathryn dropped her bag off her shoulder and sat on her made bed, smoothing her hands along the magenta-flowered quilt, her fingertips lingering on the threads. Once again, the memories flooded her mind of crashing back onto this bed after he punched her. There was no escaping it. He had come into her safe place this time, and it would be singed with that betrayal forever.

She skimmed her room; it looked different than she had left it—cleaner. The heap of worn clothes wasn't in the corner next to her newly organized desk. Vacuum tracks patterned the thick, brown piling of her carpeting. Her books were neatly arranged on her nightstand that was absent of her root beer cup and the popcorn she had been eating. She tilted her head at the tablecloth that looked unnaturally wrinkle-free. Kathryn's gaze continued to drift, and she eyed the dark wood shelves adorning the wall across from her dresser; nothing was exactly where she had left it. Her music boxes were shifted, the unicorn figurines her dad had bought for her faced the wrong way, and her encased baseball was on the lower shelf rather than the upper. Her trinkets and memories no longer sat among a thick coat of dust she didn't care enough about to clean.

Kathryn sighed and lay back on her pillow, the vision of her mom alone in her room in her absence bringing an ache to her chest. She stared up at the glow-in-the-dark stars stuck to her ceiling, following them with her eyes as they formed carefully designed music notes. Mittens jumped on her bed and curled up on Kathryn's stomach, her purrs vibrating along her skin. In complete silence, the two of them lay, Kathryn's mind on everything and somehow nothing at all.

A knock came to the door, and Kathryn gasped, sitting upright and sending Mittens flying under the table again. "Who...who is it?"

"It's Mom, honey."

Kathryn took a steadying breath and got up to open the door.

Her mom, seemingly completely unaware of Kathryn's reaction to a simple knock, beamed at her daughter once again on the other side of her door.

"If you'd like, I was thinking we could go pick up your new doorknob, whichever one you want. And we could look at some paint swatches too."

"Okay."

"Brandon is still in the basement. I already checked."

"Thanks."

They started down the stairs, and the flashes returned, prompting Kathryn to wonder how much longer these upsetting visions would haunt her.

Opening the front door, Jane turned to Kathryn. "So, what color are you thinking you'd like for your walls?"

"Pink, obviously."

Jane tightened the last screw. "Go in and lock the door. I'll test the key."

Kathryn went in her room and closed the door, the singers on the boy band poster tacked to the back now staring at her. On the other side, her mom jiggled the doorknob, and Kathryn flinched as her heart rate quickened.

"It's definitely locked," she called through the door. "I'll try the key now."

Within seconds, she pushed the door open. "There you go. No one can get in without the key." She held out the set and dropped it in her daughter's hand.

Kathryn clasped the keys in her palm and placed them in a small, heart-shaped box lying on her side table for the time being until she could decide on a more hidden spot.

"Look at those swatches in different lights, and you can decide on one after we pick out your carpet. Oh, and if you have some laundry, just make a pile outside your door." She started to leave and turned back, a soft smile painting her face. "I'm so happy you're here, sweetie."

She hoisted her suitcase onto her bed and began separating her dirty clothes from the few that could be hung back up. After forming the pile outside her door, she grabbed her pink dress and a few shirts and stepped into her walk-in closet. The usual pile of fallen clothes she was too lazy to pick up was gone, revealing the brown carpeting underneath. The shelving that held her jeans was reorganized, and a familiar smile met her from the corner. She reached for her baby doll, his sweet face resembling others in his patch.

"Hi, Benji," she said, looking into his blue, never-blinking eyes, her fingers trailing over his bald little head, down his overly loved face, and ending on his single tooth. "Were you lost among my mess? Sorry, buddy. I'm glad Mom found you." She gave his small, squishy body a hug.

"Why can't I have Benji back, Daddy?" the young voice asked over the phone.

"You can have him back the next time you come to see me, baby girl."

"But Mommy says she doesn't know when I can come over again, and I miss him."

"Then tell Mommy you need to come see me so you can have him back."

Kathryn took one hand off Benji and reached forward, brushing the frayed yarn hair off another doll's cotton shoulder from her spot on the shelf. She smiled.

"I don't want it, Mommy," she said, observing the doll behind the plastic box, her brown yarn hair covering her cabbage-shaped head.

"But, Kathryn, Mitch knows you miss Benji, so he thought maybe this doll could keep you company until you can have him back. Her name is Kimberly. Isn't that pretty?"

"I don't want it. I want Benji. I want to see Daddy, and I want Benji."

"I know, sweetie, but—"

"I said I don't want it!" She grabbed the box in her small hands and threw it on the ground, the plastic window cracking with the impact of her anger.

She scooped up the doll, holding both in her arms. "I see you've been keeping Benji company, Kimmy. I'm glad you have each other."

With every intention of spending the whole evening alone, aside from Mittens, Benji, and Kimmy, of course, she settled into her bed and flicked on the TV. Behind that lock was the only place she wanted to be this first night back, and it was where she would stay until she had to face him.

As night darkened the world outside her window, she tucked Benji under her arm and rolled over in her bed, careful not to disturb Mittens sleeping by her feet, and pulled the blankets up to her chin, comforted by the familiarity, the feeling of being back in the room that was all her own. She was home.

Splintered

Incessant barking roused her from a deep sleep, and Kathryn moaned, now preferring the blinding morning sunlight from Sam's window.

"Otis, come on! I want to sleep!" She rolled her face into her pillow.

"Otis! Quiet down!" he shouted.

Kathryn swiftly pushed herself up and spun to her back, pressing herself against the cool wall.

A knock came to the door.

"Kathryn?"

She sighed. "Yeah, Mom?"

"Can I come in?"

Kathryn flipped the blankets off her and opened the door.

"Good morning, sweetie. I was hoping I could make you breakfast. Your favorite eggs. How does that sound?"

"Okay."

"Kathryn, he's downstairs. I'll be with you the whole time. I promise everything will be okay."

She nodded slowly and followed her mom down the stairs, her heart pounding in her ears, staying close behind her. Upon entering the kitchen, she peeked around her mom's shoulder, spotting his slim, black-clad form leaning against the counter, chasing after the last drop of milk, the cup pressing into his wire-rimmed glasses. Her eyes shot to the floor as he brought the cup down.

"Hey," he said plainly.

She slid her foot a few inches to the right, their mom still in between them, and forced her eyes to meet his. "Hey."

"Kathryn, I'm not going to bother you, all right?"

"Um...okay."

Brandon stepped toward them, and Kathryn flinched, pressing up against her mom's back. He strolled past them and retreated to the basement.

Jane turned to face her daughter. "See. Not so bad, huh?"

Kathryn inhaled a shaky breath before sitting at the kitchen table, and Jane went to the refrigerator to grab the eggs.

"So," she said, cracking an egg and dropping it into the pan, "you didn't tell me too much about your week at camp. How about you start with that tall, cute boy I saw you hugging after the concert."

"That was Zac, and he's just a friend. Don't give me that look," she said, laughing. "I'm serious. He liked me, but I just didn't feel the same."

"That is sweet, but you're really too young to be dating anyway. Enjoy being a kid for as long as you can. There will be plenty of time for boys one day."

"When did you start dating?"

"Twenty-five."

Kathryn rolled her eyes and shot the same look back at her.

Jane grinned. "I was probably around seventeen, I think. Maybe sixteen. Let's not set anything in stone for you yet. We'll see how things go, okay?"

"I wasn't asking to date anyone."

"Yeah, but I could see the wheels turning in that pretty head of yours."

Kathryn laughed. "I missed this."

Her mom turned from the stove, a gentle smile gracing her lips. "Me too."

Jane set two plates on the table and sat next to her daughter. "Didn't break any this time."

"Looks great, Mom."

The recap of Grace's little love story was interrupted by the phone ringing.

"I'm not answering that. I don't want to talk to any of his stupid friends."

Her mom nodded and picked up the phone, answering it before handing it to her. "It's Aunt Hannah."

"Um...I think I'll take it in my room. Thanks for breakfast."

"Of course, honey."

Kathryn took off upstairs to pick up the phone in her room, kneeling on her bed.

"Hi, Aunt Hannah."

"Hello, Kathryn," sang her sweet voice. "I just wanted to see how everything is going over there."

"Everything is actually fine. Mom installed a better lock on my door that can only be opened with a key. I even saw Brandon this morning. Nothing happened. He told me that he'll leave me alone."

"Oh, good. It's a relief to hear you've seen him and it went okay. For you too, I'm sure. I've been worried about you."

"You have?"

"Of course I have. We all have. I'm so glad to hear you're doing well."

Kathryn paused for a moment. "I hope you're not mad at me."

"Oh, of course not, dear. You did what you thought was best for you. I would never be mad at you for that. I just want you to be safe and happy. That's all I ever wanted through all this."

"Thank you." Once again, the words felt grossly inadequate.

"Well, I won't keep you. Take care, and I'll see you soon. I love you, my dear."

"I love you too. Bye."

She placed the phone on the hook and leaned back on her bed, the encounter with Brandon and her conversation with her aunt replaying through her mind. She needed to escape.

She pulled the chair from her desk and set up her music stand as it creaked with weeks of disuse. With her cello in her hands once more, all else vanished from her mind. It was just she and her cello as they made beautiful music together.

As the summer break became shorter and shorter and the beginning of tenth grade loomed ever near, Kathryn settled back into life in her home in Edgebrook, New York. Her cello became her main focus, prompting her mom to suggest she stop practicing and get out of her room more often.

"Give Rachael a call," her mom said as they sat across from each other in the living room.

Kathryn rubbed her sore bowing arm and stretched her legs out on the loveseat. "I don't know. We kind of had a thing when I was at Aunt Hannah and Uncle Alex's."

"A thing?"

"She introduced me to some guys. They were jerks. I got mad about it."

"Hmm... Rachael's your oldest friend. I'd hate to see that end."

"We're still friends. It's just kind of weird right now. Plus, she's still close with Val."

"Still close? Are you not? Did something happen between you two?"

"Oh…we're not friends anymore."

"What? Really? When did that happen?"

"The last day of school. I got sick of the way she treated me. We kind of blew up at each other on the bus and haven't talked since."

Her mom stayed silent.

"What?" Kathryn asked, propping herself up on her elbows.

"I just…well, I didn't really care for Val." She shook her head lightly. "I should rephrase that. She was…a bit rough around the edges. I didn't care for the influence she had on you."

"You were right to be worried."

"Just try it. Come on. One's not going to hurt you." Val thrust the lit cigarette toward Kathryn.

She recoiled, almost falling off the curb of the newly paved cul-de-sac in the ritzy development across from Kathryn's house. "I'm not saying it's going to hurt me. I just don't want to. It's gross."

"It is not. You just have to get used to it. Just one drag. Come on. Don't be a loser."

Kathryn rolled her eyes. "If I try one, will you leave me alone?"

"Yup, I'll leave you alone."

"Fine then." She took the cigarette from her friend's hand, put it up to her mouth, and sucked in. Coughing exploded from her throat, and she pitched forward, gasping for breath. "That's disgusting!"

"That's because you didn't do it right!" Val said, gasping equally but in between hysterics. "You have to breathe it in slowly like this." She drew the cigarette to her lips, took a slow inhale, and let the smoke pour from her open mouth. "See? Now try it again."

Kathryn groaned. "I don't want to."

"Oh, come on! Everyone coming over to the party at my house this weekend is going to be smoking. They're going to think you're so lame if you don't."

"I don't care what they think."

Val scoffed. "Yes, you do. Don't pretend you don't. I know you care what they think of you. They're going to think you're a stupid little child."

"Val, we kind of are. We're fourteen."

"Oh, please. I've been smoking since I was twelve and got drunk on my thirteenth birthday."

"Seriously?"

"Stop being such a prissy little goody two-shoes. I don't even want you

coming if you're not going to fit in with everyone else, and they won't want you there either." She held out the cigarette again.

Kathryn sighed and took it.

"She was a terrible friend, Mom, and she did try to get me into things neither of us should have been into."

"I had a feeling. You should try to surround yourself with friends who are interested in the same things as you. Like Lexie. I've always liked Lexie. You're still friends with her, right?"

Kathryn breathed a light laugh. "Yes, of course. She's been an amazing friend to me through all of this. I've talked to her a lot since getting back, but it would be fun to get together with her."

"Yes! You really should. You've been shutting yourself away, sweetie."

Kathryn pondered that for a moment. "I guess I have."

"I know you love playing the cello, and I know you need your alone time, but I don't want you to completely close yourself off to everyone. Definitely give Lexie a call and try to set something up. Invite her over. I could even drive you to the mall if you'd like. Give you a little spending money. Oh! I could drop you off at a movie. Whatever you two decide."

"Whoa. Okay, Mom. Thanks. I'll go upstairs and give her a call." She headed for her room and stopped halfway up the stairs at her mom's voice.

"Wait, Kathryn. You should know I…I have my mammogram tomorrow."

"What? Why didn't you tell me sooner?"

"I didn't want to worry you, sweetie."

Kathryn returned to her mom's side. "You don't have to protect me from this. I want to know what's going on. Please don't hide anything from me."

Jane gazed upon her daughter, the young woman in her shining through more and more often. She reached up and tucked her daughter's hair behind her ear. "You're right. You're not a little girl anymore. I'll be upfront with you."

"Thank you. Okay, I'll go call Lexie. I'll let you know if we plan anything."

"Good. Or I could even take you girls out to eat at your favorite restaurant."

Kathryn laughed. "Got it, Mom."

When Lexie's dad's voice came over the line, instructing her to leave a message after the beep, she hung up the phone. Flopping back on her pillow, she reached to her nightstand for her book and flipped to her marked page. After reading the same paragraph multiple times, she closed it, resigned to the worrisome thoughts swirling in her mind at her mom's upcoming mammogram.

She tossed the book back on the nightstand and went straight to her cello, the need to escape pulling her hands into position on the neck and bow. Closing her eyes, she let her body take over, playing her favorite piece by memory. Just before the coda, a knock sounded on the door, and her bow slipped off the strings.

"Kathryn?"

"Yeah, Mom?"

"Can I come in?"

Kathryn leaned her cello against the chair and unlocked the door.

"Did you talk to Lexie?"

"She wasn't home."

"Oh, that's too bad. Well, if you'd like, we could watch a movie together tonight. Maybe one of our favorites."

Kathryn lifted to her tiptoes in innocent enthusiasm. "*Princess Bride*?"

"Perfect. I'll get it started."

"I'll go grab some snacks."

Mother and daughter laughed together at all the same places just as they always did no matter how many times they saw the hilarious, fantastical fairytale.

Kathryn turned to her mom as she popped a handful of chips in her mouth mid laugh. "Are you nervous about your mammogram?"

She swallowed and pointed the remote at the VCR, pausing the movie. "A little bit. I'm always a little nervous when I have to get a mammogram. After getting a positive result, I'm quite sure I always will be. But after all I went through, I know that if my cancer were to come back now or at some point in the future, I can fight it. I mean, it was the most difficult thing I've ever faced, and it was horrible and scary, especially considering how young you two were. But if I had to do it again, I just would. I'd do anything to be here with you and Brandon."

"I'm not sure I remember a lot of it. Just pieces."

"Well, like the divorce, as we've discussed before, you may not remember a lot of it, but that doesn't mean you weren't affected by it. I tried to shield you from what I could. You were so young. I didn't want to burden you with it. I didn't want it to define your childhood. But it's impossible to have your mom go through that and not feel the effects to some degree even if you weren't sure what was going on all the time."

"What if it shows something?"

"There's no reason to think it will, and there's no reason to worry about something that may not even happen. If it shows something, then we can worry. Until then, let's try to stay positive."

"Okay," she said, wrapping her arms around her mom.

"Let's finish up the movie. They're about to storm the castle."

Kathryn laughed and squeezed a little harder before releasing her and lying back on the pillow next to her, settling in for the rest of the movie.

Mittens mewed and emerged from under the nightstand, the pink tablecloth draping over her back as she crawled out to her best friend. Kathryn climbed into bed, and Mittens hopped up to be with her, turning in a circle before curling up and snuggling against her side. Kathryn's hand found Mittens' belly without looking, and the black cat laid its white chin on her arm.

"She can't go through that again, Mittens. I can't watch her go through it again."

Splintered memories of that time made an incomplete picture in her mind —mere pieces of a puzzle displaying an image of dread, sorrow, and uncertainty. All the pieces didn't need to be there, though; the fragments that her consciousness held on to all these years were enough.

Kathryn held her grandpa's hand as they walked toward the hospital. Long, menacing icicles lined the soaring roof concealing the winter sky from her view. Stepping through the automatic sliding front doors, her senses were hit with unfamiliar sights and sounds: large, bright, clean, foreboding. She tightened her grip on his heavily-veined hand as her young eyes scanned her surroundings, darting around to the overwhelming details assaulting her. Embellished fixtures cast warm light down upon them from high ceilings, gently reflecting off soft gray walls. Navy blue chairs stood clustered near a vending machine in the back corner. A dark couch accompanied a wooden coffee table and matching end tables upon which fresh, red flowers were presented in glass vases, their beauty doing little to calm the young girl's nerves.

"Hi there," he said to the receptionist, lightly drumming his fingers on the curved desk. "Bill Spahn and Kathryn Lucas to see Jane Spahn."

"Sure. Let's see... Room three forty-two."

Their shuffling footsteps scraped across the tiles as distant piano music floated overhead. Miscellaneous chatter surrounded them, and a woman's agony echoed from behind closed doors. He led her through a long hallway adorned with symmetrically hung paintings and photographs of white-coated doctors. Stopping in front of the elevator doors, he pushed the arrowed button.

When the doors parted, her grip tightened on her grandpa's hand as she scurried alongside him. Bill reached forward, pressed the button next to the number three, and looked down at her through blue, bespectacled eyes.

"Kathryn, remember what we talked about," he said with his usual soft calmness. "Your mom will be lying in a hospital bed. She's going to be hooked up to some machines. She might look tired, but that's because she just had surgery. She's okay though. You can give her a hug but be gentle."

"Okay, Grandpa," she answered, pulling his arm into her with her free hand.

"How about when we're done seeing Mom, we go back home and play Go Fish or War. I'm going to win one of these times," he said with a chuckle, squeezing her hand.

Her half-smile broke as her stomach dropped with the jerk of the elevator resting on the third floor. He guided her through an open hallway, past women dressed in blue, who smiled and tilted their heads at her as she hid behind his arm.

"Here we are," her grandpa said as they approached a wooden door. He held out a small, black box tied neatly with a gold bow. "Do you want to hold this? I know she's going to love it."

Kathryn took the box and forced a smile.

Bill pushed the door open, and she buried her face into his side.

Then, she saw her.

Her mom, lying in bed, turned to them, and a smile lit up her weary face.

"Kathryn!"

"Mommy!" She let go of her grandpa's hand and scurried over to her. Jane winced as she cautiously pulled herself up, and Kathryn came to a halt a few feet before the bed. She frowned, taken aback by her mom's appearance—her brown hair matted, her blue eyes tired and sunken, her face drained of color.

"Come here, honey. It's all right."

She slid closer to her, and she leaned forward, hesitantly placing her arms around her mom.

"I'm so happy to see you, sweetie. I've missed you so much."

"I've missed you too. Um...are you okay?"

144

"I'm tired, and the surgery is making me hurt a little bit, but I'm all right." She slowly shifted herself over and patted the space next to her. "Come on up. It's okay."

Kathryn carefully climbed up and sat on the bed, kneeling as she faced her mom, toes dangling off the edge.

"How's school going?"

"It's good," she said just above a whisper.

"That's it? Just good? That's not your normal rundown of all the day's events." She reached out and took her daughter's small hand.

"Well, I got a ninety-eight on my spelling test. And I spent the night at Alicia's house over the weekend. We had a lot of fun making up new dances."

"Oooh, new dances. How fun. I can't wait to see some. Maybe Alicia can sleep over some night after I get home."

She forced a slight grin. "What happened to your arm?" she asked, nodding to the large bandaging on her mom's left arm.

"They needed to take what are called lymph nodes from under my arm to check them for cancer. My arm is a bit sore from that, so they have it wrapped for me."

"Do you know when you get to come home?"

"Not for a few more days. They still need to take care of me a little longer."

Kathryn bit the inner corner of her lip and looked up, sweeping a few stray strands of hair off her face. "I can take care of you."

The little girl's serious expression melted away into one of confusion as her mom looked down in silence for a moment, brushing her cheek with her fingertips before gazing upon her daughter once more.

She reached out her hand, stretching the tubes connected to the IV, and slipped Kathryn's hair behind her ear. "I know you could, my sweet girl. But it's the doctor's job to take care of me. Your job is to be a little girl and have fun with your friends, make up dances, and play beautiful music on your cello."

Kathryn nodded with a weak smile and handed the small box to her mom. "This is for you."

"She picked it out herself," Bill said, rocking on his heels.

Jane untied the gold bow and opened the black box. She gasped. "Oh, Kathryn, I love it. It's just beautiful." She skimmed her finger over the teardrop-shaped, amber pendant nestled against the black velvet. "Thank you so much."

Jane opened her arms, inviting Kathryn to lean forward, but a spot of bright red spreading along her teal nightgown halted her advance. "Mom, what's that?" she asked, pointing to her chest.

Jane looked down. "Oh, goodness. I'm sorry, sweetie. I'm bleeding a bit. It's okay, really. I'll call the nurse."

Kathryn felt her grandpa's hands on her shoulders as he helped her down and led her to a chair, stationing himself at her side. Her eyes stung as he reached over and took her hand.

One of the blue-clad women from out in the hall swept into the room and quickly attended to her mom.

"Did this just start?" she asked.

"Yes. Well, we just noticed it. My daughter saw it first," she said, nodding toward Kathryn in the chair across from her.

"Oh, I didn't see you there."

Kathryn looked up, fear shining in her eyes.

"Aw. Don't you worry your pretty little head, sweetheart," she said with a wave of her hand. "It's just a little blood. Nothing to be concerned about."

Kathryn leaned her head to the side, laying her cheek upon her grandpa's hand resting on her shoulder, tears dripping onto his delicate skin.

The vision of her mom so weak, so frail, in so much pain...so defeated was the last thing she saw as she finally drifted off to sleep.

So Lucky

A faint knock and the sound of her mom's voice pulled Kathryn out of sleep the next morning. "Kathryn, I'm sorry to wake you. I just wanted you to know that I'm leaving."

"Oh, okay," she replied, rubbing the sleep from her eyes. She pushed her glasses on and stumbled over to the door to open it. "Do you want me to come with you? I can just throw some clothes on."

"Thank you, honey, but this isn't something you should have to deal with," she said, taking Kathryn's hands. "I was thinking we could pick out a carpet and make a final decision on your paint today. We could go out to lunch. Maybe even choose your bedding if you'd like."

Kathryn eyed her mom, unsure if she was living in her typical state of denial or just trying to stay positive. "Yeah, okay. I'll shower and get ready for when you get home."

"Perfect. See you in a bit." Jane gave her a firm rub on her back and headed down the stairs.

Kathryn placed her glasses on the bathroom sink before disrobing and turning on the shower. When it was almost too hot to stand, she sat on the bathtub floor and held her knees to her chest, letting the steaming hot water cascade down upon her. As she sat there, the water hammering against her head and back, her mind continued to drift, another branch of her life taking form in her mind.

147

"*Mom?*" *Kathryn gently pushed the door open, revealing Jane lying in bed, propped up against a ridiculous number of pillows, a worn book in her bruised hand.*

"*Is there anything I can get for you before I get on the bus?*"

"*No, thank you. I'm fine.*"

"*You sure? Some fresh water? More saltines? Nothing at all?*"

"*I have enough here. Grandpa said he'd come check on me around lunchtime. Don't you worry about me at all. I'm just going to catch up on soaps and grade some papers.*"

She stepped up to the bed, bumping into the recently cleaned wastebasket that stayed by her side while home these two weeks. "Grade papers? You should be resting."

"*I can't allow these two weeks on chemo to get me too far behind. It'll just make my two weeks back in class more stressful.*"

Kathryn observed her carefully, the exhaustion and illness clearly taking its toll on one who was usually so upbeat and vibrant. Every two weeks, back and forth. It had been months of this. She never truly had a chance to recuperate.

"*They're announcing the winners of the writing contest today, aren't they?*"

"*Yeah, in Morning Program.*"

"*Good luck, sweetie.*" *She held up her weak arms, inviting her daughter in for a hug. "I can't wait to hear all about it." As Kathryn pulled away, her mom quickly snatched up her glass of ice water and took a few gulps as extreme pallor assaulted her face. Jane closed her eyes, breathing in through her nose and out her mouth, and she forced a smile as her heavy lids slowly fluttered open. "Have a nice day and remember not to go to the after-school program today. Just take the bus home.*"

"*Right.*" *She walked to the door leading to the hallway and turned around. "I love you.*"

"*I love you too.*"

Kathryn sat cross-legged with her fifth-grade class in the midst of hundreds of other elementary school students gathered in the gym. As Mr. Stephens, the school principal, stood at the microphone in the center of the room, the roar of children's voices gradually tapered off.

"*Welcome, children. It's so wonderful to see your happy faces this morn-*

ing. Here's to a fabulous start to what I'm sure is going to be a great week. Now, as you all know and have been anxiously anticipating, we're going to announce the winners of the 'I'm in Trouble' writing contest." He broke off as the children clapped and cheered. Holding his hands out, they quieted down, and he continued. "When local author Joanne Kelly came to our school a few weeks ago, we all loved listening to her funny stories about being in trouble. But how exciting it was to be presented with an opportunity to explore your own imaginations and express yourself through writing your very own stories about being in trouble! The other teachers and I absolutely loved reading your creative stories. Oh, how they made us laugh! You all did a wonderful job, and it was extremely difficult to choose just two from each grade. But unfortunately, we had to narrow it down. So, without further ado, here are the selected winners. But remember, you're all winners in my book."

He pulled an envelope from his back pocket and began reading off the names of the winners. As he came to the fifth grade, Kathryn held her breath as he read one name and then another. She released the air and frowned as the two winners in her grade stood up and made their way to the empty circle at the center of the room to collect their certificates.

After the winners from the sixth grade were announced and everyone returned to their spots, Mr. Stephens continued.

"Congratulations to all our chosen winners. This contest was so much fun, wasn't it? Give yourselves a round of applause." He paused for young squeals and hollers. "I'd like to change gears and take a minute if I could to talk about one child's story that touched our hearts. A majority of the stories we read were about silly, funny times you were in trouble. One of you lost your cat but then found it hiding under your bed among all the toys you had previously shoved under there when your mom and dad told you to clean your room." He stopped to let the kids laugh, continuing to rotate in place to view all his students. "One of you kicked a ball in the house and broke your mom's favorite picture frame." He grimaced and pretended to bite his nails. "One of you even slipped on a banana and slid into the kitchen cabinet and ended up with a cake on your head! I mean, what are the chances?" he asked, chuckling. "However, sometimes, someone's problems aren't silly, and they aren't funny. Sometimes, people have problems that are scary. Sometimes, people know someone who is sick. That's a different kind of problem, isn't it? It's a different kind of trouble. There's one young lady here who wrote about that kind of problem. She wrote about how her mom is really sick and how much she loves her. This young lady very bravely wrote about her mom's journey fighting cancer. We are so proud of her strength and courage, and we would

like to give her a special award for her well-written, powerful story. So, Miss Kathryn Lucas, would you please come up here?"

Kathryn tried to close her opened jaw and bring her eyes back to their normal size to no avail. Everyone clapped for her as she stood up and walked to the middle of the gym, her mouth still agape in shock.

Mr. Stephens gazed down upon the newly eleven-year-old girl. "Kathryn, we all think you did such a great job writing your story, and we applaud you for sharing your trouble with us. You should be very proud of yourself. We certainly are. And I'm sure your mom is as well."

Kathryn could hardly form words as she scanned the room packed with kids all looking at her.

"If you don't mind," Mr. Stephens said, "I picked out some lines that sum up your story, and I would like to share them with everyone. Is that okay?"

"Yes. That's okay," she replied, a blinding smile on her face.

Mr. Stephens held a paper up in front of him and cleared his throat. "'I'm in trouble because my mom is sick. She has cancer. The doctors took all the cancer out of her body, but when I went to visit my mom in the hospital, she was bleeding, and it scared me. Now she gets medicine so the cancer doesn't come back and hurt her. The medicine makes her really sick, and that makes me very sad, but I know she needs it. She started it five months ago, and she only needs it for one more month. I'll be so happy when she's not sick anymore. I love my mom a lot, and I want her to be healthy again so she can be happy and play with me.'"

He brought the paper down and began clapping, soon followed by the rest of the students and teachers. "You are very brave to share this and write so openly about what your family is going through." He knelt down and gave her a hug and handed her a piece of paper. "This award is especially for you. Please tell your mom that we are all thinking about her."

"Thank you!" Kathryn said, admiring the bright gold sticker on her certificate.

Everyone applauded for her again as she walked back through the mass of kids to sit with her class.

"Wow!" said Alicia, her eyes bright as Kathryn sat back down. "That's really cool! You're so lucky!"

Kathryn took a seat at the back of the bus, wishing she could have stayed in the after-school program with Alicia. Her fingertips glided over the shiny, embossed seal on her certificate, and she smiled.

"You know, they only gave you that thing because they feel bad for you. You totally got it out of sympathy."

Kathryn turned around, coming face to face with a boy she hardly knew. "No, they didn't. They said I did a good job writing it."

"I know they said that, but they lied. It was just out of sympathy."

"It was not. Just leave me alone."

A girl from her class popped up from the seat next to him, twirling her short hair with her finger and smacking her gum. "Yeah, sympathy. Totally just because of sympathy," she said, dragging the last syllable.

"That's not true!"

They cackled as she whipped her head away from them, tears forming in her eyes. She grabbed her backpack and sped to the front of the bus, taking the empty seat behind the driver.

That boy's menacing face and that girl's annoying voice flashed in her mind during school the next day, and her stomach twisted at the thought of having to take the bus home again.

Half the day was over without incident, and no one had mentioned her story when she set off for lunch with Alicia.

"Maybe we can do a step-ball-change followed by a high kick next time. Right when the chorus starts," Alicia said, discussing changes they could make to their most recently made-up dance.

"I'm not sure what those are," Kathryn said, laughing.

Alicia's blond head fell forward as she giggled. "I'll show you. I'm sure you'll get it."

"I won't be in the after-school program until Mom goes back to work in two weeks, but we can do it then. Or maybe I can come over sometime and—"

"Hey, Cancer Girl."

Kathryn and Alicia looked toward the voice at the back of the line.

"Yeah, Cancer Girl, I'm talking to you!"

"What?" Kathryn asked, her brow furrowed. "Me?"

"Yeah, I'm talking to you, Cancer Girl."

Kathryn gasped.

"Who is that?" Alicia asked, her hands on her hips.

"He's a kid from my bus." She faced back to the boy. "Why are you calling me that?"

"Because that's your name, right? You're Cancer Girl. Hey, guys, don't go near her. She'll give you cancer!" He laughed, his hand slapping into his

midsection. The horde of boys surrounding him broke into fits of laughter along with him.

"My mom has cancer. I don't have it. You can't get it from her or from me anyway. Just leave me alone." She faced forward, tears once again threatening to break through.

"Oh, we would leave you alone, but everyone needs to know they should stay away from you or else you'll give them cancer. Don't go near her, everyone. She'll give you cancer!"

"Shut up!" shouted Alicia.

"Aw. What's the matter, Cancer Girl? Are you crying?"

Kathryn tore down the hall.

"Kathryn! Wait!" Alicia called after her.

She didn't stop to turn around. She simply ran. When she reached the girls' bathroom, she smashed into the door and stumbled on the tiled floor.

Kathryn placed her hands on the corners of the sink, leaning on it for stability through her cries. When she heard the door open, she ducked into the closest stall. She stayed there through lunch and only dared to leave when she heard a crowd of voices passing in the hallway. Slipping into the group of kids, she went back to her class for the remainder of the day, hungry and defeated.

Kathryn took a deep breath and stepped up into the bus, choosing a seat toward the front so as to try and avoid that jerk from the back. Her stomach sank when she saw him board, and he smirked at her as he passed by, sliding into the seat behind her.

"Pssst...Cancer Girl."

"Why won't you just leave me alone?"

"Aw. Are you sad again? Are you sad because your mom is going to die?"

Kathryn whipped her body around, her eyes narrow. "She's not going to die! The doctors are making her better!"

"No. No, I don't think so. She's going to die. At least I hope she does."

Kathryn gasped and merely stared at him, his face twisted with cruelty. She snatched her backpack and sat once again in the seat directly behind the bus driver, the boy's sadistic laughter floating through the air, sending chills down her spine.

The now lukewarm water brought her attention back to her shower, and she quickly washed her hair before the water turned too cold.

After doing her hair and makeup, she instinctively got out her cello. Running through all the pieces in her folder did little to calm her nerves, though, and she gave up and went in search of Mittens—the other cure to whatever ailed her.

Kathryn crawled on her bedroom floor, looking for her cat, but when she couldn't find her in the normal hiding places, she went into her mom's room to check there. By the dormer window, Mittens was curled up in a tight ball on the back of her mom's blue reclining chair, the warm August sun filtering onto her black fur as it absorbed the heat.

She knelt on the chair and leaned against the tall back, smushing her face into Mittens' belly. The cat released a soft moan as she stretched out her six-toed paws and laid them on Kathryn's head, kneading her hair.

The soft rumbling purr offered Kathryn a few calming moments before a car door slamming outside the window caused her to pop her head up, and she saw her mom heading for the house.

She bolted downstairs, meeting her mom at the front door.

"What did they say?"

"Why don't we go sit on the couch?"

Her heart began to race, her legs instantly feeling weak. "Mom, just tell me."

She placed her swollen hand on her daughter's arm and sighed. "They found some abnormalities on my mammogram."

"What does that mean?"

"It may mean nothing at all. I have to go back for another test early next week. They have to perform what's called a core biopsy. Then they'll be able to find out more information."

"But...I don't understand."

"Sometimes there is just abnormal tissue that shows up on the mammogram, and that's all it is. In that case, there's nothing to worry about."

"And if it's not just abnormal tissue?"

"Let's not get ahead of ourselves. Let's just wait and see what happens."

"But—"

"Sweetie," her mom said, holding her gaze, "it might be nothing at all. There's no point in worrying over something we can't control."

"So, now what?"

"Grandpa will take me to the biopsy and bring me home. It's not a difficult procedure. It's not surgery. There'll be minimal recovery. I may just be a little sore."

"Then?"

"We wait." She shrugged. "But let's keep ourselves busy and try not to think about it too much. For today, let's get out and do something. Let's go grab some lunch and pick out the last of what you want for your new room."

"I guess so. If you feel up to it."

"Good. Grab your purse."

Ties

Jane's biopsy went well, but waiting for the final results was torturous. Kathryn's dad's offer to take her clothes shopping was a welcome distraction, and she was finishing up getting ready when she heard the beep from outside.

"Mom, Dad's here. Do you need anything?"

"I really am fine, sweetie. Still a little sore but okay," Jane said, folding a shirt from the laundry piled on her bed. "I promise. Go have fun."

Kathryn nodded, embraced her mom gently, and walked into the hallway with one more glance back before descending the stairs and going outside.

"There's my baby girl," her dad said, his hazel eyes softening as she stepped out the front door into the hazy morning. He took one last inhale of his cigarette before flicking the lit ashes off with his forefinger and tossing it in the back of his blue pickup, his free hand raking through his dusky hair. Turning, he opened his arms to his daughter. "I haven't seen you all summer. I've missed you."

The strong stench of fresh and stale smoke scrunched her nose, but she hugged him back tightly, closing her eyes and resting her head lightly on his chest. "Definitely too long, Dad."

"So, you ready to spend my money?"

"Yup!"

He laughed, his bad habits reflected in the lines of his aging face. "Of course you are."

She climbed into his truck, and he turned down the oldies station on the radio.

155

"So, where to?" he asked, backing into the street.

"I was thinking maybe the mall? There's a cool store there that Mom takes me to sometimes."

"Then the mall it is. So how is everything? Seems like you've been really busy, huh? We haven't talked much since you got back from your camp," he said, tapping her knee. "I'd love to hear a bit more about it. I assumed you must have been having lots of fun since I barely heard from you."

"The line for the phone was always long. I called you twice. I only called Mom three times the whole week."

"I know how it is. It's okay. It's fine. I have my plants and my artificial knee to keep me company."

"Oh, stop," she said, rolling her eyes.

"I'm just messing with you." He reached over and grabbed her knee, squeezing it in the right spot, making her screech and jerk her leg away, laughing. "Seriously, though, how was camp?"

"It was a lot of fun. And it was amazing finally making it to the Honors Recital."

"Only one of five quartets chosen to perform before the final recital," he said with a chuckle in his voice. "My daughter, star cellist. Wait till the guys at the bar hear all about this."

"I'm sure they'll be terribly impressed."

"Well, some of them probably won't even know what a cello is, but I'll use small words. They're not exactly what I would consider cultured."

"You'll have to school them with your vast wealth of knowledge, Nurse Lucas."

"That's right. I'm not as dumb as I look," he said, tapping his head with his finger. "And that's a good thing, right?" He leaned over and elbowed Kathryn's arm.

"Yes. Absolutely."

"Oooh, ouch. Busted my knee on the job, nine knee surgeries, and barely took any of those garbage pain meds, but *that* really hurt." He brought his fist to his heart twice.

Kathryn threw her head back laughing. "You said it, not me."

"Fair enough." He joined in with her and gave her hand a quick squeeze. "I really am glad you had such a nice time, and I'm sorry I couldn't make it. It's just so far for me to drive, and you know I need to clean the bar in the mornings. Plus, Gary has me mowing lawns every weekend. It's crap money, but I take what I can get."

"I know, Dad. It's okay."

"Anything else exciting happen over summer?"

Kathryn shifted. "Um...no, not really."

"It seems like you've spent a lot of time at your aunt and uncle's."

"Uh...yeah. I guess. Well, Jake's one of my best friends, and Sam's really fun to hang out with too, so I've just been wanting to spend more time there to see them and hang out with them, and we also play our instruments together." She inhaled deeply and mentally rolled her eyes at her nervous rambling.

"Hey, I'm glad you have a good relationship with Hannah and Alex. They've always been nice to me. I'm sure they weren't happy with me when I was being such an ass when your mom and I were splitting up, but they were still good to me."

"Okay... Well, they're good people," she said, pushing through the awkward mention of his past indiscretions.

Kathryn sighed in relief when he turned into the mall. Lies and half-truths —the familiar discomfort burrowed into her stomach.

He pulled into the closest handicap parking spot, and Kathryn met him on the other side as he carefully got himself out of the truck, using his strong arms to support his left knee.

"Lead the way, baby girl."

Kathryn sifted through the racks of clothes on display at Expressions and began hanging her selections on her arm.

"Looks like that pile's getting a bit heavy," her dad called from where he was leaning against the wall.

"I'm just trying them on. Doesn't mean I have to get them."

He meandered over to his daughter standing along the wall of high shelving holding numerous jeans selections in different styles, colors, and cuts. He took a folded pair off one of the shelves, bringing the tag closer to his squinting eyes. "Fifty bucks? These jeans are fifty bucks?"

"Dad," she whispered loudly, her eyes wide.

He placed the pair back. "Oh, sure. That's fine. I don't need to eat this month."

Kathryn rolled her eyes. Hunting through the sizes, she found hers and draped it on her arm with the rest of the clothes. "I'm going to try these on."

He nodded. "Looks like this month's car payment."

"Clothes shopping was your idea, Dad," she said, closing the dressing room door.

"These kids think we're made of money," she heard him say, presumably to another parent there with their kid.

157

Kathryn slipped on the jeans and pulled on a lilac purple V-neck, smoothing it across her stomach. She turned to the side and smiled before taking a tan sweater coat off the hanger and putting it on, inspecting it.

"How's it going in there?"

"Good. I think I found a few things." Four more shirts she had brought in with her fit her nicely, but she chose her favorite two, a pair of jeans, and the sweater coat. She redressed and exited the dressing room, her favorites on her arm, leaving the remaining pieces on the rack near the dressing room door. "I'd like these if that's okay. If not, I can put a shirt back."

"No yellow? I love you in yellow."

"I didn't even see any yellow."

"All right. Well, as long as you like these."

"Thanks, Dad." She stepped forward and gave him a hug. "You're sure they're not too much?"

"It's fine, baby girl."

"Are you all set?" the cashier asked as they approached the counter.

"We are. I guess I don't need to pay my bills as long as this lovely lady here has nice clothes to wear to school."

Kathryn's cheeks stained pink, and the cashier let out a little giggle. Her dad reached over, pulling the embarrassed teenager to him with one arm and kissed her head. "But this one's worth it."

On the ride home, their conversation ranged from morons at the bar, to baseball statistics, to players, to when her dad played baseball, to how he taught her mom to play softball, to how when Kathryn played for the town league she was a good catcher with a good arm but needed to work on her swing, to cello, to Shakespeare, and somehow ended up on the Revolutionary War. Kathryn nodded most of the way as she tried to follow along, unsure of where they might end up.

"Kathryn?"

"What? Sorry."

"I said your mom had her five-year mammogram recently, didn't she? Or it has to be coming up at least."

"It's…uh…she has an appointment soon, I think."

"Yeah, I thought it was coming up. Can you let me know how it goes?"

"Sure."

"You know, just because your mom and I aren't together anymore doesn't

158

mean I stopped caring for her. She's the mother of my children, and I'll always love her."

She walked along the large wooden railroad ties bordering one of the many gardens spread over her dad's yard. With her small arms held out for balance, she concentrated hard, determined not to fall off again and to make it to the end this time. When she heard the crunching of the gravel in the driveway, she looked up, almost losing her footing. "Mommy!" she shouted at the red car as it pulled toward her.

Kathryn took another slow step and wobbled, throwing her arms around, trying to stay on. She could hear her mom coming her way, but perseverance held her focus on the beam as she neared the edge. "I just want to get to the end, Mommy. Mommy?" The little girl stopped and looked around, finding her parents talking near the car.

She continued on. Almost...almost... "Mommy! Daddy! Watch this!" Her toes slid up to the end of the plank, and she jumped into the air as high as she could. Kathryn's little feet hit the pebbles as she raised her hands above her head like a four-year-old gymnast sticking her landing off the balance beam. She swung around to see their excited expressions, but her smile faded when she saw neither of them was watching her triumphant feat.

Kathryn skipped toward them but halted at the tone in her dad's voice.

"One more chance, Janie. I can do better. I still love you."

"Daniel, Kathryn's right there," her mom whispered harshly.

Kathryn spun on her toes and leapt away as if part of her routine.

"I know you do, Dad. I'll let you know when we hear anything."

"Thanks, baby girl."

Kathryn stood on the front steps of her house and waved at her dad as he pulled away and out of sight. Her mom sat reclined on the couch in the living room, newspaper shielding her face from view as Kathryn entered, bags around her wrists.

Jane lowered the paper to her lap. "Hey, sweetie. Did you have a nice time with your dad?"

"Yeah. Look at everything I got." She pulled the jeans and purple top out of the bag and held them up to her.

"Very cute. Are you going to wear those the first day of school?"

"I was thinking I might."

A low growl brought her attention to the doorway between the living room and kitchen. "Those look like clothes every other girl wears. Where's your originality?"

"Brandon, don't start," their mom said.

"I'm just saying. Why do you want to be like every other girl?"

Kathryn took a breath, struggling to keep her expression and tone even. "I don't. I don't care what other girls are wearing. I like these clothes."

"Well, you look like a teenybopper copycat of every fifteen-year-old girl."

She shrugged, her palms flipping toward the ceiling. "Then so be it."

"Brandon, really, that's enough. She likes the clothes. Let it go."

He narrowed his eyes and shook his head. "Whatever."

"Where did Dad take you for these clothes?" her mom asked.

"He took me—"

"Wait. Dad took you shopping for these?" He threw his hands up and let them slap to his thighs. "Of course he did."

"What does that even mean?" Kathryn clenched her teeth, beginning to lose her composure.

"I'm just not surprised that Dad took his precious princess out for expensive clothes."

"Brandon, that's enough."

"So he took me shopping. So what? He'd probably take you somewhere if you bothered to ask."

He took a step forward, his eyes shining with a look of rage she knew all too well. "Why the hell would I want to go anywhere with that damn drunk?"

Kathryn recoiled, stepping back toward her mom.

Jane got to her feet and placed her arm around her daughter's shoulders, holding out a firm hand. "Brandon, stop!"

"Oh, give me a break! I'm not going to do anything. Like I'm going to risk going to jail. Lighten up." He feigned a quick step toward her and laughed before turning and retreating to the basement.

Kathryn drew a deep breath, her shoulders relaxing, and spun around to her mom. "What was that about?"

Jane shook her head. "He has a lot of anger where your dad is concerned. You know that. But that's not your problem or anything you should worry about."

Kathryn grabbed the bag of clothes and stomped up the stairs. "He ruins everything!"

"So, how's everything going? Still okay?" Lexie asked.

Kathryn switched the phone to her other ear. "Yeah, I guess. Brandon's still a jerk, but he's leaving me alone for the most part. Although, he did go off on me earlier today because he doesn't like the new clothes my dad bought for me."

"What does he care what clothes you wear?"

"He said they're not original and they're like everything all fifteen-year-olds wear."

"Um…okay. So…again, why does he care?"

Kathryn scoffed. "I have no idea."

"That's so weird. But he didn't do anything to you?"

"No. He just always seems to ruin everything. I had a nice time out with my dad, I come home to show my mom my new clothes, and he has to be all stupid and annoying and put me in a bad mood. And I'm already worried about my mom."

"When will she hear for sure?"

"Friday morning at nine. Mitch isn't here. He couldn't take time away and fly in, so I offered to go with her, but she said it wasn't something I should have to deal with. I wish she'd stop."

"Sounds like she's just trying to protect you."

"That's exactly what she's doing, but she doesn't have to, not when it comes to this." Kathryn groaned. "Let's talk about something else. Anything new with you? How's your sister doing?"

"Good days and not so good days. She actually has an evaluation soon. My parents are trying to get to the bottom of her issues. Mom said with all Anne's problems at school and social issues, her doctors think there's something more going on."

"Goodness. I hope they figure it out. She's such a sweet girl."

"She really is. Just…different." She exhaled deeply. "So, other than that, the summer's been pretty uneventful. It flew by way too fast. But I bet you're so excited to see Liam."

Kathryn smiled. "Just a bit."

"You have your outfit picked out?"

"Yup."

"You're getting up early to beautify yourself?"

"Of course."

Lexie let out a squeak. "I'm so excited for you!"

"Nothing has even happened, and who knows if anything will?"

"*I* know." She giggled.

"I'm not as confident, but let's go with it. It'll just be nice to see him again. I miss talking to him."

"Hold on a sec. Yeah, Mom?" she yelled. Lexie moaned. "I have to go. My sister...she's struggling again. I can hear her melting down. We'll talk again before school starts, okay?"

"Definitely. Call me later to talk about it if you need to. And let me know what Anne's evaluation shows."

"I will. Thanks. Bye, Kath."

"Bye, Lex."

Kathryn pulled her new sweater coat from the bag and slipped it on, admiring it in the mirror. A twinge came to her stomach, and she tossed the sweater on her bed before walking into the hallway, headed downstairs for a snack.

"Kathryn?"

She stopped and spun back to see Jane propped up against a stack of pillows on the bed, a book resting against her folded knees casting a shadow on her chest. "Yeah?"

"Did your dad say anything about my mammogram? I thought he might bring it up."

She leaned against the doorframe. "He asked if you had it. I didn't tell him anything, just that it was coming up. He doesn't know anything about the biopsy or that you're going in for the results Friday morning."

"Thank you, honey. We'll tell him everything once it's all over. I don't want to worry him or anyone else if there's no need."

"He said he was concerned because even though you aren't together anymore, he still cares about you and that he'll always love you."

Jane's eyebrows pulled together. "He said that?"

She nodded, walking to her mom's bed and sitting next to her. "I've heard him say it before, but it also made me wonder...if he loves you, why did he do such bad things when you left and when we were little?"

Jane folded her book. "I'm not sure I can adequately answer that for you, and I know you don't want me to say negative things about your dad. It's... complicated." She sat quietly for a few moments, looking as if she was carefully considering what to say next. "We've talked a bit before about how our marriage had problems. We didn't know each other well enough when we got married, and we weren't as good of a match as we thought. That became clearer over the years, to me anyway. When I would try to tell him that, he wasn't good at hearing it. When I suggested we get help to try and work on our problems, he wasn't so good at hearing that either. As you know, it got to

162

a point where I felt you, your brother, and I would be happier and healthier living away from your dad. He disagreed."

"That's when you packed us up and left."

Jane nodded. "It was an awful situation, and your dad, understandably, didn't handle it well."

The vision of her dad coming home from work that day had haunted her for years—the house empty, closets bare, drawers cleared out, his family… just gone.

Her mom sighed. "He was…very upset, very distraught. It was only compounded by his heavy drinking."

Kathryn looked down to her lap.

"I'm sorry, honey. I'm not trying to make you feel bad. I'm trying to be honest. I don't want to bash your father, but there are some details that are important if you want to understand the situation. Answering why he did what he did has many layers."

"Okay."

"Your dad is an alcoholic. You know that. That played a part in what he did. Alcoholics aren't able to put others first even if they love them. They aren't able to have normal, healthy relationships. His dad was an alcoholic too. It's a vicious cycle and a horrible disease. During this time, he did things that I know he regrets to this day, but he still did them. It was very scary, and I don't think you want details. You know a few things because you either remember them or heard them from Brandon because he witnessed them. It's so complicated and can be difficult to understand, but these bad things he did don't necessarily negate the fact that he loved me." She paused again. "I'm not sure if an alcoholic can really love in the typical sense, in a healthy way. He was overwhelmed with anger, his mind distorted with rage. I…I don't know if I'm explaining it well."

"No, I get it. I mean, I kind of get it. I don't understand how someone does something horrible to someone they love, but I get that he almost kinda lost his mind."

"In a way, I suppose. I'd say his anger took over. He couldn't see beyond his own pain."

"Was it normal for him to get that angry when you were together?"

"Not at me. I saw him angry at others, so I knew he had a temper and treated some people badly. He has been ostracized by all his brothers and sisters except one. He has burned a lot of bridges. From what I was told, he was awful to his siblings."

"He was awful to his siblings?" Kathryn's eyes tilted down, the thought twisting her stomach.

Jane gave her daughter's hand a comforting squeeze. "But as for me...I didn't let him get that angry at me. If I noticed him getting mad at something I was doing, I just stopped. I changed the behavior. That was my role. When the roles changed and I was no longer enabling him, his anger was then directed at me."

"You really seem to know a lot about all this."

"Lots of books and years of therapy, honey."

"So, if he can't love in the normal sense, does he love me?"

"Oh, Kathryn, of course he does. Loving a spouse and loving a child are different forms of love. Loving a child is instinctual and automatic. I know he loves you with everything he has in the best way he knows possible. You're his everything...which can be wonderful, yet it can be difficult, too, can't it?"

Kathryn nodded, smoothing a tear across her cheek.

"Oh, honey." Jane pulled her daughter into a tight embrace, her hand stroking her hair. "Even if you don't realize how much it affects you, it still does. It's the curse of the disease. Your dad's not a bad person. He's done bad things, and he's paid for those dearly. He's still paying for them. But there's not a doubt in my mind that he loves you."

She held her daughter, rocking her gently.

Kathryn slowly pulled away. "I'm sorry. I didn't mean for it to turn into this."

"No need to apologize. It's all buried in there. There's no telling what will set it free. You've been through a lot lately. I suspect you're a bit...emotionally fragile."

Kathryn breathed a laugh through her tears. "Uh...just a bit. I feel like all I do lately is cry."

"Having to deal with our past and those who have hurt us is exhausting and draining."

"How do I shut it off, make it all stop?"

"Denial has worked well for me." She let out a light laugh. "You may not be able to. It's all within you. Dealing with it, letting yourself explore it, feel it, might actually be good for you."

"It doesn't feel good. It feels awful."

"I know it does. But it gets better. I promise it does. Working your way to the other side of trauma and pain is difficult, but it's also worth it in the end. Maybe I should take you to see someone—someone who can help you through all you've been dealing with."

"Like a shrink?"

"A therapist. They work wonders. Think about it. Sit with the idea. We can talk about it again another time if you'd like."

"Okay." She slipped her leg out from under her and stood from the bed. "I'm going to grab a snack and get some sleep. Night, Mom."

"Goodnight. I love you."

"Love you too."

Mittens moaned, startling awake at Kathryn's touch as she knelt next to her on the carpet. Her mom's interpretation of her dad swirled and stabbed at her, rapidly forming a memory she wished she couldn't access. But it was there, just as her mom had said, and like too many others, it had been set free.

"Oh no! I missed!" Kathryn cried, her small arms flopping down to her sides as the softball spun out of the living room and hit against the dark wood kitchen cabinets, original to the house her mom and dad built together.

"That's okay, baby girl. Just try it again." Her dad grabbed the ball, placing it where the yellow tile met the off-white carpet, and pushed it, sailing it past the greenhouse doors to the little girl's outstretched hands.

"No! You only get three tries!" Brandon shouted from the plaid couch where he sat pouting.

"Brandon, stop it. She can have another turn."

The boy scowled, his blue eyes narrowing, and he stalked off into the adjoining kitchen. With her back being warmed by the wood-burning fireplace, Kathryn bent over and rolled the softball toward the last three standing juice jugs at the other end of the living room. The ball spun around and around until it hit the empty jugs, and all three fell down.

"I did it! I did it, Daddy!" she yelled, squealing as she jumped up and down.

"Yay, Kathryn!" Daniel ran to his daughter, picking her up and twirling her, her little legs fanning out behind her.

"That's just because you got an extra turn."

"Really, Brandon, that's enough. Juice jug bowling is supposed to be fun."

He scoffed as he leaned against the ivory tiled countertop, his arms tight across his chest. "Whatever."

"All right, you two. Your mom is going to be here soon to pick you up. Let's go outside for a few minutes until she gets here."

"Yeah! I want to jump on the colored stones!" Kathryn said, bouncing on her toes.

Her dad held the door open as she leapt onto the first red flagstone that made up the walkway in front of the country ranch.

"Cringer," she called to the tawny shepherd mix, *"you're in the way!"*

"Don't yell at my dog!" Brandon roared.

"I just wanted him to move," she said, hopping onto the next stone. Cringer trotted up next to her, and she slid her hand over his long, orange fur as he sniffed her other hand. *"Ew!"* she squealed, wiping his slobber on her pants as Brandon called him over.

Cheyenne, their black sheepdog, moseyed up to her and followed alongside as she jumped from stone to stone, trying to stay only on the red ones. She leaned on the dog's back to help her reach a few, her young hands disappearing in the ebony fluff. *"Thanks, girl!"*

Her dad waited for her at the end of the pathway. *"Did you have a good time with Daddy today, baby?"*

"Yes, I did!"

"You really love jumping on these flagstones, don't you? We had a lot of fun, right? We sang songs, went on the swing set, and took our walk over to the tree in the corner. It's growing really fast, isn't it?"

"Yeah, and Cringer and Cheyenne chased me around!" she said, giggling.

He scooped her up into a hug. *"So, you're happy?"*

"Of course, Daddy."

"I'm so glad."

"Oh, no!" She tightened her grip on his shoulders. *"I forgot Benji!"*

"I'll get him for you, baby girl. I know how much you love your dolly."

"Thanks, Daddy."

He placed her down, and she jumped along the blue stones on the way back toward the house. As she reached the last stone next to the garage, she heard the familiar crunch of gravel and turned to see her mom pulling into the driveway. Kathryn cocked her head to the side when she saw both her mom and grandpa get out of the car. The little girl shrugged and decided to take the green stones back to the driveway to meet her mom.

"Why is he here?" her dad asked, the harsh tone in his voice causing Kathryn to look up.

"I felt like I needed him here with me today," her mom replied.

"Why? You think I'm going to do something?"

"I don't want to do this right now, Daniel. Brandon, Kathryn, it's time to get going home. Say goodbye to your dad."

"Just one more stone, Mommy!" She leapt and made it onto the last green stone with the tip of her shoe. Smiling at her accomplishment, she skipped over to the car and held out her arms to her dad. He lifted her up and gave her a squeeze.

"I love you the mostest, my Kathryn."

"I love you too, Daddy." She tightened her arms around his neck as much as her young strength would allow, and he placed her back down.

"In you go," her mom said, holding the driver seat forward as she climbed into the back seat of the small coupe. "Brandon, can you help your sister with her buckle?"

"Sure," he said, leaning across her for the seatbelt.

Jane shut the door.

"Oh, no! Daddy never got Benji for me. I need him!"

"Shh," Brandon whispered.

Kathryn noticed his eyes looking out the window next to her, his brows furrowed, and she followed his gaze.

"Brandon, why are they yelling?"

"I don't know." He clicked her belt into place, and the two children watched the scene unfolding before their innocent eyes.

The shouting was muffled as it filtered in through the closed windows, making it difficult to hear what they were saying. Kathryn looked back at Brandon, his face tight with worry, making her even more uneasy.

"What's going on?" she asked, her voice shaking.

"I—"

The driver's side door opened, and the screaming flooded in at full volume.

"We're not done yet!" their dad bellowed.

Jane screamed as Daniel's hand came toward her, slamming the car door closed, exploding with a thunderous bang.

Kathryn ducked, and her hands flew up to her ears as the window shattered, shards of broken glass raining down on her.

"KATHRYN! What did you do, Daniel?" her mom screamed.

"Kathryn!" came Brandon's cracking voice next to her.

The commotion around her was smothered by the deafening crash, the blend of shrieking and deep voices shouting and calling her name drowned by her cries. She held her head tightly, scared to move against the fragments digging at her thighs as the car backed up and pulled forward with a jolt.

Her mom hysterical, her brother crying, her grandfather's hand brushing at her knee, Kathryn sat frozen, pieces of glass peppering her lemony brown hair.

It would be over a year before she saw her dad again—over a year before she would hold her Benji again—her doll held hostage by the father who was incapable of putting his beloved daughter before his own pain.

Thinking back on that man didn't feel real. That was not who he was to

167

her. To her, he was the loving, doting daddy who would do anything for his baby girl.

She walked across his yard, her long, dirty blond hair hanging down her back, tousled by the light breeze. Her favorite yellow dress swung down to her ankles. Her daddy took her hand in his, and she looked up at him, squinting against the bright sunlight.

"Let's go this way, Daddy! I want to lift our hands over the tree again," she said, tugging on his hand, holding her Benji in her other arm.

"Of course, Kathryn. Anything you want, baby girl."

They strode hand in hand, weaving around the gardens spread throughout his land, zigzagging through the tall trees that littered his lawn.

When they got to the tree in the back corner, they both lifted their hands in the air and said, "Up and over!"

He smiled down upon her as she laughed and pulled his hand to her cheek. "I miss you, Daddy."

"I miss you too, baby girl."

They continued on, walking across his back yard, past the vegetable garden to their right and a line of ancient pine trees to their left. She pulled free of his grip and ran ahead.

"Push me on the swing, Daddy!"

He helped her climb onto the swing, and she placed Benji in her lap, clutching him with one arm.

"Why don't I hold Benji for you while you swing?"

"But he's my favorite dolly in the whole world, Daddy, and he likes to swing with me too!"

"I know. I just want you to hold on with two hands so you don't fall."

"Okay. But take good care of him."

"I will. I promise."

She held on tightly as she felt his hand against her back, pushing her high, high, high up to the sky.

Kathryn felt a tear drip down onto her hand as she lay on the floor next to Mittens, who was sound asleep. Walking with her dad and lifting their hands over the tree in his back yard was her very first memory. Her second was when he shattered the car window, covering her in broken glass.

She climbed into her bed and pulled the covers over her head, wrapping herself into a ball, her knees tight to her chest, waiting for sleep to take her. As she fell into darkness, she was suddenly once more pulled into blazing light.

The sun shone harshly against her young, pale skin as they walked along the garden lining his garage, Kathryn's small fingers trailing the cedar siding.

"Let's go this way, Daddy. I want to lift our hands over the tree again," the little girl said, tugging at his hand. But with a blink of her blue eyes, she pulled on air, and her hand fell to her side. "Daddy?"

She ran across the grass to the driveway, kicking up pebbles as she sprinted toward the street, scanning the yard. The girl jumped up onto the thick railroad ties that lined the driveway and bordered yet another patch of carefully designed flower arrangements. "Daddy? Daddy! Where are you!"

"Kathryn? Kathryn, where did you go?" his rough voice called.

"I'm here, Daddy! I'm over here!"

"Kathryn! Kathryn!"

"Daddy!"

She spun back to the house, and her flaxen hair twirled and whipped in the burst of flames that erupted in front of her. She fell into the bed of pebbles and cowered before the fire as it spread wildly along the railroad ties and grew upward and across the stone driveway, creating a wall between her and the house, fueled by an invisible element.

Through the dancing reds and oranges, the images of her dad, mom, and brother swirled behind the heat-streaked air as sparkling embers drifted into the sky suddenly overtaken by darkness. The hem of her yellow dress got caught up in the churning wind, and she jumped back, screaming and flailing on the ground. At a safe distance from the inferno, her tiny fingers trailed along the blackened hem, the soft, innocent yellow singed and damaged beyond repair. She pulled her hand away, inspecting her soot-covered finger-tips before stumbling to her feet.

"Mommy! Daddy! Help me!"

"Kathryn," her dad said with unnatural calmness, his stoic expression illuminated by the blaze. "Come on, baby girl. Come to us."

"I can't get through! It's too hot!"

"You can do it, sweetie," her mom said, echoing the serenity of her dad's tone.

Kathryn stepped forward, reaching a hand toward the flames but recoiled at the intense heat. She knelt on the stone driveway, the pebbles digging into her bare knees. "I can't," she said through her tears drying instantly upon her overheated cheeks. "I don't know how."

Her mom wiped a single drop of sadness from her eye, took her son's hand, and turned, walking the grassy pathway between the house and garage to the back yard. Kathryn watched in horror as they melted from her sight.

"Daddy, please don't leave me."

"Never, baby girl."

The conflagration rose higher, thickening and releasing ebony smoke into the blackening sky, billowing forth, rushing at her like a charging wave, encasing her in its grasp, choking her, completely blocking her view of her dad. She extended her hands to the sides and met a wall of darkness. Kathryn pushed against it with all she had left in her, but it continued to solidify and close in on her.

"No! Daddy! Daddy!"

Then there was blackness.

Nothingness.

Slow Motion

She awoke Friday morning immersed in helplessness after yet another night of fiery nightmares. It was too much. It was all too much. Brandon, her dad, her mom... Kathryn closed her eyes, the blackness closing in on her again; it was always closing in on her. Even a flickering moment of happiness was defeated, overpowered, robbed from her and whisked away with the darkness that seemed to invade her life, collapsing in on her wherever she turned. When would her life not be plagued with pain? The question swirled in her mind, the answer utterly out of her grasp, leaving an emptiness, a dark stain upon her soul that would only expand, little by little, swallowing what was left of her innocence, her childhood, and, if she wasn't mindful of it, her future.

Her eyes popped open, and she rushed into her mom's room. The bed lay vacant, the clock on her nightstand pushing the air from Kathryn's lungs—9:12.

She's gone.

Frozen in the doorway, her eyes fell shut, the silhouette of the bed etched in the darkness, the apparition of two figures hunched on the edge flashing into the image behind her eyelids.

Kathryn's hands grasped at the walls as she staggered back into her room, and without thinking, she gravitated to her cello. She came to the last piece she had in her folder, and as Mozart flowed through her fingers, her mind wandered to the image that had appeared behind her eyes in her mom's doorway—yet another vision of a memory that ate away at her innocence.

171

The bow slipped off the D string with a screech. She reached for the box of rosin, finding it almost empty. As she approached her mom's bedroom to tell her she needed more, Kathryn heard voices through the cracked door.

She peeked in and saw Jane and Mitch sitting on the side of her bed, her mom's head hanging down while Mitch's arm draped her shoulders racked with uncontrollable sobs.

"I can't leave them, Mitch. I can't. They need me. Brandon won't survive without me. He won't make it. I have to be here to help him. To help him be the best he can be. And Kathryn... She's just...she's just a little girl. I have to watch her grow—to see her graduate from high school and college, to get married. I have to be here when she has her first baby. I can't leave them." Her hands cradled her face as her body folded, and she released despondency foreign to Kathryn's young ears. Her usual essence was gone, overtaken by fear. With each sob, she sank lower into Mitch, her tear-tracked face sliding against his thick beard, as if hope were escaping with every drop that trickled off her chin.

Mitch pulled her close with both arms, the hat she wore to hide her thinning hair knocking his glasses askew. "You will be, Jane. You will be here. You will be here to watch your babies grow up. Brandon will not be alone, and you will watch Kathryn walk across that stage and walk down that aisle. You will hold your grandchildren in your arms. You are strong. You are fighting this. We are fighting this together. You're not going to leave them. You're not going to leave me." His heavy breathing fogged his glasses as he buried his face into her covered head, crying alongside her.

Kathryn backed away slowly and crept to her room, closing her door as quietly as possible. She fell back against the door and slid to the floor, hugging her knees to her chest, fearing for the first time since this nightmare began that her mom may actually die.

A tear dropped onto the shoulder of her cello. Resigned to the fact that nothing could distract her from her fears, she placed her cello on its side against the chair and started to pace around her room.

She can't leave me.

She looked over at the clock—10:03. She paced quicker.

The walls of her bedroom felt as though they were collapsing in on her, and she threw her door open, venturing downstairs. Brandon was just coming out of his room as she walked into the kitchen.

"Is Mom back yet?" he asked, rubbing his tired eyes.

"No, not yet. Seems like she should have been though. I'm sure she'll be home any minute."

He went past her and plopped onto the couch.

Kathryn continued pacing, making a circle around the kitchen, back through the living room, and around again.

"I overheard Mom and Mitch on the phone last night," Brandon said.

"And?"

"She doesn't sound worried."

"Yeah, she basically said the same thing to me."

"Do you believe her?" he asked, looking into his lap.

"No. She's hiding it from us like last time." As she continued back and forth, her legs started to burn under the strain; she welcomed the distraction.

"Would you stop doing that?"

"Stop what?" she replied breathlessly.

"Pacing. It's annoying!"

"No. You don't like it, then go back to bed!"

"What is your problem?"

"My problem? Seriously?"

Brandon's angry expression softened, and he leaned back against the couch, observing his fingers twist around a loose thread on his T-shirt.

Kathryn slowed down her pacing and took a seat on the other side of the couch, spinning her Claddagh ring. "She just has to…"

"I know."

Her slowing pulse eventually synced with the wall clock across from them in the kitchen.

Brandon suddenly thrust himself upward. "I'm going downstairs to bang on some drums."

As Brandon's footstep creaked against the top stair, a car door slammed. The siblings raced to the front door, their hands fighting for the doorknob. Pushing into the illuminated afternoon, they tripped to a stop as she came up the walkway. She smiled. They ran to her, leaping into her embrace, lightly weeping into her hair. She hugged her children tightly, one in each arm.

Forty-Six

The phone rang, interrupting their movie, and Jane handed the cordless to Kathryn.

"It's your dad."

"Hey, Dad."

"Well hello, my sweet Kathryn. I just wanted to call you and tell you what a great time I had shopping with you the other day."

"Oh, yeah, me too, Dad." She sighed, the tone in his voice once again with that certain quality she knew too well; he had been drinking.

"I have some bad news though. I'm sick."

"Sorry, Dad. With what?"

"Oh, just a virus, most likely. Nothing to worry about. I don't suppose you'd want to come over and take care of me, now would you?"

The phone rang one cold, damp night as Kathryn sat cross-legged on the living room floor, rocking Benji and giving him a bottle of milk after his bath.

"Kathryn, it's your dad."

She jumped to her feet.

"Hi, Daddy!"

"Hi, baby. How are you?"

"I'm good. Just getting Benji ready for beddy-bye."

"You're such a good mommy. I'm glad you're good, but Daddy isn't feeling so good."

"What's wrong?"

"I'm sick, baby girl. I'm coughing really badly. I'm even coughing up blood. I'd love for my special nurse to come over and take care of me."

"Of course I'll take care of you, Daddy."

"You will? You're just the sweetest. Go ahead and pack a bag for the night, and I'll be over in just a little bit to pick you up."

"Okay. Bye."

She hung up the phone and ran into the kitchen. "Mom, Dad is really sick, and he's coughing up blood, so I'm going to go over to his house to take care of him."

"He's coughing up blood?" her mom asked.

"That's what he said. I have to go take care of him. He'll be here soon to get me."

"Kathryn, you should not be the one to take care of him, especially if he's so sick."

The little girl followed her out of the kitchen, pulling at her hand. "But, Mom, he needs me."

Jane grabbed the phone and started dialing, glancing down at her. "He needs a doctor, not a nine-year-old girl. I don't want you going over there tonight."

"He doesn't have anyone else!"

She put the phone to her ear. "Sweetie, there's nothing you can do for him. This is not your responsibility." She scoffed and clicked the phone off, tossing it onto the couch and turning to face her daughter. "I'm sorry, honey. You're not going."

Kathryn gasped through her tears. "But who's going to take care of him? He's all alone."

Jane leaned down, placing a hand on her shoulder. "It can't be you, Kathryn. It just can't be."

The little girl threw her hands over her face and took off up the stairs and into her room, flinging herself on her bed.

Her cries had died down when she heard the double beep of her dad's truck in the driveway, and she ran into her mom's room to look out the front window. His headlights cast a heavy glow on the scene. Her mom stood solid, hands on her hips, and her dad flailed his arms, screams muffled by the closed window. He suddenly got back in his car and drove off, his tires screeching against the wet pavement.

"Kathryn?"

"Sorry. What?"

"I was asking if you wanted to come take care of me."

"Um…no, I'm good."

"You won't come over and take care of your sick father?"

"Nah."

"Oh, well, thanks a lot." He laughed. "Good thing I'm just messing with you. I'm going to work in the greenhouse for a little while and then get to bed. Hopefully, I'll feel better in the morning."

"Okay. I hope you feel better too."

"Thank you, baby."

"Oh, Dad, Mom's tests came back clear. She's officially five years cancer free."

He exhaled loudly. "That's great news. Please tell her I'm very glad to hear that."

"I will."

"Thank you, baby girl. See you later, alligator."

"After a while, crocodile."

"I love you, my sweetest."

"Love you too."

"Thank you."

"You're welcome. Bye."

"Bye."

Kathryn gave her mom the phone. "Go ahead and play the movie."

"Everything okay?"

"Yeah, it's fine. Just play it."

Kathryn couldn't sleep as the all too familiar darkness seemed to seep in under her locked door, gliding up onto her bed and surrounding her. Materialistic reminders of her dad were sprinkled all around her room—music boxes, unicorn statues, cat figurines, a baseball encased in a plastic box. Her eyes stopped, focusing in on that ball, and she smiled. That man in those memories, he wasn't the man she knew anymore. She knew full well what he had done, but the man she knew was different. Who he had become did not negate what he had done in the past, but the man she knew was a man trying to salvage the most important relationship in his world.

. . .

Kathryn brought the brush through her hair one more time and slid on a touch of lip gloss as she heard the double beep of his pickup outside. "Mom! Dad's here!"

"I'll be right there!"

Kathryn limped out into the hallway and waited for her mom to come help her. "This is ridiculous," she said as her mom grabbed on to her arm. "How am I even going to do this?"

"Do you not want to go?"

"No. Dad and I have been planning this game for weeks. He'd be so disappointed if we didn't go. And it's been so long since we've been to one together. I'll make it work. Can you carry my mitt down?"

Jane helped Kathryn down the stairs as she used one of her crutches to support herself. She opened the door for her daughter as she wobbled out into the summer afternoon.

"What happened to you?" he asked, concern etched on his sun-kissed face.

Kathryn rolled her eyes. "I stepped on a bee. What happened to you?" She nodded to the brace on his knee.

"Ah, my darn knee is acting up again."

"Quite a pair you two will be at the game," her mom said with a snicker.

Jane helped Kathryn into the truck, and father and daughter set off for the baseball game with the oldies station playing lightly in the background.

"So, eighth grade coming up, huh? You excited for school to start?"

"Yeah, I guess. It'll be easier to make first chair because Cari moved up into high school. She was really good."

"You better get first or else."

"Or else what?"

"Or else I'll go over to your school and make them give you first chair," he said in a low, deep voice, shaking his fist.

"Yeah, you do that," she said, laughing. "I think I'd rather make it on my own, though."

"That's probably a better idea." Daniel gripped the wheel tighter and glanced in his rearview mirror. "Hey, get off my tail! Would you look at this guy? He's right on the back of my truck."

Kathryn turned to look behind them and grimaced. "Eek. Maybe it's because you drive so slowly," she said, stifling a laugh.

"Hey, I don't drive slowly. I drive the speed limit. There's a difference. If some jerk is in a hurry and wants to speed, well then that's their problem. I don't speed, especially with my precious baby girl in my truck. Which reminds me, are you ready to count cars?"

She burst out laughing. "Yes! Yes, I'm ready! When should we start?"

"Let's wait until we get on the Thruway."

Jonny Maestro and the Crests serenaded them as they pulled onto the Thruway entrance.

"Okay. Get ready," he said.

She laughed. "I already counted two."

"Two cars passed us already? We just got on!"

"Yup. Now it's five."

"Oh, come on."

"I think the record for how many cars that have passed us driving to a game was about fifty. Maybe we'll beat that this time."

"Well, that's just fine by me. Let them pass me. I'm staying the speed limit."

They were nearing the exit as Kathryn continued to count cars whipping past them. "Thirty-three, thirty-four. Hey, look! You passed that one!" She giggled.

Daniel's head whipped around. "It doesn't count when it's a broken-down car on the side of the road," he responded, laughing along with his daughter.

They pulled up to the parking lot across from the baseball field at car number forty-six. "Ugh! So close to beating our record! Maybe on the way home."

"Challenge accepted!" He put the truck in park and looked over at his daughter, beaming with joy. "You ready to go?"

"Yup. Let's get a hobblin'."

Daniel came around to the other side of the truck and helped her down. "You're on crutches, but you still managed to bring your mitt."

"Of course! I'm not letting a chance get by. Could you imagine if I didn't bring it just one time and the ball came to us? No, no, no. Not taking that chance. We're catching a ball one of these years."

"I'd just catch it with my hand."

"And break it?"

"Maybe. But I'd still catch it. I may not be as young as I once was, but I was a hell of a ballplayer. Mostly shortstop and sometimes—"

"Sometimes first. I know." She winked at him.

"Oh, so I've mentioned that before?"

"Just a few times," she said, a smile breaking through her attempt at keeping a straight face.

Getting through the turnstile with her crutches was interesting, but when she got to the other side, her senses were overwhelmed with the sights, smells, and sounds of so many wonderful memories with her dad at Buffalo Bisons

179

games—buttered popcorn in red-striped buckets, giant hot pretzels doused in thick salt, footlong hot dogs drowning in ketchup and mustard, nachos smothered in cheese. Young kids wearing foam fingers ran around their parents, and royal blue baseball caps topped the chattering crowd of people filling the hallways beneath the stands.

People parted slightly as they saw the father-daughter pair coming.

"Well, look at that. Your crutches are pretty useful."

She shot him a look. "Very funny."

He chuckled. "So, you really stepped on a bee?"

"I was running around Jake and Sam's back yard."

"Without shoes on?"

"We were swimming and getting in and out of the pool, playing a game yesterday. It looked like a bumble bee. The stinger was huge and got stuck in my foot. It started swelling and has been super painful to step on since."

"Oh, my Kathryn. What am I going to do with you?" He shook his head and cracked a smile. "This is us here," he said, pointing up at the blue section number painted on the concrete wall.

She followed him through the tunnel, her eyes squinting against the blinding glare emerging with every slow, strained step. The thick grass spread out before them, a brilliant deep shade of emerald green, mocha-toned dirt standing in stark contrast to the snow-white chalk lines shooting off the batter's box. Blue and red chairs ascended into the clear sky, some groupings meeting the glass-encased box seats topped with gray roof tiles.

Kathryn stopped to take it all in, observing the baseball players speckled around the diamond, playing catch, taking practice swings, and doing sprints. She spotted the catcher crouched down low, and she smiled as the ball slapped against the mitt—one of her favorite sounds.

Her dad limped up next to her. "That could be you someday."

She scoffed. "Playing catcher in the town league isn't exactly the same thing, Dad. I think I'll stick with the cello."

"You don't want to be the first girl accepted into the major leagues?"

She simply closed her eyes and shook her head.

Daniel shrugged. "All right. Guess not." He looked down at their tickets and nodded to her right. "We're this way. Looks like we're behind the dugout."

She frowned. "Well, we might have a shot at catching a foul, I guess."

As they made their way to their seats, he cautiously backed his way down the steps, keeping right in front of her, his hands held straight out.

"I'm okay, Dad."

"Hey, it's my job to keep you safe. If you trip on those crutches...well, I won't be able to catch you, but I'll break your fall."

Kathryn stopped on the last step, laughing. "Now you're really going to make me trip!"

"Hey! Sir!"

Daniel whipped around to meet the deep voice behind him. One of the Bisons stood in front of the dugout, looking up at them—the thirteen-year-old girl on crutches and the middle-aged man with a giant knee brace.

"Here!"

The player lobbed a baseball toward him, and Daniel caught it with his bare hand.

He flicked the brim of his cap up a smidge. "Thanks for coming out today."

"Hey, thank you, sir!" Daniel turned to his daughter and gently tossed her the ball.

She easily caught it, her eyes wide with excitement. "We finally caught a ball!"

Kathryn smiled. He had bought the case for her at the gift shop on the way out "so you can always remember this wonderful day we had together," he had said. She knew he had done horrible things. She knew he had hurt them. But he was her dad. Kathryn knew he loved her in every way he knew how to love someone, and that was what mattered to her. Taking the good with the bad, she would love him for who he was now despite who he used to be.

Mittens snuggled up to her side as she started to drift off into unconsciousness, welcoming the relief, but a booming crash came from the basement, and the atrocious mess of random noises mashing together flooded up through the floor vent.

Mittens scampered off the bed and under the nightstand as Kathryn sharply threw her blankets off her. "Oh, come on!"

Bracing

Kathryn stomped across the hall. "Mom," she whined, "why are they here?"

"I'm sorry. I told Brandon he could have his friends over tonight. He hasn't had them here in weeks because I wanted you to settle back in."

"Couldn't they have just stayed away? It's almost eleven. I want to sleep. They're going to keep me up."

"I'll tell them to keep it down."

She rolled her eyes. "Yeah, 'cause those idiots are actually going to listen to you." She trudged back into her room with a huff and slammed the door, fury bubbling up from within. Those moronic, disrespectful, inconsiderate jerks elicited a raw, uninhibited rage within her, rivaling that of the anger she felt for her brother.

Every Friday night, every damn Friday night, they would come over and abuse their instruments while in a drunken stupor in a feeble, pathetic attempt at making what they foolishly considered to be music.

And her mom let them. If she knew what Kathryn knew, though, she doubted she'd be so open to invite them into her house. But Kathryn wasn't allowed to tell her—one more smothering secret she was forced to keep that made her feel like a prisoner in her own home.

"All right, so remember the rules, you two," Jane said as she spun around the living room, making sure she had all the bandages to contain the edema in her arm while she was away for the weekend. "Kathryn, Valerie can come over

and spend the night. I know she smokes, but please don't let her smoke in the house."

"Got it. I won't."

"Brandon, you can have four friends over, but that's it. No big parties. It could get out of control really quickly. Don't let anyone smoke in the house. They can go outside." She paused to look at him squarely in the face. "And no drinking."

"All right. Fine, Mom."

Kathryn eyed him, turning away sharply when he looked over at her.

"You have the phone number at Mitch's house. You can call any time you need anything. I'll be back Sunday night. I'm trusting you two to take care of everything, okay?"

"Okay, Mom," Kathryn said with a nod.

Brandon sighed. "Yeah, sure. We got it."

"Good. Have a nice weekend, and I'll see you in two days. I love you both." She gave them each a hug, grabbed her luggage, and walked out the door leading into the garage.

Without a word to each other, Brandon retreated to the basement while Kathryn went upstairs to her bedroom.

Music was already starting to waft through the floor vent in Kathryn's room when Val arrived, and she went down to let her in. Val was distracted by Brandon and his three friends huddled in the kitchen.

Kathryn rolled her eyes. "Come on, Val. Let's go up to my room."

"Ugh. Fine." She gave them one last look as she reluctantly ripped herself away and followed up the stairs. "Do you know if Shawn is coming over tonight?"

Kathryn shrugged. "I don't know. Probably. But Brandon is only supposed to have four friends over."

"Do you think that's all he'll have?"

"Of course not."

The girls talked for a while in Kathryn's room, but as the music downstairs got louder, Val became more impatient.

"Come on. I want to go downstairs," Val said, whining.

"I don't want to. Why can't we just stay up here and hang out? Just because you want to see if Shawn is here?"

"Well, yeah. Come on. Please?"

"I don't want to. Why would I want to hang out with Brandon and his friends?"

"Uh...because they're cool and fun? Not to mention hot."

Kathryn grimaced. "They are none of those things."

"Ugh...give me a break. Just for a little while. Please, please, please?"

Kathryn shook her head, once again sucked into Val's need to be in the middle of Brandon's stupid parties. "Fine," she said, aggravation digging into the syllable.

Kathryn gasped as they neared the bottom of the stairs. The living room and kitchen were packed full of people, most she didn't even recognize, a majority clutching beer cans. She waved the cigarette smoke out of her eyes as she made her way through the crowd, scanning for Brandon. Val weaved through the mass ahead of her and zeroed in on one of the guys sitting at the kitchen table, a cigarette in his hand.

"Hey, Shawn," Val said, her voice higher than usual.

Shawn took the cigarette out of his mouth and let the smoke ooze through his teeth. "Hey, Val. What's up?"

"Oh, nothing much. Can I bum one of those?" she replied, grasping at the tips of her hair with her fingers.

Kathryn's jaw fell. "Val!"

"God, Kathryn. Lighten up. It's a party." She slid a smoke from Shawn's pack and put it to her heavily painted lips.

Shawn grabbed a lighter from his back pocket, swinging it up to Val's cigarette before observing Kathryn. "What's your problem?" he asked, a scowl on his already unpleasant face.

"What's my problem?" Kathryn snapped back.

Val's eyes narrowed. "Kathryn, don't."

"My problem, Shawn, is that you guys shouldn't even be here. And you shouldn't be smoking in my mom's house!"

"Kathryn, shut up!" yelled Brandon from behind her.

She spun around to face him. "Mom told you she didn't want you to have too many people over, and she didn't want anyone drinking or smoking in here. She says it every time, yet you keep doing it, and I'm sick of it! Do you have any idea how much trouble she could get in if anyone found us all like this? She trusted you!"

"Oh, calm the hell down. No one is going to find out. I know you certainly aren't going to tell anyone, are you, Kathryn?" He had that look in his eyes.

She took a step back. "You all make me sick," she said through gritted teeth. Pushing past everyone in her way, she stomped up the stairs, leaving Val right where she wanted to be.

The horrendous racket continued to vibrate the house, and Kathryn's rage only grew. Away from home, she could let what they've done to her disappear into the far corners of her mind. But being thrust back into a life where they invaded her home brought all those memories flooding forth, feeding the dark knot that was infiltrating her soul. When her mom was there, it was kept under control. It was when her mom went away for a weekend to visit Mitch that the chaos ensued.

"Is Valerie coming over tonight, Kathryn?" Jane asked.

"No. She's sick. It's just me tonight. But that's fine with me. I'm just going to get some food together and hang out in my room." She looked away, trying to hold in how scared she was for her mom to leave again after what happened last time. Kathryn wanted to shout it, scream it, tell her mom everything that happened when she wasn't there—the cigarettes, the drinking, the pot smoking, the way Brandon's friends took advantage of Val, and last time what they did to Kathryn herself.

"That sounds good to me. Brandon, like always, no parties, four friends, no drinking, and no smoking in the house."

"Fine," he said.

Kathryn stared at Brandon, and he stared right back, knowing just as well as she did that he was not going to follow her rules and equally knowing Kathryn was too afraid to say anything about it.

It wasn't long before the music was blaring, and she could already smell the smoke drifting throughout the house. Kathryn hesitantly descended the stairs and peeked around the corner. The house was overflowing with people, more than she had likely seen there before. She kept her head down and charged into the kitchen, trying to avoid looking at anyone.

"What are you doing down here?" Brandon asked her.

"I just wanted to get something to eat and drink. Then I'll take it upstairs."

"Fine. As long as you're not staying."

"Like I'd stay down here after what happened last time. I don't really feel like spending the night feeling like death because your friend's girlfriend thought it would be funny to trick me into getting drunk."

"I wasn't happy about that either, okay? Just get what you want and go upstairs. Stay away from everyone. I told them not to mess with you."

He almost kind of sounded like he might have cared. She shook the absurd thought from her mind and made herself a sandwich and grabbed a bag of chips and some root beer and escaped toward the stairs, weaving around the strangers in her living room.

Although Kathryn stayed upstairs in her room all night, Mittens at her side, anxiety racked her body—the pounding drums, the amped instruments blaring into the middle of the night, even groups of people outside in the back yard, sitting around the fire pit that Kathryn could see from her window. As her clock read two in the morning, she still couldn't sleep through all the noise. If someone called the police, if they came into the house and found all these teenagers drinking and doing who knows what else with no adult there…

Blasting classical music on her CD player only slightly muffled the crappy music and chaos downstairs. But by three, it sounded as though people were clearing out, and the music was lowered to a dull roar, allowing Kathryn to finally fall asleep.

She stayed upstairs for as long as she could the next morning, but her stomach got the better of her. After getting herself fully dressed, knowing there would be strangers sleeping on her couches in the living room, she went downstairs to grab some breakfast, or lunch, as it was almost noon.

Kathryn crept past the sleeping forms on the couches, and she was startled by the sight of Brandon sitting at the kitchen table. "You're already awake?"

"I didn't really sleep much."

"Okay?" She walked past him and grabbed a box of cereal off the top of the refrigerator.

"I'm sorry the party got so out of control last night. I guess word got out, and a lot of people I didn't even know showed up."

"Yeah, I noticed."

"Well, I didn't mean for that to happen. I was really pissed and told off some guy for bringing a bunch of the people over. They won't come back."

"I won't hold my breath."

"Oh, shut up. I said I was sorry."

"Why are you sorry? You've never been sorry before."

"Because"—he exhaled deeply—"last night, I came upstairs and noticed one of the guys that wasn't invited was going up the stairs to your room."

"What? Why?"

"When I saw him, I stopped him and asked him what the hell he thought he was doing. He said he was going upstairs to see you."

A wave of nausea flowed over her, the air leaving her lungs.

"I told him, 'The hell you are,' and I made him and his group leave and told them never to come back. I'm sorry. I really didn't mean for it to get so out of control."

"What if you didn't come upstairs and see him, Brandon?" she shouted.

"I know. But I did come upstairs, and I did see him. If he ever comes back, I'll make him leave."

She turned the dial up on her CD player, hoping some of her favorite cello concertos would help dull the atrocious noise from beneath her. The fact that

Brandon seemed genuinely upset didn't make the memory any less terrifying and disturbing, and she tried not to allow her mind to wander into the darkness of what if.

It was a few months before her mom left to visit Mitch again, and Kathryn didn't want to risk staying. But being away from her home during the parties didn't protect her from the destruction either.

"Kathryn? Pssst...Kathryn?"

She fought the heaviness of her eyelids at the whispering voice in her ear. "What?"

"Do you want to get up and watch TV with us?"

She pried her eyes open to see Jake's smiling face. "What time is it?"

"Six thirty."

"In the morning? I'd rather keep sleeping."

"Oh, okay."

She heard footsteps walk out of the room as she closed her eyes again.

Kathryn nearly fell out of bed at the high-pitched beeping sound attacking her ears. She slammed her glasses on and ran toward the sound, finding Aunt Hannah standing on a chair, waving a yellow-flowered hand towel at the smoke alarm, a light fog creeping along the kitchen ceiling.

"Oh, Kathryn, I'm so sorry. I was making breakfast, and this darn smoke alarm went off. It goes off so easily. It's such a royal pain. Poor Max was so scared he meowed at the back door, begging to be let outside."

"Can't hear the TV, Mama!" Sam yelled in from the living room.

Aunt Hannah rolled her eyes and walked over to the doorway between the kitchen and living room. "Oh, I am so very sorry to have disturbed your TV watching, my son. My most sincerest apologies," she said with a dramatic bow to her sons, who were sitting cross-legged on the rug in front of the TV.

Jake leaned over into Sam. "I don't think she means that," he whispered loudly, his hand poorly cupped to the side of his mouth.

Sam jabbed him back with a playful elbow to the ribs, and they joined in with their mother's laughter.

"Breakfast is almost ready, boys." Aunt Hannah bustled back to the counter. "I hope you're hungry, Kathryn. I made waffles. Well, the first batch is a little...overdone," she said with a giggle.

"Sounds great. I do have to get back to check on Mittens, but that can certainly wait until after waffles."

"Wonderful. Would you mind setting the plates on the table for me? Just four. Uncle Alex is teaching a piano lesson."

"Okay." Kathryn grabbed the plates off the counter. "Thanks again for letting me spend the weekend here."

"You know you're always welcome." Aunt Hannah lifted the lid of the waffle iron. "Okay, guys, the next batch of waffles is ready."

"Yessss!" the boys shouted in unison. They darted into the kitchen, stopping feet from the table to slide across the linoleum flooring on their socks.

The boys set to work, and Kathryn enjoyed a nice breakfast with some of her favorite people.

"That was really good, Aunt Hannah. Thank you."

"You're very welcome." She looked at her sons, tilting her head down and keeping her eyes locked on them.

"Thanks, Mama," Jake said.

"Yeah. Thanks, Mama," Sam added, syrup dribbling onto his chin.

Kathryn stifled a laugh. "I'm going to go back home for just a bit to check on Mittens, maybe hang out with her for a little while."

Kathryn walked to her house that late March morning, a touch of chill in the breeze tickling her arms. She went in through the unlocked door, meeting a deep bark.

"Otis, it's just me. Relax."

The black lab panted at his moment of exertion and retreated back through the kitchen toward Brandon's room.

Kathryn's lip curled as she scoffed at the guys passed out on the couches and went straight to the stairs, stumbling to a halt at the top landing. Her door was open. Her heart rate sped up, knowing she had locked Mittens inside with food, water, and her litter box.

Kathryn hesitantly placed her hand on the door and slowly opened it, her heart sinking with every inch revealed. Her room was trashed. Cedar chip bedding for her guinea pig was scattered over her entire room, blanketing every surface. Unfolded maxi pads were stuck to her walls and the wrappers strewn about. Her mouth hung open as her eyes began to tear, her throat constricting. As she continued to process the scene, she felt the air knocked from her lungs. A basketball-sized hole had been punched through her wall.

She felt her feet carrying her into her room, wood shavings crunching beneath her sneakers, surveying the damage, trying to catch her breath. She found her TV on its side, and her Sega Genesis was gone—stolen.

Kathryn gasped. "Mittens!" Dropping to her knees, cedar chips rustling beneath her, she looked under the bed. Mittens wasn't there. Kathryn looked *under the nightstand. She wasn't there. She crawled over to the closet, frantically searching for her in any of her usual hiding spots. Nowhere.*

Hoisting herself up, she dashed into her mom's room, scanning from the blue chair to her usual perch atop the vanity mirror before checking under her bed. "Mittens? Baby girl?" Nothing but darkness. "Oh my God."

Kathryn ran down the stairs, banging every step as she went, and burst into Brandon's room, flipping on the light. "Mittens is gone! And what happened to my room? Get up! Answer me!"

Brandon rolled over, his arm covering his eyes. "What the hell, Kathryn?"

"I can't find Mittens anywhere! She was locked in my room when I left, and now I can't find her. And who destroyed my room!"

"I don't know. Some guys we didn't know showed up, and it got out of control. I'm sorry, okay?"

"No! It's not okay! They totally wrecked my room! And my baby girl..." Tears began to gather as her breath came in sharp jabs. "Where is she? And there's a hole in my wall! And my Sega is gone!"

"Shit. It is?"

"Yes! How could you let this happen? You said you weren't going to let these parties get out of control anymore. What if I had been here? Would whoever did that still have broken into my room?"

"You weren't here, okay? I said I was sorry. I'm sure Mittens is just hiding somewhere. And I'll help you clean your room."

"I don't want your help! I hate you!"

Her throat ached, and her ears pounded as she stomped into the kitchen, looking up as her strength to stand nearly abandoned her. The side door was open. "Mittens!"

She sped into the garage, scanning quickly before dashing to the expansive back yard. From the fire pit to the oversized shed, across the thick rows of trees bordering the yard, she saw nothing. She sprinted to the tree line, her eyes wide as she tried to keep her tears from distorting her vision. "Mittens," she called softly in the voice she saved only for her. "Come here, baby girl. Come on, sweetie. It's okay."

Silence.

After sweeping the entire yard and surrounding trees, she came up on the left side of the house, panic wrenching at her chest, her face drenched with the fear she would never see her baby girl again. Bricks lining the garden shook under her feet as she caught her balance and searched through the patches of purple anemone flowers under the dwarf weeping cherry tree. "Mittens? Please, baby girl. I'm here."

She stopped suddenly when she heard it, freezing her movements and holding her breath. It came again—the deep, unique voice of her best friend.

"Mittens? Oh my God."

Her beautiful face peeked up from between the bushes against the house, and she took a tentative step on the unfamiliar earth beneath her muddied paws.

Kathryn knelt down, reaching her hand forward, and Mittens came closer, another scratchy mew emanating from her throat. She pressed her black nose into Kathryn's hand and rubbed against her, arching her back. With cautious movements, Kathryn scooped up Mittens, her hand sliding under her white belly, and held the terrified cat against her chest, burying her face into her, dampening the ebony fur. "My sweet girl. Thank God you're okay. I love you so much."

She carried her through the front door, and Mittens immediately sprang from her grasp, her back claw slicing into Kathryn's forearm as she flew up the stairs and into the bedroom.

Wincing at the scratch on her arm, Kathryn turned to the people now stirring on the couches. "Get out of my house!" She took off up the stairs and slammed her door over and over again until she broke down and fell to her knees, hysterical.

After a few moments, she picked herself up, her eyes wet but hardened. She brushed the wood shavings off her jeans and grabbed the phone.

"Hello?"

"Mitch?"

"Kathryn? What's wrong?"

"Can I talk to Mom?"

"Of course."

"Kathryn?"

"Mom, when I came home, Mittens was gone! Brandon had a huge party last night. They left the door open, and she got out."

"What? Did you find her?"

"Yes. I searched the yard and found her, but she was so cold and scared. It looks like she was out all night. And they trashed my room! Someone broke into my room and destroyed it. There's a huge hole in my wall, and my Sega is gone!"

Jane gasped. "I can't believe this. Hold on a second, honey."

Her heart pounded against her ribs, fear spreading through her with every pulse, the uncertainty of what Brandon might do to her stabbing at her chest. But this was too far. They violated her safe place, and she could have lost her best friend forever, left to die out in the cold, alone.

"Kathryn, I'm coming home. I'll catch the next flight. I should be there by dinner time. I'll see you soon, sweetie. I will take care of this, okay?"

"Don't tell Brandon you're coming."

"I won't. I love you, and I'll see you soon."

"Love you too."

Kathryn lured Mittens out from under the small table and took her into her arms. "Come on, baby girl. No way we're staying here."

The cacophony of abused instruments finally began to wane, but Kathryn was far from being able to sleep, the memories of those parasites seeping into her blood, evoking a level of vexation that shook her to her core. The danger Brandon put her in didn't stop at his own hands; he brought these thugs into their house, into her life, forcing her into situations she should not have been placed in. Whether she went downstairs, hid in her room, or left, she could not escape. In her own home, she never felt completely safe, never felt fully comfortable, never knew what new tribulation would find her next.

Only amid their mother's rage did Brandon admit it had actually been one of his close friends who had trashed her room in a drunken outburst—someone who had once told Kathryn she was like a little sister to him. Despite her mom's anger, discipline for Brandon, and assurance it would never happen again, the damage was already done, and there was no way to completely eradicate the black seed that drifted over and latched itself onto the darkness brewing beneath her pale skin forever invisibly stained with far too many tears of betrayal and violation.

Veiled

The next ten days blended into one another, cello and her mom taking up most of Kathryn's time—hours, minutes, seconds ticking by at an unbearable pace as if in slow motion. She talked on the phone with Grace a few times, hearing all about her budding relationship with Craig, and she called Zac once, a disappointing air of awkwardness in their superficial conversation. Kathryn was in touch with Lexie often, and they spent a day together, shopping and going to see a movie, and although she had fun, upon returning home, she retreated to her room, shutting herself off from the world for as long as she could. In her solitude came simultaneous contentment and loneliness.

At night, she lay awake, her eyes following the pattern of stars on her ceiling until they began to lose their glow, their essence, and she watched them gradually die into nothing before sleep would finally claim her. The mornings brought new waves of numbness that swept over her, subtly increasing with each passing day, expunging any trace of a smile until she reluctantly forced herself out of bed and found her way to her cello—one of the final things in which she found even a trace of joy. The darkness was taking her.

The day before the new school year started, Kathryn laid out what she planned to wear the next morning. With as much enthusiasm as she could muster, she settled on the outfit her dad had bought her over the summer.

She turned her music down when she heard a knock on her door.

"Kathryn, Rachael is on the phone for you."

Sighing, she picked up the phone.

193

"Hey, Kathryn!"

"Hey, Rach."

"I haven't talked to you in like forever. So, you're back home?"

"Yeah, for just over a month now."

"How's it going?"

Kathryn paused. "Um...it's fine. I try to mainly avoid Brandon when I can. His stupid friends still come over, but I stay upstairs."

"And everything with your mom?"

"It's much better."

"Oh, good. That's awesome."

Silence.

"Kathryn, are you okay? You're really quiet."

"I'm just tired."

"Ugh. Me too. We started school here last week. I'm so not a morning person."

Silence.

"So, um...have you talked to Val at all lately?"

"Not since the last day of school. Why?"

"Well, I was just talking to her, and she was saying she misses you."

The numbness started to give way as anger developed in Kathryn's words. "She misses me? No. She misses being able to come over here and hang out with Brandon's friends. That's what she misses."

"Oh, come on. She was your friend."

"She wasn't a friend to me. She treated me like garbage, Rachael. I'm no good to her anyway since I refuse to have anything to do with Brandon and his damn friends. If she knew that, she wouldn't miss me."

"That's not the only reason she was your friend. We had a lot of fun together. Remember when we all climbed out on your roof and watched the fireworks? And all the sleepovers we had together?"

"Yeah. At my house when Brandon had all his friends over. Practically every Friday, she just had to be over here because she knew they would be here. You really think she would have come over so much if they weren't here? The only time we went to her house was when she knew they weren't coming over. She never wanted to just hang out with me. She *always* had to be with them. They used her, they took advantage of her, you know they did, and she still kept going back."

"I still think—"

"Stop, Rachael. Seriously."

"Can't you just give her a call? She said she wants to talk to you."

"I don't want to talk to her! Look, if you still want to be friends with her, whatever. But I don't want to talk to her or see her. She tried to drag me down with her every chance she got, and I'm not going to let anyone treat me like shit anymore!"

"Okay. Okay. I got it."

Silence.

"Are we still friends?" Rachael asked.

"I always want to be your friend, but you need to stop trying to get Val and me to be friends again. Please. I just can't have anything to do with her."

"Okay. I won't. I promise. I'm sorry I upset you. I…guess I'll talk to you later. I really am glad you're home and doing better."

"Thanks. We'll talk again soon, okay?"

"Okay. Bye."

"Bye." Kathryn clicked off the phone and threw it onto her bed.

She paced around her room, fuming, wondering how Rachael could still want to be friends with Val and, most of all, how it could have taken Kathryn so long to finally break free of Val.

"Come on, Kathryn. Everyone's starting to meet over at the garage. The kegs are here, so let's go!"

"Yessss. Let's go!" Kathryn followed closely at Val's heels.

Breaking free of the old farmhouse, the young teenagers hurried across the yard. The chickens stirred in their coop as Val called to them on her way by. She shrieked at the huge turkey behind the fence, and it waddled into the barn.

The massive garage that housed their awesome parties was in running distance, and Val tore off toward the large group of people already gathered at the opening. Kathryn broke into a jog to catch up. Reaching the crowd, she followed Val, weaving around a wide range of people from adults to other fourteen-year-olds. They entered the garage practically big enough to fit her house, the music booming off the structure and echoing through the large pieces of equipment randomly scattered about, rust nearly flaking off the walls with the vibration of the bass. Broken-down cars and a tarnished tractor served as tables to hold everyone's plastic cups of beer fresh from the keg.

"Hey, Mom," Val said, running up to a thin brunette.

She blew smoke carelessly at her daughter. "Hey, girls. Go help yourself to some beer."

"You don't have to tell us twice," Kathryn said, laughing as she followed Val to the keg. She nodded to some of the regulars and grabbed a cup, filling it to the top, thick foam flooding over the edge.

"Cheers!" Val sang and clinked her cup into Kathryn's, spilling more foam to the rocky soil at their feet.

Kathryn smiled and raised her cup to her mouth as the stale smell flooded her tightly sealed upper lip. She brought it back down while Val continued to chug the whole cup.

"Geez, Val. Pace yourself."

"Why would I do that?" she asked, laughing and spilling some down her front. "Damn. Good beer, isn't it?"

"Oh...yeah. This is good. Mmm... I'll be drinking a lot of this tonight."

"It's gonna be a great night for sure. Not so great of a morning though!"

"Ha! Got that right!" Kathryn shouted with a hoarse laugh.

"Remember when that girl at your house got you drunk? You said you'd never drink again. I knew you didn't mean it. Drinking is just way too fun to resist."

The sickening sting of that terrifying night flashed through her mind, and Kathryn stared at Val for a moment before smiling and releasing an exaggerated laugh. "Ha! Yeah. What was I thinking? This is waaay too much fun. I was stupid. Yeah. How dumb am I?"

"Right? Let's get some more!"

"You go. I'll be right there."

"Okay. Woo!" Val screamed, throwing her hands in the air, exposing her flat belly as she returned to the keg.

Kathryn looked over her shoulder and slid back a few feet behind one of the many pieces of farming equipment. She scanned the garage for any prying eyes. When she was fairly certain she wouldn't be spotted, she slowly tipped her full cup forward, spilling the nasty drink to the ground while still keeping an eye on the crowd.

When most of it was dumped out, she merged back into the gathering, filled her cup again, and joined Val sitting on ripped lawn furniture surrounding a makeshift fire pit just outside the garage on the pebbled driveway.

Val leaned over and rested her head on Kathryn's shoulder, peeking into her cup.

"Hey! You got more!" she screamed in her ear.

Kathryn kept her eyes from widening at the stench of Val's stale, smoky breath as it poured out of her obnoxious mouth.

She sat around, watching more than talking, not having much to say to these people. However, they did provide a certain level of sad, pathetic entertainment as they continued to pour the alcohol into their bodies as if it were water on a sweltering day. As the night went on, Kathryn observed their eyes drooping, their speech slurring, and their balance going straight to hell.

Kathryn's upper lip reeked of beer, as did the ground right next to her chair.

"Hey!" Val shouted in Kathryn's face. "You cup's nempty! To the keg!"

Kathryn stood and stumbled toward the garage, making her ankle go to the side just enough and threw her arms out to catch herself on Val's shoulders.

"Ha! Kathryn's wasted!" shouted one of the regulars.

"Oh, you know it! Woo!" Kathryn yelled back, raising her cup. Her eyes rolled back into her head as she turned away from the crowd. She kept her arm around Val's shoulders to keep her friend steady, but she was careful not to walk too straight either, approaching the garage and a small huddle of men leaning against an old pickup.

"Take it easy there, girl. You're looking pretty hammered," said Val's dad to Kathryn.

"This will be my last. I want to at least be able to get up to bed tonight, right?" She laughed, forcing it to a higher pitch that hurt her own ears.

It was hours before Val decided she wanted to go up to bed. The young girls walked over to the house, stumbling and bumping into each other, all the while laughing hysterically.

"Great night, wasn't it, Kaffafferyn?"

Kathryn cracked up again. "What did you call me?"

"I don't even know. I'm so wasted."

"I can tell."

Kathryn shifted, her arm weakening under Val's weight. Helping her up the stairs to the bedroom, she let her collapse on the bed, swinging her legs up and covering her with the blanket.

Arms raised, she bent, stretching her back. After spreading some blankets on the floor, she got out her book and propped herself up against the wall with her pillow.

She lit a cigarette, placed it in the ashtray on the floor next to her, and pushed it away as it burned down while she read. When it was gone, she spread the ashes around, smushed the butt a little with her fingers, and placed it back in the tray. It only took one chapter of her book for the night to catch up with her, and she lay down, folding the pillow over her head in an attempt to drown out Val's snores.

Kathryn shook her head, a sick feeling churning within her. Even though her memories were somewhat recent, it felt like a different life.

She headed downstairs for something to eat, passing Jane sitting in her usual spot on the couch, hidden behind a newspaper.

197

"Hey, Mom."

"Hi, sweetie." She brought the paper down from her face. "Wait. How's Rachael doing?"

"She's fine. Already started school."

"You guys okay?"

"She was on my case about talking to Val. But I don't want to talk to her. And how can Rachael still even want to be friends with her after she's been such a horrible friend to me? She's only going to do the same to her."

Jane patted the spot on the couch next to her and folded her paper, placing it on the armrest. "Val hasn't hurt Rachael the way she's hurt you. I'm sure Rachael is upset for you, but that doesn't automatically mean she's going to just stop being her friend. That's not really fair of you to ask of her, either. You don't have to be friends with Val, but don't let your relationship with Rachael be hurt by the fact that she still wants to see Val for the two months a year she comes up from Florida to visit."

"Yeah. I guess so. I still don't get it, but I really don't want to lose Rachael."

"That's very mature of you."

She shrugged.

"You know, you told me that I had been right to worry about her, that she was a bad influence on you, that she tried to get you to do things. I didn't want to press it at the time, but...would you share with me what those things were?"

Kathryn hesitated. "I...um...I used to kind of smoke with her. I mean, I didn't do it a lot, and most of the time, I just let it burn down, but... I'm sorry."

Her mom sighed. "I thought you might try it. It's hard to be around someone who is doing those things and not do them yourself, which is why she worried me. I was afraid you would feel pressured into doing those kinds of things with her."

"I never did anything really bad. I promise. I did try beer, but I hated it. It's disgusting. When we would hang out at her house, though, everyone was drinking, and I felt like I had to fit in, so I would take really small sips sometimes. But mostly, I would pretend to drink and then act drunk. I know how ridiculous that sounds."

"Better than actually doing it."

"But I wish I didn't even try to fit in with them. It's like I saw myself doing it and knew I shouldn't, but I still did it, and I don't even know why. I never even liked it."

"I think we've all been there at some point. Peer pressure is real, and it's hard. It may sound cliché or like an after-school special, but it's real life."

"I'm just so upset with myself for even doing it."

"But you stopped, and nothing really bad happened, right?"

"Yeah."

"Then it's a lesson learned. Quite a hefty lesson to learn at fifteen, but I guess you've had to learn a lot of lessons at a young age."

"I don't want that life—Val's life, Brandon's life. I don't want it."

Jane took her daughter's hand. "I'm proud of you, Kathryn."

"Proud? How can you be proud of me after what I've done?"

"Because you learned such a valuable lesson from it—something that it takes some people years and years to learn, and some people never do. You may not really know exactly what you want to be yet, and that's okay. You're only fifteen. But you know what you don't want to be, and that can be just as valuable."

"I guess so." She looked down at her fidgeting hands. "But why though? Why was I able to do it?"

Jane placed her hand under her daughter's chin, lifting it to catch her eyes. "You're a strong young woman. I like to think I had something to do with that, but you still deserve the credit for standing up for yourself and not settling for less. I also think your childhood has a lot to do with it. You've seen what drinking and that kind of lifestyle can do. You've seen the way it has hurt your father and our family."

"I don't understand why people drink. It tastes so gross and makes people act stupid."

"Well, there are some people who can have a drink responsibly, and it's just their way of winding down. That's not the case for the people you've been around. People who drink to get drunk like the ones you've seen are usually trying to escape something, to forget their problems. A child from an alcoholic family can fall into the trap, using it as a way to escape their problems, or they can avoid it, seeing it as the root of theirs."

"So...book...or counseling?"

Jane nodded. "Both. It's hard to go through what we've been through and not try to understand it on a deeper level. That's why I mentioned counseling before. I know you don't necessarily see all the ways your childhood has affected you, but it's there even if you don't. And obviously everything that happened with Brandon is certainly taking a toll." She paused. "I see you disappearing again, Kathryn. You did it when you were a little girl, a little lost child. I feel like I was able to help you, along with your counselor at the time, but I think I see it happening again. It's worrying me."

199

"I'm fine, Mom."

She tucked Kathryn's hair behind her ear. "Just keep it in mind. It's always available."

"Okay. I will."

Jane returned to her paper, and Kathryn grabbed a small bowl of pretzels before she started back up the stairs, something her mom said resounding through her mind. A nagging feeling pulled at her chest, words that felt hauntingly precise spreading a cold rush through her veins—a lost child.

What Becomes

Kathryn stepped into the shower after a restless evening of night-before-school nerves and more fiery nightmares. The thought of seeing Lexie...and Liam...lifted her spirits enough that she felt somewhat excited for the first day of school. As the darkness threatened to extinguish her spark of happiness, she forced thoughts of Lexie's laugh and Liam's smile into her mind, pushing it deeper within.

She slipped into her new outfit and did her hair and makeup, remembering some tips she learned from Grace.

"I'm heading out, Kathryn. Have a wonderful first day of school."

"You too," Kathryn said, embracing her mom.

She ran her fingertips through the front of her daughter's hair with a gentle twirl. "You look lovely. I love you."

"Love you too."

After a quick breakfast and reapplying her lip gloss, Kathryn walked into the warm September morning to face her first day as a sophomore in high school. The difference between the final day of school last year and this day struck her suddenly as she looked down the street and saw Jake waiting at the end of his driveway. It didn't feel as though it could have possibly been two and a half short months ago that she stood with him and Sam on their last day.

She saw the bus in the distance, and her heart rate quickened. After it pulled away from Jake's, it stopped for her, and she crossed the street and climbed in. Risking a glance toward the back, she spotted Val's dark eyes peeking from behind the high seats. Without a flicker of emotion, she looked away and to Jake, smiling as she sat down next to him.

"Yay! You're in high school!" she said, hugging his arm.

He laughed. "Right? I'm so excited. Crazy nervous but excited."

"Once you know where all your classes are, you'll be fine. And we have lunch together fifth period. Oh, and so does Lexie!"

"O-oh...she does? Awesome."

"You don't have to play it cool with me, Jake. I know. She's an awesome girl."

"Is it that obvious?"

"Maybe only to me. Just talk to her. Show her what an amazing guy you are."

As the bus slowed to a stop again, Kathryn noticed a familiar girl get on; her brown hair whipped from side to side as she searched for an open seat, her deep blue eyes tight with unmistakable anxiety.

"You can sit with us if you'd like," Kathryn called to her.

The girl's breath washed out past her smile as it crept across her face, the freckles delicately scattered on her cheeks rising. "Thank you so much."

"No problem. I think I've seen you before, right?"

"Yeah. You usually sat in the back though. I'm Melanie."

"I'm Kathryn, and this is my cousin Jake."

"Hey," Jake said with a goofy wave.

Kathryn held back a laugh. "You're in tenth grade, right?"

"Yup."

"Me too. What's your schedule like?"

The girls got their schedules out to compare.

"Cool," Kathryn said, pointing to Melanie's. "We have lunch and math together."

"Awesome! My friends Kristin and Joselyn have lunch fifth period too. I'll introduce you. Oooh, I love your Claddagh ring. It's gorgeous. I have one too." She held out her right hand, displaying the gold ring very similar to Kathryn's. "Are you Irish?"

"There's Irish on my dad's side, but really I just think it's a pretty ring."

"Do you know what it all symbolizes?"

Kathryn shook her head, smiling at how Melanie was so quickly breaking from her original shyness, her voice gaining speed and volume, her features brightening.

"The crown is loyalty, the heart is love, and the hands are friendship. And if you wear it the way we are with the crown facing you, that means you're

202

single. If you flip it around and wear it with the heart toward you, that means you're taken."

"I didn't know any of that," Kathryn said with a laugh. "That's really cool though."

Jake looked up from Melanie's schedule. "You're in band too?"

"Yeah. I play the flute. You?"

"Percussion."

"Very cool. I guess I'll be seeing you every morning in band and then in lunch. And you're in orchestra, Kathryn? What do you play?"

"Cello."

"Nice. I also love to sing."

"Me too!"

"Really? How fun!"

When they arrived at school, Jake split from Kathryn and Melanie at the top of the stairs, taking a right into the familiar red locker-lined hallway. Going straight, the girls searched unclaimed blue lockers to nab for themselves. Kathryn's search was over when she spotted Lexie at her new locker, loading her backpack.

"Kathryn!" she shrieked and ran toward her, hands flailing. "Sophomore year. Let's do this! I saved you a locker right next to mine."

As well as her morning went, Lexie had a unique way of brightening her day, and she started to feel more like herself as she looked into those fluttering emerald eyes.

"Have you seen Liam yet?" Lexie asked, shaking Kathryn's arm.

"No. Not yet."

"I have, and he's even cuter than he was a couple months ago."

Kathryn laughed, trying to rein in her giddy glee at the thought of him, but her heart rate soared, and her stomach danced knowing she'd see him again. She had played their first encounter over and over again in her mind—what she might say to him, how she'd try not to look like a nerd and embarrass herself, what her response would be if he asked what she did over the summer.

"Lexie, do you know Melanie?"

"Yeah. We've had some classes together."

"Awesome. She has lunch fifth period too. I was thinking she could sit with us," Kathryn said.

"Of course. Oh! The locker right next to Kathryn's is still open if you want it."

"Really?" Melanie sighed. "Perfect!"

Lexie slung her bag onto her shoulder. "You two better just throw your stuff in though because first period is in like five minutes."

"I have band right across the hall, so I'll walk with you."

"I'm totally trying out for cheerleading this year," Lexie said. "Tryouts are in just a few weeks. You should try out with me, Kathryn!"

She lightly shook her head. "Not really my thing, Lex. But yeah, you totally should. With your dance background and your overflowing pep, you'll make an awesome cheerleader."

"Thanks! I'm so excited. Plus, I get to watch all the hot football players."

The three girls laughed as they entered the music wing. Melanie waved and turned right into the band room while Lexie and Kathryn went left. A rush of energy flooded over Kathryn, feeling revitalized just by being back in the orchestra room.

"Never fear, Mr. Darrow! We have arrived!" Lexie said, her hands in the air.

"Oh, yay. I am so excited," Mr. Darrow said robotically.

Lexie nudged his arm with her elbow. "Aw. You know you love us."

"Yes. Love. That's what I'm feeling right now." His freckled face held stern. "Now go get your instruments and tune up!" he yelled as a smile cracked along his tight lips.

The girls giggled and scurried off dramatically to get their instruments.

Everyone was starting to fill in as Kathryn grabbed a seat next to Cari, her stand partner from last year, and Lexie waved from the back of the second violin section.

Mr. Darrow flicked his stand with the baton and cleared his throat. "Okay, everyone. Welcome back. Here's your A." Despite the gravelly tone, it was a perfect A as usual, and the orchestra tuned to it, a mashup of strings that hadn't been tuned properly in quite a while. "Goodness. Did no one tune and play the entire summer?"

"I practiced every single day, Mr. D!" Lexie shouted, waving her bow in the air as her pink highlighter rolled off her lap and clinked against the floor.

"If you practiced every day, then Kathryn didn't practice at all."

The excellent acoustics of the orchestra room amplified the students' laughter as all eyes snapped toward Kathryn.

She blushed. "It wasn't *every* day."

Mr. Darrow chuckled. "All right, guys. Keep tuning before we run out of time." He reached his long arm out to the first student of many needing help tuning their instruments.

Kathryn and Cari helped the other cellists tune up quickly.

"Well, that was painful, and I'm glad it's over. So, let's get to what most of you probably forgot how to do—play your instruments. There's some new music on your stands. Let's give it a try. Put some of those sight-reading skills to work. F major, three-four time."

He silently counted two measures with the beat of his hands, and the students started together on the downbeat, following him closely. Once they reached the end of the piece, he held his hands up, leaving them suspended, waiting for someone to drop their bow prematurely.

Mr. Darrow released his hands. "So you *do* retain what I say. Impressive." A smile broke through his flat expression. "Seriously, great job, everyone. I wasn't expecting to get through that so easily. Now what? We've still got twenty-five minutes." He sifted through the sheet music on his stand. "All right. I suppose we can go on to another piece. Let's try the Brahms." His wide smile and amber eyes shone brightly upon his class. As he raised his baton into the air, his expression snapped back to his stony mask, and his lips tightened. "Don't make me regret this."

Kathryn left the orchestra room with a full grin gracing her face and a burst of hope for the new school year, images of those she held dear at the forefront of her mind as her eyes danced around, hoping to see Liam. Yet something still lurked close by, waiting…waiting…

She walked the halls to her next class, a light bounce in her step, unburdened of fear, unencumbered by those trying to drag her down, to break her. Yet still it seeped through the halls, gliding silkily above the speckled tiles, undeterred by shuffling feet, oozing under the classroom doors, spiraling in the calmness, and wrapping her in its ebony mist.

The girls grabbed their lunches from their lockers and headed for the cafeteria. Once again, disappointment sank in Kathryn's chest, wondering if she would cross paths with Liam at all. As she attempted to shake it off, she noticed an unfamiliar sadness falling across Lexie's features.

"Is everything okay, Lex?"

"Um…yes and no. We got Anne's evaluation results back a few days ago. I'm sorry I didn't tell you sooner. I was…processing it all, I guess."

Kathryn halted and turned to her friend. "Does that mean it's bad news?"

"Not exactly. We found out that she actually has something called Asperger's syndrome. It's like a mild form of autism."

"I've heard of autism, but I don't know that much about it."

"It's mainly a social disorder, and certain things are harder for her. Honestly, it all makes sense. It explains some of her differences and her struggles. It's actually a bit of a relief for my parents to know what's going on so we can move forward. It's still overwhelming, but they're working to get her the extra help she needs."

"She's lucky to have such wonderful support."

"Thanks, Kath. Anne is such an amazing girl. We just have to figure all this out. It's just a lot. She needs...a lot more of my parents' attention. A sibling who demands attention... You can certainly relate to that."

Kathryn offered a gentle smile. "Yup."

"And I know it's not her fault, but...it's still hard."

"Of course it is."

Lexie brushed a tear aside. "I just want her to be okay."

Kathryn leaned in and embraced her. "She has the best big sister to help her and guide her."

Eighth period arrived with no sign of Liam.

"There's only one class left," Kathryn said, leaving history with Lexie.

"There's still time. Maybe you'll still get to see him."

Kathryn gasped. "Oh my God."

His tall, olive-skinned form was walking toward them, his ebony hair gelled to perfection, his chocolate eyes as soft as she remembered them. Liam's lips parted into a smile as he adjusted the black strap of his backpack on his defined shoulder. The blond boy at his side made Liam laugh, and his dark head tipped forward.

Kathryn's heart sped at the sight, longing for that smile to shine upon her, for him to hold her in his kind gaze again. As he came closer, she slipped her hair behind her ear. Closer and she smiled. Within a few feet, she looked up at him and into those eyes. He saw her.

"Hey, Liam."

He averted his gaze and walked past her without a single word.

Kathryn's breath caught, and her hand flittered to the invisible force compressing her abdomen.

"What was that about?" Lexie asked, her brow furrowed. "He looked right at you."

"I...I don't know. That was strange, right? He saw me and just...kept walking."

"Maybe we didn't see it right and he didn't actually see you," she said, her voice laced with uncertainty.

"I swear he saw me, but...it's like he...looked right through me."

"I'm sorry that didn't go as you had hoped. Don't worry about it too much. There's probably a good explanation."

"I guess."

"What's your last class?"

"Math."

"Blah. Then I'll see you at the lockers, and we'll walk to the bus together."

Kathryn nodded.

"Try not to let it get to you. I'm sure everything's fine."

She offered a weak smile before taking the hall to the right toward the math wing.

Upon entering, Melanie waved her over, and she took the empty seat next to her.

"Hey, Melanie. How's it going?"

"Pretty good. I have a friend in all but one of my classes, so that's a relief. You?"

"Eh, pretty good, I guess." Liam's eyes darting away from hers as his face lay stoic flashed across her mind.

"I've heard this math teacher is tough," Melanie said, taking out her red binder.

"I heard that too. Math is not my thing. Let's hope this doesn't suck."

For as much as Kathryn detested math, the period went by relatively quickly, and the end bell startled her. The class stood and began packing up and heading out into the busy hallway.

Kathryn grimaced. "I can't believe we already have homework."

Melanie's blue eyes rolled, and she scoffed loudly. "Seriously. Yuck." Melanie veered off to her locker. "Kathryn?"

"I'll be there in a sec."

Kathryn passed her locker, continuing on as if being pulled by an invisible string. Liam leaned against the lockers, talking to his friend, the one Kathryn recognized as Josh, the blond jock who pulled him away from her on the last day of school. She flipped her hair off her shoulder and took a deep breath as she drew closer to him.

Trying to keep her composure amid the closeness of his beauty, she smiled and found her voice. "Hi, Liam."

He looked at her, his usual kindness disappearing within the grooves of his furrowed brow, his brown eyes cold and narrowed, absent of any warmth they typically cast upon her, that smile replaced with a slight curl of his lips. "Um…hi?"

His friend slammed his locker door, and the two boys started off, Kathryn swinging around to watch at their backs.

"Who was that?" Josh asked.

Liam shrugged. "I'm not even sure. Some girl from one of my classes maybe."

Kathryn stood frozen as Liam looked back at her over his shoulder, just a hint of the quality she had come to know in his eyes, and then he faced forward once more, walking off down the hall with his friend.

"What the *hell* was that?" Lexie asked, practically yelling as she stepped up beside Kathryn.

"I have no idea. He acted like he didn't even know me. Like any of the time we spent together just never happened."

"What an asshole!"

"I don't get it, Lex."

"I'm so sorry. He's such a jerk. He doesn't even deserve you."

Kathryn spread a solitary tear across her cheek. "If he doesn't like me like I like him, fine. But I thought at the very least we were friends."

"I always thought so." Lexie put her arm around her friend. "Come on. We have to get out to the bus."

"So, Jake, how was your first day of high school?" Melanie asked.

"It was amazing! My best friend, Jake, is in almost all my classes with me. This year is going to be awesome."

"Your best friend's name is Jake?"

He chuckled. "Yup."

"That's so funny," she said, laughing.

Kathryn sat quietly next to Melanie, the scene with Liam playing over and over again in her mind as the two talked and laughed loudly at her side, Melanie's melodic voice singing in response to Jake's.

"You okay, Kathryn?" she heard Jake ask.

"What? Oh, yeah. Everything's fine."

"Well, I know you better than that, and you're lying. Is everything okay at home?"

"Sorry. Yeah, home's fine. I promise," she added when she met the worried tilt of his eyes. "Today just didn't quite go the way I had expected."

She threw herself on her bed, tears flowing down her cheeks. Mittens moaned as she jumped up next to her, nuzzling into Kathryn's hand.

"What did I do, baby girl? He's always been so nice to me—talking with me, joking with me. Last time I talked to him, he was the one who approached me. Now he acts like he doesn't even know who I am? I don't understand what changed."

Kathryn shuffled along with the current in the heavily packed high school hallway as students traipsed to their lockers, the tiles wet with slush carried in on snowy sneakers and boots.

Last night's fight replayed through her fatigued mind—screaming, his hand ripping at her hair, the unforgiving wall as her shoulder crashed against it. She flinched as she felt a tug on her hair and snapped her head to the right to see white bandaging stark against tan skin. Looking over her shoulder, she saw his wrapped hand fall and met his chocolate eyes, her heart palpitating.

Liam took a quick step, coming up to her side. "Hey, you."

Her attempt to control her smile was worthless as he brushed aside a stray piece of his shadow-colored bangs speckled with melting snowflakes. "Hey. What happened to your hand?"

"I...uh...fell on the ice and fractured it."

Her eyes widened. "Seriously? Geez. I'm so sorry."

"Yeah, my little sister tripped me, and I slipped. I caught myself, but my wrist paid the price."

"Your sister tripped you? On purpose?"

He shook his dark head. "No, of course not. We were just messing around and didn't realize our driveway was so icy."

"Ouch. Looks like it hurts."

He shrugged. "It's not too bad now. And the doctor said it should heal by baseball season. I shouldn't have any lasting effects. The worst part is having to admit how it happened. Like I couldn't even hurt myself in a cool way like taking a pitch or something."

Kathryn couldn't help but chuckle.

"Oh, thanks." He threw his arms up. "She's laughing at me now. See, and I thought we were friends," he said, playfully shoving her with his good hand.

She only giggled harder. "I'm sorry. The visual is just...well, kind of hilarious."

He barked a laugh. "It probably did look pretty funny. My sister and dad laughed at me too. At least my mom cares." He feigned a sniffle. "How about we keep the fall between us? Then I can tell my buddies I did it snowboarding or playing hockey." He brushed his arm against her shoulder as he looked down at her, his eyes crinkled in the corners.

A flutter in her stomach spread through her limbs. "It'll be our secret."

Mittens snuggled beside her best friend as she sobbed, each tear eroding away at the joy that kept the darkness from finally claiming her.

The Lost Child

The school days flowed into one another, and soon the trees were peppered with evidence of the ever-changing seasons, the crisp November air bringing the familiar scents of autumn.

Kathryn struggled to open her eyes against the heaviness of the invisible force as her mom's voice attempted to pull her awake.

"Up and at 'em. Better get in the shower or you'll miss your bus. You need to make it a quick one. I don't want you to have to call Grandpa to drive you in again. Come on. Up, up, up."

She rolled over, facing the wall, drawing her blankets to her chin and nodding off again.

"Kathryn, honey, it's time to get up. You're going to be late."

"I don't feel good," she said, whining.

"You've already missed too much school lately. You just can't miss another day. If you don't have a fever, you have to go."

Kathryn groaned and forced herself out of bed. She slipped into her jeans atop a pile on the pink carpet and grabbed a shirt from her closet.

"You're not taking a shower?"

"Whatever. I took one yesterday. I'll just throw my hair back."

Her mom's vision hung on her a moment. "Well, okay. It was going to be cutting it close anyway. Better pack up and grab something to eat."

"I'm not hungry."

Jane sighed, dropping one hip. "Kathryn, you need to tell me what's going on with you."

"Like I've told you over and over again, Mom, I'm fine, okay?"

"No. It's not okay. You're not fine. This is not you. It's been weeks and weeks of this, honey. I'm worried."

"Don't be," Kathryn responded, any indication of emotion stripped from her words.

"I have to get to work, but this isn't over. We're going to talk more when I get home tonight."

"Whatever."

Jane gave her daughter a kiss on the forehead and scrambled down the stairs.

Once again alone, Kathryn applied some makeup and pulled her hair into a ponytail. She stared at her reflection. Just stared. With a prolonged blink, she turned from the mirror and grabbed her bag before heading outside.

The teenagers sat in silence on the bus, Kathryn mindlessly staring out the window and Jake playing air drums on his lap.

With the final drum roll, Jake nudged Kathryn's arm, and she ripped her attention away from the scene outside.

"So...um, do you know if Melanie is going to be on the bus today?" he asked.

"As far as I know. She didn't say anything when I talked to her on the phone last night."

"Oh, you talked to her last night?"

"Like most nights."

"Oh. So, um...has she ever said anything about me?"

"Like what?"

"I don't know. Just anything about me."

"Not really."

His eyes fell to his lap. "Oh, okay. I was just wondering."

"I mean, I know she likes talking with you if that's what you mean."

His head shot up, his blue eyes wide. "Really?"

"Of course." Kathryn tilted her head, realization sweeping over her. "Wait. Do you like her?"

"Shh... She's getting on," he whispered, frantically waving his hands.

"Hey, guys," Melanie sang as she sat next to Jake.

"Hi, Mel," he responded, his voice doing that high thing reminiscent of when he used to talk to Lexie.

As the two chatted, Kathryn's focus returned once again out the window, but she kept a listening ear on her friends, unnerved by how she could have possibly missed Jake's feelings for Melanie.

Kathryn weaved through the students already in their seats spaced throughout the orchestra room and quickly grabbed her cello and took her seat in the fourth chair she had earned at auditions a few weeks prior. She avoided Mr. Darrow's eyes, not in the mood to meet his disapproving glare again.

"Are you in tune, Kathryn?" he asked.

"Yeah. It's fine."

"Then let's get started. From the top of the program. We only have two weeks, people, and it's just not where I know it can be."

They began to play, but when they came to the rare shining moment for the cello section, he waved his hands, signaling them all to stop.

"Cellos, try it by yourself. From the first measure of your solo."

The cello section started out in unison, but someone fell behind, the notes mashing in disharmony.

"I'm sorry," Kathryn said, her eyes holding the sheet music and evading stares. "I don't know why I can't get this. I'll get it down. I promise. I'll practice it more at home tonight."

"All right. From the last repeat, everyone."

Although she didn't quite get it, she held on enough to push through, and Mr. Darrow continued with the piece.

The rest of her day followed the same trajectory—focusing next to impossible, passing on questions in science, tripping over her words, missing every foul shot in gym.

After getting changed, she left the locker room and found herself heading away from the cafeteria and toward the orchestra room without much conscious thought.

"Kathryn?"

Her eyes snapped up, meeting Melanie's.

"Aren't you going to lunch?"

"I'm going to the orchestra room to practice, so I won't be in lunch today. I keep messing up this part. Mr. Darrow said he'd help me. I'll see you later." Kathryn continued on without waiting for a response.

"Okay," Melanie said behind her.

She shoved her shoulder against the door to the orchestra room, pushing it with strained strength, and ambled into the emptiness, creeping toward the back room.

"Back so soon?"

She gasped. "Oh, hey, Mr. D."

"Kathryn," he said, nodding.

"Just heading into the file room for lunch if that's okay."

He hesitated, his eyes focusing on hers. "Sure. You know the drill though. Turn the light off when you're done."

"Okay."

Kathryn stepped back into the small room, her safe haven from almost six months ago, a similar yet different sensation overwhelming her as she breathed in the familiar scent of old sheet music in which she used to find the solace she had hoped she'd never need again.

She pulled down her usual chair and started on her lunch. Without even bothering with her book, she sat in complete silence as she ate, her eyes zeroing in on a swirled imperfection on one of the filing cabinets. The stillness, the nothingness calmed her. Closing her eyes, she let it consume her.

When her time was running out, a rush of heat fell over her, dreading having to leave her sanctuary. Knowing she had no choice, she dried her face, put the chair back, flicked off the light, and grudgingly reentered reality.

She exited the orchestra room before the bell had rung, and as a cruel twist of fate, in the empty hallway leading to sixth period English, she came face to face with Liam, his bright orange fleece pullover striking against the white hallway.

As if she didn't have control over her feet, she came to a stop as his dark eyes found and held hers, and he slowed. Kathryn smoothed a stray tear across her flushed cheek, unable to shake the invisible pull toward him, to find comfort in his eyes, to bring that smile to his beautiful face just one more time as he made her forget even if only for a moment. With fire singeing every nerve in her exhausted body, she ripped her gaze from his, and finding her strength to move again, she pushed past him.

For the remainder of the day, she once more played the role of a normal fifteen-year-old, an act she thought she had retired. She forced herself to smile, to interact; she even accomplished a laugh when talking with Jake and Melanie on the afternoon bus ride.

When she finally got home, she went straight up the stairs and into her room, locking the door behind her. She crawled into bed, bringing the covers over her head, taking in the darkness and letting it take her.

"Kathryn?"

Her eyes slowly flickered open, and she pulled the blankets off her face, her hair plastered to her forehead with sweat. She drowsily looked around the room, disoriented by the dim evening sky out her back window.

"Mom?" she asked, her voice harsh.

"Yeah, sweetie, it's me. Can I come in?"

Kathryn stumbled to her feet and unlocked the door.

"Were you asleep?"

"I guess so. I just lay down when I came home, and...I must have dozed off."

Jane took her daughter's hand and led her to the bed, sitting on the edge, facing her. "I'm worried about you. There is something going on with you whether you see it or not. But be honest with yourself. You have to see there's something...amiss."

Kathryn looked down at her entangled fingers in her lap, her eyes beginning to moisten. She looked up at her mom, unshed tears in her blue eyes. "I don't know what's wrong with me." Burying her head into her mom's shoulder, she wept.

"Oh, honey. We'll figure this out together. I promise we will," she said, stroking her daughter's hair. "Can you try to describe how you're feeling?"

Kathryn pulled away, sniffling, drying her cheeks with her sleeve. "It's hard to explain. I'm just...not happy. Things that usually make me happy, they don't. There's this...emptiness. Sometimes I'm sad or angry, but sometimes... there's nothing. I'm just numb. I've barely practiced in weeks, and I keep messing up in orchestra. I mean, I got fourth chair. *Fourth.* I've never gotten fourth. I can't seem to stay focused in my classes. I stay up late just staring at the ceiling and can hardly wake up in the morning. And...I've started hiding away in the orchestra file room again."

"Again?"

She sighed. "I used to go to the file room during lunch at the end of last year so I could be by myself. Pretty much every day."

"I didn't know that."

"I didn't really tell anyone. I was going to try and go to the cafeteria with my friends today, but the thought of being in there with everyone—I felt like I couldn't breathe. I just couldn't do it. So Mr. Darrow let me eat in there again."

Jane squeezed Kathryn's hand. "How long have you been feeling like this?"

"I don't know. It's kind of been building, I guess. At least a few weeks, maybe more. Today just seems to be the worst it's been for some reason."

"I'm obviously not a doctor, but from my own experience, it sounds as though you might be depressed."

"Depressed? But everything is better now. I'm home, Brandon leaves me alone, I'm away from Val, I have Lexie and Melanie and the girls. I don't have any reason to be depressed."

"It's not always that simple, sweetie. It can be very complicated. I'd like to make you an appointment to see my doctor if that's okay. I think she can help us get to the bottom of this. Is that okay with you?"

Kathryn nodded. "If you think she can help me not feel like this anymore." She fell forward, sobbing into her mom's shoulder.

Jane wrapped her arms around her, holding her close, her own tears dripping into Kathryn's hair.

Kathryn drifted in and out of consciousness, never fully asleep but never fully awake. A muffled yelling infiltrated her subconscious as she was falling deeper and ripped her eyes open.

"They won't want to come over here anymore!"

"Well, I'm sorry, Brandon, but some rules have to be set. I know you're struggling right now, but so is Kathryn. Her needs have to be considered here too. Your friends will just have to adjust."

"This is bullshit! Maybe I'll just try to kill myself again! Maybe this time I'll succeed!"

"Brandon, don't talk like that! No. Don't walk away after saying—"

A door slammed.

Kathryn walked downstairs and peeked around the corner into the living room. "Mom?"

Jane looked up from the couch, pulling her face from her hands, sniffling and wiping at her eyes. "Goodness. Did you hear that?"

"It was kind of hard not to."

She patted the couch next to her. "Come here."

Kathryn sat next to her mom, her eyes watering at the sight of her mom crying.

"I'm sorry you had to hear that."

"What's his problem?"

"Drop the tone. We need to cut him a little slack."

Kathryn scoffed.

"Stop. I know you're going through a lot right now, but so is Brandon.

And I know it's hard for you to hear it, but everything that's happened has hurt him too."

"That's not an excuse for what he's done to me."

"I am absolutely not saying it is. I would never say that. But there's an underlying reason to why he has done what he's done."

She rolled her eyes. "That sounds like an excuse to me."

"Honey, please. I'm not making excuses. Please hear me. He's damaged. He's in pain. He's struggling right now with a lot of things. He's having a difficult time in college. He's into something with some of his friends, and he got into another argument with your dad. Plus, he doesn't like his job. He has a lot going on, too."

"He wouldn't really try to kill himself again, would he?"

"That's not the first time he has said that. I…" She shook her head. "No. I don't believe he would. He's angry. He's a very angry person. He always has been. Your dad—"

"Come on, Mom."

"I know you don't like to hear it, but what he did was very hurtful to your brother."

"I know. I was there too."

"But he was older. He saw more. You don't know everything he saw. He…" She closed her eyes and inhaled deeply. "Okay. Let's take a breath here. You've heard all this before. The reasons don't need to be rehashed right now. He's an angry person, and he's struggling right now, so he's lashing out. But I don't think he'd harm himself. I'm going to go talk to him though."

"What was he even yelling about?"

"I told him that his friends can't stay past nine on weekdays and eleven on weekends. He wasn't too happy with me. He said his friends won't want to come over anymore."

"Wouldn't that be a shame."

"To him, it would. But I told him they'd just have to deal. I don't want you put out by his friends being here."

"I'm always put out by them. I just want to be able to come downstairs in my nightgown in my own house without worrying there's some guy asleep on the couch. Is that really so much to ask?"

"No, it's not. I can't guarantee there won't ever be someone sleeping on the couch, but I'll talk to him about that."

"I hate them, and I don't want them here…ever."

"I know that, but they are his friends, and unless I knew there was something going on that made me decide otherwise, they're allowed here, but now there are some rules attached to make it a bit easier on you. I'm not crazy about their loud music either, but I'm letting him express himself."

Kathryn exhaled harshly. "Does he have to express himself with such crappy music?"

Jane tilted her head to the side with a short bob. "He likes it, so yes."

"If you really don't want me to feel put out by them, let me start locking the doors at night."

She nodded. "Go ahead and lock the doors at night. He shouldn't have friends coming in at all hours anyway."

Finally feeling heard, Kathryn sighed, a rush of relief pulling her lips into a smile. "Thank you, Mom."

"You're welcome." She tapped Kathryn under her chin. "I'm going to go check on Brandon."

"Okay. Goodnight."

"Goodnight, sweetie. I love you."

"Love you too."

Kathryn lay in her bed, once again observing the pattern of stars written on her ceiling. Thinking about what Brandon said, that night flooded her mind.

"I'm at the hospital with Brandon."

"Why? What happened?" Kathryn asked, her fist clenching around the phone.

"He...he tried to kill himself."

"W-what? I... How...?"

"He swallowed too many pills at school. I'm sorry. That's all I know right now. He's going to be okay though. I have to leave him at the psychiatric ward tonight, but I'm staying with him until they can take him. Because he's only sixteen, I'm required to give my consent for treatment, so there's a lot to handle, and I don't know when I'll be home. I want you to pack a bag and go over to Aunt Hannah and Uncle Alex's."

"Um...okay."

"Yes, I'm right here. Kathryn, I have to go. The doctor is here."

"Okay."

The phone clicked off. Kathryn stood in the middle of the living room, the phone still up to her head, beeping in her ear.

Approaching the Shadowed

"How long would you say you've been feeling like this, Kathryn?"

"Um...at least a few weeks. It wasn't really bad at first though. It was just a little bit, and then it got worse kind of quickly."

Jane's hand rested on her daughter's and offered a supportive squeeze.

Dr. Halloran jotted on her pad of paper. "I see. So you said interrupted sleep patterns, trouble focusing, loss of pleasure in your favorite activities, avoidance of family, friends, and peers. No significant change in weight. Have you had any thoughts of hurting yourself?"

"No," Kathryn answered quickly. "Not at all."

"That's always good to hear," she said with a smile. "How about an overall feeling of worthlessness?"

Kathryn looked at her mom and shrugged. "I'm not sure. I guess I haven't felt great about myself if that's what you mean."

"I mean more like a loss of self, a feeling of insignificance, feeling as if you don't have value, as though you're not good enough."

The question spun in her head. "I...I don't really know. Maybe." The doctor's words continued to swirl around her, spreading through her and pulling at her chest.

Not good enough.

"Do you find yourself pretending to be happy, putting forth a fake smile when you're around others?"

Her words struck Kathryn deep within her soul, constricting her breath.

219

Acceptance gathered in her eyes, releasing down her cheek with a hard blink. "Yes."

Dr. Halloran's pen skated across her notepad again. "Well, Kathryn, considering your symptoms and the duration, it's my professional opinion that you have Major Depression, also called Clinical Depression."

"That's what I was thinking it could be," Jane said. "I've dealt with depression long enough to recognize the signs."

"But why?" Kathryn looked from her mom back to the doctor.

"It can be brought on by any number of things. Sometimes it's caused by grief of a loved one, social isolation, major life changes, personal conflicts, physical, emotional, or sexual abuse. Sometimes there's a chemical imbalance. It can also be genetic. Often, it's a combination of those. There are many causes, and they vary among each person. Are any of those striking a chord with you?"

"Well, I went through something with my brother this summer."

"What happened?" Dr. Halloran asked.

Out of the corner of her eye, she saw her mom shift slightly, and Kathryn opened her mouth to answer.

"Her brother has a pattern of physical abuse toward her," her mom said before she could speak.

"I see. When was the last occurrence?"

"Last June," Kathryn said. "Nothing has really happened since then though."

"Have you been feeling upset about it recently? Feeling down or overly focusing on what happened?"

"No, I really haven't. I mean, it's always there, but I'm trying to move past it."

"She's also been exploring some past issues with her father," Jane said.

"Yeah, but that's all old stuff. We're fine now."

Dr. Halloran leaned back against the counter in the small office, her hands at her side. "Well, it can still be a factor. There hasn't been anything else specific that you can think of that would cause you to feel depressed?"

Kathryn shook her head.

"Well, there are two possibilities that I can see. One is that it could be a hormonal imbalance, which could be related to genetics, seeing as there's a history of it in your family."

Jane nodded. "Besides me, her grandmother has experienced depression too."

"So that could certainly be playing a role. However, considering the situation as well, I would say another likely possibility is that the trauma is, in a way, catching up with you. Sometimes as a way of surviving the pain, we kind of just deal with it in the moment while we're going through it. Often, it isn't until later that we feel the effects from it. I suspect in your case, it's a combination of both possibilities. It's important to try to understand why this is happening, but either way, we treat it the same. If it's okay with you, Kathryn, and you as well, Jane, I'd like to prescribe you antidepressants, and I'm also going to strongly encourage you to receive therapy."

"I think that sounds like a solid plan," Jane said. "Kathryn?"

She nodded.

"Good. Antidepressants can be very effective. Unfortunately, though, there can be some negative side effects. Not every medication works for everyone, and it's possible we'll have to try a few different ones before finding what's right for you. It's important that you talk openly with your mom if you feel the medication isn't helping or especially if you begin feeling worse. That is a possibility with antidepressants. If you're not noticing any positive changes within a month, we'll try something new."

Kathryn's eyes widened. "A month? I have to feel this way for a month?"

"Sometimes it's two weeks. Most likely three to four though. These medications just take time to work."

"Okay," Kathryn said just above a whisper.

Jane reached over and took Kathryn's hand, offering a reassuring smile.

Kathryn couldn't return it. Her lips wouldn't move. She wanted to feel hope in this moment, but she was left only with the familiar darkness that swirled deep within her and the fear that she would never again see the light.

It had been just over four weeks since Kathryn began the antidepressants, and the weight upon her chest felt as though it had increased. A constant ache dispersed through her body, making everything difficult—getting out of bed, school, talking with her counselor, being around people, eating, caring about...anything. The emptiness was spreading.

Kathryn pulled on a black top and her jeans, having to tighten her belt an extra notch. She brushed her hair into a ponytail and swept a bit of powder over her reddened cheeks before picking up the phone and dialing.

"H-hello?" he said, his dry voice straining.

"Grandpa? I'm sorry. I woke you up again, didn't I?"

"It's okay, Kathryn. Did you miss the bus again?"

"Yes. I'm so sorry."

"It's okay. I'll be there soon."

Kathryn clicked off the phone and placed it atop the disorganized mess on her desk. She gazed into the mirror, expressionless, the reflection of some foreign girl staring back at her from her own room.

She ambled into the kitchen and grabbed a handful of cereal from an open box on the counter. The lack of flavor scrunched her face, and she spit it out into the garbage. Nothing had taste anymore. No scents, no beauty, even colors were dull and pointless. Life…pointless.

Almost four weeks had passed since Kathryn started the second round of medication, and the weight upon her chest was unbearable. The darkness consumed her. Simply getting up in the morning was physically painful as she dragged herself out of bed, moaning, forcing herself to get ready for school. She couldn't miss another day. Yet the mere thought of school was suffocating, the heaviness on her chest pressing the air from her lungs struggling to draw breath. Plagued by a constant ache in her head and every muscle in her fragile body, she was regularly on the verge of tears and avoided anyone and everything she possibly could. But today couldn't be avoided. She had to hand in her English paper. Her grades were suffering already this term, and her paper could not be late. At least, that's what her mom told her; Kathryn couldn't find the strength to care.

After throwing herself together, she stared at herself in the mirror but quickly looked away. She couldn't look at the girl staring back. It wasn't…her.

Kathryn glanced at the clock and gasped. She rushed down the stairs and out the door to see her bus speeding past her house. "Damnit!"

Retreating inside, she knocked the snow off her sneakers, grabbed the phone, and dialed.

"Hello?"

"Hi, Aunt Hannah. I'm so sorry, but I missed the bus again. Would you be able to give me a ride to school?"

"Sure, dear. I'll be there soon."

Kathryn threw the phone on the loveseat. She paced a few steps before turning toward the couch, leaning forward, and unleashing her tightened fists upon it, a scream emanating from a space so deep, so dark, pouring out through her mouth and into the world that had betrayed her. Over and over again, she assaulted the cushions with unrelenting force.

Two months of trying to find the right medication and nothing had worked. She was drowning, slipping further and further from who she used to be.

She stood and attempted to calm her rapid breathing and slow the rageful tears.

"Um…are you okay?"

Kathryn whipped around to face Brandon. "I'm fine."

"You don't look fine. You just beat the crap out of the couch."

"I said I'm fine!"

"Fine. Geez." Brandon returned to his bedroom.

When Aunt Hannah arrived, Kathryn grabbed her backpack and jacket and went outside to meet her.

"Thank you, Aunt Hannah. I'm really sorry to do this to you again. I just didn't want to bother Grandpa."

"You've missed the bus quite often lately. Talk to me, my dear."

She used to be able to put on her mask, conceal the pain, paste on a smile that she had become so good at presenting to the world, belying her true self…but no longer. Her mask, like her hope, had become another victim. Kathryn immediately gave in to the despair, breaking down into sobs.

"Goodness. What is it? Is it Brandon?"

"No. No, it's not," she said in between gasps for air. "This medicine just isn't working. And counseling isn't helping. If anything, I'm worse than before I started. I…don't know what to do anymore."

Aunt Hannah placed a gentle hand on her niece's shoulder. "Oh, Kathryn. It'll get better. I know it will."

"How can you possibly know that? What if it doesn't?"

"I have true faith that somehow, someway, you will overcome this. You've overcome so much already. You're stronger than you know. I know you can beat this."

Kathryn slouched in the seat, uncertain about everything.

Aunt Hannah drove her the ten minutes to school as the winter morning brought thick flakes down upon them, and she took her to the back entrance closest to the orchestra room, giving her a quick hug before Kathryn got out of the warm car.

Fresh snow had blanketed the walkway, and her right foot slipped, carving a gash into the soft powder as a vision of Liam's bandaged wrist fought its way into her mind. Her expression remained flat, indifferent to the memory.

As she walked into school, the halls were already emptied. She hustled to the orchestra room, a wall of sound meeting her upon opening the doors. Keeping her head down as she made her way past all the string players, trying her best to avoid bowing arms, she grabbed her cello from its locker and took her spot in the fourth chair.

Avoiding Mr. Darrow's eyes, she attempted to jump right in, blending with the rest of her section. When first period ended, she quickly escaped from the room without a look or word to anyone.

"Kathryn!"

She kept walking.

"Kathryn! Wait!"

She felt a hand on her shoulder and reluctantly slowed to allow Lexie to fall in step beside her.

"Still?"

"It's just not getting better. I don't know what to do anymore," Kathryn said without looking at her.

"When do you see the doctor again? Obviously you need to try something else."

"I don't know how much longer I can do this."

Lexie grabbed her friend's arm and pulled her into a nearby doorway, out of the flow of foot traffic. Her green eyes shone with ferocity. "You will do this for however long it takes. I know it seems impossible right now, but I know you can do it. I know it."

Her face remained void of emotion. "Everyone seems to know I can do it. But what if I don't want to?"

Lexie's eyes narrowed. "Don't talk like that. I mean it. Stop. Don't let this consume you."

"I don't know how," she said, her voice starting to crack.

"I don't know either, but if anyone can, it's you. Do you know what my mom has said to me? She's amazed by you. 'With everything Kathryn has been through, she's such a sweet, kind girl. She has such strength and courage for someone so young.'"

Kathryn's eyes fell to the floor. "I don't feel strong."

"I know you don't. But you're so much stronger than you realize." She reached forward and gripped Kathryn's shoulders with both hands. "You have to keep fighting. Please, Kathryn. You have to keep fighting."

Kathryn nodded.

"Come on. I'll walk you to your next class."

"Won't you be late?"

She spun Kathryn forward and linked her arm with hers. "I don't care."

224

The door creaked as she entered the orchestra room, lunch in hand, and she gripped the handle of the file room as Mr. Darrow stepped out from his office.

"Kathryn, can I talk to you for a minute?"

She followed him, and he closed the door before leaning back on his desk, folding his arms across his wide chest.

"Kathryn, you've been coming in late a lot the past couple of months, you don't know your music, you slipped down to fourth chair, you're locking yourself away in the file room again. I have to be honest. I'm concerned. I didn't want to push, but I've been concerned for a while. This isn't like you." His deep voice, usually drenched with sarcasm, rang with an unfamiliar tone as his eyes softened, and his head tilted slightly.

"I'm just...going through some stuff right now."

"Okay...?" He paused, observing her.

Avoiding his amber stare, she fixated on the florescent light reflecting off his orange hair.

"I want you to know you can talk to me if you need to. You can trust me with whatever is going on."

Her focus was drawn to him, a man usually equal parts jokes and snappy wit, standing before her, exuding compassion, reaching out to her. She held his strong gaze in her own and spoke as her voice broke. "I've been diagnosed with Clinical Depression. I've been dealing with a lot of stuff this past year. Um...family stuff. My brother...he's"—she swallowed—"he's abusive. My doctor put me on medicine. I'm on my second one in two months, and nothing is working. I feel worse than ever. I just feel...so lost." A tear spilled down her cheek as she held her eyes on him. "But...I'm trying." She inhaled sharply as her voice caught in her tightened throat. "I'm doing the best I can."

With a resolute stance, he offered her an almost imperceivable nod. "Keep doing the best you can, Kathryn."

She nodded silently, unblinking as she held there for a few moments, beholding her teacher with unwavering deference. He responded with a slight upturn of his lips, and she disappeared into the file room.

Kathryn closed the door, not bothering to turn on the lights, and was lost within the darkness of the solid enclosure. Her breath washed out as she slid to the floor, the berber scratchy against her hands. Unable to hold back, she let her emotions burst forth, agony in each scream, devastation in each cry, unconcerned with those who could most likely hear her outside the room.

As she began to still within the tranquility of the nothingness that encircled her, she reflected on Mr. Darrow's actions. He reached out to her. He listened. He didn't try to make her smile; he didn't draw on her face. He simply showed her he cared.

Three other faces swirled within her chaotic mind—her mom, Aunt Hannah, Lexie.

She spoke into the emptiness, to the darkness that consumed her, encased her, unrelenting determination lacing every word. "I'm going to keep doing the best I can."

Deciduous

"How did that make you feel?"

"Horrible. Angry. Confused. Even almost two years later, I don't understand why he did it. Why he hated me so much to break into my room and attack me." Kathryn followed the detailed edge of the crown molding lining the perimeter of the office she had come to know well over the past eighteen months. She shifted on the plush, gray couch, sitting up from a slouching position and untwisted the hem of her top from her finger, her hand gliding to her beaded bracelet, pulling at the clasp. "I know I keep coming back to this."

"It's okay to revisit this as often as you need to."

"But I want to get past it. I don't want it to haunt me anymore. I've dealt with practically everything else. But this…" Kathryn sighed, watching the tip of her sneaker rapidly tap against the closest leg of the white coffee table. "Why can't I just move on?"

Linda leaned back, her blond bun inches from the top of the leather highback chair on the opposite side of the coffee table, her pen twisting leisurely in her hand. A notepad rested on her crossed legs as she observed her patient through delicately rimmed glasses. "Have you ever asked him why he chose to do what he did?"

"No," she said, shrugging. "We don't talk about anything. We really just coexist and have ever since it happened."

"Maybe you should ask him."

Kathryn shook her head. "I don't think that would go over well."

227

"I'm not saying it would be easy. I'm afraid, though, that this will never resolve and you'll never receive closure until you have an answer to your question."

"How would I even start a conversation like that?"

"How did you start the conversation with your dad that led to your healing? How did you start the conversation with your mom?"

"But those were my parents. I love them, and they love me. With Brandon, I feel…almost indifferent. Apathetic. I don't wish anything bad on him, but he also doesn't really mean anything to me." She looked down. "That probably makes me sound like a horrible person."

"No. You sound like someone who is healing from abuse at the hand of someone who isn't supposed to inflict that level of anger upon you. You sound like someone coming to peace with the limits of your relationship and the limits of your ability to care for someone who has hurt you so badly. That's actually progress."

"Really?"

"Kathryn, when you came to me, you were only just beginning to explore the root of your depression and the depth of the emotions that brought it forth. Look how far you've come. The right medication and painstakingly dealing with the events of your past with me over the past year and a half has brought you to this place." She uncrossed her legs, placed her notepad on the table, and leaned forward. "Are you happy, Kathryn? Right here and now, are you happy?"

"I feel like I'm getting there. I mean, I'm not unhappy. Things aren't perfect, but they're not anywhere close to where they used to be. I have good friends, my cello, a good relationship with my mom and dad, a part-time job that I enjoy going to."

"Those are all great accomplishments, ones you've worked hard for. I'd really like to see you resolve the issues with your brother though. I think that will lead you to be a happier person in the long run. Think about it. We can discuss it more next session if you'd like."

"Okay."

Linda met her at the door. "Well done, Kathryn. You should be proud of your progress."

"Thanks. See you next week."

"Looking forward to it. Have a nice weekend. Oh, and happy belated birthday. Here's to seventeen being a great year for you."

Kathryn smiled. "Thanks. Let's hope so."

Her left foot held the clutch down as she shifted into gear, inhaling deeply at the roar of the car beneath her. The excitement of getting her license the day prior was still coursing through her, and having her own car, being able to get out of the house whenever she wanted was a freedom she had never known. She cranked the volume on the CD player, and she set off to work, singing along with her favorite boy band.

Kathryn drove into the parking lot, pulling up next to her friend's red convertible.

Chris leaned back against his car, arms folded across his firm chest, waiting for her as she approached him. "Jamming to boy bands?" He mockingly flipped his caramel hair off his brow.

"Sure am! I got my license yesterday. I get to jam to whatever I want."

"Yes! That's awesome!" He held up his hand, inviting a high five. "Well, not for people on the road because I'm willing to bet you're a wild woman behind the wheel, but it's awesome for you, I guess."

"Ha. Ha. Very funny."

He elbowed her in the arm and breathed a laugh. "No, seriously. Congrats. That's really great. I figured you passed when I saw you pull up. I remember when I got my license last year. It's a great feeling. You ready for a fun-filled evening at your favorite entertainment store?"

"You know it."

The pair walked through the automatic sliding doors of JAMM Media. Just beyond the row of cashiers, the large, tiled center aisle ran the length of the store, leading back to the warehouse. There were four departments—video games and computers, nicknamed hardlines; movies; music; and books. Each occupied a carpeted corner of the store sectioned off by an intersecting aisle crossing at the center. Within each quartered segment stood a kiosk placed squarely in the middle, behind which one of her colleagues was perched, ready and waiting to help customers and stock shelves with new inventory.

"Hey, Evan!" Kathryn said to the guy on her left behind the desk in hardlines just beyond the cashiers.

He looked up from the video games he was organizing. "You get it?"

"I sure did!"

"Yes! Look out, world. Kathryn's got her license."

She laughed, facing Chris. "Why does everyone keep saying that?"

"There must be something about you."

"Shut up. I'm a good driver," she said, playfully pushing him away.

"Hey, Aubs," Chris said, nodding to Aubrey, also from Kathryn's school, who worked in movies across the aisle from hardlines.

She giggled and twinkled her fingers at him.

Kathryn tilted her head down at Chris.

"What?"

"Nothing."

"It's not my fault I have a way with the ladies."

She nearly choked on a laugh. "Not this lady. This lady thinks you're a conceited jerk."

"Then she'd be right, but she adores me anyway."

"You're such a dork," she said, rolling her eyes.

After clocking in, they dropped off their things in the breakroom in the front left corner of the store, grabbed their red aprons off the wall hooks, and checked the cashier assignments for their designated registers.

"We're at the twin set together," Chris said as he slid his apron over his head, catching it on his round glasses.

"Awesome."

The first hour dragged on with few customers to tend to, but Chris had a knack for filling time.

"Someday, I want to be the person who designs the pictures on credit cards," he said after a customer went through his line.

"What?"

"No, really. How cool of a job would that be?"

She chuckled. "Wow, Chris, that's quite an ambitious dream of yours."

"What can I say? I'm an ambitious guy." He nodded behind her. "Customer."

"Oooh. This one's mine."

"All yours."

"Good afternoon. How are you today?" Kathryn asked with a smile.

"Fine. Thanks," the man said, flipping an empty video game display case on the counter.

"I just have to go get your copy of this game from the drawers over there," she said, pointing behind her and to the right. "I'll be right back."

With her back to the customer, her face scrunched, feigning crying, and Chris seemingly fought to suppress a smile.

Opening the "K-O" drawer, she breathed a sigh of relief when uncharacteristically she was able to find the game quickly among all the different colored, crazy fonts printed on the spines of numerous rows of games.

She sidled behind Chris as he silently clapped for her, open-mouthed astonishment on his cute face. Trying to ignore him so as not to punch him in the chest in front of a customer, she stepped behind the register, forcing a smile.

"Here it is," she said, scanning the barcode. "Your total is fifty-three forty-eight."

He handed her his credit card, and she ran it through the reader at the top of her keyboard. As he was signing the slip, Chris nudged her and pointed to the credit card in her hand, decorated with a picturesque mountain scene.

She shook her head, her slight smile teetering on the edge of losing her composure, and handed the card back to the man. "Thank you. Have a great night."

Chris turned from the door after watching him leave. "Geez. What a grump. He could have at least said thank you."

"Right? Especially because I had to go through the Giant, Black Drawers of Doom to find his game."

"But quite a picture on that credit card, huh? What a great choice. That could have been me!"

"Kathryn," Rich, their boss, called from behind them. "Go ahead and take your break. Chris, take yours when she gets back."

"Okay. Thanks," she answered as he turned and retreated to his office. "It's all you now."

"I'm not sure I can handle this on my own." He swung his hand out, drawing her eyes to the desolate store.

"I believe in you. You've got this."

"I shall do my best."

She giggled. "Dork."

Kathryn walked past the drawers, shooting them a murderous look, and pushed her way into the breakroom just beyond them.

"Oh, hey, Aubrey. I didn't see you come in here."

"Yeah. You were talking with Chris." She leaned her head back, taking a swig of pop. "So, how's it going? How's your spring break been?"

Kathryn slid four quarters into the vending machine. "I'm doing okay. Just got my license yesterday." She pressed "C10" for a chocolate candy bar.

"Really? Congrats. I have my test next week. I'm super nervous."

"It's really not too hard if you've taken driver's ed."

"That's what I've heard."

Kathryn took the seat across from her.

"I like your bracelet," Aubrey said before popping a chip into her mouth.

"Thanks. My mom got it for me for my birthday last week."

"I have a blue one just like it. It's supposed to bring good luck in school. The pink's good luck in love, isn't it?"

"Really? I didn't know it meant anything," Kathryn said, observing the pink beaded bracelet. "I just picked it because it's pink."

231

Aubrey smirked and crunched on a few more chips. "So, are things getting better with you and your brother?"

"Oh, um…yeah, I guess. I mean, I mainly just avoid him. But it's okay."

"That sucks that you have to hide from him though."

Kathryn shrugged. "Yeah, it does. Just how it's going to be."

"Do you know if you're working at all next week?"

"I think just Monday and next Saturday. You?"

Aubrey laughed. "Tomorrow and Wednesday."

"Of course." Kathryn dug into her candy bar.

"So, um…I saw you and Chris laughing together."

"Yeah. He's fun to work with. Such a dork."

"He's pretty hot too."

"A hot dork then." Kathryn cracked up at herself.

"So…?"

"So…what?"

"Is there something going on there?"

"With Chris and me?" She shook her head. "No. No, we're just friends."

"Really? That's it?"

"That's it."

"So you don't mind if I um…try to get to know him better?"

"Go for it."

She blushed. "Cool."

Chris looked back over his shoulder as the girls exited the breakroom. "Oh, Kathryn, thank God you're back. I've been swamped. I almost had to call Evan over to help me."

Aubrey giggled as she sauntered past, glancing back over her shoulder and flashing a smile at Chris.

"Really?"

"Yes. I've had three customers in fifteen minutes," he said, dramatically pretending to wipe sweat off his brow and knocking his black-rimmed glasses askew.

"I'm very proud of you for making it through all that by yourself," she said seriously as a single-sided smile broke through.

"I'm pretty amazing, you know."

She rolled her eyes as deeply as possible, and the friends burst into a fit of laughter.

The rest of the night remained slow, but she hardly noticed while having fun with Chris and calling Aubrey and Evan on the intercom system when Rich was in his office.

When nine o'clock came, the four of them walked out together, Aubrey scurrying up on the other side of Chris. Deeper into the parking lot, Aubrey and Evan split off in the other direction toward their cars.

"Bye, guys," Kathryn said with a flick of her wrist. "See you at school on Monday."

Kathryn and Chris strolled over to their cars parked next to each other.

"Now, you drive safely, Kathryn. Don't let those girly boy voices cloud your brain."

"Hey now. Don't dis my boys."

Chris chuckled, rapping her gently on the arm. "See ya, Kathryn."

"Night, Chris."

"One second. She's right here. Kathryn?"

She closed the front door behind her and tossed her purse on the loveseat. "Yeah?"

"It's your dad."

"I'll take it in my room." She hiked upstairs and flopped onto her bed with the cordless in hand.

"Hey, Dad."

"Hello, my Kathryn. Do you have something to tell me?"

"Uh…like what?"

"Kathryn," he said with phony severity.

"Oh, yeah. That's right. I passed!"

"You did? Oh, great. As if I don't worry about you enough, now I have to worry about you driving, too."

"Yup. Sorry about that, but I'm excited. I'm going out with Melanie, Joselyn, and Kristin tomorrow. Probably out to eat and mini golfing."

"Well, you better be careful all the time, wear your seatbelt, obey all traffic laws, check your mirrors, wear a helmet, and you better have cars passing you left and right. You better beat my record, young lady."

She smiled. "I know, Dad. I know."

"You don't know. You don't know what it's like to worry about a child. It's terrifying knowing that my baby girl will be out on the road all by herself."

233

"Dad, I'm not a baby anymore. I just turned seventeen."

"You'll always be my baby. No matter if you're seventeen or seventy, you'll always be my baby. You'll understand someday."

"All right. Well, I'm going to get to bed. I've had a long day."

"Okay. Do you know how much I love you, Kathryn?"

"Yes, Dad."

"No, you don't. You don't know how much I love you. There's no way you could fully understand."

"Hey, I know what it is to love people. I love Mom and you and my family and friends."

"It's not the same. Trust me. Love for a child is not the same."

"Well, then I guess I don't know. Do you want me to do something about that?"

"Absolutely not!" he shouted with a laugh. "I unequivocally do *not* want you to do something about that. You'll understand one day when you have your own kids when you're thirty-five."

She giggled. "I'm just messing with you, Dad."

"You better be. Well, goodnight. I'll talk to you soon. You be careful tomorrow and every day forever."

"I will. I promise. I'll talk to you soon."

"I love you, Kathryn."

"I love you too, Dad."

"Thank you."

"You're welcome."

"Bye, baby girl."

"Bye, Dad."

Kathryn hung up the phone, a whisper of a laugh lingering on her lips as a smile of contentment formed, thankful for where she and her dad had fought to get to.

He sat balancing on the edge of the lavish chair, his knee bouncing, his rough hands twisting. Kathryn watched him, her heart racing, a piece of folded lined paper clutched in her clammy hand.

Linda snatched her notepad and pen from the coffee table and placed them on her crossed legs. "Daniel, welcome. I'm so glad you were able to come in today. You're an important part of Kathryn's life and, therefore, her recovery. I know it means a lot to her that you're here."

Daniel looked over at Kathryn on the gray couch, and she offered a delicate smile that he couldn't seem to return. He simply wiped his brow and looked back at Linda.

"I suggested to Kathryn that she write you a letter to read to you today. It's a useful tool in situations such as these. It helps to keep thoughts organized and make sure she says everything she needs to say."

"A letter, huh? Is this what you did with Mom too?" he asked.

Kathryn nodded.

"Well, okay then. You're the only one I'd ever let bash me. Let's get to it. Lay it on me."

"Dad—"

"Daniel, Kathryn's intention is not to bash you. She simply wants to get a few things out in the open that she feels the need to work through."

"All right. All right. Let's hear it."

Kathryn unfolded the paper carefully, slowly, hesitantly. She laid it on her lap and smoothed out the crinkles with an open hand. Bringing the paper inches from her face, she cleared her dry throat. "Dad, you know how much I love you. Everything that I'm going to say is not to hurt you but to try and understand my past and heal from it and move on together." She inhaled deeply and released. "You have done things to hurt me. I know you didn't mean to, but you did. The one that sticks in my mind the most is when you slammed the car door and glass fell on me."

"I...I didn't even know you remembered that. I never meant for that to happen. I would never ever want to hurt you, baby girl."

"I know, Dad."

"Daniel, I know it's hard not to comment, but let's let Kathryn get through her letter, and then we can discuss."

"Right. Sorry. Guess I'm not very good at this. Go ahead, honey."

"Another time you hurt me was when you wouldn't let me have Benji back. I remember crying for him, and I didn't understand why you wouldn't give him back to me. Looking back on it now as a sixteen-year-old...it was a...selfish thing to do." She kept herself from looking at him. "Every time you missed one of my concerts, you disappointed me. My cello is very important to me, and I wanted to share it with you." Kathryn relented and met her dad's eyes, the pain within ripping at her chest. Quickly setting her sight back on her letter, she let her eyes travel down the page, skimming past a bulleted list of painful memories and hurtful actions that would only twist the knife in her daddy's heart further. She couldn't do it.

Skipping to the end, she continued. "Hurting my mom and Brandon, although I wasn't directly involved or remember, still hurt me too. It all affected me even if I didn't realize it at the time. It's all still a piece of who I am. Despite the ways you've hurt me or disappointed me, I have never doubted that you love me. I just needed to get these things out so we can both talk about them and move past them." She quickly folded the letter and set it on the couch next to her, pushing it aside as though it may turn on her.

"Daniel, I know that was a lot to hear. Would you like to respond?"

He threw his hands up, letting them slap to his knees. "I'm not even sure what to say."

Kathryn's breathing increased as her throat tightened.

Her dad turned to her. "You're right. About everything. I hurt you and your mom and brother. I know it was all my fault. Everything. Losing your mother and you two. I did it."

"W...why?"

"I have no excuses, baby girl. When all that was happening, I was so lost. In pain, angry. Losing your mother was hard enough, but losing you guys... It was the single worst thing that has ever happened to me. And I did it to myself."

"But you didn't lose us."

"In a lot of ways, I did, though." He looked down, seemingly avoiding her gaze. "I lost out on so much. I didn't get to tuck you in at night, to make you breakfast every morning, to send you to your first day of kindergarten, to just be a constant part of your life like I could have been if I hadn't screwed everything up so badly, if I had been better to your mother."

Kathryn then witnessed a completely foreign sight. He wiped a tear off his reddened cheek.

"I'm not trying to make excuses. I did all those things, and I shouldn't have." Her daddy brought his tearful hazel eyes to hers. "I'm...sorry. I can't lose you, Kathryn."

Kathryn slid to the end of the couch, closer to him. "You could never lose me, Dad," she said, her voice breaking. "Never. I promise."

"Even though I f...screwed up your life?"

"You didn't screw up my life. If anything, Brandon did."

"And he probably did because I screwed up his life."

"No. He made his own choices."

"That I set in motion with the shitty things I did."

"Daniel, let's stay focused on Kathryn."

"Sorry. This is all..." He took a deep, rattling breath and roughly wiped at his eyes. "So, now what?"

Kathryn reached her hands out, taking his own. "We move forward."

He looked down at their entwined hands. "You can do that?"

"Of course. That's all I want."

"I am trying to be better for you."

"I know you are. And you have been. At this point, that's what matters to

me—who you are now and who you're trying to be. What you've done in the past isn't important anymore. I don't care who you used to be. You're my dad, and I love you no matter what. I forgive you, Dad."

His fists dug at his wet eyes again. "I don't deserve you."

"Well, you've got me anyway."

He finally looked up. "And I'm the luckiest dad in the world."

Unveiled

After a fun weekend of driving around and hanging out with Melanie, Joselyn, and Kristin, Kathryn popped up for school when her alarm went off Monday morning. She showered, did her hair and makeup, and was off to pick up Melanie at her house.

"You left your sunglasses in my car, Mel," Kathryn said as her friend closed the car door.

She groaned. "I was looking everywhere for these. I totally blamed my brothers for taking them. Oops." She shrugged. "Oh well."

Kathryn chuckled and started their favorite CD, and the teenagers harmonized their way to school.

The halls were crowded when they came in through the back doors, currents of students moving in opposite directions.

"See you later, Mel." Kathryn waved as she sidestepped her way through the hall to reach the orchestra room as Melanie entered the band room.

Kathryn opened her cello locker and set her backpack down, turning behind her to the young man whose height nearly surpassed the bass in his large hands. "Hey, Sam."

"Morning, Kathryn," he said, his deep voice in competition with his instrument's low register. "Mama wanted me to mention that we're having a party for Papa's birthday in a few weeks. She was hoping you'd come."

"Of course."

"We're thinking of making it a game night."

"Oh, it better be," she said, feigning an attitude.

239

The cousins laughed together.

"Good morning, Kathryn."

"Morning, Mr. Darrow," she said as she tightened her bow.

He leaned his tall form against the doorframe of his office. "And how's my first chair cellist this morning?"

"Doing pretty well."

"I'm glad to hear it. Now, clean out that cello locker of all your school papers before I lose what's left of my mind."

Kathryn tried to harden her expression, but a smile broke through her tightened lips. "Yes, Mr. D."

Lexie growled and slammed her locker door.

"What's up, Lex?" Kathryn turned the lock on her yellow locker.

"These stupid college applications. How the hell am I supposed to make a decision like this that's going to affect the rest of my life? I'm seventeen!" Her back fell against the lockers, books clutched tight to her chest. "I hate this."

"Sorry. Is your dad still putting pressure on you?"

"Oh, just every day, all day. It's not like I don't want to go to college. I do. But it's so much pressure. What if I make the wrong choice?"

"Do you have any ideas what you want to go for?"

"I...I kind of thought about maybe looking into cosmetology. Maybe become a hairstylist."

"Lex, you'd be so good at that!" She shoved her English notebook in her bag. "I think that's an amazing idea."

Lexie's green eyes widened, painting her face with excitement. "You do?"

"Absolutely! You already highlight your own hair," she said with a laugh, flicking the hot pink streak she was working on in orchestra practice that morning. "And you'd get to style hair and gossip for a living!"

Her face scrunched in a giggling fit. "Right?"

"Seriously, though, I love that idea."

"Thanks, Kath. Still planning on WNYU for music?"

"That's the plan. If I can get in, that is."

"Of course you will. You're... Oh, ew. Don't look behind you."

"What? Why?" She turned and glanced over her shoulder, spotting Liam among a group of his friends.

Lexie grabbed her arm and pulled. "I told you not to look."

"Lex, it's fine. I'm over it."

She tilted her head, her hand floating up to her hip. "Yeah, right. Because I don't know you well enough to know you're lying."

Kathryn playfully shoved her. "I'm trying, okay?" She sighed. "He just looks so good in black. Matches his hair."

"Stop it," Lexie whispered harshly, pointing a stern finger at her friend.

"I know. I know." She scoffed. "What's wrong with me?" She moaned, switching out a few books she needed for homework.

"Hey, ladies!" shrieked Aubrey as she pranced over to them from across the hall. "Kathryn, have you seen the new super cute guy in hardlines? Oh my God. *So* cute. Tall, dark blond, blue eyes. Dreamy," she said in a singsong voice.

Kathryn shook her head. "No, I haven't."

Evan slid between the girls. "*Sooooo* cute!"

"Oh, you stop!" Aubrey said, punching him in the arm.

"Sorry. But yeah, she's right. He's one tasty dish."

The girls roared, and Aubrey pushed him away from the group. He walked backward and dipped to a dramatic bow, waving goodbye to his audience before turning around and walking off.

"Anyway, as I was saying, we worked together on Saturday. I don't even know his name, but he's—"

"Super cute?" Kathryn stifled a laugh.

"Yes!"

"I'm working tonight and Saturday, so I'll be sure to keep an eye out for a super cute, tall, dark blond, tasty dish in hardlines."

A group of girls swooped in from behind Lexie and called her name, pulling on her arm. "I have to go, Kathryn," said Lexie.

"Call you later?"

"I have practice." She nodded toward her cheerleading squad. "I'll see you tomorrow though."

"Okay." Kathryn watched as Lexie skipped off and disappeared around the corner.

"Why do you think you put on such an act for Val?"

Kathryn shrugged as she looked away from Linda and leaned deeper into the gray couch. "I don't know. To get her to like me, I guess."

"Why did you want her to like you?"

"I don't even know anymore. I just know that at the time, I did. She was… exciting? Not like any of my other friends."

241

"Yet you say you couldn't be yourself around her."

"Nope." Kathryn shook her head and caught her therapist's gaze again. "Any time I was, she'd put me down."

"So you changed who you were."

"I wouldn't say I changed who I was, but I acted like a different person around her."

"But wouldn't you say that carried over a bit into other parts of your life? If you're doing things you wouldn't normally do, even if you don't want to do them at the time, aren't you still changing? Those actions had to have had an effect on other areas of your life."

Kathryn's fingers tapped against the armrest as she pondered that for a moment, a sick feeling stirring within. "Yeah, I guess they did. She talked me into things—smoking, drinking, lying. And I did it, to a point at least."

"But then you put a stop to it. Why?"

"I guess I just saw it clearer when I left my house for that month. She didn't want to come over to visit me because she couldn't drink or smoke. She never came over once. I saw what I probably had known for a while. She was using me as a punching bag and for my brother's friends."

"The ones with whom she was involved."

"She was pretty much involved with most of them."

"That's unfortunate, especially at such a young age."

"She didn't see anything wrong with it. I bet if I had still been friends with her last year when two of Brandon's friends…propositioned me…she would have said it was no big deal and that I should have…done what they wanted." A harsh shiver spread through her body. Two separate friends of his, two separate times—their eyes…the curl of their lips when they asked her for something she would never give them. A wave of nausea assaulted her, and her hand fluttered to her stomach.

"She may have, but you were stronger than she was. You said no. Thankfully, they listened. That's not always the case."

She quivered at that horrid thought. "It wasn't strength. It was that they're disgusting, and I hate them," Kathryn said through clenched teeth.

"Well, whatever the reason, you made a much smarter decision. How was Val's home life?"

"Pretty awful."

"That's not surprising. Not an excuse but typically the pattern." Linda uncrossed her legs and scooted to the edge of her leather chair. "So, you've been done with her for a while now, haven't spoken to her at all. Why do you think she is still so heavily on your mind?"

"You're the one who brought her up."

242

"Only because I feel there's something deeper we need to find. She's part of that time in your life that we've been working on dissecting. I think it's worth exploring if you're up for it."

"I guess."

"How did you feel about yourself at the time you were friends with Val?"

"I don't know."

She looked at her patient over the top of her glasses. "Kathryn, you know."

Kathryn threw her hands up, and they fell crossed over her chest. "I felt lost, worthless, not myself, not good enough."

"Keep going."

"I couldn't just be me around her."

"Why?"

"Because she didn't like who I really was."

"How did that make you feel?"

"Like I said—worthless and not good enough."

"Do you see where this is leading, Kathryn?"

She stared off toward the window on the other side of the room, following the flow of the sheer drapes cascading to the hardwood floor. She looked at Linda, tears welling up in her eyes. "I wasn't good enough for anyone! Brandon hated me, and I have no idea why. Val, who was supposed to be my friend didn't like me for me. I wasn't good enough the way I was. Even Liam apparently decided I wasn't worth his time and pretended he didn't even know me. I mean, what the hell is that about? Why wasn't I good enough? We couldn't have at least been friends?" Kathryn gasped through her tightened throat. "Why wasn't I good enough?" She reached forward and took the tissue Linda offered and laid her face in her hands.

"You've never mentioned Liam before."

"I didn't see much of a point. He was just this guy who I was friends with, or at least I thought we were friends."

"And what changed?"

"I don't know. We had a class together and got to know each other, and then the school year ended. He even talked to me on the last day before the buses left. *He* came over to talk to *me*. Then when the next year started, I didn't exist anymore. I tried to say hi to him in the halls, and he ignored me. Then later I went up to him to talk to him, and right in front of me, he told his friend he didn't know me. That's pretty much it. It sounds stupid now that I say it all out loud. So a boy didn't like me back. Big deal."

"It clearly is a big deal. You brought him up for the first time when you were talking about the people who made you feel not good enough. It's clear

243

that he hurt you. That's never no big deal. You obviously cared for this boy."

She spun her Claddagh ring, the crown digging into her knuckle. "More than any other boy I've ever met. And then he didn't want anything to do with me, and I don't know why."

"Just one more person you weren't good enough for."

She felt the air pushed from her lungs, and her tears began again. "How is talking about him helping? I thought I had almost moved past it all. When I see him in school, I'm okay now."

"Do you still feel a pull toward him?"

"Sure, but it doesn't make me feel like my heart's being ripped from my chest anymore. At least until now."

"It was always there, and it will be until you deal with your unresolved feelings."

"I don't want to deal with it. It's over and done. He doesn't want anything to do with me. Fine. Okay. I want to move past it. It was almost two years ago."

"Pain doesn't have a timetable, Kathryn. You felt you had a connection with this boy, a friendship."

"Well, I was wrong. So why can't I just let this go?"

"It's a pattern in your life. If you feel rejected, you feel as though you're not good enough. You place the blame on yourself. It can't possibly be on the other person's end. It must be you."

"Well, isn't it? If it's a pattern and I'm the constant, it must be me."

"I can't tell you what Liam was thinking. You know he knew you, so why he acted like he didn't, I can't say. He's a teenage boy. Maybe he cared for you and was scared. Maybe he got mixed in with a new crowd and thought he wouldn't be accepted if he got involved with you. Maybe he knew you liked him but only wanted to be your friend and didn't know how to handle that. There are many reasons, and I wish I had answers for you, but I'm afraid it'll just take time to truly move on from your first broken heart."

"I...I never thought about it like that. My first broken heart."

"Well, isn't that what it is?"

"Yeah, I guess so."

"It will take time to mend. Or maybe if a new young man enters your life, he can override that part of your heart. Time will tell. But don't put this on yourself. You don't know what happened, and although that's difficult for you to accept, finding every way it could have been your fault will only hurt you more."

Kathryn drew a ragged breath, her voice breaking. "He made me forget. If only for a little while…he made me forget it all."

"This was two years ago, you said? When everything was going on at home."

"I started having feelings for him earlier in the year, but yeah."

Linda nodded, staying silent for a few moments. "I wonder if perhaps you held on to him a little too tightly. Perhaps idealized him as the one who could sweep you away and make you happy."

Kathryn's hand floated up to her mouth.

"That doesn't make your feelings for him or your heartache any less real, but you need to make yourself happy first. A boy can't truly do that, not in any way that's going to last."

"I recognize I wasn't happy back then. I mean, obviously. But I feel like I'm closer than I've been in…well ever…to being happy. The pain is still there, yet I'm able to feel happy again. The pain isn't pulling me down and keeping me from feeling joy like it used to."

"That's wonderful. You've worked hard to get here. Everything you've been through, you're here now. And as for Brandon and Val, I do believe I know the core reason they treated you the way they did. They're both very damaged people, Kathryn. In different ways, I'm sure, but they are. That's absolutely no excuse for treating you the way they did, but it doesn't change the foundation upon which their behavior was built—pain. You just happened to have the bad luck of being on the other end of that pain."

Kathryn was suddenly overcome with a wave of exhaustion. The session had built into something she hadn't expected, taken a path down a road she hadn't been prepared to travel.

"You are good enough, Kathryn. If they can't see that, it's on them, not you. Everything bad that ever happens to you is not automatically your fault or somehow a reflection on you. Look how far you've come, what you've overcome, all that you've achieved. You are good enough, and the people meant to be in your life will see that and love you for exactly who you are— the good, the bad, for your strengths and your flaws. You already have people in your life like that, right? Lexie, Melanie, Joselyn, and Kristin. Your mom and dad, of course. Your aunt and uncle and cousins. You don't have to pretend or be someone you're not. You only have to be Kathryn. That's enough for the people who truly care about you, and that will attract the right kind of people you deserve to have in your life."

Kathryn sat there silently, letting her therapist's words wash over her.

"This was a lot, wasn't it? Let's end there. It may not feel like it, but you did excellent today. You're facing everything with honesty and thoughtful consideration. Well done. I do still want to talk about setting up a time for your mom and Brandon to come in and discuss some issues for your own personal well-being, but we can discuss that next week. Let's let all that settle. Just know that you're not alone in your feelings. It can be quite common for people, adolescents especially, to feel inadequate, not good enough."

Kathryn stared at Linda, her eyes motionless. "So...I wasn't the only one?"

Linda shook her head gently. "No."

Her head fell into her hands, and she drew in a slow, deep breath, a slight smile tickling the corners of her tear-tracked lips.

Silhouetted

Mid-April weather was usually a hit or miss in the Western New York town of Edgebrook, but Kathryn pulled into the JAMM Media parking lot for her Saturday shift, surrounded by nature's beauty. The air seemed to smell sweeter as it wrapped her in warm comfort, and fledgling flowers pierced the surface of the earth, reaching toward the sun to bathe in its brilliance.

Upon entering work, she followed her typical routine—punching in, placing her purse in her locker in the breakroom, and tying on her red apron. Taking her place at her assigned register, she waved to Evan, who looked bored out of his mind with his face smushed in his hands, his elbows resting on the counter.

Kathryn looked over to see a stout woman approaching, her silver ringlets bouncing on her shoulders. "Hi, Mae," she said to JAMM's assistant manager.

"Hi, hon. I'm heading out for the evening, but Rich is around here some-where, probably making someone organize something. Anyway, have a nice night."

Kathryn grinned. "Night, Mae."

Customers trickled in, keeping her attention at the front of the store. Even when there were lulls in activity, Rich had her organizing the front shelves of magazines, new bestsellers, and an assortment of candy.

Kathryn had just finished lining up the magazines on the bottom rack, effort that would soon be undone by the first toddler zipping by with the need to touch everything, when she spotted a customer walking toward her. She held a smile on her face despite the dreaded game display case in the woman's

247

hand swinging at her side. Kathryn pushed herself off her knees and brushed at her jeans. As the woman got closer, she hurried around the counter to her register.

"Hi. How are you this evening?"

"I'm lovely. Thank you, miss. Am I supposed to bring this up here? I'm sorry, but I'm buying this game for my grandson, and I'm clueless about this stuff. His mom just gave me a name."

Kathryn offered a polite chuckle. "Yes. You bring the display case, and I go over to that cabinet to get the actual game," she said, pointing to the drawers.

"Oh, good."

"I'll be right back with your game."

"Thank you so much, dear."

The fact that the woman was so pleasant only slightly eased her annoyance at the Giant, Black Drawers of Doom. She headed over, game in hand, and went all the way to the last drawer butted up to the breakroom doorframe. Wrenching it open, she scowled at the bright mash of colors and random-sized fonts printed on the spines of the fifty video games laid out neatly before her. Looking into the evil abyss, all seemed hopeless, time ticking by as the sweet lady waited for her to return. In a moment of blessed intervention, the breakroom door opened.

"Evan, thank God. Can you help me find this stupid game? I'm ridiculously bad at finding games in this thing."

"Sure," he said, laughing.

Before he could find it, a large hand was before her, clutching the allusive game.

"Here you go."

Kathryn looked up and was instantly taken in by the handsome stranger, his eyes a deep blue as they held her, his thick hair sandy blond and adorably ruffled, trailing down his fair skin and dispersing into a light stubble encircling his full, smiling lips.

She slowly reached for the game. "Um…thanks."

"Sure. No problem," he said, his deep voice like a humming cello.

She watched Evan and the stranger turn to walk back toward their department.

Evan slapped him on the back. "You beat me to it, man."

Kathryn stood frozen for a moment, air finally filling her lungs again. She looked down at her hand and snapped back to reality. Turning on her heel, she scurried back to the waiting customer.

"I'm so sorry for the wait, ma'am. I always seem to have trouble finding these games," Kathryn said, her cheeks flushing pink.

"Oh, that's fine. I'm in no hurry. I appreciate your help."

Kathryn rang up the game, gave the woman her change, and slipped the receipt into the small bag.

"Thank you, young lady."

"You're very welcome. Have a great night."

She checked to see if there were any more customers, and her eyes flashed to the hardlines kiosk where Evan and the stranger were laughing. Evan waved her way, causing the stranger to spin toward her. He offered her a nod, and she felt her face heat up as her heart rate increased, her legs feeling as though they were going to collapse under her weight. Her hands found the counter, and she smiled back before the guys resumed their conversation.

As the evening continued, customers were scarce, and the whole front area was immaculate. Kathryn leaned against the counter, her chin in her hand, her fingers tapping out the cello part of her favorite piece for the final orchestra concert of the school year. Her eyes seemed to be acting of their own accord as they danced back and forth to the mysterious guy, her stomach a mess of knots and flutters.

Intently fixated on him, she was startled by Rich slapping his hand on the counter.

"Kathryn, you're off twenty minutes early. You can go ahead and shut down your register for the night. Stephanie is on the lead register until close. That's all we need."

"Okay, sir. Thanks."

The thought of losing twenty minutes of being in the same building with him affected her in a way that made absolutely no sense to her whatsoever. She had no idea who this guy was; she knew nothing about him. All she knew was she couldn't fight the inexplicable urge to be near him. She didn't want to.

After closing up her station and clocking out, she grabbed her purse from the breakroom and went back out onto the floor. She perused the greeting cards on the outskirts of his department and stopped to admire some cute bumper stickers near the central kiosk. Moseying through the shelves of video game display cases, she giggled to herself that this was where the damn things started. Her stranger was nowhere to be found. With a last walk around the rows of printing supplies, she sighed and started for the front doors.

"Leaving so soon?"

The leap her heart performed bordered on painful, and she quickly turned around to see him walking toward her. She drew a sharp intake of breath, steadying herself, her legs once again threatening to fail her.

"Yeah. Rich told me to clock out a little early. I was just looking around."

"Find anything you like?" he asked, stepping around to the other side of the kiosk.

She couldn't possibly stop the smile that spread beyond her eyes. "I thought this bumper sticker was kind of cute," she said, reaching to the display on her left and grabbing a silver, glittering oval that said "DIVA."

He laughed, the sound floating toward her, gliding on the air as it widened her smile. "Nice."

She held the sticker in her fingertips, sliding them along the edge as she took a few steps closer to him. "So, how long have you worked here? I haven't seen you around before"—she stole a glance at his name tag—"Adam."

The right corner of his mouth tilted upward. "Since December."

"December? Seriously?" Her voice pitched up a bit higher than she had planned.

"Yeah, but I've mostly been in the back warehouse. They only brought me out to work in hardlines the past month or so."

"Oh, okay. How do you like it out here?"

"Much better than the warehouse." Their eyes locked a moment. "How long have you worked here?"

"About a year. My mom made me get a job as soon as I turned sixteen."

"You're only seventeen? Wow. You don't look seventeen."

Her smile held with no sign of departing. "Really?"

"Yeah. You look…more mature, I guess."

"How old did you think I was?"

"I'd guess twenty."

"Really? Well, how old are you?"

"Twenty."

"See, and I would have thought you were seventeen," she said, closing the space between them a bit more.

They laughed in unison, the tones blending harmoniously in her ears.

His eyes broke from hers, hovering over her shoulder, and he grabbed a stack of games off the counter. Kathryn looked back and saw Rich eyeing them.

"Sorry. I'll let you get back to work."

"It's okay," he said quickly.

"I don't want to get you in trouble, and my mom will be expecting me soon anyway."

"Oh, okay. Hey, wait. I never caught your name," Adam said.

"Kathryn."

"Kathryn." He smiled. "It's nice to meet you, Kathryn. I hope to work with you again soon."

"Me too, Adam." Her gaze lingered on him a moment longer until she forced herself to turn from him. After buying the bumper sticker, she walked through the sliding doors, risking a glance over her shoulder, and their eyes met briefly as she exited into the evening air, cool on her flushed skin. She faced forward into the darkness, trying to contain her excitement—at least until she got into her car, where she screamed like a giddy little girl who just won a purple unicorn at the fair.

"Hi, honey. How was work?" Jane asked as Kathryn closed the front door.

She tossed her purse and backpack on the loveseat and danced over to her mom standing at the kitchen sink, washing dishes. "It was pretty amazing, actually."

"Amazing?"

"Well, I kinda met this guy."

"Ah. And here I thought you just loved your job that much."

"I do now." She giggled.

"Aw. Well, that's exciting."

"There's just one thing. Um...how would you feel about me dating a twenty-year-old?"

She placed the last bowl in the drying rack. "Did he already ask you on a date?"

"Well...no. We just talked."

"Quite the planner, aren't we?" Jane shut off the water and snatched the hand towel from the counter. "If I'm being honest, I actually dated a guy who was twenty when I was seventeen, so you may have lucked out."

Kathryn's eyes widened, and she softly grabbed her mom's swollen arm. "Really? You'd let me?" Her high-pitched voice hurt even her own ears.

"I'd have to meet him first before he takes you anywhere, though."

"Yes," she said, nodding at rapid speed. "Absolutely."

"So, tell me about this twenty-year-old who has my girl all giddy."

"I don't really even know much about him. I mean, he's obviously gorgeous, but...I don't know. There's just something about him. It's not like I've never seen really good-looking guys before. This is...different. I can't even explain it."

251

"Wow. Speechless. You? He really does have an effect on you. I mean, look at that smile."

"My face hurts so much," she said, laughing.

"Sorry to bring down the moment, but do you still have homework to do?"

She moaned. "Yeah. Fine." Kathryn grabbed her backpack and purse and started up the stairs.

"Keep me updated on… Wait. You didn't even tell me his name."

"Adam."

"Well, I like how Adam is lighting up my girl's face."

Kathryn's shoulders scrunched up, and she squealed uncharacteristically as she raced up to her room.

Throwing her stuff on the floor, she grasped the phone and dialed Melanie's number. Homework could wait.

"Well, this won't do," Melanie said. "You're not working with him at all this week. Who knows when you'll be scheduled with Adam again. We need a plan."

"A plan?" Kathryn closed her locker and gave the lock a tug before slinging her bag onto her shoulder.

"Yup. We need to know when he's working."

"I may have snuck a look at his schedule and saw that he's working tomorrow from five to nine."

Her blue eyes widened as she bounced on the balls of her feet. "That's it! We'll go to JAMM tomorrow after school. We'll just act like we're there to browse or buy stuff. Then you can run into him and talk to him!"

"So we're gonna stalk him?"

Mel breathed a laugh. "Yeah, pretty much."

Kathryn nodded. "I'm in."

"The plan is to go to my work and run into him. Am I completely crazy?"

"A little." Rachael laughed through the phone. "But that also sounds like fun! I wish I could be there to stalk with you."

"I think that may be one of the few things we've never done together. See what you miss out on when you can't come visit for the summer."

Rachael scoffed. "I know. Having to work through the summer sucks. I'm going to miss you."

252

"I'll miss you too. You haven't heard anything from the college you applied to? I can't remember all the letters."

"EFSC. And no. Nothing yet. I'm going crazy waiting."

"Well, I better be your first call."

"For sure. And you'll have to call me tomorrow and let me know how it went with Adam. If you're not in jail, that is."

Kathryn burst out laughing. "That makes me feel much better. Thanks for that."

"What else are friends for?"

Melanie and Kathryn huddled together among the noisy chatter of the cafeteria.

"This is crazy, Mel."

"You mean genius. It's perfect. We'll just casually walk into JAMM. We're just there to browse and maybe pick up a CD. It needs to seem natural. Like, 'Oh, Adam! I didn't realize you worked today. What a coincidence. Meet my amazing friend Melanie. Do you have any cute, single friends?'"

Kathryn nearly choked on her sandwich, and Mel slapped her on the back as they cracked up, attracting the attention of the surrounding tables despite the uproar of a huge room full of high schoolers. "Yeah, that's exactly what I'm going to say. Gah...I'm so nervous. Maybe we shouldn't do this."

"No, we have to! Come on, Kathryn. Look, do you like him?"

"Well, yeah, you know I do."

"When's the next time you'll be scheduled with him?"

"I have no idea."

"Well then we have to go see him today. It could be months before you're scheduled together. Or what if he quits and then you never get to see him again. Do you want that to happen? Do you want to never see him again?"

She giggled. "Okay. I get your point. Geez." Anxious excitement tightened her fists, and she pressed them to her lips. "Okay, let's do it! But seriously, I'm not going to say that to him."

"Yeah, fine." Melanie laughed. "But something along those lines."

"I don't want to lie to him though. I can say I'm there to get a gift for my mom's birthday. It's coming up soon anyway. We can pick something up for her while we're there."

"Perfect."

253

Kathryn stood near the back doors off the music wing where Melanie had instructed her to be, nerves flooding her body as she rocked on her heels, waiting for Melanie to arrive. She felt a clap on her back.

"You ready?"

"No, not really."

"Well, we're doing this. I'm not letting you back out now. Come on! Let's go!" Melanie said, hopping out the door and onto the concrete pathway leading to the parking lot.

Kathryn couldn't help but laugh at her friend's bubbly enthusiasm, and she followed her, hoping this wasn't going to be a complete and utter disaster.

Her hands gripped the wheel of her parked car standing just feet from JAMM Media. "I can't do this."

"Yes, you can, Kathryn. And you're gonna. I know you're scared, but you look gorgeous, and if you don't go in there and talk to him, you'll totally regret it. And I've got your back. Not that you need me though. If he hasn't figured it out from your first conversation, you're pretty awesome."

Kathryn looked over at Melanie and smiled. "Aw. Thanks, Mel. Ah! Okay! Let's do this! Wait! I need lip gloss." She pulled her pink sparkly lip gloss from her jeans pocket and slid it back and forth over her lips, popping them together before getting out of the car. She looked up at the tall building and felt Melanie's hand on her back, pushing her toward the store before linking her arm with Kathryn's and leading her onward.

As the girls came under the florescent lighting, Kathryn walked straight down the center aisle instead of to the left.

"Where are you going? You said he's in computers and video games," said Melanie.

"I know, but I want to hang back a bit and see where he is first."

They fumbled around the stacks of books in the department kitty-corner to hardlines, pretending to read the blurbs on the back covers.

"Oh my God. There he is. Shh… Don't look."

"He can't hear us, Kath. And he definitely can't hear us looking."

Kathryn clapped her hand to her mouth to muffle her laughter. "Oooh, he's going in the breakroom. Maybe we should go over there now so when he comes out, we're just there. Maybe it won't seem too suspicious."

Melanie nodded. "Good plan."

The girls weaved their way through the bookshelves, taking the tiled walkway across the wide center aisle. They casually meandered through the rows of CDs and arrived in the hardlines section.

"Kathryn, stand up straight. You're all hunched over like you're trying not to be seen."

"Am I really?"

"Try not to look so uncomfortable."

"But I am uncomfortable, Mel. We're literally stalking this guy. We're crazy people."

"Hey now. We're only crazy if this doesn't work."

"I don't think that's true."

"Eh, well, whatever. Let's go get your guy!"

"Shh! You're so loud. I know these people," Kathryn whispered harshly.

Melanie buried her face into Kathryn's arm, trying to smother her laugh, and Kathryn felt herself bend down again.

"Gah. I really am hunching over."

Melanie couldn't get a word out through her hysterics.

"Thank God he's still in the breakroom," Kathryn said with difficulty, choking on her laughing fit. She took a deep breath. "Okay. Come on. We need to pull it together." She scanned the area. "Let's go over by the card rack. It's tall and tilted away from everything."

With Adam still out of sight, they made their way to the greeting cards and each grabbed one, pretending to read it while peeking over the tops.

"What is this card rack doing in the computer section?" asked Melanie.

"I don't know. Maybe they wanted it close to the front of the store for easy accessibility."

"Just seems like an odd place for it."

"Okay, focus, Mel. Adam. We're here to talk to Adam."

"Right. Um...speaking of..." She nodded behind Kathryn.

She gasped, whipping her head around, and her breath escaped her...as did her balance, and Kathryn banged her foot into the metal base of the card rack. Melanie grabbed her arm to keep her steady and snorted into her friend's shoulder.

"Oh my God," Kathryn said, her hands fluttering to her forehead. "This is ridiculous. He's going to think I'm such a loser."

"Shh..."

They stayed silent as Adam approached, seemingly completely unaware of their presence.

"Oooh, he *is* cute," whispered Melanie.

Kathryn observed him carefully, and as he came closer, she felt herself straighten, her lips upturn, and a calmness settle over her.

"Hey, Mel, maybe I'll get this one for my mom," Kathryn said, opening a card.

"Oh…uh…yeah, that's a nice one. I'm sure she'd love it."

Kathryn walked on stable legs to the other side of the card rack, risking a glance in Adam's direction as he neared the kiosk.

He looked over and saw her, a smile spreading on his face, his eyes a shade of blue she felt certain hadn't been named yet. "Hey, Kathryn."

The sound of her name in his voice threatened her stance, yet she surprisingly remained calm. "Hey, Adam." She felt a jab to her arm. "Oh, this is my friend Melanie."

"Hi, Melanie. So what are you two ladies doing here?" Adam asked, his gaze holding on Kathryn.

"I'm looking for something for my mom. Her birthday's in a few weeks. Thought I'd get a head start."

"That's awesome. What's she into?"

"The Beatles. She's in love with Paul McCartney."

He chuckled, sending her heart into a spin. "I'm sure there's some Beatles stuff in music and books. Not sure you'll find much over here."

"We were looking at cards over here. Yeah. We thought we'd pick her up a nice card too. Right, Kath?" Melanie rammed her elbow into Kathryn's side.

"Ow. Uh…yeah. Yup. A card."

"Well, don't let me keep you guys."

"Oh, no. You're not. It's okay. We're in no rush," Kathryn said, waving off the very idea that she would rather be doing anything else in that moment.

Their eyes held each other's for a moment longer until Adam's shot slightly to her left. She followed them over her shoulder to see Rich standing toward the front of the store, looking in their direction. She offered him a little wave before turning back to Adam.

He rolled his eyes. "Why does he always seem to be lurking around when we're talking?"

Kathryn laughed.

"It's like he's stalking you two," Melanie said with a snort.

Kathryn slowly turned to her friend, her eyes wide, and tried to suppress a fit of hysterics begging to burst forth.

"Okay," Kathryn said, turning back to Adam. "We don't want to get you in trouble. We'll go walk around and look for that gift for my mom."

"Hello, you two," Rich said behind her back. "Kathryn, if you're going to stand around here chatting, you could at least pick up some inventory and help Adam put it away."

"Ha. Maybe next time. We were actually just leaving."

"Adam, I have Philip bringing the new shipment of ink cartridges from the warehouse for you to put out on the floor tonight."

"Sure thing, sir."

"Ladies." Rich nodded to the girls and turned back to his office.

"Yeah, we better go," Melanie said, pulling on Kathryn's arm.

"It was nice seeing you again, Kathryn."

"You too."

Melanie led her friend toward the back of the store. "Kathryn," she whispered out the corner of her mouth, "walk forward."

"What?"

"You're walking backward. Play it cool, girl. Turn around."

She ripped her vision from his smiling face and stumbled into Melanie, laughing at herself. "Doesn't my name sound different when he says it?"

Melanie shook her head. "Wow. You are so hooked."

The Long and Winding

Kathryn traced over the "A" in his name along the margin of her notebook for the fifth time as Jake stood over her shoulder, startling her out of her reverie where she only saw Adam and the way he looked at her a few days prior.

"The bell rang," Jake said, nudging her.

"What? Oh, chem's over? That's a shame."

He laughed. "I'll let you borrow my notes."

"Having a super smart cousin who can jump into higher-grade classes is paying off."

The cousins merged with the crowd of students in the hall, clearly in a rush to get to the last class before it was officially the weekend.

"Kathryn!"

She felt a hand on her shoulder. "Hey, Jos."

Jake offered Joselyn a quick nod. "I'm going this way, guys. Oh, Kathryn, the party for Papa's birthday is next weekend. You coming?"

"Absolutely. I'll be there. See ya later, Jake," Kathryn said before Joselyn started pulling on her arm.

"So?"

Kathryn sighed. "We're not working together this coming week. I guess we'll see about the week after."

"Oh, come on. That's annoying."

"Seriously. But at least the big meeting is this Sunday. It's mandatory, so he has to be there. Oh, there's Evan. Hey, Evan!" she said, waving her arm.

"Sup, Kathryn?" he asked, switching out his textbooks at his locker.

259

"You're going to the meeting this weekend, right?"

He grimaced. "Yeah. Seven freaking thirty in the morning on a Sunday."

"I know, right. Totally sucks. So, um…Adam should be there too, right?"

"I don't see why not. Rich is being a tight ass about… Wait. Why?" His eyes widened, and his mouth opened dramatically. "You have the hots for Adam? Ha! Told ya he's a tasty dish."

"Knock it off," she said, punching him in the arm.

"Does he know?"

"I don't know, but I have no idea when I'll be working with him again, and I really want to get to know him better."

"Dude, leave it to me."

Joselyn laughed. "What does that even mean?"

"No clue. But I'll come up with something. Just meet me outside in the courtyard after school."

Kathryn eyed him and nodded as she and Joselyn headed toward eighth period.

After class and gathering what she needed for homework over the weekend, Kathryn walked out into the courtyard, flanked by Melanie, Joselyn, and Kristin.

"What does he mean by that?" asked Kristin, flipping her dark, springy curls off her slender shoulder, a thick novel clutched tightly in one arm.

"I have no idea. But we're about to find out. What's Aubrey doing there with him?"

The girls advanced on the pair huddled together in the far corner of the courtyard near the buses.

Aubrey caught her eyes and squealed. "Oh my God, Kathryn. We have the *best* plan."

"Plan?"

"Yeah, so this is what we're going to do," Evan said, his hands doing most of the talking. "After the meeting, I'm going to ask Adam to come out to breakfast with me. You know, a little bro time or whatever. And then you and Aubrey are going to come over to us, and I'll be like 'Hey, ladies. I have a brilliant idea! You should both come out to breakfast with us!' And then we'll all go hang out, and you two can have some time together."

"Isn't it perfect?" Aubrey asked, bouncing and clapping. She gasped. "Can we invite Chris too?"

"Focus, Aubs."

Kathryn let it sink in a bit—a whole morning with Adam away from work. The corners of her lips glided upward. "That's perfect."

Kathryn, Evan, and Aubrey walked out of JAMM Media around eight thirty Sunday morning. A sick feeling pulled at Kathryn's stomach. "Why wasn't he here? You don't think he quit or was fired, do you? What if I never see him again? I don't even know his last name."

"Whoa. Calm down," Evan said. "I worked with him Friday night, and he didn't say anything about quitting."

"And you didn't ask him if he was going to the meeting?" Aubrey asked.

"I didn't want to risk sounding weird. I don't know. Just don't panic, okay? I'm sure there's a good explanation. I'm working a few days this week. I'll let you know if I see him or find anything out."

"Thank you all for coming today. I'm glad we were able to arrange to get you all here," Linda said, settling in her leather chair.

Kathryn spun her Claddagh ring from her chair off to the side, Jane roughly twirled her hair with her fingertips, and Brandon slouched next to his mom on the gray couch, looking as though he'd rather be anywhere else.

"Understandably, one of the main things Kathryn and I have discussed is her relationship with you, Brandon, and the incident that made her move in with her aunt and uncle."

Brandon scoffed. "Jumping right into it then, huh? We're here to talk about what a huge asshole I am, right?"

"Brandon, stop," Jane said.

Kathryn's heart rate increased, that familiar tone in his voice spreading a fire through her body.

Linda raised a gentle hand. "Absolutely not. We're not here to attack you or even to rehash the whole event."

"Then why the hell are we here?"

"We're here because Kathryn has a question for you, and she felt it best to ask in a controlled environment with your mom and me here."

"Oh, give me a break, Kathryn."

"Can you blame me?"

Brandon's fists closed tightly, and his face hardened. She could see it coming. She had seen it too many times to not recognize the signs.

261

"Let's all try to calm down," Linda said. "This is supposed to be a safe place to talk freely, but we also need to be mindful of our reactions."

"Brandon, please." Jane placed her hand on his. "Let's just hear what your sister has to say."

Brandon kept his eyes focused toward the coffee table, his arms folded across his thin chest, even more slouched than before.

Linda turned to Kathryn. "What is it that you wanted to discuss?"

"I...I just had a question." She twisted her ring on her finger, noticing the light ricocheting off the gold beveling of the crown. "Why?"

Silence.

Brandon finally turned to her. "Why what?"

"Why...do you hate me so much?"

Brandon shot up off the couch. "I'm not doing this. This is bull."

Kathryn rose to her feet. "No!" She would not allow herself to cave under the fear his glare heaved at her. "Tell me! What did I do? *Why* do you hate me so much?" Tears began forming in her eyes, but she stood firm.

"All brothers hate their little sisters, okay? You're a pain in the ass. Brothers and sisters fight. What the hell is the big deal?"

"Brandon, if I may," Linda said, "you're right that brothers and sisters fight sometimes. I have an older sister and a younger brother, and we certainly didn't get along all the time. But what you've done, it goes beyond typical arguing siblings."

"Give me a damn break. She pisses me off, okay? I guess I didn't handle it well."

Kathryn scoffed. "You guess?"

"Oh, shut the hell up."

"Not until you tell me!"

He bent forward, his head lowering, his eerily calm tone laced with malice. "Just the fact that you exist pisses me off."

"What am I even supposed to do with that?"

"I don't give a damn what you do—"

"It goes back to their father," Jane said, her voice shaking.

"What?" Kathryn asked, her face pinching. "What does Dad have to do with why you hate me?"

Brandon turned from the group and stalked toward the window over-looking the parking lot. "I'm not doing this."

Jane sighed. "Brandon, please."

"I said I'm not doing this!"

Kathryn flinched at his screams, the tone that typically accompanied pain. "I deserve to know," she said, her voice catching in her tightened throat. "What does Dad have to do with any of this? You barely even talk to him."

"Oh, but *you* talk to him all the time, don't you?" He turned around sharply, his eyes filled with familiar rage.

"What's that supposed to mean?"

"What? Daddy's little princess doesn't know what I mean? Daddy's baby girl doesn't know what I mean!" he yelled, his volume increasing.

"I'm not... You're not making any sense."

"I think we may be getting somewhere here, Kathryn," Linda said. "Brandon, please continue."

"Continue? Oh, yes, let's continue. Let's continue talking about how Dad hates me. Let's talk about all the shit he did to Mom when we left him."

"Brandon..." Jane shifted uncomfortably.

"No, Mom. Why shouldn't she know? Why does she get to go around thinking Dad is so perfect?"

"I don't think he's perfect. I know he's done horrible things. I'm trying to see past them. He's trying to be a better dad."

Brandon laughed. "Well, it's too damn late for that!"

"I don't care if you have a relationship with him or not! Do whatever you want. But what does that have to do with why you abused me?"

"*Abused* you? Oh, come on."

"Yes! Abuse! Hitting me, punching me, stabbing me in the ankle, beating me with Otis's dog rope, grabbing me by my hair and slamming me into the wall. What would you call that?"

He took another step toward her, his lip curling into a snarl. "Well deserved."

"That's enough!" Jane pushed herself up, standing between her children. "This isn't helping. I can't stand to listen to you two talk to each other like this."

"He's the one saying horrible things to me! God! You're always taking his side!"

Jane turned to her daughter. "Kathryn, that's not true."

"Then why did I have to move out! Why did *I* have to be the one to leave?"

"I thought we had moved past this, honey. I... It was an impossible situation. I—"

"Because she'll always take my side. Just like Dad always takes yours. Don't you see, Kathryn? It's always been me and Mom against you and Dad."

Kathryn stood frozen, utterly incapable of forming words.

"All the shit he's done to Mom, to me, to you. Everything he put us through. You still go to him. You still want to spend time with him. You don't give a damn about what he's done to your own mom."

"That's not true. Of course I care."

"Bullshit! If you cared, you wouldn't want to have anything to do with him."

"It's not that simple. He's still my dad."

"Well, he's not mine!"

"Fine! What do I care? But that doesn't mean it's me and him against you and Mom. That would mean there's no me and Mom."

"You said it, didn't you? You were the one who moved out. I stayed. You left. What does that tell you?"

Jane gasped. "Brandon! Stop this right now! I love you both, not one more than the other. You are both my children." She turned to Kathryn, tears streaming down her face. "I didn't know what to do. It was an impossible situation. The two people I love most in the entire world, the two people I would give my life for, one threatening the other, making her scared to live in our home. I didn't know what to do. I knew he was in the wrong. He had no right to hurt you. But where would he go if I made him leave? He had nowhere to go. You at least had a place to go. I knew you'd be safe and well cared for with Hannah and Alex. I know that's not good enough. I know I wasn't enough. I wasn't what you needed me to be. But it's all I had to give. I'm so, so sorry, Kathryn."

Overwhelmed, her adrenaline plummeting, Kathryn's legs gave out, and she fell to the chair, her elbows hitting her knees as she sobbed into her hands. She felt a hand on her back.

"Sweetie, I know I can never make it right. I can never make up for the mistakes I've made. I hope one day you can forgive me. For now, though, please know how much I love you. I need you to know how much I love you."

"This is ridiculous," Brandon said, his rough voice cutting through their cries.

Jane swung around. "That's enough, Brandon! No more! It's not you and me against them. She is my daughter, and I love her the same as I love you."

"And you're just okay with her and Dad? After all he's done?"

"He's her father, and she has every right to have whatever kind of relationship with him she wants. You have the same right. What you both do with it is up to you."

"Whatever. Can I go now?"

"This is probably a good place to stop for today." Linda closed her notebook.

"Great. I'm out of here. I'll be in the car." He slammed the door behind him.

Linda knelt next to the mother and daughter crouched beside each other. "It may not seem like it right now, but I believe this was a big step toward healing. I truly do. However irrational, he gave you his reasoning. It's not accurate. He has concocted this in his mind over the years, and it's clear that he's hurting greatly. But he believes it, and at least now that it's out in the open, hopefully, it can be discussed again at some point, and you all can continue to heal from this."

Kathryn looked up, her face splotched red and tear tracked. "I don't see Brandon and me ever healing. It's too far gone. Too much has happened."

"Never say never," Linda said, tilting her blond head. "Maybe when you're older, adults with your own separate lives, maybe you'll find a way to have some kind of relationship. It's up to you to define it. For now, though, the relationship right here, that's the one worth nurturing. This is the one worth saving."

Kathryn leaned her head against her mom's. "I know."

"He didn't quit or get fired, so calm yourself," Evan said to Kathryn as she opened her locker. "I worked with him last night. He had some Easter thing last Sunday with his family or something."

Kathryn exhaled deeply, a smile of relief lighting up her face. "Thank God. Waiting this week has been torture. Wait. But Easter was earlier in April."

Evan shrugged. "Don't know. That's what he said. He talked to Rich and didn't have to go. Either way, he's still working there, so you can breathe easy. He's working again tonight, Tuesday, and Thursday."

"Thursday? Really? Ah! Me too! I just called to check my hours last night!"

Evan shrieked and jumped up and down.

Kathryn tried to keep a stern face. "Are you done?"

"I think so," he said, calmly tugging at the hem of his T-shirt and pretending to fix his heavily gelled hair as he winked at a girl walking past them.

"Smooth."

He feigned a bow. "Oh, crap. I have to be across the school for history. Talk to you later."

Kathryn laughed and snatched her English book and binder before closing

265

her locker. A familiar laugh grabbed her attention, and she peered down the hall, spotting Lexie dressed in her red and white cheerleader uniform, encircled by the other cheerleaders. Their heads flung back in laughter almost in unison, tossing their perfect hair about. Lexie caught her eye and grinned, raising her hand and wiggling her fingers. Kathryn smiled back, returning the wave, and started down the hall in the opposite direction.

"Happy birthday to you," they sang in three-part harmony.

"Blow out your candles, Papa!" said Sam. "Don't make us wait any longer for that cake."

Jake chuckled. "He's only here for the cake."

Sam feigned a gasp. "That's not true. There's also ice cream."

"All right, you two. Alex, make a wish," said Aunt Hannah, rubbing his back.

"I don't know what else I could possibly wish for, darling." He bent down and kissed her.

"Very sweet, Papa."

He took a deep breath and blew out the candles to applause.

Aunt Hannah picked up the cake off the kitchen table. "Kathryn, would you help me slice and serve the cake and ice cream, please?"

"Sure." Kathryn grabbed the ice cream from the freezer and met her aunt at the counter.

"So, how are you, my dear?" Aunt Hannah asked, slicing the first piece. "How's everything been going for you lately?"

"Pretty well actually. I'm...doing better, feeling stronger...happier." She plopped a scoop of ice cream next to the piece of cake.

"I'm very happy to hear that. My goodness. So, so happy. Home, work, school—everything is going well?"

Kathryn served Uncle Alex and Sam their cake and ice cream and returned to Aunt Hannah's side. "I still just stay away from Brandon when I can, but when we're together, we're civil. School's good. My grades are good this term, and, of course, our orchestra concert is coming up."

"We couldn't be more excited to see our first-chair cellist and our second-chair bassist perform."

Sam fist-pumped into the air as he shoved half the slice of cake in his mouth.

"And work?"

Kathryn set a plate of cake and ice cream in front of Jake. "Work's good too. I…uh…actually met a guy there recently."

"Oooh, do tell."

"His name is Adam," Jake said before licking frosting off his fingers.

Aunt Hannah and Kathryn laughed.

"Yes, his name is Adam. I've only seen him twice, but I'm hoping to get to know him better. We're both scheduled this Thursday."

"That's wonderful. How fun and exciting. You'll have to keep me updated."

"I will. And I'm sure Jake will be able to fill in any blanks for you, too," she said with a giggle.

When all the cake had been eaten and ice cream spoons thoroughly licked clean, Jake leaned back in his chair, rubbing his stomach. "Great cake, Mama. Worth the wait. Game time!"

"Yuuss!" Sam pushed away from the table and bolted into the living room.

"What are we playing?" Kathryn asked, entering the living room, a glass of ice water in her hand.

Sam twisted his face dramatically. "What else? The Game of Life! I call blue!"

Jake threw his hand up. "Red!"

Kathryn sat on the loveseat next to Aunt Hannah while the boys knelt on the floor beside the coffee table, organizing the money and doling out cars to everyone.

"White for you, Mama. Kathryn, you get yellow. Papa, here's your green car."

"Oh, come on," said Sam as he fumbled with the tiny blue peg, trying to put it in his car with his oversized hands. "Why can't I ever get these darn things in?"

"Roadkill!" shouted Aunt Hannah.

The family laughed at the standing joke never losing its hilarity regardless of how many times over the years it was and would be spoken, no matter how many times they huddled around that table in that house with one another. Kathryn's spirit soared with familial adoration for the people—these wonderful people—who saved her, thankful for them with every beat of her heart.

Kathryn parked and pulled her break before popping her pink, glossed lips in her rearview. She took a deep breath and got out of the car, smoothing her soft purple V-neck top, nearly tripping into Chris as his hands shot up to her arms.

"Geez. Sorry. I wasn't paying attention."

"Clearly. Got your head in the clouds?"

"Something like that. You just getting off shift?"

"Yeah. It's dead in there, and Rich and Mae knew you were coming, so they said I could take off early."

"Lucky you. Except now you don't get to work with me. So...maybe not so lucky," she said, scrunching her face.

Chris smirked, walking backward toward his car. "I'll be okay...someday." He offered a wave as he turned. "See ya, Kathryn."

She ambled through the automatic sliding doors, keeping her head up—confident, determined not to let her giddy mess of nerves show. After punching in, she put her purse in the breakroom locker and tied on her red apron. As she slid behind her assigned register, she still hadn't risked a glance, but the anticipation overtook her, and she couldn't stop herself.

There he was—his sandy blond hair brilliant in the bright overhead lights. He fidgeted with his pen as he talked to a shopper, and his eyes darted over, meeting hers briefly before he returned his attention to the customer, clearly unable to overpower the smile that spread across his adorable, stubbly face as he helped the man choose the right printer.

Heat rushed to her cheeks, and she quickly fanned herself as a woman and a young boy approached her register with the second and third books of the latest popular series. She had no control over her smile as she scanned the barcodes on the back covers amid the beautifully detailed artwork.

"Do you like these books too?" the little boy asked her, his eyes wide with excitement.

"They're my favorite. She's my favorite author. I can't wait for the fourth one to come out. It's supposed to be released this summer."

The boy gasped. "Really? Can we get that one too, Mom? Can we please?"

"Of course."

"We'll sometimes have release parties for big books. I'm sure we'll have signs out if we decide to do that for this release."

"Fantastic," his mom said. "We'll keep an eye out. Thanks so much."

"You're very welcome." Kathryn slid the books into a bag. "Have a great evening. Enjoy your books."

"Thanks!" the little boy shouted as he scrambled to catch up to his mom.

There was a steady stream of customers on and off for the next few hours, and in between, Rich was hanging around, giving Kathryn and the other cashier a list of small tasks to accomplish before their shifts ended. After she was done wiping down her counter, straightening the magazines, making sure the candy was properly sorted, and perfecting the bestseller display, he instructed her to take the basket of returns to the warehouse the first chance she got.

"Ladies," Rich said, his hand landing on Kathryn's counter just as her line died down, "I'm leaving for the night. Mae's in her office. She's in charge. Kathryn, thirty minutes left on shift, yes? Looks like a good time to take those returns to the warehouse."

"Yes, sir." She scooped up the basket of returns as Rich exited through the front doors. "I'll be right back, Stephanie. You're okay, right?"

"Oh, yeah," Stephanie said, wiping down her counter. "Looks like it's slowed again."

Kathryn started down the center aisle, looking to her left to see if she could spot him, but he wasn't there. She sighed and watched her feet shuffle along the ivory tile.

"Had any games to find tonight?"

Her head shot up at the familiar voice, and Adam was strolling toward her, his long strides covering three tiles to her two. A light laugh escaped her smile. "A few. But I managed okay by myself this time."

"Too bad. I would have loved to come to your rescue again."

Her hair was lightly tousled by the gentle breeze his body created as he strode past her, his bicep just slightly brushing her shoulder, a clean, sweet aroma lingering in his wake. She looked back at him, unable to form words, and returned his smile. Warmth rushed through her body once again, and she fought to keep her gait straight as she entered the warehouse and placed the assortment of returned merchandise into the corresponding bins.

With only ten minutes left in her shift, panic set in. She had no idea when they'd work together again, so this could be her only chance to talk to him for a while. But she was clueless as to how to do it. She wasn't Lexie, the stunning, flirty cheerleader who all the boys chased. She was just Kathryn.

She lifted her elbows off the counter when she saw him heading her way with an elderly woman, her heart rate hastening as he drew closer.

"Here you are, ma'am," he said, sweeping his arm toward her register. "Kathryn can help you with that game for your grand-nephew."

"What a nice young man. You didn't have to walk me all the way over here," the woman said, patting him on the arm.

He glanced at Kathryn. "I know. Happy to do it though." He softly tossed the game on the counter and faced the woman. "You have a great night."

"You too," she said. "What a sweetheart that boy."

269

Kathryn nodded, still watching Adam as he turned and walked backward, pointing at the drawers before twisting around to return to his kiosk.

"I'll be right back with your game, ma'am. I have to get it from those drawers over there."

The game took her a bit longer to find than the others; she was a little distracted.

After ringing out the woman's game and wishing her a good evening, she spotted the time on the clock hanging on the front wall—8:01. Her shift was over.

"I'm off, Stephanie," she called over to her.

"Okay, Kathryn. Have a nice night."

"You too."

She punched out and hung her apron on one of the hooks in the breakroom before grabbing her purse from the locker. Without further thought, she found herself walking back onto the floor and gliding toward him cutting a yellow piece of paper into strips.

"You know, you could have just taken her to actually get the game from the Giant, Black Drawers of Doom."

He snickered. "The what?"

"That's what we cashiers call those evil drawers."

He buckled over in laughter. "That's amazing. I figured you'd appreciate the practice."

"I thought you wanted to rescue me again."

"On second thought, you don't seem like a girl who needs to be rescued."

Words failed her.

"So, you're off the clock?"

"Yeah. How long are you here?"

"Until ten. But it's okay. I have all these display tags to cut, all these game cases here to tag," he said, slapping a hand on top of the stack on the kiosk, "and every one of them to put on display. And those"—he pointed to the box behind him—"are the games I have to put away in the...what did you call it? Drawers of Death?"

She laughed. "Giant, Black Drawers of Doom."

"Ah, yes. How could I forget?"

"You have to do all that by yourself?"

"Yeah. I'm the only one on until ten."

"That kinda sucks." She fiddled with her ring, pushing the crown with her fingernail. "Um...I could stay and help...if you want."

"Really? And not get paid for it?"

270

"I don't really want to go home anyway. My brother's a jerk. I don't feel like dealing with him tonight."

"Uh…yeah, sure. I don't mind at all. Not sure what Rich will say though."

"He left a little while ago. Mae's in charge."

Adam smiled. "Awesome. Uh…here." He handed her the scissors and yellow paper. "You can cut the price tags out."

"You play the cello? That's really cool. My mom made me play clarinet in elementary school."

She held in a laugh. "I can't really picture that."

"I was awful. Didn't make it past fifth grade. She must have known how bad I was because she let me quit."

Kathryn grabbed a game from the pile. "And your dad didn't fight for you to stick with it and become a concert clarinetist?"

Adam breathed a laugh while taping a display tag on the front bottom corner of the last game in his pile. "Not quite. He…wasn't around much. I mean, he was, but he wasn't."

She nodded. "Same."

"Divorced?"

"Yeah. It was mainly just me, my mom, and my brother."

"Who's a jerk."

"Major jerk."

"Sorry. The plus of being an only child."

"We have a few tags left over," she said, straightening the pile of small yellow pieces of paper in her palm.

"I'll hang on to them." He slipped them from her hand and shoved the tags into his apron pocket, scooped up the stack of games, and met her by the empty shelving.

One by one, she took a game off the pile in his arms and placed it on the shelf. "Let me know if I'm not doing this right. I have no idea what I'm doing."

"Looks perfect to me. So…uh…seventeen means you're still in high school? Where do you go?"

"I'm a junior at Edgebrook High."

"Ah… I went to Maysville High. I guess we're rivals. But I suppose I can let it slide."

"That's big of you."

"Eh, that's the kind of guy I am," he said with a tilt of his head.

She laughed again, her face sore from smiling so much in his presence. "You're in college then?"

"Yeah. Buffalo University. I started in graphic design but switched to IT."

"Design? You're an artist?" She set the last game on the shelf, moving it over so it was even with the others.

"I like to draw, but the design program just wasn't what I thought it would be. I like what I'm studying now though."

They walked out from behind the shelf, coming face to face with Mae.

"Kathryn? I thought you clocked out."

"I did, but...um...I wasn't really in a hurry to get home, and Adam had a lot of work to do, so..."

The short, stocky woman looked over her thick glasses, her dark eyes darting from Kathryn to Adam and back again.

"I...uh...hope that's okay."

Mae looked behind the pair, and Kathryn and Adam followed her gaze to the shelf they had just finished stocking. "I suppose. As long as you're not... too distracting to this young man here."

"No, not at all. We were just about to put the games away in the drawers." He turned to grab the box on the kiosk.

Mae took a step toward Kathryn, her voice hushed. "Not at all? Then you're not trying hard enough, hon." She winked and spun on her heel, heading back to her office.

Adam returned to her side, the box in his arms. "What did she say?"

Kathryn smiled, suppressing a laugh. "Just that it's fine if I stay and help."

"Cool. You ready to dive into the Huge, Dark...Doom...Drawers?"

Kathryn nearly pitched forward in amusement. "Giant, Black Drawers of Doom. Come on, man," she said, gently shoving him. Her hand lingered on his bicep longer than she had intended, and she withdrew it sharply. "Let's do it."

"Do you think putting these away might help you find them more easily?"

She shook her head. "Not likely. I hate this thing with such a passion. Good-for-nothing, stupid drawers."

"I wouldn't say 'nothing.'" He met her eyes.

If her heart flipped once more tonight, she swore it would burst.

"So...um...are you hanging with your friend Melanie this weekend?"

"Oh...not that I know of. We haven't planned anything. She...I think she's even busy this weekend. Family stuff or something. I guess it'll be a pretty boring weekend."

Adam grabbed the final game from the box and parted two games with his fingers, sliding it into the right spot. "Do you think I could maybe call you? Maybe we could hang out."

She bit the inside of her bottom lip to try to keep from smiling way too widely. "Sure. I'd like that."

"Cool." He grinned and picked up the box, catching sight of his watch. "Geez. It's almost ten already."

"It's been two hours? Wow. Didn't seem like it."

"So, I'll call you tomorrow. We can set something up for Saturday."

"Actually, I'll call you. I don't really like answering my home phone. Um...long story."

"No problem." He rifled around in the pockets of his apron and pulled out a yellow tag. "Come here," he said, motioning toward the kiosk. He grabbed a pen off the counter and scribbled on it before folding it in half.

He held out his open palm, and she took it, letting her fingertips brush against his skin.

"Thanks. So, I'll call you then."

"Looking forward to it."

"Yeah, me too." She tried to move from that spot, to fight the invisible pull, but she was powerless in that moment, longing to stay lost in his smile.

"Quitting time, you two," Mae said, appearing as if from nowhere, snapping Kathryn back to reality.

Adam nodded to the wall clock behind Mae. "I still have ten minutes."

"Is all your work done?"

"It is."

"Then clock out. Walk a lady to her car."

Adam faced Kathryn once more. "My pleasure. I'll just punch out. Meet you by the doors?"

"Okay." She bit her inside lip harder.

When he was a safe distance from them, Mae nudged Kathryn's arm. "You're welcome."

"This is mine here. The little red one," Kathryn said, walking up to her Mazda.

He chuckled. "That's mine there." He gestured to the white Mustang parked next to her, its lines reflecting that of an older model.

273

Kathryn's eyes widened. "Seriously? Wow."

"A gift from my dad for my eighteenth birthday."

"That's an awesome car."

"Well, you'll get to ride in it when I pick you up Saturday." He led her to her driver's side.

"Can't wait."

"Talk to you tomorrow, Kathryn." He seemed to hesitate for just a moment before he walked away from her and got into his car.

She tossed her purse on the passenger seat and waved at him as he backed up and drove off.

Alone in her car in a nearly deserted parking lot, she gripped the wheel and screamed before falling into a giddy fit of laughter. "Oh my God!" She stamped her feet as she pushed against the wheel, letting out another gleeful shriek. Kathryn started the engine and cranked up her boy band, singing along, releasing her joyous energy with every note, reveling in the feeling Adam evoked within her. At the first stoplight, she snatched the yellow slip of paper off the seat and opened it, tracing her finger over his phone number and giggling at the exclamation point he put after his name.

Breathe

"Mom! Do you know where my black scoop neck is? Or maybe the pink one? And where are my favorite dark jeans with the embroidery on the back pockets? I can't find them anywhere."

Jane leaned against her daughter's open doorway. "You're wearing them."

"What?" She looked down. "Oh my God. I need to chill out."

"That would be a good idea. I just hung up both your black and pink scoop necks last night."

"Which one should I wear though?"

"Whichever one you feel comfortable in. They both look lovely on you." She approached Kathryn and rested a hand on her shoulder. "Sweetie, breathe with me. He clearly likes you or else he wouldn't have asked you out. Try to relax."

"But he's going to be here in twenty minutes. My hair is still in rollers, and I don't know which shirt to wear. Oh! Where's my lip gloss?"

"Check your pocket."

Kathryn's hand snapped to the outside of her jeans, and she sighed when she felt the tube through the denim.

"If I had to choose, I'd say go with the pink. You always look so nice in pink. Plus, it goes nicely with your bracelet. I'm sure your rollers are done. Let's take them out." She unclipped a roller and let it unravel into her palm, leaving bouncy fullness in the strip of Kathryn's hair.

When all the rollers were out, her pink top lay smoothly over her shapely frame, and her lips were well glossed, Jane threaded her fingers through

275

Kathryn's hair from behind her, sweeping it forward onto her chest. She met her daughter's eyes in the mirror. "He won't know what hit him."

Kathryn laughed. "Thanks, Mom." She gasped at the doorbell. "Oh my God. Oh my God."

"Relax. Breathe. Come introduce me."

Kathryn led the way down the stairs to the front door, spotting his car through the picture window.

"He drives a Mustang?"

"It's okay, Mom. Breathe."

She opened the door, and there he stood, his eyes matching his blue polo, a yellow stripe across his chest.

"Hi," he said breathily.

"Hey." Despite her nerves, a calmness settled over her as she examined the dark flecks scattered through his irises so blue she couldn't think of an accurate word to describe them if she tried.

"Ahem."

"Oh, sorry. Adam, this is my mom, Jane Spahn. Mom, this is Adam Lyndon."

"It's nice to meet you, Ms. Spahn," he said, extending a quivering hand.

"Jane, please. It's very nice to meet you too, Adam. So, where are you two going?"

"I was thinking of starting with lunch if that sounds okay."

Kathryn slipped on her ivory sandals. "Sounds perfect."

"Okay, well, you two have fun." She reached for Kathryn and pulled her into a hug. "He's cute. Be safe, sweetie."

"I will, Mom. Breathe."

"'Livin' La Vida Loca!'"

Adam dropped his hand on the small dining table. "You beat me again! I'm going to get one of these before you do by the time we're done."

"Oooh, big talk."

"Hey now. I know the songs. You're just too fast with the titles."

She bit the tip off a french fry. "I guess you'll need to be quicker."

He chuckled. "She's got a competitive side. Okay. All good info to learn on the first date. So, you were saying before you beat me again?"

"What was I...? Oh, just that my parents divorced when I was three, and it's just been my mom, brother, and me."

"Was your brother...?"

"Brandon."

"Brandon. Was he at the house when I picked you up?"

Kathryn fingered her pink beaded bracelet, tugging on the clasp. "He was probably in the basement. He pretty much lives there." She lifted the pink lemonade to her lips for a quick sip. "You're so lucky to be an only child."

"I always wanted a brother or sister, actually. My parents divorced when I was two. It's just me and my mom. My aunt, her sister, has always been around a lot though. I guess I kind of had two moms."

"And your dad?"

"He was around. I'd go to his house, have sleepovers." He dipped a fry in a blob of ketchup. "Yours?"

"Same, I guess. It's…kind of complicated."

"Okay. Maybe it can be fifth or sixth date material."

"Fifth or sixth?"

The corner of Adam's mouth upturned into an adorable half-smile. "Yeah."

She was drawn into his one-sided grin, into his eyes, into his words, completely taken by this young man she hardly knew.

"'Amazed!'" she shouted before clapping her hand over her mouth, reacting to how loudly it slipped out.

"Oh, come on. That's not fair." He shook his head. "I wasn't even paying attention."

Kathryn shrugged. "Not my problem." She fought to keep her expression flat, but she cracked, letting a laugh break through, joining with his. "I love this song."

"Me too."

"So, you know about my favorite things, but what are some of yours? I noticed the football keychain."

He nodded, finishing a bite of his burger. "Love football. Hockey too."

"Do you play?"

"Not really. I mean, just around the back yard with my friends growing up. But I love watching and following all sports. Being born and raised here, I'm obviously a diehard Buffalo Bills and Sabres fan."

"Of course. My dad loves sports too, baseball especially. He used to take me to Bisons games."

"Very cool."

"Are we all set here?" the waitress asked, pulling his attention from her.

"Yup. Thank you. I'll take that," he said, reaching out his hand for the check.

"You don't have to do that."

"I know." He flashed that cute smile again as he reached into his back pocket for his wallet. "So, where to next?"

"I was thinking we could maybe just walk around the mall? Lots of different things to do there."

"Sure. The mall it is."

"We've been friends for almost two years. Mel's the best."

"She seemed very cool…for the two minutes I spent with her."

The pair leisurely strolled through the mall, Kathryn in no hurry for their date to end.

"I actually live a few doors down from two of my best friends," Adam said.

"Really? That's awesome. No siblings but friends close by." She slowed. "Can we look in here? I need a gift for my mom for tomorrow."

"Tomorrow?" His eyes widened. "Oh, geez. Tomorrow's Mother's Day."

"I guess you need to pick something up too."

"It completely slipped my mind."

They walked through the aisles, perusing the trinkets and figurines, neither of them finding anything.

"What's your mom into? Besides The Beatles, of course."

Kathryn stopped and turned to him. "You remembered."

Adam smiled. "Of course I did."

She bit her inner lip. "She really loves lighthouses."

"My mom's into cardinals. There are some suncatchers over there," he said, nodding toward the display. "I think my mom would like something like that."

"Mine too." She scanned down the array of colored glass on one side and spotted a cardinal sitting on a branch with leaves crawling along the edges. "Here's a cardinal," she said, leaning around to the other side with the suncatcher held up for Adam to see. She laughed. "Seriously?"

"I found a lighthouse." He chuckled, the circular glass lightly swaying in his hand.

"I guess we're all set for Mother's Day then."

By their second lap around the mall, both the lower floor and the upper, Kathryn knew quite a bit about Adam, but she was overwhelmed by the desire to learn more and more, to soak up every single word and detail he could possibly offer her. She had successfully skirted around a few issues but had opened up to him just as much, reveling in his apparent craving for the same from her.

They ended up back at the entrance through which they originally came.

He slowed his pace to a halt as they both eyed the doors. "Is there somewhere else you wanted to go?"

"I know I don't want to go home yet."

He smiled. "Me neither. I have an idea. Come on."

She felt his hand delicately brush up against hers, and she responded to it, moving toward him. Kathryn's heart fluttered as his fingers interlaced with hers, and she closed her hand around his. Adam led her outside into the dazzling May afternoon, rich with sunlight, not a dark cloud in the sky.

The cool, smooth mist cascaded around them like the branches of a weeping willow. They stood leaning against the guardrail, the purr of the rushing water plummeting to the rocky earth below strong in their ears, the haze of the rising water droplets billowing upward. Living twenty minutes from such a natural wonder had dulled its magic over the years, but in that moment, with Adam by her side, her hand fitting perfectly with his, Niagara Falls had never looked so miraculous.

Kathryn let out a small squeal as a gust of wind whipped the mist toward them, and Adam stepped between her and the falls, shielding her from the spray. She looked up into his eyes so close she could see every variation, and her breath caught as he skimmed a stray strand off her cheek speckled with moisture. "Do you want to take a walk down one of the paths?"

Adam nodded slowly. "As you wish."

He took her hand once more, and they continued down the pathway along the rim of the falls, disturbing the loose pebbles with every step.

They walked across the bridge that carried them over the Niagara River, stopping halfway to take in the view of the charging water that would soon plummet over the falls, Canada as its backdrop.

"I don't mean to be presumptuous, and I know this date isn't even over yet, but I'd really like to take you out again," Adam said as they strode from the bridge and broke the wooded threshold off the path, looking for a grassy area to sit.

"I'd like that too."

"Phew!" He wiped his brow. "So, I'm doing okay?"

She laughed and squeezed his hand. "Absolutely."

Kathryn let her fingers lightly dance against the buttery flowers of a row of forsythias as they came upon a small hill leading toward the riverbank separated with large boulders acting as a barrier from the rushing waters. She sat hugging her knees to her chest, leaning against the rough bark of a giant maple while Adam dropped cross-legged in front of her, the couple engulfed in the shadow of the canopy overhead speckled with a small flock of goldfinches. There they stayed for what felt like hours yet only minutes all at the same time, not a silent or uncomfortable moment between them. Their voices carried throughout the small tree-lined nook, scattering like veining on the leaves that dangled above them.

When the foot traffic at the top of the hill died down significantly and the spring air began to cool, a slight shiver crawled along Kathryn's alabaster skin.

"Are you cold?"

"Maybe a little. Goodness," she said, looking around, only then noticing the evening sky beginning to dim. "What time is it?"

Adam glanced at his watch and sighed. "Eight thirty."

The first moment of silence.

"Come on. I should probably get you home." He stood and offered her his hands, leaning back as he helped her up. "This is a pretty ring," he said, running his thumb along the gold crown sitting atop the heart held within two hands.

"Thanks. I love it. I never take it off." They started up the grassy knoll, their fingers entwined. "I still can't believe we worked at JAMM together for so long and never saw each other until just recently."

"Actually, I saw you when I first started working there."

"You did? Where?"

"In the warehouse. You brought some returns back there when I was pricing CDs."

"Really? I had no idea."

He shrugged lightly. "You didn't see me."

"You remember that from five months ago?"

Adam smiled that smile. "Of course I do. I watched you place all the returns in the correct bins. Most people just toss the box on the counter and leave. But you put them all away. I...remember thinking I could never get someone like you. That you were too good for me."

Kathryn halted as they reached the top of the hill and turned to look up into his eyes. "You thought *I* was too good for *you*?"

He nodded.

"That's crazy. I'm not too good for anyone. I'm...just...me. Nothing special."

"Then you have no idea how amazing you are."

Kathryn couldn't stop the smile pulling at her lips, and she looked down, pink staining her cheeks. Adam brought his hand under her chin, lifting it, holding her in his strong gaze. He lightly traced her jawline with the back of his finger. Heat flushed through her body as she attempted to steady herself against the weakness in her legs.

Adam led her back onto the stone path, taking their time on the bridge, the rapids of the Niagara River underfoot.

With Niagara Falls in Adam's rearview, he drove south, heading back toward Kathryn's house.

"I don't really want to go home. Don't take the Interstate. Take the long way back."

"You got it." He switched lanes, bypassing the Interstate. "That seems to be a theme with us, not wanting to go home. I mean, it's working out for me... but is it because you don't want our date to end"—he nudged her with his arm —"or because you don't want to be home with your brother?"

"Both. But more the first."

"So, what's the deal there? If you don't mind me asking."

"With Brandon?"

"Mmm hmm."

The truth held in her throat, aching to be freed, to tell this man everything, to fully let him into her life, to reveal all her secrets so he could know her completely. But the words died on her tongue, too many uncertainties, too much fear censoring her response.

"He...he's just awful to be around. Lots of snide remarks, teases me, puts me down. I try to spend as little time with him as possible. Probably similar to other siblings." The taste of her dishonesty twisted her stomach.

"That sounds miserable. I'm sorry."

"It's not really my favorite topic."

"Then what is?"

"Mittens or my cello."

"Ah, yes, the instrument you've been playing since you were ten and your...black and white cat who hates everyone."

"She doesn't *hate* everyone. She just loves me so much there isn't room for anyone else."

Adam laughed.

"She's my...animal soulmate. I've had her since I was six. We've...been through a lot together."

"That's really sweet. So, when do I get to meet Mittens who will most certainly hate me?"

"Oh, I don't know. That's a big step. I don't just let anyone meet her."

He nodded. "I see. Well...hopefully I'll make the cut."

"I think you have a pretty good chance," she said, tugging at the beads of her bracelet.

"You've been fiddling with that bracelet all day."

Kathryn looked down at her left wrist. "Yeah, I mess with it a lot."

"Is that a special bracelet?"

"It was just something I picked out for my birthday. I thought it was cute. And it's pink, so that's always a plus for me."

"Mittens, cello, pink. Got it. I'd love to hear you play sometime."

"I'd really like that. I actually have a concert in June if you'd like to come." She watched as his lips upturned amid the stubble.

"I'm there." He reached over and took her hand again. "So, cello's a pretty big deal then."

"I love it. It's my favorite thing to do. I go to a summer orchestra camp every year. My good friend Grace goes too. I think this'll probably be our last year there together though. This time next year, we'll be getting ready for college. I'm applying to WNYU's music program. I want to be an orchestra teacher."

"That sounds perfect." He brought his hand back to the wheel as the sun continued its descent, his bright lights slicing through the darkness.

Kathryn's right hand gravitated to her left wrist, pulling on the beads again. "I have an awesome orchestra teacher, and I just love strings so much. It would be amazing to make it my career."

"You certainly sound passionate about it."

"I've been thinking about it for a while and—" She gasped. "Oh, no!" Pink beads sprang in every direction, bouncing off the roof and the windshield, dropping to the car floor. "My bracelet." She groaned. "I shouldn't have messed with it so much. I must have weakened the string." She leaned down, picking up all the pieces she could, collecting them in her hand. "You're going to have pink beads in every crevice of your car."

"Don't worry about it. I'm sorry about your bracelet."

"I'm sorry about your car."

"Don't be. I'll just have lots of little reminders of you."

He pulled into her driveway and slid the gear into park. Their heads swiveled toward each other, their eyes locking.

"Come on. I'll walk you to your door."

"Such a gentleman."

"Yup," he said, shrugging, "that's me."

Every step up the walkway felt heavier and heavier as if she had to force her legs to take her home and away from Adam.

He swung around to face her at the door, taking both her hands in his. "I had a really nice time today, Kathryn. Like the best time I've had in as long as I can remember."

She couldn't possibly suppress the bliss gracing her face. "Me too. I can't remember the last time I smiled and laughed so much."

"I know tomorrow's Mother's Day and all, and I suppose I'm supposed to play it cool or whatever, but I'd like to call you tomorrow if that's okay. We can talk about our next date. Maybe Monday?"

"Monday's perfect."

"Perfect. Bye, Kathryn." He took a small step to her side and leaned forward, his stubble brushing against the side of her face, feeling softer than she had expected, and he tenderly kissed her cheek.

She opened her eyes as he pulled away, holding his gaze a moment longer —a moment not nearly long enough. "Bye, Adam. Thank you for the perfect day."

"My pleasure."

"And then he kissed me on the cheek."

"Ah! Oh my God. That has to be one of the best first dates in the history of first dates!" Joselyn's hand flew up to her heart.

"And you're going out on another date with him again tonight?" asked Kristin.

"Yup."

Melanie slapped at Kathryn's arm. "Oooh, oooh! Tell them how the bracelet that's supposed to give you luck in love just happened to explode on your first date with this guy. I mean, come on. Guess you don't need it anymore."

"Hey, Kathryn."

She turned to face the familiar voice. "Hey, Lex!"

"So, what's this I hear from across the hall? A date?"

"I met a really amazing guy at work."

Lexie's emerald eyes widened, and a trill of excitement brought a bounce to the balls of her feet. "Eee! That's so amazing! I'm so happy for you."

"We have to get to class, Kathryn," Melanie said, looking to Joselyn and Kristin.

"I have my free period now, so you guys go on ahead. I'll talk to you later."

"I have lunch next, so I can be a few minutes late," Lexie said. "I want to hear all about him!"

"His name is Adam, and we went out on our first date on Saturday. Oh my God, Lex. He's...incredible."

"Wow. You are falling hard for this guy. I've never seen that look in your eyes before. Not even for Liam."

"Liam was...not...real. An idealized fantasy. I've spent many hours on a therapist's couch coming to grips with that. I've seen him in the halls since meeting Adam, and I can't say I all of a sudden feel absolutely nothing, but there's this...dullness. Adam...Adam is real."

Lexie squealed and grabbed Kathryn's hands briefly. "So, are you two together together? Like boyfriend and girlfriend?"

"I know I want to be. I guess I have to see how he feels. But it seems like he likes me a lot. Of course, my judgment on that has been a tad off in the past." She rolled her eyes.

"Like you said, this is different. I'm so, so happy for you. If there's anyone who deserves to be happy, it's you." Lexie reached out and wrapped her arms around her friend, embracing her.

"Thanks, Lex. That means a lot." Pulling apart, she reached up and lightly flicked the red and white ribbon in Lexie's hair, holding her blond locks streaked with hot pink highlighter in a high ponytail. "I see you have a game coming up then?"

"Yeah, we do. An away game."

"Next time there's a home game, I'll come see you cheer."

Lexie smiled. "That would be awesome. Oooh! Bring Adam! Maybe Liam will be there too, and you can rub your newfound love in his stupid face."

The halls echoed with the teenage girls' squeals of laughter.

"I miss this," Kathryn said.

Lexie sighed. "Me too."

"Hey, Lex!" a voice called from down the hall.

Kathryn turned to see four members of the cheer squad near the stairway.

"You coming to lunch? We're going to talk about something new for the routine."

"Yeah, I'll be right there." She turned toward Kathryn once more. "I guess I have to go. I want to hear all about your date tonight. Can you maybe call me when you get home? I should be home from the game by nine."

"Absolutely."

Lexie gave Kathryn one last quick hug and scampered off to be with her cheer friends, leaving Kathryn staring off after her.

Kathryn held up the black top in front of her, then the blue, then the black, then the blue. She groaned. "Mittens, which one looks better?"

The cat kept on purring happily atop Kathryn's pillow.

"You're no help at all." She laughed. "I think the blue brings out my eyes." She took off the purple shirt she had worn to school and slipped on the blue top as she heard the front door close. "Maybe Mom can help since you're too busy sleeping and being pretty." She ran her newly manicured hand over her sweet kitty, and Mittens' voice trilled as she brought her head up, her jade eyes half open. Kathryn gave her a kiss and a rub on her nose. "Sorry. I'll let you sleep."

Kathryn ventured downstairs, peeking around the corner into the living room. "Mom?" She walked into the empty kitchen, swinging her head until she heard voices coming from the basement. With her hand on the doorknob, she opened it, intending to call her mom, but she stopped at the tone in his voice.

"I thought it was all over, and then I'm getting dragged into some shrink's office and getting yelled at."

"No one was trying to gang up on you, Brandon. Kathryn needed some answers, some closure."

"But it was two damn years ago."

"Yes, but in a way, not to her. It's still very current for her, still very painful."

"But then why do *I* have to talk about it?"

"Because she's working with her therapist to heal."

"'Cause I hurt her so badly that she can't possibly move on from the crap I did two years ago?"

"Yes, Brandon. Yes."

There was silence as Kathryn stayed still.

"What about all the shit that's been done to me, huh? She's not the only one who's going through crap. Dad doesn't accept me for who I am. That's some messed up shit right there. Oh, but not Kathryn. No. She's perfect. Why aren't *I* good enough?"

"Brandon...you are good enough. Your dad...he doesn't... If he doesn't necessarily see the value in something, if he doesn't understand it, he has a hard time accepting it. He told me once that he never felt accepted by his father. He never felt good enough for him. It's a cycle that he should have broken instead of carrying it on. That's not fair to you and has created a deep rift in your relationship with him. He should have done better for you. You are your own person, and that's okay. You know that's who I want you to be. Kathryn...she just fits in more with your dad's ideals of who he wanted her to be. That's just who she is, and it's not her fault. You and your dad butt heads. Kathryn wants to save him. That shouldn't be held against her because you don't understand why."

"I'm just so angry...all the time. He makes me so angry. Messing with my mind and making me feel like shit."

"I know. But your issue is with your dad. You need to keep it with him. I'm sorry to say it, and you may not want to hear it...but what your dad is to you...that's what you've become to Kathryn."

The phone ringing startled Kathryn, and she jumped back with a gasp. With her heart beating rapidly beneath her hand, she ran up the stairs to her room.

"Did you like the movie?" Kathryn asked as Adam's Mustang headed off to his house.

"I did. It's not usually the kind of movie I go for, but it was very sweet. And obviously, being with you made it better."

"Obviously," she said with a giggle.

Within minutes, they were back at Adam's house, and he came around to open the door for Kathryn. He took her hand and walked her toward her car parked in the street.

"I'm sorry we have to cut tonight short. I have a paper to finish."

"Sometimes I forget you're still in high school. You seem so much older. I actually have a class in the morning myself. But do you want to maybe do something tomorrow?"

She frowned. "I have an appointment tomorrow, and then I have a shift right after. What about Wednesday?"

"Wednesday's perfect. I'll come pick you up at your house this time."

They stopped at her car and turned to face each other.

"I had so much fun tonight," she said, spinning her ring.

"I did too." He took a step toward her. "You liked the restaurant?"

"I did."

"Good. Maybe it'll be our place."

A light breeze caught Kathryn's hair, floating it in front of her face, and Adam swept it behind her ear, his hand lingering on her cheek.

Her right foot took her inches closer.

"So, I'll call you tomorrow?"

"I hope so." She blinked slowly at the delicate touch of his hand still on her face, and her breath caught.

He closed the distance between them with one step, and his other hand glided along the small of her back. As if in slow motion, she felt his strength drawing her closer, closer than she had ever been to anyone, his eyes unblinking, and after a slight pause, he lowered his head as she tilted hers up, his fingertips guiding her to him. Now so close she could taste his sweet breath, Adam leaned in and gently brushed his lips against hers, pressing into her for only but a moment before releasing her.

Her eyes fluttered open to see his smiling face pull back, and he held her in his arms and gaze a moment longer. He grabbed the handle and pulled open her car door.

"Goodnight, Kathryn."

"Goodnight."

She slipped into her car, and Adam closed the door before walking into his driveway. Kathryn glanced at him shrinking in the rearview and turned left at the next street. Pulling over before the main road, her heart beat rapidly, her knees weak. She laid her head back upon the seat and grazed her lips with her fingertips, closing her eyes against the moment now ingrained in her memory forever.

"He kissed you? Ah!"

Kathryn pulled the phone away from her ear a few inches as Lexie got it all out.

"What was it like?"

"It was so perfect and sweet. He's so perfect and sweet!"

"Can I call him your boyfriend? I want to call him your boyfriend!"

"I don't know. How do these things even work?" she asked, laughing. "What makes him my boyfriend?"

287

"You just have to ask him if that's what you are. Like if you're only seeing each other."

"I guess I can ask him on Wednesday."

"You're not seeing him tomorrow?"

"He asked me to, but I have my appointment with Linda after school, and then I'm working until nine."

"Boo. Well, Wednesday will come soon enough. Ah!" she screamed. "I'm so crazy excited for you!"

"Thanks! I'm pretty excited for me too!"

The girls giggled as though no time had gone by, as though no distance had ever been placed between them by life's twists and turns that unexpectedly took the friends down diverging paths.

Her Fire

"He sounds wonderful." Linda observed her, pausing and narrowing her eyes slightly. "I sense there's something more you want to say though."

"Is he too perfect? Like, for me?"

"How do you mean?"

"He's so normal. Normal family, normal home, normal life. I mean, sure his parents are divorced, but that's pretty normal now anyway."

"And you're not normal," she said without the inflection of a question.

Kathryn shook her head. "No, I'm not. I'm messed up."

"You still feel you're messed up?"

"Not as much as I was. I know I'm better. And I'm happier now, even before meeting Adam. But it's all still there—Brandon, my dad, my mom. Even though I've healed a lot and have moved past the issues with my mom and dad…" She kicked off her sandals and brought her feet onto the couch, hugging her knees to her chest. "It feels like it's just waiting right below the surface, and I don't know what could trigger it—the depression. I'm scared it's going to come back."

"That's an understandable fear. But the steps you've taken to heal and deal with your pain and past trauma are the best way for you to recover and hopefully stave off a recurrence. It's often those who do not seek treatment who continue to struggle so greatly. There are exceptions, of course, but you've undergone intensive therapy and interventions. Your chances of success are greater because of that."

She let her folded legs fall to the side and sat silently for a moment, her vision drifting to her hands. "I had my nightmare again a few nights ago. It's been so long since I've had it, but it's back again. What does that mean? That crazy dream must mean I'm royally messed up, right?"

"Of course not."

Kathryn sniffled, observing her ring in her lap, her voice just above a whisper. "It's always the same. It always starts with my first memory with my dad—that one where we lift our hands over the tree in his back yard. It's this beautiful moment, and then it's chaos and terror."

"Tell me more about that first memory."

Kathryn finally looked up. "I've already told you the dream."

"I know. But I want to hear about the memory, not just the dream."

She paused. "I...I only really see it as a dream now. I'm not sure I know what's the memory and what's the dream anymore."

"Well, the dream always sounded...exaggerated, I would say, by the way you described it."

"You don't think the actual memory was as perfect?"

"Oh, I believe it was a perfect moment for you when you were a little girl. You had a special relationship with your dad even then, and you enjoyed your time with him. I would never diminish the importance of that memory."

"But...?"

"But I wonder if you've taken a special moment and created an idealized recalling of it." Linda sighed, sympathy pulling at her brow. "Everything that was going on around you was awful. You had just left your dad and your home, Brandon was out of control, your mom was struggling greatly, and your dad was doing some scary things even though you weren't aware of them at the time. You were just a little girl in the midst of mayhem. So while this sweet moment with your dad was beautiful and powerful, it was a small spark of happiness within the darkness, and you've held on to it as tightly as possible."

Kathryn stilled for a few long moments, considering this as her reoccurring dream shown through her mind. The small child's hair lit a magnificent shade of golden brown in the bright sun as she looked up at her daddy, and her innocent eyes flashed an unnaturally exquisite blue as she watched their hands lift gracefully over the tree, birds singing above them, their songs wrapping them in harmonies too perfect for a mere bird to produce. The light's brilliant glare blurred their silhouettes like an artistic camera effect as Kathryn blinked hard and met Linda's eyes.

"Are you okay?"

Kathryn shook her head softly. "Has it all been a lie?"

"No," Linda said sharply, her brown eyes stern. "No. Absolutely not. That moment was real. Your relationship with your dad is real. Your love for him and his love for you is real. That tree is real. It's still standing, yes?"

"In the far back corner on the left side of his land. It's enormous. I can't even fathom it being so small that I could have lifted my arm over it."

"Then it stands firm as proof of that moment, growing and changing as you have. I only meant to analyze your romanticized recollection of the memory, not the actual memory and what it means to you."

Kathryn nodded ever so slightly. "But then why does my nightmare always start with that moment?"

"In your mind, that's kind of where your life starts. You don't remember anything before it." Linda leaned forward in her chair, her eyes soft, her blond head tilted. "It's where your story begins, Kathryn. And it was very shortly after that you started to become aware of all the bad that was going on around you."

Kathryn drew a deep breath as exhaustion pulled at her chest. "What does the nightmare even mean? They say dreams mean stuff, right?"

"Some believe so."

"You don't?"

"I believe our subconscious is complex, and it's not out of the realm of possibility that it can dive into our worst fears or buried memories and bring them to the forefront in some form."

"Then what's that nightmare trying to tell me?"

"I've concocted a theory. It...may be difficult to face."

"I've faced everything else."

"Yes, but your dad is a tricky subject with you. I know you only want to focus on the good, not on the bad."

"I want to know what you think."

"I'm no expert in this area, but if I were to wager a guess, it has come to my mind that possibly you feel there's something standing in the way of you and your family."

Kathryn hesitated, her mind whirling. "The fire?"

"The fire would be representative of what you feel stands between you and them. Do you have any idea what that could be? It could represent something different for each member."

She shrugged. "I don't know."

"I think maybe you do."

Kathryn scoffed. "If you know, just tell me. I'm...exhausted...with all of this." She fought through the break in her voice and the tears welling up from within. "You're right. It's too difficult. I don't know how much deeper I can go. This is too damn hard. Once I think I've come to terms with something, it's like something new is waiting to take me down again. It's just a dream."

"I know it's hard. But look how far you've come. Stay with me. Maybe it is just a dream, but perhaps you can still learn from it. What do you think the fire represents if we were to dig deeper and analyze the dream? Let's start with your mom. What stands in the way of your relationship with her?"

"That's easy. Brandon. He's the only real problem we have—how she has handled him."

"Good. That's a start. And what stands in the way of you and Brandon?"

"Brandon does—his insane notion that it's him and Mom against me and Dad."

"I would say that's true. It's his irrational perspective that he has created in his mind." She paused. "And your dad?"

"The things he's done to my mom and Brandon?"

"But you didn't actually witness those. Those aren't your experiences with him. They're theirs. That's their fire. What's yours?"

"I don't know."

"I know you've chosen to accept him for who he is—the good and the bad. You've forgiven him, which shows your growth and maturity. But I believe it's important to find the root of all this, of this cycle. What keeps you from having a better relationship with him?"

Kathryn rolled her eyes. "Just tell me," she said, whining.

"This is your fire, and you need to see it on your own."

She shook her head as her gaze fell to her lap. "It's too hard."

"I know it is."

Kathryn hesitated, flashes cycling through her mind: tree, glass, Benji, crying, baseball, an empty seat. She smoothed a tear across her cheek. "Alcohol."

Linda nodded. "Even though you don't have true memories of all the things he did, you're still affected by his alcoholism."

She exhaled forcefully. "How is this helping? If anything, it's showing me exactly what I said—that I'm still messed up. How can I expect Adam to be able to handle all my crap? Why should he want to?"

"That's how you heal, how you become a more complete person. Isn't that why you came to see me in the first place? You can't just bury it. You have to face it. So what does your reoccurring nightmare mean? It means you're still fighting. You're still trying to move on toward happiness because of and in spite of your past. You said yourself that it's all still there. It's all a part of you. We're all made up of our little moments. Like trees made up of thousands of leaves, each branch a year of our lives, each leaf a memory, the veining the little moments. They may fall away as time charges forward, as the seasons change. But they're always there beneath the surface, ready and waiting to burst through."

Kathryn sat quietly for a moment, absorbing her therapist's words. "Wow. That's deep," she said with a breathy laugh.

Linda feigned a small bow of her head. "There are lots of ways to say the same thing—everyone is made up of and shaped by their experiences. That one's always been my favorite. Nice imagery." She smiled. "But just because those scars are there doesn't mean you have to let them define you, to let them define your future. You have a young man who seems to care a great deal about you. You seem to care a great deal for him."

"I do."

"Don't let your past define your future, Kathryn. Don't let it take anything more away from you."

"What do I do?"

"Talk to Adam. Be honest with him. Don't make up his mind for him. Don't push him away because you don't think he can handle your baggage. Let him be the one to decide that."

"Tell him everything?"

She nodded. "Everything. It can push him away or bring him closer. If you're truly scared it'll do the former, it's better you find out now rather than get too invested, even fall in love with him only to find out he can't handle what difficulties your past may bring with it. The decision is in his hands. Do you really think he'd just walk away?"

Kathryn shook her head. "No, I don't. But I still want him to know everything there is to know about me."

"I agree. But remember, it's only one piece of who you are—one branch, one veined leaf."

Kathryn tossed her purse and backpack on the loveseat and headed up the stairs with only half an hour to get ready for her date. As she touched up her makeup, the phone rang, and she let it go, certain her mom would get it.

"Kathryn! It's your dad."

She grabbed the phone and continued with her eye shadow. "Hey, Dad."

"Hi, sweetie. I got your message last night too late to call back. What's up?"

"I don't have much time, but I wanted to tell you something. I...um...met a really nice guy."

"Oh, boy. Okay. I knew this day was coming. What's this kid's name? Does he need to know I own a gun?"

"Dad!"

"What? It's not loaded, and I don't even use it. I hate the thing really, but he doesn't need to know that."

She swept on a touch of blush. "No, Dad. Let's not. His name is Adam, and he's actually very sweet, and he's super into sports. He loves the Bills."

"Well, that's a plus. I can go with that." He paused. "Is he making you happy?"

She smiled. "He is."

"Then I'd like to meet him."

"I'd like that too. I think you're really going to like him."

"Well...no one is truly good enough for my girl, but we'll see if he comes close."

Kathryn laughed. "I think he will." She held the phone with her chin and passed a brush through her hair. "Adam is also coming to my orchestra concert in June. I thought maybe you could come too."

"Oh, I don't know, honey. You know I don't like driving at night, and it's hard for me to sit in those little seats with my bad knee."

"I know. It would just mean a lot to me. I'm first chair this time. Please?"

He sighed. "You know I can't say no to you. All right. I'll be there."

"Really? Thanks, Dad. Geez, he's going to be here soon. I need to get changed. I'll call you later."

"You have fun and be safe." He groaned. "My baby girl...dating. He better know how lucky he is. I love you so much, my Kathryn."

"I love you too, Dad."

"Thank you."

"You're welcome."

"Bye, baby girl."

"Bye, Dad."

"Adam's here, Mom. I'll see you tonight."

"Have fun, be safe, and be home by nine thirty."

"I will," she shouted back as she closed the front door behind her. Kathryn stumbled to a stop at the bottom stair, almost falling into him.

"Well hi," he said, laughing.

She joined in. "Hey!"

Adam put his arm around her shoulders, leading her to his car. "Anything special you wanted to do today?"

"Um...there's actually something I wanted to talk to you about. Maybe we could go to someplace quiet, like a coffee house?"

"Yeah, sure." He stopped as he went to open her door. "Should I be worried?"

Kathryn bounced forward on her toes, pushing herself upward, lightly kissing him. "No."

He smiled down at her. "The coffee house it is then."

"Can I get you something?" Adam asked, pulling out a chair for Kathryn.

"A hot chocolate with a shot of vanilla, please."

"Sure thing."

Kathryn slung her purse over the back of her chair, watching him walk toward the counter, her heart racing. She drew a deep breath, strengthening her resolve. Her short fingernails tapped out her favorite piece from the upcoming recital against the table as she scanned the coffee shop. Round, wooden tables adorned in centerpieces of archaic-looking books were topped with burned-down candles in glass holders, and coffee drinkers sat scattered about—some talking with others, a few buried in their books.

"This is a nice place." Adam set her hot chocolate in front of her. "I see why you picked it."

"I actually haven't even been here before."

He smirked. "Then why'd you pick it?"

"I just wanted someplace quiet."

He took a sip of his iced cappuccino. "So, what did you want to talk about?"

Kathryn brought the hot chocolate to her lips, the steam stinging her nose, and she pulled it away quickly. As her fingers continued to beat against the surface, she could feel Adam's attention on her.

His hand crawled across the small table, resting on hers, calming her fidgeting. "Kath, You know you can tell me anything, right?"

She nodded, taking another deep breath, tracing his face with her eyes, trying to memorize every line, every beautiful feature. "I really like you, Adam. I'm having so much fun getting to know you. I feel like we have this amazing connection. I can't even really explain it." To her relief, he smiled.

"I feel the same way."

Kathryn's nerves steadied, feeling safe to be her true self with this man. "I

295

want to be honest with you about something. I didn't exactly tell you the truth about my family. My brother, he's not just a jerk. He...he hits me." She watched his kind eyes shift and slant in concern. "Or at least, he did for a long time. I had to move out of my house when I was fifteen because I was too scared to live there. I moved in with my aunt and uncle and cousins. I obviously eventually moved back, and he hasn't done anything since. But...I'm still kind of messed up from it all." She looked down at her ring, spinning it with her nail. "I was diagnosed with depression. I'm on medication. I see a therapist. I'm trying to heal from it all, but I'm not there yet, and I wanted you to know all this so you know what you're getting into with me. I don't want to scare you away, and I know we've only been on a few dates, but"—with unshed tears lining her sapphire eyes, her gaze floated up to meet his—"I'm completely falling for you, and I needed you to know all this...in case maybe you thought it was too much to handle."

Adam reached his other hand across the table and took hers, lightly shaking his head. "I'm so sorry. Geez. I'm not even sure what to say. I'm just sorry that happened to you." He lifted their hands, sweeping a tear off her cheek with the back of his finger. "I'm not going anywhere. My life has been pretty...uneventful. I have no idea what it's like to go through anything like you have. But I'll be here for you in any way you need me to be."

A single tear dripped off her smile. "Really?"

"Of course. I care about you." He caught the tear before it slipped off her chin. "I told you I was raised as an Orthodox Christian, right?"

Kathryn nodded. "That's why you missed the meeting at work. It was your Easter that day."

"Yeah. When I was growing up, my mom always told me that our religion believes that when someone suffers in their life, they're rewarded at some point. I'm sure that reward is different for everyone, but I've always felt it was a nice thought—that people who go through something horrible can hold on to hope that things will get better someday."

"That is a nice thought. I hope you're right."

"Your reward will come. I know it." He ran his thumb over her Claddagh ring, shifting the crown slightly. "Thank you for opening up to me. It means a lot that you trusted me with all this."

"Thank you for being so understanding...and for taking a chance on me."

"You're worth it." He let go of her hand and swept her hair behind her ear, drawing his finger down her cheek. "I have to say, though, I'm not looking forward to meeting your brother."

"Just don't say anything."

Adam quickly shook his head. "Oh, I wouldn't. I can be civil." He stirred his straw around in his iced drink. "Speaking of meeting people...I thought maybe we could go back to my house for a bit. You could meet my mom."

She grinned. "I'd like that."

"Mom?"

"In the kitchen," a voice called as they walked into the foyer.

Kathryn's eyes widened as she looked around. "Your house is beautiful. Oh my goodness."

"Why, thank you," Adam's mom said, coming through the kitchen doorway, her short blond hair brushing her chin. She extended a hand. "It's nice to finally meet you, Kathryn."

"Pleasure to meet you, Mrs. Lyndon."

"Natasha is fine. So, Adam tells me your mom is a teacher as well."

"Yes. Fifth grade. You're a French teacher, right?"

She nodded. "That's right. Middle school."

"That's really cool."

"Well, come on in. Can I get you a drink? Have you two eaten? I can make up something."

Adam chuckled. "We're fine, Mom. We're just going to watch a little TV before I have to take Kathryn home."

She held her hands up. "Okay. Just checking. Well, I have some things to attend to upstairs. It was lovely meeting you, Kathryn. I hope to see more of you."

"You will," Adam said.

Natasha gathered a stack of papers and fled up the stairs.

Adam intertwined his hand with Kathryn's and led her into the back as she continued to observe his home in awe. Walking into the family room, the fireplace caught her eye first, following the ivory brick wall up to the high ceiling. He brought her to the couch across from sliding glass doors that occupied most of the opposite wall, opening up to the back yard where a grand maple stood among the well-manicured lawn, the setting sun peeking through the minute breaks in the thick leaves.

They sank into the plush couch, and Kathryn leaned against Adam's arm. "Your mom kind of left to go upstairs in a hurry."

"I don't think she knows how to act. Probably just didn't want to feel like she was watching over us."

"Didn't know how to act? So, you...don't bring girls around here often?"

"You're the first."

297

She smiled with relief. "Really?"

"Why do you sound surprised?"

"I don't know. You're twenty...and adorable."

He laughed. "Well, as adorable as I might be, I haven't really dated much. Haven't met anyone I wanted to...until you." He cleared his throat. "Have... uh...you...dated much?"

She smirked and shook her head. "Nope."

Adam exhaled deeply. "Glad to get that talk out of the way."

He wrapped his arm around her, pulling her toward him, and she scooted closer, laying her head on his chest, calmed by the strong rhythm of his heart.

"Wanna watch some TV?" he asked.

"Sure."

Kathryn could hardly pay attention to what was happening on the screen, far too distracted by his warmth, his arm draped over her, and the movement of his body when he laughed. She hesitantly rested her hand on his chest, and his hand found hers, his soft touch vibrating through her. Closing her eyes, she breathed him in, never before hearing the beat of a man's heart against her ear as his chest rose and fell beneath her cheek, never before feeling such peace.

"What does your ring mean?"

She opened her eyes and saw him twisting her Claddagh ring.

"The crown, heart, and are those hands?"

"Yeah. The crown symbolizes loyalty, the hands friendship, and the heart love. It's Irish."

"How do you decide which way the crown points? It's facing toward you and kind of looks upside down. Just wondering if there's a reason or if you like it that way."

She moved back a little, finding his eyes intently focused on her. "Oh, well, Mel told me that if you're single, you're supposed to wear it with the crown facing in toward you. If you're taken, you turn it the other way so the heart is closer to you." A smile slowly graced her face as it came to her. She slipped off the ring and dropped it into his lap.

Adam watched it fall and picked it up, spinning it in his fingertips. "Okay." His hand slid under hers, lifting it, and he placed the ring on her middle finger, the crown pointing away, the heart closer to her.

Kathryn admired the new view of her ring and met his gaze as he lowered his head, kissing her smile, parting his lips slightly as she leaned into him.

He rubbed her nose with his. "How cute are we?"

She giggled. "Yeah. We're pretty cute."

298

With her curfew only fifteen minutes away, the couple reluctantly got into Adam's Mustang and headed back to Kathryn's.

"Since we already met each other's moms," Kathryn said as they got closer to her house, "maybe we take this to the next level. Do you want to come in and meet Mittens?"

He barked a laugh. "Absolutely. I'm honored you have found me worthy."

"Well, I figured my best friend should meet my…boyfriend."

He reached over and took her hand. "I like the way that sounds when you say it."

"I like saying it."

As they pulled into the driveway, Kathryn groaned.

"What's wrong?"

She flicked her head to the front picture window. "Looks like you'll be meeting someone else tonight too."

"It'll be fine."

Kathryn got out of the car and closed the door. "I just don't want him to ruin what's been such an amazing night."

"He won't. Nothing could." He took her hand, leading her toward the front door.

"What if Mittens claws your eyes out?"

He chuckled for a moment, but then his face fell flat. "Wait. Would she?"

Kathryn burst out laughing. "No! Don't be silly. She doesn't have front claws. Teeth though, those are still pretty sharp for an old girl."

"I can't tell if you're kidding."

"Just come in the house," she said with a laugh, playfully pushing his arm.

Jane and Brandon turned at the sound of the door.

"Hey, Mom."

"Hi, sweetie. Adam, it's nice to see you again. You two have a nice night?"

"We did. Thank you," Adam said.

Kathryn turned to face her brother, Adam tight to her side. "Brandon, this is Adam. Adam, Brandon."

Adam held her hand firmly with his left hand as he extended his right. "Nice to meet you."

Brandon took his hand with a clap. "Yeah, you too, man. Cool car you got there."

"Thanks. Ninety-three Mustang."

Brandon nodded deeply. "Nice."

"You into cars?"

"Nah, not really. Music's my thing. But I can appreciate a cool car. Well"

299

—he clapped his hands together—"if you'd excuse me. I was heading downstairs to jam for a while. It was cool meeting you, Adam. Peace," Brandon said, raising two fingers.

"See ya, Brandon."

"Mom, I was going to take Adam up to my room to meet Mittens."

She grimaced. "Good luck, Adam."

He nodded. "I've already been warned."

"Oh, stop, you two. It'll be fine…maybe. Let's go!" Kathryn skipped to the stairs and pulled him up behind her. "Okay, so let me go in first and just be really quiet. When you see her, maybe crouch low to the ground and hold your hand out so she can sniff you. She probably won't bite your hand."

"You're not helping."

Kathryn opened her door ever so slowly and peeked around the room, looking for Mittens. She clicked her tongue twice. "Mittens? Come here, pretty girl."

A low moan came from under the nightstand covering. Kathryn knelt down and lifted the tablecloth. "There's my sweetie girl. Come here. I want you to meet someone." She held out her hand, and Mittens pressed her nose to it before getting gracefully to her six-toed feet and arching her back against her best friend's touch.

"Come on," she said to Adam, just above a whisper, waving him over.

He took a few slow-motion steps and crouched down a couple feet away from them. He held out his hand, keeping it stable as the cat studied him.

Mittens' eyes opened wide, her pupils nearly eclipsing the soft jade. She brought one white, mitten-shaped paw closer to the stranger, her head bowing low. Mittens took another step, then another, then another as she tentatively brought her nose to his fingertip. Then Kathryn watched in fascination as Mittens pushed her face into his hand and arched her back against his palm.

"Oh my God. What is happening?"

Adam grinned. "She's not biting my hand off," he said quietly with an excited bounce in his voice.

Kathryn reached out and tickled Mittens under her chin. "What a good girl you are."

Mittens floated straight to her, and Kathryn ducked down, allowing Mittens to press her nose against her forehead. Kathryn scratched the back of her head and kissed the white triangle shape between her eyes.

Adam gently reached forward, and Mittens stepped into his hand again, rubbing into him before hopping up on the bed and curling into a tight ball on Kathryn's pillow.

"I can't believe she just did that. She's never done that to anyone. Not even my friends who've been coming over for years."

"I guess I've just got something about me."

"That you do."

Adam got to his feet and held out his hands to help her up. His arms wrapped around her waist, pulling her in closer until their faces were inches from each other. "I had an amazing time tonight, girlfriend."

Pure delight pulled at her mouth. "I did too, boyfriend." She felt his hands on her lower back tighten around her, drawing her into him as his lips found hers, kissing her deeper than he ever had.

When he pulled away, she bounced to her toes and threw her arms around him, embracing him tightly, her lips brushing against his neck. Adam hugged her back, slightly swaying as he held her.

"I don't want you to go."

"I don't want to go."

After what wasn't nearly enough time, they separated, and Kathryn walked him down the stairs and out to his car.

Adam lifted her right hand and kissed her ring. "I'll call you tomorrow."

She smiled. "You better."

With another hug and kiss, he drove off, leaving her standing in the driveway, the brightness from the picture window lighting her way back into her house.

And Always

"I'll grab the sparkling juice and meet you guys in there, and then we can hear all about Adam and your one-month anniversary coming up," Kristin said as the three other girls went into the back room.

"When I'm an adult, I'm totally having a hot tub in my house." Joselyn took off her jean shorts. "This is freaking awesome."

"Right? I so need this right now." Melanie slipped into the hot tub up to her chin and closed her eyes.

Kathryn dipped her painted toes into the steaming water, sliding under and nestling into one of the corner seats. Her breath slowly glided past her lips. "This should be like a weekly thing."

"I'm so in," Melanie said.

"Kristin!" called Joselyn from her corner. "We're all coming over and hanging out in your hot tub every week, okay?"

Kristin laughed her tender laugh, sparkling juice and four wine glasses in her hands. "I can get on board with that." She poured the juice and handed each of them a glass of bubbles before getting into the hot tub.

"Mel, let's invite Jake over next time," Jos said with a giggle. "Kath, you should set that up. Bet he looks pretty hot in swim trunks."

"Uh, that's my cousin."

"Doesn't mean he's not hot, right, Mel?"

Melanie's eyes narrowed, and she skimmed her hand along the surface of the hot water, flicking droplets at Joselyn. Fits of laughter assaulted the friends.

"Stop," Melanie said as she leaned back again. "He doesn't like me like that anymore."

Joselyn dabbed her splashed face with the corner of her towel. "But he used to, so there's totally hope."

Melanie didn't answer as she closed her eyes again.

Kristin took a light sip of sparkling juice and brushed a wet curl off her slender shoulder. "Kathryn, any plans for your one-month anniversary?"

"I think we're just going out to eat, maybe to where we went on our first date."

"How sweet. Everything still good with you two?"

A rosy hue spread along Kathryn's raised cheeks. "He's...amazing."

"Aw. You guys are sickeningly cute."

"We are, aren't we?" Kathryn leaned in toward Kristen, both girls letting out an excited squeal.

Joselyn closed her eyes and released a prolonged moan as her blond hair sank beneath the water. "Do you live in here, Kris? If I had a hot tub in my house, I'd live in it. Like, 'Just bring me my dinner in here, Mom.'" She brought her hand above her head and snapped twice.

"Don't think my mom would go for that. I use it relatively often. My parents are in it a lot. I catch them out here with wine glasses, laughing and talking. It's pretty cute."

"Aw. That is cute. Must be nice having parents who actually like each other," Kathryn said with a lighthearted laugh.

Bubbles and jets overtook the conversation for a few minutes as they relaxed in the steaming water until a faint sob brought the girls' attention to one of their friends.

"Mel? What's wrong?" Kathryn asked, her voice heavy with concern.

"My parents... They're getting divorced."

Kristin gasped. "Oh no. I'm so sorry, Mel."

"That's awful," Kathryn said. "What happened? I didn't even know they were having issues."

"They tried to hide it from me and my brothers, but we kind of saw they weren't really that happy. Always snapping at each other. Certainly not having wine together, laughing and talking. I can't believe this is happening. I just never thought I'd be from a broken home."

The girls left their corners and slid over to their friend, Kathryn and Joselyn putting their arms around her shoulders as Kristin took her hand.

"We're here for you, Mel," Kathryn said as she laid her head against her friend's. "In any way that you need us. Any time."

Melanie sniffled. "I think I'll be needing some extra hot tub get-togethers."

"Oh, that we can do," Joselyn said.

Melanie's lips upturned ever so slightly. "Thanks, guys. You're the best friends anyone could ever have."

"We'll always be here for each other...forever. Right, ladies?" Kathryn looked to her friends.

Kristin and Joselyn smiled. "Always."

Kathryn gave Mittens a quick pet and a rub on the nose.

"Bye, Mom," she said, standing in Jane's bedroom doorway.

Jane looked up from the stack of papers on her lap that spilled over onto her bed.

"Looks like it'll be a fun night for you. I'll be home by ten. Love you."

"Kathryn, wait."

She spun back around. "What's up?"

Jane patted the small section of her bed next to her that wasn't covered in fifth-grade math finals. "I just wanted to talk to you for a minute. You've been out of the house a lot, spending time with Adam. Things seem to be going well."

"They are. I really like him. He's amazing."

"So, tell me. What's so amazing about him?"

"He's sweet and funny. We have a lot in common, get along really well, and have so much fun together. I just really love being with him."

"Love?"

"I said I *love* being *with* him." She giggled. "But I've never felt like this before. Like, not even close."

"Sounds as though you're falling pretty hard. You know, I can't explain it, but...I feel as though this is it for you."

"What?"

She nodded slowly. "I do."

"It's only been a month."

"I know. I just have this feeling. It's hard to describe. You seem to be such a good match. I think he could be the one. You don't?"

"I don't know. What does being in love even mean? And how do I know if this is it?"

"When you know, you know. It's a cliché, I know. But it's also usually

305

true." She slipped her daughter's hair behind her ear. "You'll know when you can sing him the song."

Kathryn flashed back to that day in the car, singing with her mom, the sweet love song serenading them. She pictured Adam's beautiful face and smiled.

Jane embraced her daughter with a sigh. "You're growing up too quickly. Boyfriends and falling in love. I hope I'm ready for this."

"I hope *I'm* ready for this."

She looked Kathryn in the eyes. "You are. You've come a long way, but now you're right here, with a man who cares a great deal for you."

"But it's only been a month, and I'm only seventeen."

"That doesn't mean he can't be the one. You could just be that lucky. That being said, you're still only seventeen. If you're in love with him, or when you fall in love with him, I want you to embrace it and enjoy it. It's an amazing feeling being in love. But being seventeen…"

Kathryn tilted her head. "I know, Mom. Don't worry."

"I'll always worry." She hugged her daughter again. "Just make darn sure you can sing him the song."

"Mom, really. There's nothing to wor—"

"Promise?"

Kathryn grinned. "I promise. I'll see you tonight."

The doorbell rang just as she reached the bottom stair.

"Hey, you." She lifted up onto her bare toes to kiss him. "Let me just grab my sandals from the kitchen."

"Okay," Adam said, sliding his hands into his pockets.

Kathryn slipped on her sandals and turned to see Brandon coming out the basement door.

Brandon nodded. "Hey."

She eyed him. "Uh…hey."

He followed her into the living room and cleared his throat. "I was thinking maybe we could all play a few rounds of Knock Out sometime. Maybe see if Jake and Sam want to join."

"What's Knock Out?" Adam asked.

Kathryn turned to him. "It's a basketball game we used to play. You line up and try to make a basket from the foul line. If the person behind you makes it before you, you're out." She faced Brandon. "We haven't played that in a long time."

"Yeah. I just thought it might be fun."

"We already planned to go out to eat and then back to Adam's today. But…maybe next time he hangs out here. If that's okay with you, Adam."

"Sure. Yeah. That sounds fun."

Brandon nodded. "Cool. Have fun, you two." He offered a low wave and retreated to the kitchen.

Adam took her hand and led her outside.

"Uh...what just happened?" Kathryn asked, her eyebrows raised.

"I guess we're playing basketball with your brother. Didn't see that coming."

Kathryn shook her head. "Neither did I."

"Why are you standing so close? Move back." Kathryn waved her gloved hand and tossed the baseball up into the air, catching it. "Keep moving."

"I'm in the neighbor's yard," Adam said, chuckling.

"Do you want me to break your hand? Keep going."

Adam walked backward until he was almost in the next-door neighbor's driveway. "Is this far enough?" he shouted, his mitt by his mouth.

"Yeah, that should be good," she yelled back. "Ready?"

He nodded, punching the center of his glove.

Her right hand cupped the ball tightly as it rested in her mitt she had owned since middle school.

"It's too big, Dad."

"You'll grow into it. But you've gotta work on loosening it up a bit. Now... lift your hands to your chest." Daniel took his daughter's wrists and tucked them into her. "Now remember to bring your right arm back like we practiced. Good. And make sure to always step forward with your left." He tapped her on the shoulder before jogging toward their tree, halting in its shadow. He held up his mitt. "Keep your eye on me and follow through like I showed you."

Kathryn's right arm drew back, and she stepped with her left leg as her arm shot forward, following through with the throw. The ball met her dad's worn glove with a slap.

"Damn, girl!" He laughed. "That arm is getting better and better. Let's go again."

Kathryn smiled as she released the baseball off her fingertips, sending it soaring toward Adam. It hit his glove with a familiar slap.

"Damn!" He took his mitt off and shook out his hand.

"Told ya."

Adam jogged over to her and grabbed her as she squealed, lifting her up and twirling her. "You're adorable," he said, putting her back down. "And have one hell of an arm."

"My dad taught me well."

"I'll run back over for another one. Take it easy on me, will ya?"

She smirked and shook her head. "Nah."

Adam laughed as he trotted back into his neighbor's front yard. He was about to throw the ball when an older woman walked out onto the porch. "Hi, Mrs. Shannon."

"Adam! My goodness. It's been so long. Since we moved out and Juliet moved in, we haven't been around as much. How are you?"

"Doing great. You?"

"Oh, can't complain. We're loving our new downsized home, and it's wonderful seeing what Juliet has done with the place." She looked down to Adam's yard. "Who's the young lady?"

He waved her over. "Mrs. Shannon, this is my girlfriend, Kathryn."

"Hi," Kathryn said.

"Hi there, sweetie. It's nice to meet you. I've known this guy for years. You were...eight when you moved in here?"

"Yup."

"Goodness. My girls still lived here with me then. Well, my daughter Juliet actually bought the house from us about six months ago. She's living here with her family now."

"That's really sweet that she gets to raise her family in the house she grew up in," Kathryn said, tucking her mitt under her arm.

"Yes. It's wonderful to watch as a mother. So, are you from around here, Kathryn?"

"I live in Edgebrook."

"Edgebrook? So you went to Edgebrook schools? The middle school?"

"Yeah. That was a few years ago. I'm a junior now."

"My daughter teaches at Edgebrook Middle. Do you know Mrs. Hagen?"

Kathryn's eyes widened. "She was my science teacher."

"Oh my. How remarkable." Mrs. Shannon twisted around and opened the front door. "Juliet, come on out here for a moment."

"What is it, Mom? Kathryn? What are you doing here?"

"She is little Adam's girlfriend. Well, not so little now, of course," she said, waving off the idea.

"Mom, Kathryn is Bill and Lorraine's granddaughter."

Mrs. Shannon gasped.

"You know my grandparents?"

"Do I? Oh, I've known them for years. Why, I remember their grandchildren swinging on that wooden swing your grandpa made and hung on a tree in their back yard. My word. Could that have been you?"

"It could have been. I have four other cousins too, though. Two older and two younger."

"How extraordinary. How are they doing? I haven't spoken to them in far too long."

"They're doing really well."

"Please, tell them I said hi. I have to give them a call myself though. I'll jot down a little note. I just love them. Such a sweet couple. And those letters they've kept... I love that story, and your grandparents always told it with pride and so much love for each other."

Adam turned to Kathryn. "Letters?"

"My grandpa and grandma met just before he was sent off to World War Two. He was a sailor in the Navy. They wrote letters to each other the entire time he was away, and it was through those letters that they got to know each other and fell in love. It wasn't long after he came back home that they were married."

"That's really cool," Adam said. "And they still have them?"

Kathryn nodded. "All of them. They're in an old suitcase in their house."

Mrs. Shannon sighed. "I bet they're simply wonderful to read. Such history and love. Just amazing. What a story."

Juliet still wore a look of surprise. "How funny that my former student would be dating my next-door neighbor. I grew up in this house, even knew the people who lived here before Adam and his mom moved in. I used to play in your back yard as a kid."

Mrs. Shannon gasped again, and her heavily veined hand fluttered to her chest. "Oh my. This is absolutely bananas. Have I got a story for you two."

"Both of us?" Adam asked.

"Oh, yes, dear. This is a doozy. When Juliet was a child, as she said, she used to be friends with the girl who lived here before you, Adam. They used to love playing under that big maple in your back yard. Juliet snatched some seeds from that tree one spring and planted those seeds in cups. Do you remember that, Juliet?"

She nodded. "I do."

"Well, when those little seedlings grew too big to stay in those cups, she gave them away to people. And I swear to you on all that is good and holy that she gave one of those seedlings to your grandparents, and they planted it in their yard."

"Seriously?" Kathryn looked over at Adam, her look of shock mirrored on his face.

"As serious as can be! So, there's a maple tree in their yard that actually started from the maple in your boyfriend's back yard. Isn't that something? You have an amazing story just like your grandparents." Mrs. Shannon winked.

"That's incredible," Adam said, running his hands through his hair.

"Wow, Mom. That is amazing. What a twist of fate. A story for the grand-children, huh?" Juliet laughed.

Kathryn risked a glance at Adam and matched his smile.

"Well, dears, I do have to get going." She turned toward her daughter. "I told your father I wasn't staying too long. He'll be wondering where I am. It was just lovely meeting you, Kathryn. And I'm so glad I remembered that story. Please tell your grandma and grandpa I said hi and that I'll get in touch with them soon."

"I will. Thank you."

Mrs. Shannon placed her hand on Kathryn's. "My pleasure, dear."

"I'm sure I'll be seeing you around, Kathryn."

"Bye, Mrs. Hagen."

"You're not my student anymore. You can call me Juliet." She smiled and disappeared into her house.

Kathryn and Adam crossed the lawn.

"That is freaking *insane*," Adam said.

"Right? It's amazing. I mean, what are the chances?"

He grabbed her hand and spun her into him, wrapping his arms around her waist. "Like she said. It's fate."

Inches apart, their eyes held each other, unblinking, unwavering. Her breath caught, realizing in that moment what she already knew. "Can we go hang out in the back yard? Maybe check out this tree that seems to have special powers?"

"Of course." With his arm around her shoulders, they walked back through the wooden gate opening to his back yard where the maple tree stood at least fifty feet into the crystalline sky.

They lay down on the padded lounge chair on the patio. Kathryn flipped to her side, her hip pressing into the cushion, and rested her head on Adam's chest. She wrapped her arm around him and sank further into him as he pulled her closer with both arms.

"So, that's the tree."

"Our tree," he said into her hair before kissing her head.

"So, we have a tree now, but we still don't have a song. We're doing this in an odd order."

He laughed. "Do most people have a song before they have a tree?"

She lifted her head off his chest and breathed a laugh. "Yeah, that didn't make sense, did it? That was just my way of saying I think we should have a song."

"I was actually thinking about that the other day. How about 'Amazed'? I've always loved the song, and it—"

"It played on the radio at the restaurant on our first date."

He tightened his arm around her back, lifting her into him, kissing her, his hand tracing the curvature of her hip. Adam pulled away slightly and rocked his head forward, resting his forehead on hers. "Kathryn..."

She moved back a few inches, taking in every moment of him.

"I love you."

She smiled. "I love you."

Adam held her as she buried her face into his neck, breathing him in—this man, her reward.

Epilogue

They walked in sunlight. Their golden blond hair shone with brilliance, blue eyes sparkling between every blink.

"Daddy, this way! Come on! Leaves, Daddy!"

"Okay, buddy." He grabbed the little boy under his arms. "Ready?"

"Yeah!"

"One, two, three!"

The boy flew into the pile of leaves, bouncing on them as if they were made of orange, red, and yellow pillows. "Mommy! You see dat?"

"I saw it, Ethan. Come here. You have leaves in your curls, silly boy."

He scurried over to her, throwing himself into her arms as she hoisted him up. "My mommy," his little voice sang as he hugged her neck.

"My baby," Kathryn said, breathing him in.

"My turn, Nathan!" she yelled.

"No, it's my turn!" he shouted, stomping his foot.

"But you went first last time."

"No, Allie, you did."

"Mom!"

"Mom!"

"Okay, you two. Nathan, can you let your sister go first this time?"

"But it's my turn, Mom."

Kathryn gestured to her children, and they dashed over to where she sat shadowed by the large maple in their back yard. "Guys, I'm not sure whose turn it was, but, Nathan, maybe you can let Allie go first?"

"Why?" he asked, tilting his blond head.

"Because you're her big brother, and she's your little sister. And what does that mean?"

A small smile spread on his young, handsome face. "That I always need to take care of her."

"Exactly. And, Allie, as his little sister, what's your job?" Kathryn swept her daughter's yellow waves behind her ear.

"To always take care of him too." She turned to her brother. "You can go first if you want."

"No, Allie. You go. It's okay. I'll go first next time."

"Let's just go at the same time. Come on!"

Allie skipped into a cartwheel and took off with her brother at her heels. Their young legs carried them across the lush grass, lifting them into the air and down into the pile of leaves.

"I wan go too, Mommy."

"Go ahead, sweetie."

"Nafan, Awie, wait for me!"

Kathryn slipped her phone out of her pocket and snapped a picture.

"I caught another one," Adam said, carrying a younger girl over his shoulder, a tri-colored Australian shepherd at his heels. He laid her down across Kathryn's lap, snatching a kiss before taking the seat next to her and bending forward to ruffle the dog's long, ebony hair.

"Hey, baby girl," she said to her younger daughter.

The little girl giggled and grabbed her mom's face, pressing her forehead into hers, her hands flapping with delightful energy escaping out her fingertips.

"Daphne. Daphne," Kathryn said, gently turning her daughter's reluctant gaze toward her. "What do you have there? Is that a leaf? A yellow leaf? So pretty."

Daphne held the leaf close to her sweet face, her small fingers gliding over the thin veining, some darkened, some golden as evidence of the ever-changing seasons. Kathryn brought Daphne's back to her chest, wrapping her arms around her, the girl's long legs draping down past Kathryn's knees. She kissed her daughter's lemony brown hair as she squealed with joy.

"Mommy, Daddy, watch dis!" Ethan's flaxen ringlets bounced as he charged his little legs forward, propelling himself into the leaves.

"Quick! Cover him up!" Allie shouted, giggling.

Nathan and Allie scooped leaves into the air as Ethan laughed, the array of colors raining down around him.

"Daphne," Adam said, "do you want to go play with your brothers and sister?"

She hopped off her mom's lap and ran toward them, stopping to pinch a new leaf between her innocent fingers, breaking out some of her famous Daphne moves, dancing to her own unique music among the leaves crunching beneath her ever-bouncing feet.

Adam reached for his wife of thirteen years, taking her left hand, straightening her solitaire with his thumb as it shimmered in the fall sun.

Kathryn leaned against the chair, tilting her head back, watching as yet another leaf let go of its branch and drifted from the tree—their tree—to the ground blanketed with leaves and memories.

"So many leaves," Adam said with a moan.

"But look at them." She smiled, her heart overwhelmed with love. "It's worth it."

Adam squeezed her hand and leaned over, his other hand tracing her cheek and threading into her hair, pulling her into a kiss.

"Daddy! Throw me gen, Daddy!"

"Sure, Ethan." He pressed his lips to Kathryn's forehead as she closed her eyes, and he jogged over to his children. "Come on, Sadie!" The dog followed closely behind, prancing on joyful paws. Adam scooped up Ethan and swung him through the air.

A soft breeze tousled Kathryn's hair, and she tucked the strands behind her ear. She inhaled and exhaled deeply, taking in the view before her. Nathan and Allie sat half buried in the leaves, tossing handfuls at each other, laughing, nothing but happiness etched on their beautiful faces. Daphne bounced on her toes, swinging her arms with yellow leaves still pinched in her fingers, her hands flapping with excitement. Adam held Ethan up over his head, twirling him, his little legs fanned out behind him, his sweet giggles bringing a smile to his dad's lips among a thick beard peppered with evidence of the passing years.

Kathryn closed her eyes, the theater of her mind flashing in the darkness. *"Up and over!"—Mittens pressed her nose to her forehead—"We finally caught a ball!"—The doorknob shook rapidly—"Thanks, Lex." "Always."—They huddled around the coffee table, the board game spread out before them, laughing as a real family—Her bow slashed across the string, rising into the air as the final notes vibrated through the great hall—"So we're gonna stalk him?" Mel breathed a laugh. "Yeah, pretty much."—"We'll always be here for each other…forever. Right, ladies?"—She swept her daughter's hair behind her ear. "Make sure you can sing him the song." The scene shifted, leaves sprinkling down upon them as he bent on one knee. "I love you, Kathryn, more than I ever imagined possible. Will you marry me?"—Tears flooded her eyes at the sight of the miracle they had created. "It's a boy," Adam said, overwhelming emotion choking his voice.*

Kathryn opened her eyes against the sun filtering through the expanding gaps in their tree's leafy canopy. She drew a slow breath, and a single tear cascaded down her cheek, beholding her blessings, her life's greatest work, thankful for her time between the trees.

About the Author

Kathy Moczerniak is a lifelong Buffalo, New York native, where she has built a life with her husband and their four children. Originally turning to writing seeking catharsis, her love of the written word quickly grew into a passion. Kathy's determination to study her craft led her to graduate summa cum laude from Southern New Hampshire University with a BA in English and Creative Writing. On her path to becoming an author, she began as an editor, her love of literature increasing with each experience. Life as an author, editor, and autism mom keeps Kathy quite busy, and she is eternally grateful for her family and the opportunity to do what she loves.

You can follow Kathy Moczerniak at:
Website: www.KathyMoczerniak.com
Facebook: https://www.facebook.com/AuthorKathyMoczerniak/
Twitter: https://twitter.com/KathyMoczerniak
Instagram: https://www.instagram.com/author_kathy_moczerniak/

Also from the Lavish family

The Hunter Series
Sara J. Bernhardt
https://www.lavishpublishing.com/authors/sara-j-bernhardt/

Jane Callahan is a reclusive, seventeen-year-old high school student dealing with the death of her beloved brother. Her home in Southern California with her mother is a constant reminder of her loss and pain. In hopes of escaping her past she moves to North Bend Oregon to live with her father, where she meets a beautiful boy named Aidan Summers.

Jane is intrigued by his looks as well as his unusual ways of attempting to get her attention. After months of uncommon conversation and frustration, an uncertain romance brews between Jane and Aidan, but Aidan has a ghastly secret that could destroy everything.

Also from the Lavish family

Sweet Christmas Series
Samantha Jacobey
https://www.lavishpublishing.com/authors/samantha-jacobey/

Life isn't always sweet, even for girls called Candy, and in this series, romance is a family affair...

Candice Parker's life has never been easy. Plagued by losses and setbacks, each day is a struggle for the petite brunette and her young son. When fireman Gary enters her world, he is one mistake she refuses to make; but after tragedy strikes, she may not have a choice.

Gerald Ford has never been what anyone would call settled. Always keeping things simple, he lived a fast and furious lifestyle, with no intentions of slowing down. However, when he inherits his family's ancestral mansion on his thirtieth birthday, he considers the possibility that it's time for a change. Could this complicated young woman be his Christmas Candy?